FAKE EMPIRE

C.W. FARNSWORTH

FAKE EMPIRE

Copyright © 2022 by C.W. Farnsworth

www.authorcwfarnsworth.com

All rights reserved.

This book is a work of fiction. Names, characters, places, and incidents either are products of the author's imagination or are used fictitiously. Any resemblance to actual persons, living or dead, events, or locales is entirely coincidental.

For Elizabeth.

Everything I learned about being a strong woman, I learned from you.

"Great empires are not maintained by timidity."

TACITUS

CONTENTS

FAKE EMPIRE

There's rich.

Then there's the Ellsworth family. The Kensingtons. American royalty.

Money buys power, and power always has a price. The fear of those who already possess both? Losing it. The best way to ensure keeping it? Alliances. And elites don't marry down—they marry equal.

For Scarlett Ellsworth and Crew Kensington, that leaves one option: each other. Accepting that inevitability is very different from embracing it. That's the *only* thing they agree upon.

It was meant to be a union for better and for business.

Instead, it challenges everything Scarlett and Crew thought they knew about themselves, their families, and most of all...*each other*.

FAKE EMPIRE

C.W. FARNSWORTH

CHAPTER ONE

SCARLETT

M y fiancé's gaze meets mine across the crowded club. I hold his stare. I'm not in the business of backing down from *anyone*, including him.

Especially him.

It's harder to break a habit than to form one.

The thirty feet separating us shroud them, but I know the intense eyes currently fixed on me are blue. Hovering in a shade somewhere between icy and navy. Inviting, like the flat water surrounding a tropical island. One glance and you can imagine exactly how walking into that water will feel.

The first time I saw Crew Kensington, I was tempted to tell him, *You have the prettiest eyes I've ever seen.* I was fifteen. I didn't end up saying a word to him, because those eyes are the *only* attribute of his that could be described as inviting. Because they weren't—aren't—his only attractive feature, and that used to intimidate me speechless.

Crew doesn't look away, even when a busty blonde wearing a dress that barely hits her mid-thigh decides to rub up against him. The redhead who was already hanging on to his left arm shoots the new arrival an annoyed glare. Neither sight surprises me. Look up *player* in the dictionary, and you'll find a two-page spread of the billionaire slouched against the long bar top like he owns it.

I can feel the confidence radiating off him from here. The cocky assurance that comes from the Kensington name and also contains something uniquely Crew. Since he arrived a few minutes ago, he's reduced every rich, powerful, handsome man in here into a knockoff version. They're all attainable. Not nearly as gorgeous. Poor by comparison.

Everyone in here already knows who he is. But even if Crew had a different last name and a less robust bank account, I still think I would be staring.

Call it presence or charisma or good genes. I've had to fight for privileges I should have been born with. Crew has them all without trying and yet people still bend over backwards to ensure he doesn't have to work for anything.

And he knows it. *Uses* it.

The blonde is working hard to get his attention, running her hand up his arm, twirling her hair, and batting her eyelashes. Crew doesn't look away from me. The redhead follows his attention. Her pretty features twist with displeasure when she sees me.

I'm not bothered by her glare.

I *am* bothered by Crew's stare.

This has become a competition between us. A game. We've danced around each other for years. We attended different boarding schools throughout high school. Both ended up at Harvard for undergrad. He went to Yale for business school; I attended Columbia for the same two years.

The whole time, we knew we'd be inevitable. No need to fight it—or acknowledge it. That will change soon. This comfortable dynamic will shatter as easily as the thin stem of glass I'm holding.

I raise my martini to him in a silent *cheers*. Immediately, I second-guess the motion. It feels like toppling the first domino. Moving the first pawn. I don't play games until I know the rules. When it comes to me and Crew, I'm not even sure if there are boundaries in place.

One corner of his mouth curls up before he finally looks away, snipping the invisible string temporarily connecting us. For the first time in what feels like hours, I exhale. Then pull in a deep breath of the cool air swirling with the scent of expensive perfume and top-shelf liquor. Followed by a healthy sip of my cocktail.

Those damn ocean eyes. I feel them on me, even when he's not looking.

"Shit, who's *that*?"

I keep my eyes on the curl of lime peel balancing on the rim of my drink. Mostly because I know who Nadia is talking about. We've been sitting in this booth at Proof for forty-five minutes. In that stretch of time, I've only spotted one person who could possibly merit the awed tone she's using. Since I'm the single one in the booth, this will inevitably circle around to me.

"Who?" Sophie asks, looking up from her phone. She might be more dedicated to her work than I am, which is saying something.

"The hottie with dark hair," Nadia answers. "By the bar with the two hang-ons."

Sophie looks, then laughs. "Seriously? You don't know?"

Nadia shakes her head.

Sophie's eyes land on me. "That's Scarlett's future *husband*."

I flick the curl of lime off the rim with a crimson nail before leaning back against the leather booth. "Nothing is official yet."

The *yet* sounds more ominous than usual. Probably because I know my father met with Arthur Kensington last week.

Nadia gapes at me. "Wait. You mean you're actually getting *married*? To *him*?"

I shrug. "Probably."

"Do you even *know* him?"

"I know enough."

I'm not surprised Nadia looks shocked by the unexpected revelation I'll likely marry a man I've never even mentioned. Just like I wasn't all that surprised Sophie recognized Crew on sight, since she has an unhealthy obsession with New York's ever-churning gossip mill. I wasn't expecting her to know about our rumored engagement. As far as I knew, any published gossip fizzled after years of total silence from both of our families. Whispers among our social circle are another matter, but Sophie wouldn't be privy to those.

Nadia and Sophie are friends from business school. They both grew up in wealthy suburbs of Manhattan, riding around in brand-new cars and never applying for financial aid. They're the comfortable sort of well-off, where worrying about paying rent or putting food on the table is a foreign concept.

I grew up taking a private jet between my six-figures-a-semester boarding school and a multi-million-dollar penthouse overlooking Central Park.

There's wealthy, and then there's me. Crew. We're each set to inherit empires including sums of money that have a *lot* of zeroes. More than anyone could spend in a lifetime—or a thousand of them. If the Federal Trade Commission had a say in the institution known as marriage, there's no way this merger would go through. It's a melding of assets akin to a Rockefeller marrying a Vanderbilt.

Whether or not I want to marry Crew is mostly irrelevant. I

accepted it as an inevitability a long time ago. I have a choice. It *is* my choice. Marrying for love isn't an option, even if I'd ever met anyone who made me think so, which I haven't. My world would chew him up and spit him out. Not to mention, there would always be a voice in the back of my head, wondering whether he wanted me or the money.

With Crew, I don't have to worry about that. He's callous, cocky, and cold. He grew up in this world, same as me; he knows what's expected. He's known for the traits I just observed: entertaining women, always retaining total control, and getting exactly what he wants.

My father did me a favor, arranging this marriage.

It doesn't make it any less of a foreign, antiquated concept to people who live in the normal world. Nadia has been dating the same guy for the past two years. Finn is a sweet, unassuming native New Yorker who is in his last year at NYU Law. Sophie is currently seeing a cardiovascular surgeon named Kyle, who sounds like a total tool. According to her, his dexterity makes up for anything his personality lacks.

My mind wanders to stupid thoughts as I keep my gaze firmly on my glass. Like whether Crew is good in bed. He seems like the sort of guy who would expect blowjobs without reciprocating and always come first.

I'll likely find out.

The end of my drink gets drained with one gulp. "I'll be right back." I stand and stroll in the direction of the restrooms.

I'm sure Nadia is taking this opportunity to grill Sophie about my upcoming engagement. As soon as I heard my father met with Crew's, I knew there was no chance I'd keep it from them—from anyone—for much longer. Neither of our families have ever confirmed an engagement. Rumors have to be fed in order to spread.

My father hasn't broached the topic with me himself in years. He assumes I'll do what he wants without question when the time comes, and for once, he's right.

As I walk across the club, I can feel the stares on me. The gold sequined minidress I'm wearing isn't meant to blend into the wallpaper. Work has eaten up most of my time lately. The only reason I left the office before eleven p.m. is that it was Andrea's birthday tonight. None of my magazine's editorial staff—including her—will leave before I do.

I headed out at seven, which is unheard of for me. I met Nadia and Sophie for sushi at a new spot in the Village, and we ended up here, just like I knew we would. Coming to Proof and rubbing elbows with New York's young, rich, and famous is a novelty for my two companions. Less so for me, seeing as I was coming to places like this long before I was legally allowed to.

The hallway leading to the restrooms is empty, lit by muted columns every few feet. My stilettos click a rhythmic melody across the hand-painted tiles and into the lounge that serves as the entrance to the actual bathrooms. I pass the velvet-covered chairs, barely sparing the furnishings a glance, before locking myself into one of the stalls that are situated like private rooms. Each has its own sink and toilet. One wall is decorated with frames filled with dried flowers, while another holds a long shelf boasting an array of expensive sprays, soaps, and lotions.

I'm washing my hands when I hear the distinctive tapping of other heels approaching and the muted murmur of feminine voices. I shut off the water and dry my hands on one of the fluffy towels from the basket beside the sink before tossing it into the hamper. One of the women is complaining about her blisters. The other is talking nonsensically and fast, indicating she's already over-indulged. It costs a small fortune to get wasted in a place like this, so she's probably someone I know.

6

I open my clutch and pull out a tube of lipstick to slick my lips with my signature shade of red. Even if I didn't share a name with a hue of the color, I like to think I'd still be the sort of woman who walks around with crimson lips.

It makes a statement.

"Did you see Crew Kensington is here?" a third voice asks. My hand stills halfway across my lower lip.

"He's hard to miss. Anna St. Clair was over there in seconds." That surprisingly sober sentence comes from the woman who was spilling gibberish about some film premiere seconds ago.

"I'm surprised he's here. He hasn't been coming out much. Kensington Consolidated just bought that new electronics company. Isn't he taking that over for his father, along with everything else? Talk about a slap to the face for Oliver."

"I thought that was just gossip. Like the engagement to Scarlett Ellsworth."

"No, I heard *that's* true. He's really going to marry her."

"Then why hasn't he?" the woman formerly complaining about her heels asks.

"Maybe Crew is trying to get out of it. She's not exactly his type. He likes his women a little...looser." She laughs. "Not the princess of Park Avenue and her perfect pedestal."

"Who cares? He'll still sleep around, just with a few extra billions in his pocket."

"God, can you imagine having that much money? Scarlett is so lucky."

"She's already as rich as he is," one of them points out.

I smile at that. *Richer.* Crew has to split his inheritance with his older brother Oliver. I'm an only child.

"How greedy can she be? Doesn't she already have enough money?"

They're jealous—and drunk. But still, I want to lecture them about the hypocrisy. *Crew* isn't greedy? Just *me*?

"She's not even that pretty. I've never seen her smile or flirt—ever. At the Waldorfs' holiday party, she spent the whole evening talking business. Margaret said she was bored out of her mind."

"Margaret is always bored out of her mind. I would be too, if I were married to Richard."

"I'm just saying—she probably can't get anyone else to marry her. Her father needed to dangle *billions* to snag a catch. Pathetic."

I cap my lipstick and drop it back in my clutch, tucking the bag under one arm and opening the door to head for the lounge. Being the subject of gossip is nothing new to me. Everyone has an unhealthy obsession with wealth and power—and those who have it—even if they tell themselves they don't.

A thick skin and *fake it until you make it* mentality are requisites for surviving in this world—especially if you have higher aspirations than spending a trust fund, which I do. No one wants to do business with a coward. The women's movement hasn't seen much movement in the upper echelons of society. Business is a boys' club.

The only reason I have any foothold in it is the fact I'm the sole heir to the Ellsworth empire. Complications during my birth prevented my mother from ever conceiving again. Even a man as cold-hearted and indifferent as my father couldn't stomach filing for divorce on those grounds alone. It's one of the main reasons he's pushed for my marriage to a Kensington, though. There was never any question—in his mind, at least—that I would marry well. The antiquated elite see no value in their children marrying anyone with less money than they do. Marrying *down*. Especially when it comes to a son who will carry on the name to the next generation.

For my family, the closest economic equivalent is the Kensingtons. It's an arrangement advantageous to both sides, which is unique. Usually, one party gains more than the other. More money, more assets, more status.

Crew is my best option. Our situation is different because I'm also *his* best option. I have more power than most women entering an arranged marriage and no intention of ceding a single inch of it.

I stroll into the lounge with my head held high. All three of the women perched on velvet look familiar, but none of their names come to me right away. The only social events I attend are the ones I'm required to. Most of Manhattan's elite feel fortunate to be invited to the endless slew of functions that act as an excuse to show off how much money you can spend on or in one evening. I only attend the parties where my lack of presence would be an insult.

As soon as I appear, all conversation ceases. Six eyes widen. Three sets of lips purse. A few harsh comments sneak to the tip of my tongue, but I swallow them. You can't expect anyone to see you as above them if you lower yourself to their level. Insults say more about the speaker than the intended recipient.

I sweep past the three surprised women and out of the lounge without a word or a stumble. Rather than head straight back to my booth, I pause at the bar, stopping about twenty feet from where *he* is standing. One of the black-clad bartenders immediately rushes over to me.

"Gin martini, please," I order.

"Right away, miss," he replies.

He spins and immediately sets about making my drink, indicating he's worked here long enough to appreciate Proof's patrons don't tolerate being kept waiting. I watch the dimmed lights twinkle off the line of colored bottles behind the bar as another bartender smoothly measures a stream of vodka and squeezes grapefruit atop it.

"Ellsworth."

My stomach dips like the floor fell out beneath me as soon as I hear the deep, confident voice. I focus on everything tangible: the hard surface my arm is resting on, the pinch of my heels, the splash and smell of alcohol being poured. Without looking over, I instantly know who is standing beside me.

"Kensington." I angle my head to the right so I can appraise him, keeping my casual pose in place.

Before tonight, the last time I saw him was at the Waldorfs' holiday party four months ago. Crew looks the same, except he's wearing a pair of navy slacks and a white button-down with the sleeves rolled up instead of the tux standard at society events. He looks like he came here straight from the office.

If there's one thing I respect about Crew Kensington, it's his work ethic. For someone who has had everything handed to him his entire life, he appears to pull his own weight at Kensington Consolidated. While wearing an entitled smirk, but still. His father, Arthur Kensington, values success over nepotism. He wouldn't be grooming Crew for future CEO if he didn't have what it takes to thrive in the role.

I glance past him, down to where he was standing before. "So, who's the lucky lady tonight? The redhead or the blonde?"

Those blue eyes appraise me as he casually props one elbow on the varnished wood of the bar top, mirroring my relaxed posture. Crew swirls a tumbler of what smells like bourbon before he replies. "Or both."

"Underachiever."

The left corner of his mouth creases with a hint of amusement as the bartender sets a fresh martini down in front of me.

"Thank you," I tell him.

Crew holds eye contact with me as he reaches into his pocket. His hand emerges with a hundred-dollar bill, which he slides across the smooth surface. "Keep the change."

"Thank you, sir." The bartender departs quickly, unwilling to give Crew a chance to change his mind. Even at a place as upscale as this, it's an outrageous tip. People are happy to drop whatever amount they're charged for overpriced liquor. More than the obligatory twenty percent tip to service staff is usually another story.

I say nothing. If he's trying to impress me, money is the wrong way to do it. I don't know *what* he's trying to do. He approached me, all but confirming the outcome of our fathers' conversation last week.

Crew watches me closely as I raise my glass and take a sip. A high-pitched, whiny voice interrupts our silent staring contest.

"Crew, you said you'd be right back."

He acts like nothing was said. I hold his gaze for a few more seconds, then glance at the woman who's approached us. The redhead who was hanging on him earlier has one hip cocked and a smile pasted on her face. Neither completely masks the irritation wafting off her—presumably about his choice to leave her side and approach me instead.

I savor another sip of my martini before acknowledging her unwelcome presence. "It's rude to interrupt."

The redhead gives me a snotty look. "And who are *you*?"

"Crew's fiancée." The two words roll off my tongue like I've said them before, even though I haven't. They still sound strange.

That title shuts her up fast, especially when Crew doesn't deny my claim. He just continues to watch me, unreadable emotions swirling in cerulean depths as he ignores her.

The redhead flounces off.

"Happy?" Crew drawls.

"Disappointed, actually. I was hoping she'd slap you."

Another corner of his mouth curl. I'm beginning to think it's his idea of a smile.

"So…" He steps closer.

I want to breathe, but there's a brief moment where I can't.

"You're my fiancée now?"

"Aren't I?" I take another sip of gin. At this rate, I'll be finished with my second drink before I make it back to the booth. Maybe I'll break my two-drink limit as an engagement gift to myself.

"Prenup paperwork is being drawn up as we speak." Crew pauses. "Your father didn't tell you?"

"The less he tells me, the more power he can pretend he has." I look away, back at the long row of bottles behind the bar. "His secretary called my secretary about lunch. I'm guessing I'll get the happy news then."

"Glad to hear you and Hanson are closer than ever."

I scoff. "Not all of us ask *how high?* when Daddy says *jump.*"

"Have you always had this much of an edge, or is it a recent development?"

"If you'd ever done more than compliment me on my dress in the past decade, you'd know the answer to that."

Crew makes a show of looking the gold minidress I'm wearing up and down. "It's shiny?"

"Have you always been this terrible at coming up with compliments, or is it a recent development?"

For the first time—ever—I get a full-blown smile from Crew Kensington. He looks damn good pouting. Amusement—genuine, not mocking—softens the sharper angles of his face. Throw on a backwards baseball cap and a t-shirt, and he wouldn't look like a ruthless billionaire.

As quickly as the grin appears, it fades.

I want to stand here and coax another one out of him, which is what convinces me to leave. He'll be my husband, and this is the first conversation we've ever had that encapsulates more than polite small talk. Curiosity is one thing, interest another.

"Thanks for the drink," I tell him, then walk away.

Sophie is practically bouncing in the booth when I return to my seat. "Ah! What did he say?"

"He bought my drink and then gave me a half-assed compliment." And confirmed our engagement is imminent and incoming, but I keep that to myself.

"Sounds like he likes you."

"More like he's trying to figure out how much of a pushover I am."

Nadia laughs. "He's in for a surprise, then."

"Maybe." I'm only half-listening now, busy scanning the tall tables below the wall of champagne bottles. It's more than a maybe. Crew and I know a lot about each other. But we don't *know* each other.

I've never wondered what he thinks of me—until tonight.

I've never considered he might surprise me—until tonight.

The two realizations are unnerving, uncomfortable. I don't like the implications, and I need a distraction.

A group of guys strolls inside. One toward the front, a blond, makes direct eye contact with me. He's wearing a full suit that looks custom made—tie, jacket, and all—which seems like trying too hard to me. If you have money, there's no need to flaunt it. Especially in a place like this. But he has an appealing face and a decent body, which are my main criteria at the moment, so I smile at him. He smiles back. I look down, take a sip, and then glance back up. He's still staring at me. I pretend to be self-conscious about his eyes on me, glancing away and shifting in my seat like the attention is overwhelming rather than exactly what I was hoping for.

After ordering a drink, he heads our way.

"Incoming," Sophie teases, spotting him. Nadia looks as well. All three of us watch him saunter over.

"Is this seat taken?"

Not the most original opener, but the way he addresses us all while talking only to me indicates he's no newcomer to picking up women. I'm not interested in his conversation skills, although some would be a plus.

I shake my head in response. He slides into the seat beside me, sitting close enough the stiff material of his pants brush my leg. It's a deliberate, practiced move, one that should probably prompt more of a response than light chafing. Unfortunately, I'm distracted by the feel of eyes on me, eyes that don't belong to the guy beside me. I don't succumb to the strong urge to look at the bar.

The blond beside me introduces himself as Evan. He, Sophie, and Nadia chat as I work to act like I'm listening to their idle conversation, not slowly simmering beneath blue flames. I've talked to other guys in front of Crew Kensington before. Why should this time be any different?

"What do you do, Scarlett?" Evan eventually asks.

"I run a magazine."

"Really?" He looks intrigued. "What sort of magazine?"

"Fashion."

His eyes run over my dress. "Not surprising. You look stunning."

"Thank you." *Shiny, my ass.* If I weren't personally appalled by the idea, I'd order a sequined wedding dress just to spite Crew. I take a fresh stab at conversation. "What do you do, Evan?"

That question prompts a weird look from Sophie that makes

me think the answer might have been covered while I was "listening" earlier. Evan launches into a spiel about his job as a tax attorney. It's wholly unfamiliar, so I either blocked it out resoundingly enough or Sophie was frowning about something else. I try to pay attention at first. But I feel my attention drift, even before Crew leaves the bar and approaches our booth, followed by a different blonde than the one from earlier. Once he does, Evan could be belting Beyonce and I wouldn't notice.

My whole body tenses. Preparing for what, I don't know. We've swerved so far off script I can't remember what our lines are.

Crew doesn't stop walking until he reaches the edge of our booth. He crowds the space like he has every right to be here. Evan glances up at him mid-sentence, clearly confused by what is happening. There's a long pause where everyone is silent.

Then, Crew holds a hand out. "Crew Kensington."

Recognition washes over Evan's face, quickly followed by reverence. "I—oh. *Wow*. It's an honor to meet you. I'm Evan—Evan Goldsmith."

Crew glances to me as Evan babbles, amusement obvious in his expression. I imagine Evan is fanboying in hopes he'll be able to announce to a managing partner he snagged *Kensington* business for his firm. It's wasted time—Kensington Consolidated has an in-house legal team. Evan is mid-sentence when Crew leans down and whispers something to him I am certain involves me.

Crew straightens with a self-satisfied smirk that makes me pray a punch will mess up his perfect bone structure. If not for me, on behalf of average-looking men everywhere. That sort of symmetry is an unfair standard to be held to. I thought Evan was attractive...until I saw him next to the table's uninvited guest.

Whatever Crew said to Evan leaves him pale. "Enjoy your

night, ladies." Crew *winks* and walks away, with the blonde trailing right behind him.

"Nice talking to you." Evan grabs his drink and disappears.

"Well...*that* was interesting," Sophie muses. Nadia looks like she was just spun around in circles: wide-eyed and off-kilter. Exactly how I'd appear—if I weren't excellent at schooling my emotions.

I shouldn't look over my shoulder, but I do. Crew is standing right next to the glass doors that lead out onto the street. The blonde is nowhere in sight; he either ditched her or she's waiting outside. Crew doesn't move or react when he sees me staring at him. He holds my stare for a few seconds before turning and disappearing out into the night. It's unnerving—because it's exactly what I would do.

We're similar, me and Crew Kensington.

Guarded.

Proud.

Stubborn.

Cynical.

We've grown up with the same privilege and expectations. We know what's expected. What it takes to thrive in this world, not just survive.

That's the reason I agreed to marry him.

And the reason I *shouldn't*.

CHAPTER TWO

CREW

P eople scatter as I step off the elevator on Monday morning. Kensington Consolidated employs a workforce upwards of five hundred, not to mention the many companies we serve as the parent entity of. Less than fifty employees have offices on the executive floor. Men and women twice my age scurry away like skittish mice as I stride down the carpeted hall toward the main conference room. One perk of having your name displayed on the side of the skyscraper. It commands respect, even when you haven't earned it.

My father and brother are sitting at the centered table when I enter the conference room. The three of us start every Monday with a "chat." That's what my father likes to call them, at least. Lectures would be a more fitting descriptor. He uses them as an intimidation tactic toward everyone else with an office on this floor. Forcing them to be in on time and fueling speculation about what we're talking about. Promotions. Acquisitions. Firings.

"You're late," my father announces as I take a seat across from him. I resist the urge to direct his attention to the clock above the projector screen used for presentations.

It's ten seconds past eight a.m.

Instead, I say, "Sorry. Hope you two had some golf stories to swap."

My father's eyes narrow, trying to decide if I'm being glib or genuine. The fact he can't tell is a source of pride.

He and Oliver love flying investors and potential partners around to different courses, hashing out business over eighteen holes. Those outings often involve polo shirts and bets. I prefer to do business in a stiff suit inside a boardroom.

"The paperwork is all set?" he questions, letting the jab slide.

"Yes," I answer. "I went to Richard's office on Sunday." Just how I wanted to spend my one day off in two weeks, signing a two-hundred-page document explicitly laying out how each asset will be distributed in the event my upcoming union ends in a divorce.

My father hums, which is the closest to a sound of approval he gets. "The Ellsworths will be over for dinner on Friday night. Make sure you have a ring by then."

"I want Mom's."

Not much gets to my father anymore. A mention of the woman he buried two decades ago seems to be the one thing that always does. The glimmer of surprise in his eyes disappears quickly. "It's in the safe."

I nod.

"Can we move on from the marriage talk?" Oliver requests. The snide way he says *marriage* answers any questions about how he's handling the upcoming addition to the family.

Two years older than me, he should be the one embarking on the archaic tradition of an arranged marriage. Probably to Scarlett Ellsworth, a prospect that didn't bother me at all before I exchanged more than a few dozen words with her. Her sharp tongue would be lost on my staid brother. Before, our engagement was a hypothetical. A probable outcome, but far from certain. That's changed, and the tick in Oliver's jaw says it bothers him.

Our father decided I was going to be the one who married Scarlett years ago, and Oliver and I learned far earlier than that not to question his decisions. What Arthur Kensington says, goes.

The muscle above my father's right eye twitches, a surefire sign he's displeased. "This marriage is crucial for the future of this family, Oliver. You know that."

No matter how old you get, I don't think the perverse satisfaction of a sibling getting scolded for a slight against you ever fades. It hasn't after twenty-five years, at least.

"I do, Dad," is Oliver's hasty answer.

Our father nods. "Good. Now, we need to go over the team for the Warner Communications transition. I was planning to have Crew oversee everything, but he'll be busy over the next few months, before and after the wedding."

My brain homes in on the phrases *few months* and *after the wedding*. "There's a date set for the wedding?"

"Nothing official yet. We'll let the engagement announcement settle for a few days before announcing one. The wedding planner said she could pull something together by early June."

June? "June?" It's mid-April. I'm not opposed to marrying Scarlett. Mildly intrigued, even, following our conversation at Proof on Friday night. But six weeks feels close—claustrophobic. I wonder if her father has even told her we're officially engaged yet.

"This agreement has been in place for nearly a decade, Crew. If you had objections, we're far past the point to raise them. The press release is going out tomorrow." I love how my father makes pushing your sixteen-year-old into a future engagement sound normal. I don't even remember what our conversation back then consisted of. Probably lots of nodding on my part.

"I'm not objecting, Dad. Just asking."

"Josephine Ellsworth is handling the wedding logistics. Scarlett is her only child. I'm sure she'll keep you appraised, probably with more than you want to know. Now, what do you think about assigning Billingston to lead Warner? He had the experience at Paulson with..." My father continues to talk through the strengths and weaknesses of all the executives not currently on assignment. I lean back in the chair and scratch notes on a legal pad to refer to later.

Eight fifteen a.m., and I'm ready to call it a day.

I walk into my office and stop. Take a few steps back. Glance at the nameplate. "For a second, I thought I had the wrong office. But no. This *is* my office."

"That joke gets funnier every single day you do it, man."

"*Off.*"

Asher Cotes doesn't move his feet from the corner of my desk. "Good morning to you too."

"I mean it, Cotes. I'm not in the mood."

"Was Roman thirty seconds late to pick you up again?" my best friend teases.

I snort as I stalk toward my chair. "I was late for a meeting with our entire accounting division on Friday because of that delay."

"Too bad your name's not on the letterhead. I'm sure they chewed you out."

They didn't, and we both know it. The vice president actually apologized, thinking he got the time wrong. I don't tell Asher that.

"That's how my dad runs things. Not me." I unbutton my suit jacket and take a seat behind the massive mahogany desk.

Asher settles back in one of the leather chairs facing me. Feet still up. "What pissed you off this morning, then?"

I pick up a Montclair and spin it around one finger, debating on what to say. Fuck it, he'll find out soon enough. "My engagement is getting announced tomorrow."

Asher's eyes widen to a comical size. "To Scarlett Ellsworth?"

I nod. Set the pen down, then pick it back up. "She was at Proof on Friday night." *That* fact won't be included in the engagement announcement. I don't know why I say it.

"Damn," is Asher's initial reaction. "I knew I should have skipped dinner with my folks. How did she look?"

Like a fantasy. "Fine."

"That good, huh?" Asher isn't being sarcastic. His tone has turned admiring. He may not come from the sort of money Scarlett and I do, but his family is still wealthy. He's attended events she's been at before. He's seen the thick dark hair and the perennially red lips and the figure that hijacks rational thoughts.

I don't want to be married to a woman every guy I know is lusting after. A woman *I'm* attracted to. It's a complication I don't need or want in a part of my life I've always kept simple and easy.

Scarlett Ellsworth isn't simple. She's most definitely not easy. She's smart and fiery and determined and sassy. And wherever she goes, she's always the most stunning woman in the room.

She's the sort of woman men go to war for, yet I didn't have to do a single thing to win her. Our fathers decided our fates for us nearly a decade ago. I could fight it, but for what? The Ellsworths and the Kensingtons are the two wealthiest, most prominent families in the country. Marrying anyone else besides Scarlett would be marrying down.

"I talked to her," I admit as I spin the pen around my pointer finger.

I've avoided conversation with her for years. We've exchanged small talk. Pleasantries. Compliments, like she pointed out. Nothing of substance. Nothing about *us*. We both knew it wouldn't change anything.

Asher's eyebrows shoot upward. "Really?"

"What I just said, isn't it?"

He rolls his eyes at my sarcasm. "She came up to you?"

"I went over to her." I lean back in my chair, making the leather creak. "She was right by me," I add, as if that detail makes a difference. I can't recall the last time I approached a woman in a bar, which Asher is well aware of. He's by my side most nights.

Asher whistles, long and low. "She must have looked *damn* good."

She did. "I was curious. I'm going to be married to her."

"And?"

"She's…something." I don't know how else to categorize our interaction. I can't recall the last time I wanted to keep talking to someone, and they walked away. She *walked away* from me. After *I* approached *her*. I didn't chase, at least not right away, but I wanted to.

"In a good way or a bad way?"

"I'm still deciding." My computer chimes with an alert. As I switch over to my calendar, I groan. I'm fully booked until lunch. "I've got to go. I'll see you at one." We eat lunch together most days.

"Yeah. Sure."

I grab the stack of folders on my desk and head for the door, only glancing over my shoulder at the last minute. "Feet off the desk, Cotes. I mean it."

"What are you going to do? Fire me as your best friend?"

"Yep."

"Then who would you complain about slash compliment your fiancée to?"

I don't answer before walking out of the room. But his words stay with me as I walk to my next meeting. Scarlett Ellsworth is my fiancée. In a matter of weeks, she'll be my wife. It doesn't really bother me. And *that* bothers me.

I'm sitting with Asher and Oliver, talking about the Yankees' train wreck of a season and eating lunch, when my secretary Celeste appears. "Mr. Kensington?"

"Yes?" I look up from the chicken piccata the catering staff delivered for today's mid-day meal.

"Um, I'm sorry to bother you. I know you said not to interrupt you during lunch unless there's an emergency—"

"*Is* there an emergency?"

Celeste hesitates before answering. "Miss Ellsworth is here. She's requesting to speak with you immediately. You didn't leave me any instructions on how to handle—well, whether to let you know…" Another pause. "She's quite persistent."

Asher and Oliver both look at me. Asher appears as surprised as I feel. Oliver's gaze is discerning; he's attempting to assess my reaction.

"Here?" I question. "Scarlett Ellsworth is *here*?"

"Yes, sir."

"Send her into my office," I instruct. "I'll be there shortly."

Celeste nods before disappearing back into the hallway. I stand and shrug on my suit jacket, taking a few extra seconds to straighten the lapels and orient myself. *Why is she here?*

"What is she doing here?" Oliver asks, voicing my confusion.

"She's probably scoping out the place." Asher drops his fork and sends the miniature basketball he likes to carry around up into the air, then catches it. "She's about to gain a substantial stake in Kensington Consolidated."

Oliver scoffs at that. "Why would she care? She's got her fashion shit to focus on."

I say nothing before I walk out of the suite that serves as the floor's break room. The glass door shuts soundlessly behind me as I stroll down the hallway that leads to the main executives' offices, which includes mine. Employees scutter out of my way as I pass.

Celeste is back at her desk when I reach the end of the hall.

"She's inside?" I ask.

My secretary nods. I want to take a moment—to prepare to see her—but I can't. Aside from Celeste, there are at least a dozen people in this wing of the building surreptitiously eyeing me. Hesitation is weakness, and I refuse to show it. I stroll into my office like I own it—which I do.

Scarlett is standing behind my desk, staring out at the skyline. The afternoon sun shines through the floor-to-ceiling windows, bathing my office—and her—in golden light.

She turns at the sound of the door closing behind me. The silk material of her navy dress swishes around her thighs as she moves, strolling to the side of my desk. Her confident posture suggests this is *her* office, not mine. No one ventures behind the stretch of mahogany, much less leans against it, the way she is casually doing. Fifteen years of friendship, and all Asher has ever dared to do is rest his shoes on one corner.

She crosses her arms. "Took you long enough."

"Some of us have important matters to handle, darling."

"Your secretary said you were at lunch."

I grind my molars. "It was a working lunch."

"*Sure.*"

Normally, I'd immediately stride behind my desk and take a seat in the leather chair. But if I do that, I won't be able to maintain eye contact with her. If I sit down, I'll be beneath her, looking up. So I stay where I am, essentially ceding control of the room to her.

Scarlett smirks, realizing the same, then straightens. She pulls a thick packet of papers out of her handbag and tosses them onto my desk with a soft *smack*. "I need you to sign these."

I move, walking over to my desk like it was my choice to linger by the door at first. This feels like a game of chess. Fitting, since the queen is the most powerful piece. I pick up the heavy stack and flip through the first few pages. It's our prenuptial agreement. "I already signed this."

Spent two hours signing it.

"Well, I didn't. Changes needed to be made first."

Changes? I round the edge of my desk and take a seat in the chair. Leather creaks as I lean back. My left eye twitches as I page through the lengthy document. "Do you want me to do a line-by-line comparison, or are you going to tell me *what* changes were made?"

"My father neglected to distinguish *his* holdings from *mine* in the disclosures for the original document. You're entitled to a share of the Ellsworth name. Not *my* name."

I flip back to the first page before I look up at her. "Meaning?"

25

"I want to maintain total ownership of my business enterprises. My personal accounts and my magazine. While we're married, and in case we divorce."

A mixture of surprise and annoyance war within me. This, I did not see coming. "*That*'s what this is about? Your little magazine? You're worried I'll tell you how to dress your cover models or what trends are in?"

Scarlett's expression doesn't react to the taunt. She's waltzed in here, made demands she's not entitled to, and still has the gall to look at me like *I* am the one inconveniencing *her*. Something that feels a lot like respect flickers deep down.

"My father has had no involvement in the magazine. It's not his choice how it's handled. Or yours. I want full control, or I walk."

I smile at the bold proclamation. "You're going to walk away from an arrangement worth hundreds of billions, for a fashion magazine worth...what? Fifty million? At most?"

"Not all of us inherit everything we own, Crew."

"You inherited the money you used to pursue this venture."

Her eyes flash. "It's non-negotiable. I'm not bluffing. My father can make all the *arrangements* he wants. He can't *make* me marry you."

"You'd be a fool not to."

"I'm bringing more to the table. If you don't agree to my terms, you're the one who will look like a fool. I don't need you or your money, Crew Kensington. Don't forget that."

I flip through a few more pages to buy myself some time. I'm not sure what to do—and I can't remember the last time that happened. I don't care about the magazine. I *do* care about giving Scarlett the impression she's in control here. "All you changed are the magazine's shares?" I ask.

"Yes."

"I need to see earning statements before I agree."

Her eyes narrow. "Why?"

"I make informed decisions, Scarlett." I focus on her hazel eyes, because looking elsewhere won't end well. Scarlett is *distracting*. The brunette hair I can't help but imagine spread across a pillow. The pouty lips painted an enticing shade of red. The tailored blue fabric that hugs her curves. All distractions.

She sighs, then steps closer. "Move."

"Excuse me?"

"If you want to see the earning statements, *move*."

Against my better judgment, I do. I stand and step away from the computer that has full access to everything. I'm not worried she'll snoop in any secret files. For two reasons, the second more troubling than the first. One, I don't think she will. That suggests some level of trust. Two, if she wanted to spy, I expect her to come up with a more creative method to gain access to my files. Admiration, maybe even respect, is inherent in that thought.

I watch as she settles in my chair and starts typing.

"Have you talked to your father yet?"

"I headed straight from that meeting to meet with my attorney. If you're annoyed about signing for a second time, maybe you should have confirmed I approved the agreement first. Seeing as it'll be *my* signature above yours, not my father's."

I say nothing to that. She's probably right, although I had as little involvement in the drafting of the document as she did. "Did your father mention dinner?"

"Yes."

"Wedding dates?"

"Yes."

I give up on conversation and take a seat on the leather couch. The printer whirs to life.

Scarlett stands and strolls over to it. The pages are still warm when she flings them into my lap. "Here you go, *honey*."

"Testing out pet names?"

She doesn't respond, just takes a seat behind *my* desk, again. I'm stuck on the couch like a visitor.

I flip through the pages of numbers, trying not to act impressed. I know next to nothing about the fashion industry, but I do know what a significant profit margin looks like. I also know that *Haute* was close to declaring bankruptcy before Scarlett bought the magazine.

I'm impressed.

I'm *never* impressed.

"You shouldn't have shown these to me."

"I know."

"I'd be an idiot to sign away shares."

"I know that too."

"But you think I will." It's a statement, not a question.

"Yes."

We stare at each other for a few heady seconds. I'm tempted to call what I think is a bluff. To see her mostly green eyes flash and catch the ire she'll fling my way. If she was another woman— not my fiancée—I would. Then again, I can't picture anyone else pulling a stunt like this with me.

"I'm not signing until my legal team has looked at it," I say.

"But you'll sign it?"

There's no mistaking the hope in her voice. This matters to her; it's not just a power play or a test. My response will ripple past this conversation to the rest of our relationship.

I want her to like me.

The thought is bizarre. People worry about what I think of them—not the other way around. "If that's the only thing you changed? Yes."

Scarlett bites down on her bottom lip. I watch her white teeth sink into the red skin. As we stare at each other, I realize two things. One, for all her brash declarations, she didn't think I would agree. Two, I want to kiss her. *Badly.* The same awareness that swirled around us in Proof appears in my office, thickening the air until it's all I can breathe.

There's a knock on the door.

"What?" I call out. Irritation at the interruption seeps out into my voice.

Isabel, one of the board executives, opens it and pokes her head in. "Crew, I—" She stops speaking as soon as she spots Scarlett. "Oh. I—I didn't realize you were in the middle of something."

"We're not." Scarlett stands and shoulders her handbag. I'm expecting the contrary emotions she elicits in me this time. The wish that she'd stay. She thinks she makes the decisions, and I find it both amusing and arousing. "See you later, *sweetheart.*"

I smirk before replying. "Thanks for stopping by, *dearest.*"

Scarlett rolls her eyes before striding toward the doorway where Isabel is still standing. Isabel doesn't move, blocking the door half-way open.

I watch the scene unfold, immediately knowing which woman I would bet money on. It would make my life a hell of a lot easier if Scarlett had the spineless socialite personality I was expecting, but I can't summon any disappointment I ended up saddled with a spitfire. She fascinates me, and I've never been able to say that about a woman before.

Isabel Sterling is a year older than I am. She worked her way up the ranks of my family's company since starting a position here right out of college to become one of only two female members of the board. I've seen her stare down powerful men until they fold.

I don't think Scarlett isn't going to scurry through the small opening like a dirty secret, though. And she doesn't disappoint. "Move," she instructs. Her tone is haughty and her back is straight as a ruler.

Reluctantly, Isabel shuffles to the side. In a minute act of defiance, she doesn't push open the door. Scarlett shoves it ajar herself and walks out of my office.

Isabel shuts the door behind her with a huff. "*That*'s Scarlett Ellsworth?"

"Yep." I stand from the couch and grab the stack of papers Scarlett left behind. "What did you need, Isabel?"

"The Powers Corporation sent over new slides before their pitch. I thought you'd like to look at the numbers before the Andover meeting."

Looks like I won't be eating the rest of my lunch. "Fine. We can use the main conference room until the meeting starts."

Isabel nods. I follow her out of my office and stop by Celeste's desk, dropping the stack of papers consisting of my prenup on the counter, encircling her space with a *thud*. "Get these to legal," I instruct. "I want them to look through every word and get me a memo listing every difference from the original document that was drawn up. Have them tab every spot I'm supposed to sign too. I don't have time to go through it all myself. Again. Tell them to drop everything else. I want this done by the end of the day."

"Yes, of course." Celeste grabs the papers and hurries toward the elevators.

I stride to where Isabel is waiting. As we walk, she fills me in on the changes that were made to the pitch tomorrow. The main conference room is in the very center of the executive floor, surrounded by glass that's frosted during important meetings.

"What did Scarlett want?" Isabel asks as soon as we enter the room. I can tell she's trying to sound casual, but the question alone is an anomaly. Isabel and I discuss business, that's it. It's why we work well together.

I unbutton my jacket and take a seat at the table. "Some paperwork needed to be straightened out."

"She could have had it sent over," Isabel points out.

"She wanted to talk in person." I pull out the notes for the meeting.

"Are you having second thoughts about marrying her? She seems awfully needy."

I almost smile at that, picturing how Scarlett might react to being called needy. This line of questioning is giving me the impression Asher might not have been *entirely* off base the three times he's told me Isabel has non-professional feelings for me. I'm sure rumors of nepotism fly about when I'm not around, but I take my role here seriously. I don't mix business with anything else. I've never dated an employee or fooled around in my office. "Is there a point coming? About my *personal* life?" Warnings litter those two questions.

Warnings Isabel doesn't heed. "I'm worried about this woman's impact on the future of this company."

Now I *know* she's jealous. "Her impact on the future of this company will be strengthening the Kensington name by adding billions to my assets and giving me children to leave everything to."

"But you don't *want* to marry her, do you?"

I don't do things I don't want to do. There are downsides to being born into the sort of wealth most people can't comprehend. But autonomy has never been an issue. Especially when it comes to big, life-changing choices. If I didn't want to marry Scarlett, I would have found a way out of it years ago.

"She's stunning and has a shit-ton of money. I could do

worse." I'm not sure why I'm continuing to indulge this conversation. No one else has shown up early for the meeting, I guess. And I like working with Isabel. I'm eager to rid her of any notion there's a chance of anything ever happening between us. "We're colleagues, Isabel. If I wanted your input on my life outside this office, I'd ask for it."

Her cheeks turn pink at the chastisement. "Of course. Just looking out for you."

We both know that wasn't all she was doing, but other people are finally arriving for the meeting, so I turn my attention back to my notes. I'm not absorbing anything I'm reading. Not paying any attention to Isabel sitting across from me. Nor any of the greetings aimed my way.

She's stunning and has a shit-ton of money.

That's how I described Scarlett just now. Both true. The second fact is the main reason I'm marrying her. The first is a nice, albeit somewhat inconvenient, bonus. But pretty and rich are no longer the first two adjectives I'd use to describe Scarlett Ellsworth. After two conversations, I'd describe her as ambitious.

Fearless.

Vivacious.

That's what I need to look out for.

CHAPTER THREE

SCARLETT

I t would be very easy to break this glass, I decide. To watch the fragments shatter and the golden liquid spread. I roll the thin stem of the champagne flute between my pointer finger and thumb, trying to decide if the temporary thrill will be worth the inevitable mess.

I decide not to and take a sip of fizzy alcohol.

The bubbles burn a trail down my esophagus and simmer in my empty stomach. I hate caviar, and it's all that's been served so far tonight. Part of the endless posturing. I would kill for some fries. To be anywhere else.

Moonlight glimmers off the surface of the pool, bathing the perfectly even stones and pristine landscaping that surround it in a luminous glow.

I suck in a deep lungful of air as I continue staring at the dark surface of the water before me. Oxygen circulates in my bloodstream. Carbon dioxide tries to escape. I don't let it. Even once the uncomfortable sensation turns painful. Finally, I exhale.

Sweet relief flows through me. I feel alive. Refreshed. Cleansed.

"Contemplating a swim?"

I don't react to the sound of his voice, even as awareness sparks across my skin. I do bristle at the taunting comment. As far as I can tell, Crew has two settings: privileged asshole or obnoxious asshole.

"Do I *look* dressed for a swim?" I tug at the shimmering silk gown I'm wearing for emphasis. It's gold. My mother picked it out and had it sent over to my penthouse to wear tonight. Probably as a reminder to the Kensingtons I'm a trophy—a prize.

"You could skinny dip."

I snort. "I bet you'd like that."

"Yeah," Crew replies, stopping beside me. "I would, actually." His voice has turned deep and husky, and it wreaks havoc on my insides.

Crew grew up surrounded by the same beauty I did. I've seen women flit to him like moths to a flame for years. There's no way he's not getting laid on a regular basis. I didn't expect he would act like I'm anything different—like I'm special. He's probably not, and I'm misreading his tone because I'm tired and hungry and more susceptible to feigned honesty than usual. Because *I* am attracted to *him*.

"You have to buy the cow first, *honey*." I continue our nickname game with an indifferent tip of my glass. It doesn't matter what he says. What he thinks. What he suggests.

"I signed, *pumpkin*," he replies.

I don't respond. He did, and it made me wish I'd never made the changes to our prenup in the first place. I wasn't worried Crew would try to seize control of *Haute*. I *am* worried it's made things uneven between us. His refusal was supposed to give me reason not to trust him. Instead, I feel indebted. No gift comes without consequence, in my experience.

Crew hums as he looks outside. "Unseasonably chilly tonight."

"Feel free to take your weatherman audition elsewhere."

This time, the hum almost sounds like a laugh. "I was referring to your personality, *dear*."

That quip isn't deigned a response. I'm on edge enough tonight as it is. My mother and Crew's stepmother manufactured this evening. Now that our families have announced our engagement, the Kensingtons and the Ellsworths are supposed to look like one big happy family.

I've met Crew's father and stepmother before. His father multiple times, his stepmother just once. Candace Kensington is twenty-seven, only two years older than me. Perky and blonde and far more interested in her stepsons than her husband, based on my interpretation of the family dynamic during the last hour. Or the lack thereof.

I watch Crew as he takes a sip of whiskey. "Have you slept with Candace?"

He doesn't react as he swallows, which is disappointing. I was hoping for a dramatic cough or two.

"My father's *wife*?"

"Your stepmother. Yes."

Crew chuckles. Rubs a hand across his clean-shaven jaw. I wonder what he'd look like with stubble, just a little less put together.

"Why are you asking?"

I shrug as I sip more champagne, noting the lack of a no. "Just trying to figure out how much messiness I'm marrying into."

"It's *a* mess," he replies. "Not messy."

"What does that mean?"

"It means it's nothing you can't handle and nothing you can change."

"How vague and mildly complimentary of you."

Crew smirks. "Come on."

He starts walking across the marble floor toward the twin curved staircases. I follow, mostly because I'm sick of staring at the pool and in no hurry to return to the stiff small talk taking place in the drawing room.

My heels hit the smooth rock with a light tap that echoes through the cavernous space with all the subtlety of a gunshot.

The Kensington estate is stunning, but I can't muster any genuine appreciation. I've been in—lived in—mansions just as large and ostentatious as this one. If you stare at shiny objects for too long, they lose their luster.

I've been here a handful of times over the past decade. All the visits were for parties or formal events. Never when the enormous house was empty—of people and of anything besides a wide assortment of antique furniture and priceless art.

The hallway overlooking the pool and grounds is sized similarly to a hotel ballroom, with glass doors that rise to meet the ten-foot ceiling.

Halfway to the staircases that bookend one end of the hall, my stomach growls—loudly.

"Hungry?" There's stifled laughter in his voice.

"I hate caviar."

"I don't think anyone actually *likes* caviar. You just choke it down."

"I never swallow because a guy says so."

Crew clears his throat. Coughs. *Laughs.* "Good."

He takes the comment in stride, and it makes me want to push him further. I pegged Crew as brash and bossy, not easygoing. Maybe he's only like that at work. In bed.

I shove that last thought far, *far* away. I knew I was attracted to Crew. He's objectively gorgeous. But I didn't know I would be attracted to *Crew*. Admiring a guy's ass is different from noticing how he acts. What he wears. What he says.

Watching his Brioni-clad back alter course and turn down another marble-lined hall, I'm unsettled by how much of a distinction I can suddenly find between attraction and interest.

Walking into the gourmet kitchen provides a welcome distraction. I barely have a chance to take in the crystal chandeliers, marble backsplash, and shiny appliances before Crew turns to the right and opens a sliding door. He flicks on a light, and we're in a...pantry.

"Cool," I drone. "I love spending time amidst non-perishables."

"How does that silver spoon taste, Ellsworth?"

I have to bite the inside of my cheek so he doesn't know I find him funny. Or worse, clever. "Better than yours, Kensington."

Crew shakes his head as he opens a small box and holds it out to me. "Here."

I stick my hand in and pull out a circular disk just smaller than my palm. I sniff. "What is it?"

"Chocolate-covered biscuit. I get them every time I'm at the chalet in the Alps." Crew grabs another one out of the box and takes a big bite. Mine is more hesitant. My teeth slowly sink through the thin layer of dark chocolate and into the biscuit. Buttery, slightly bitter deliciousness explodes in my mouth.

"It's good," I decide. "Really good."

"Yeah. I noticed you were...*swallowing*."

I hold his gaze, but I want to look away. There's too much intensity hovering there for a tiny room. It wraps around me and threatens to swallow—pun intended—me whole. "Do you usually spend a lot of time in the pantry when you're visiting your father?"

"Depends."

"On?"

"How long I'm stuck here total."

"Not many happy memories?" I keep my tone light, but I'm really asking. I haven't seen Crew interact with his father and brother much. At parties, they're usually schmoozing separately. Each socializing in their own way. Tonight, they've interacted more like colleagues than a close family.

"Plenty, in this pantry."

I wrinkle my nose. "How charming."

Crew's mouth curl appears but quickly fades. "I meant with my mom. She loved baking." The sudden stoicism dares me to ask more. Warns me not to.

"You never answered me about Candace."

I expect him to accuse me of being jealous, but he doesn't. "Why do you care?"

I shrug. "You know how people are. If there are rumors about you and your stepmother floating around at the Waldorfs' holiday party this year—the way they were last year—it would be nice to know how horrified of a wife I should act." I crunch another biscuit.

"It's probably a better question for Oliver."

"Really?" I don't hide my surprise. The elder Kensington seems more the type not to step a toe out of line.

Crew reads it on my face. "I don't know for certain. Just that he's been over here while Dad is out of town."

"Does that surprise you?"

"Yes and no." Crew sighs. "He's careful not to show it, but this…" He gestures between me and him. "It should be him. Getting married first, becoming CEO, all of it."

My face stays carefully neutral as I reply. "Do you think he'll do anything? Sow opposition in the board?"

"No, I don't think so. Oliver is rational—maybe too rational. He sees the big picture. I don't think he wants to get married. I'm not even sure if he wants to inherit CEO. It's the principle of it... it all *should* have been his."

Unfamiliar guilt churns my stomach. At sixteen, I didn't think this all the way through. I didn't think about the other people who would be affected by my impulsive demand—by my exerting the little authority I had. Expending the small amount of power I'd gained.

"You want it, don't you?" I ask.

He tilts his head to look at me better. I've heard the gossip about Crew's bossiness. His looks. His assurance. People don't talk much about his intelligence. The shrewdness staring at me now suddenly seems like his most dominant feature. It sees me, sees through me. Past the protections that keep everyone else out.

Certain choices are one luxury our lives don't afford. I realize he might think I'm asking about a different decision than I am.

"CEO?" I clarify.

He doesn't have a choice when it comes to *me*. Not anymore. The announcements have been made. The planning is already underway. It would be a scandal of shocking magnitude for either of us to back out of this marriage now—a blow to both of our families' reputations. It shouldn't matter—shouldn't bother me— that he doesn't have other options anymore.

"I want it," he confirms.

The loud crunch of another bite punctuates the statement. "Great." My voice is full of false cheer and real sarcasm. "We should go back. They'll wonder where we are."

"They'll assume it involved milking."

I shoot his charming smile a disgusted look in return.

"Actually, we can't go back yet."

"What do you mean, we *can't* go back yet?"

"I need to give you something."

"Oh." I realize what he's talking about, then glance at the shelves lined with colorful cans and boxes. "In here?"

"I don't think the string quartet or the champagne tower will fit."

Dammit. I thought minimizing any pageantry was one way Crew and I are on the same page. If he has some elaborate proposal speech planned, I'll probably start laughing. Making it seem like this is something that it is not is of no interest to me, especially when we're alone.

Whatever expression I'm wearing makes his crease with what looks a lot like amusement.

"Yeah, I thought so."

"Thought what?"

"Come on." Crew walks out of the pantry. We retrace our steps back to the same hall overlooking the pool and yard.

He approaches the staircase to the left. Silently, I follow. Up the stairs and down the carpeted hall and into a large room filled with dark wood walls and old books. There's a mustiness in the air that smells off-putting but isn't. It's not cozy, but it doesn't feel like a museum, the way the rest of the mansion—minus the pantry—does.

I trace the patterns in the stained glass windows while Crew walks to a painting of a fruit bowl on the wall. He lifts it off, exposing the front of a safe. I continue perusing the room while stealing glances at him.

There's a telltale beep. The safe door opens and closes. The painting returns to its place. Crew walks toward me. There's nothing that could be described as pomp in sight.

This should be as detached as signing on a dotted line. That's what it *is*—a sign of a commitment based on nothing but business. There's nothing moderately romantic about this moment—the dusty books, the stale air, Crew's blank expression—but my pulse picks up anyway. I feel *something*, when I should feel nothing.

Giddiness.

Anticipation.

Interest.

I try to pretend I'm in here with Oliver Kensington instead. If Crew's older brother was approaching me, I'd be unbothered. I wouldn't be mentally measuring the inches separating us. The inches steadily shrinking.

Maybe I messed up *my* life worst of all, I suddenly realize.

Crew stops less than a foot away. Nine inches, I'd estimate. "Here."

I stare down at the small, square, black box that he just dropped on my palm. One glance at his unreadable expression is all I allow myself before opening it. A huge diamond set in a halo of smaller ones twinkles up at me. It screams expensive without seeming garish. It's timeless and classic. Something I would have picked out for myself.

"It's beautiful," I say, truthfully.

Crew doesn't make any attempt to, so I lift the ring out of the box and slide it onto my finger. The weight feels heavy, unfamiliar, and permanent. If I took it off right now, I would still feel the lingering sensation on my skin, like a brand.

Scarlett Kensington. I roll my married name around in my mind, trying to accustom myself to it the same way I'll have to adjust to wearing a sparkling reminder of Crew on my hand.

For once, I have no idea what else to say. *Thank you*? This ring cost a lot, no doubt. But he didn't buy it because he wanted to or because I wanted him to. I don't dole out thanks and apologies as freely as most people do.

"Dinner will be served soon."

I nod, absorbing the sting of dismissal. There's no reason to feel slighted. He's behaving exactly how I expected him to all along: cold and distant. How I *wanted* him to act. If he hadn't agreed to change our prenup so I retain full control of my magazine and hadn't fed me chocolate-covered biscuits, I wouldn't be battling the bizarre urge to ask him what's wrong right now.

From Crew's perspective, I'm a prize.

Property.

A pawn.

Not a partner.

Probably not even a person. My worth to him can be boiled down to my net worth and how I'll look on his arm and the kids we'll have together who will inherit his ancestors' hard work.

I've wondered if I would ever meet a guy that would make me wish for more. That might make me resent how the marriages that last are ones built on understanding and agreements and contingencies. Not love and lust and passion.

Marriages with a purpose preserve empires.

Marriages fueled by desire are plagued by jealousy and ultimatums and whispers at the wedding that the bride must be pregnant.

I've never wondered if that guy might be *him*. Up until right now.

Crew steps to his left at the same time I move to my right. Rather than move further apart, like we both attempted to, we're closer together.

Close enough, he could reach out and touch me.

Close enough, he *does*.

Suddenly the cavernous library doesn't seem so large, after all. We're taking up the smallest percentage of space two people could. The space between us has shrunk further. Three inches, maybe four.

I watch Crew's hand rise, feel the stiff material of his suit brush against my bare arm. His thumb traces across the length of my jaw, leaving a searing trail on my skin that lingers like the lick of a flame. His other palm rises to press against my waist, anchoring me in this spot beside the fireplace.

There's no fire burning in the grate now, just clean, gray stones. That's what I thought Crew and I would be: a bare fireplace. A spot where softer, warmer emotions than duty and obligation *could* be built but *wouldn't* be.

Empty potential.

"Scarlett." His voice slides over me like warm honey, followed by a whisper of whiskey. No one has ever said my name like that before.

Like a prayer and a curse.

A secret and a sin.

A hope and a fear.

I meet his gaze and discover the mask of stoicism has slipped. When I think of passion, I picture bright, flagrant colors. Oranges and reds. Fire and heat and hearts and blood.

From this moment on, I'll imagine light blue. The sky on a sunny day with no sign of clouds. The ocean on a calm day with the barest hint of waves. That's how Crew's eyes appear. So, *so* blue. Endless. Bottomless. *Consuming.* Beneath their calm color lurks the same potential for calamity as the sky and the sea.

If I let him, he'll wreak havoc on my world.

My head.

My heart.

I'm tempted to give in. *Very* tempted. Anticipation and arousal are tangible in the air. I want to know how he kisses. How he tastes. How far he would take this—me and him in a library with our families waiting downstairs.

But I hold firm. "No."

His gaze flashes. Waves crash. Clouds form. He doesn't like being told what to do. Too damn bad—he'd better get used to it. "You're bought and paid for, baby."

Misogynistic asshole. "With money you didn't earn—just like you didn't earn me. Don't act like I had a choice in this and you didn't. We may be in this together, but I'm not yours, Crew. I *never* will be."

His hand tightens its grip just above my hip, the fingers curling possessively and pressing into my skin. It makes me want to jerk away...and press closer. "We're getting married, Scarlett. It's a done deal."

"We'll see." My tone is lofty, almost bored.

I have just as much power here as he does—maybe more. The prenup will only take effect if we divorce. Once we're married, our substantial assets will be combined. He'll be richer than his own father. I'm gaining a lot from this agreement, but he's getting more. No one will look at me and think of how much wealth I'm accumulating. They'll look at the ring on my finger and whisper my new last name with envy—not respect. In their eyes, I'm a clause in a merger. A bonus, not an equal. It's how our world works, and I'll never change anyone's opinion.

Except his.

I have power here, and I refuse to cede any of it. If he wants to kiss me, wants sex from me—wants *anything* at all from me—he'll have to work for it.

I watch him realize it. Battle it. Annoyance, then acceptance settles on his face. He's too proud to beg.

"I'm sure you'll have no problem finding a *willing* participant if you're that desperate," I taunt.

Danger dances in his blue eyes. I watch his brow smooth and his jaw tighten. "Careful, *darling*. That sounded an awful lot like a compliment."

I grit my teeth. He's right; it was one. As much as I would love to claim he holds no appeal, he does. Denying it will only look worse.

Crew moves even closer. I have to tilt my head back to hold his gaze, which I know was a purposeful move on his part. My heart pounds out a steady staccato that feels like a live presence between us.

I'm annoyed with him. I'm also enthralled. Aroused.

The push and pull between us is electrifying.

Addictive.

His hand skims my collarbone, then drops to his side. He's not touching me *anywhere*, but it feels like he's touching me *everywhere*. "You want me, Scarlett. You just won't admit it. I'll find someone *willing*. Fuck her. And when you're *willing*? When you want me? When you're wet for me, just like you are now?" The soft, hypnotic rasp of his low words emphasizes each syllable.

My expression stays indifferent. Inside, I'm hanging on to each word like it's a cliff I'll fall off otherwise.

Crew shakes his head, a mocking, harsh smile spreading across his handsome face. "Baby, you'll have to *beg* me for it."

"I won't." My voice is confident. My body is much less so.

Crew chuckles, dark and ominous and enticing. "Wanna bet?" His breath skates across my cheek.

"I'll never."

"Forever is a long time, Scarlett." He drops his hand from my waist and strolls out of the library, as if he did nothing more than hand me a ring.

Dinner is underwhelming.

It probably would have been regardless, but it's especially uneventful in the wake of the scene in the library. I'm used to men backing down from me. I'm brash and opinionated and, in most people's minds, not worth the trouble.

I figured shooting Crew down would be no different. He would move on to a socialite or a model, and that would be that. I didn't expect an *ultimatum*. Consequences. And it wouldn't matter, if not for the fact that he was right. I owe him nothing—but I want to kiss him.

The possibility of that not happening—not until I *beg*, which I won't—is not a pleasing one.

I'm seated directly across from Oliver, who has spent the past twenty minutes running one finger around the rim of his glass of cognac, trying very hard to impress my father. He's mentioned his law degree no less than twenty times and has cycled through a reel of obviously prepared topics that have ranged from international relations with China to the stock market.

I can see why Arthur sends Oliver out like a golf-playing show pony to every potential investor. My father is definitely intrigued by his perfect son act as Oliver touts Kensington Consolidated's many successes.

Kensington Consolidated has never been a direct competitor of my family's company, Ellsworth Enterprises, but business is business. And Hanson Ellsworth *never* turns down an opportunity to talk business. Not to mention, my father has a new stake in the Kensingtons' substantial assets: me.

I'm bored out of my mind, picking at the filet mignon while Oliver and my father make polite conversation. My mother and Candace are discussing the wedding, which is an equally unappealing topic.

And my fiancé is flirting with one of the female servers. I chime in on the stock market discussion simply to make it clear it doesn't bother me Crew couldn't even wait until the end of dinner to find someone *willing*.

I thought Crew would be easy to ignore—to control. I also knew we'd have a physical relationship. Novelty, at first. For kids, later. It's a prospect that's become increasingly desirable—and demeaning. I won't beg him. I refuse to. I'd rather knock myself up with a turkey baster.

All through dinner, I steal glances at the new addition to my left hand. Arthur Kensington spared a long stare at the diamond ring when I reappeared earlier. A look laced with sadness and longing and sentimentality.

Crew gave me his mother's ring.

I don't know why the possibility didn't occur to me until I saw Arthur's expression, but it didn't. Elizabeth Kensington passed away when Crew was five. I wonder how differently the three men she left behind might look today if she hadn't died so young. Would Arthur be as robotic? Oliver as desperate? Crew as callous?

"I'd *love* some more wine." I interrupt the love fest across the table.

The server startles, finally remembering there are other people in the room. She grabs my glass and scurries off.

Crew's unsettling gaze rests on me for the entire two minutes it takes for her to refill it and return. I don't look away. Our eye contact feels like a chess match, with no pieces to play and no obvious victory.

I don't know what he wants from me. I figured the simple act of marrying him would be where it started and ended. Until we have kids, nothing else needs to change. He'll work. I'll work. Our lives will look like a Venn diagram, with some overlap, but not much.

That moment in the library didn't feel like a neat separation though. It felt like a raging inferno that would incinerate lines, not just blur them. I doused it...temporarily. The embers flicker at me from across the table.

As soon as dessert has been cleared, we end up in the soaring entryway, trading goodbyes. My father is in a short mood. Like Crew said, he and I are a done deal. Hanson Ellsworth doesn't spend time chasing those. This evening was a courtesy, an invitation it would have been too rude to refuse.

I get nodded farewells from Arthur and Oliver and a hug from Candace. I wonder if she can tell I'm so tense I could snap in two. It's becoming increasingly difficult to remain indifferent about my upcoming nuptials. For years, I've told myself it's nothing more than a contract. A business deal. A blending of assets.

With Oliver—with anyone else—it would be.

With Crew, it's different.

My heart hammers when he approaches me. Stops when his thumb catches and rubs against the diamond resting on my left hand. "It looks good on you, *sweetheart*," he whispers, before his lips graze my cheek. The mocking edge to the words destroys any genuine intent.

There's a huge family portrait hanging in the center of the marble staircase, just above the split in the steps. It's of the original Kensington family: Arthur, Elizabeth, Oliver, and Crew. My eyes settle on Elizabeth's left hand, resting on a much younger Crew's shoulder. The diamond on her hand is an exact replica of the diamond on mine.

"Thank you," I manage.

Crew's eyes follow my gaze and flick to the portrait as well, his jaw tightening with realization.

Does he regret giving it to me?

Is he worried I'll think it means something it doesn't?

Was he simply too lazy to go buy me a new one?

Rather than ask for answers to any of those questions, I follow my parents out of the marble foyer and into the crisp spring air.

My mom is talking to me as we walk toward the fountain where our cars are parked. I nod along to whatever she's saying. Something about a dress fitting? I'll get a couple dozen texts reminding me of whatever it is, no doubt.

I thought I'd take more of an interest in my wedding when the time arrived. Barring some catastrophic event, it's the only one I'll ever have. I used to think any apathy toward the event would stem from a lack of significance. That the indifference I felt toward the groom would seep outward and color everything else. Instead, I'm terrified of the opposite. Nervous that caring what white dress I wear or how many tiers the cake is or which flowers are in my bouquet might reveal I care about *him*.

My parents depart first, my father's omnipresent impatience a hasty urge. I linger in the driveway for a few more minutes, looking up at the stone façade of the Kensington manor. Stiff and hard and unreadable—just like its inhabitants. Just like the world I grew up in, the world I'm stuck in.

I have a say here, but not enough of one. Not enough to stop this from happening. I'm expecting the swell of rebellion in my stomach. I'm stubborn, and it's a trait I encourage rather than tamp. But the rebellion doesn't drown out the pinprick of relief.

I don't want Crew to marry someone else. I don't want to marry someone else. Then, I'll never know which of us will break first.

We're getting married. It's a done deal.

His words echo in my head, even when he's nowhere in sight. With a sigh, I climb into the car and instruct my driver to take me back to the office.

I spend the whole drive staring at the ring on my hand. Replaying the words that were spoken—and the words that weren't—after I put it on for the first time. I'll never be able to shake that moment. Not as long as I'm wearing this ring.

Forever is a long time.

No shit.

CHAPTER FOUR

CREW

The cardboard boxes that have lined the front hallway for the last week are piled directly in front of the elevator when the doors to my penthouse open.

What the hell?

I push two stacks aside, wondering if the movers messed up the dates. The building staff would have notified me if they showed up early. The only way up here is through the front desk or with the code only a few people have.

The mystery is solved when Asher appears, wearing basketball shorts and a ball cap reading *Best Man*.

"What are you doing here?" I grumble, dropping my briefcase atop a box and pulling off my jacket. "And what the fuck are you wearing?"

He grins. "I told you I was throwing you a last hurrah! Farewell to bachelorhood and all that jazz."

"And I told *you* that we'll keep getting drunk and picking up women *after* I'm married, so there's really no point in doing anything."

"Well, I didn't listen. Pizza will be here soon. So will Oliver and Jeremy."

I can feel a headache forming as I walk into the kitchen. "You invited *Oliver?*"

"Yep."

"And he said yes?" I open the fridge, debating what to eat. While I deliberate, I grab a beer.

"I wouldn't drink that," Asher tells me.

I pause. "Why?"

"Because I've been reliably informed it's a bad idea to do the activity we'll be partaking in tonight, drunk."

"What the hell kind of bachelor party is spent sober?"

"We go out and get drunk all the time, like you said. I got creative."

With a sigh, I stick the beer back in the fridge. "I'm going to change. Don't move any more boxes around."

"Put on something you'd exercise in!" Asher calls after me.

I grumble a response as I walk down the hallway toward my bedroom. Boxes litter this room too. I've lived here for less than a year, since I graduated business school at Yale and moved back to the city for good. It's strange to see it so empty. Most of my belongings are being shipped to Scarlett's, since she insisted on remaining in her place after our wedding. I was informed—via her attorney telling mine, our main mode of communication—that I was welcome to stay in my own penthouse following our marriage. I have no burning desire to cohabitate with a woman. The only urge outweighing it is the fact I don't share Scarlett's apparent willingness to leave our lives completely unchanged once we share the same last name.

There was a time my younger self dreaded marriage as a prospect involving a clingy wife and no freedom. Fucking laughable, in hindsight. Scarlett seems loathe to so much as to talk with me.

I change out of the suit I've been wearing all day, into a cotton t-shirt and a pair of joggers. New York has been unseasonably cool for June. Candace even called me on Monday to ask if Scarlett was reconsidering her strapless dress. I let a long silence answer for me.

In the short time I've known my father's second wife, I've come to the conclusion she lives in a fantasy world. One where my father views her as a comfort, not a convenience. One where Oliver and I look at her with lust. One where I give any thought to what dress Scarlett might wear on our wedding day and how warm or cold she'll be.

That last one isn't much of a stretch, though.

I went so far as to search photos of *strapless wedding dresses*, just to know what to expect. I've never seen Scarlett look anything short of devastating. I have a whole lot of apprehension about seeing her on our wedding day that I'm certain most grooms don't grapple with.

Lines between us have blurred. Boundaries have sharpened. I can barely think straight when I'm around her. I'm hoping that's a problem that will magically disappear soon.

When I reenter the kitchen, Jeremy and Oliver have arrived. Jeremy Brennan has known me almost as long as Asher has. He's not a native New Yorker; his family is from Boston. We went to the same boarding school in New Hampshire, then both ended up at Harvard. He remained in Boston after Asher and I left for Yale, graduating from law school there a couple of weeks ago.

Jeremy grins as soon as he sees me. "Here's the groom!"

I roll my eyes as I give him a hug and a slap on the back. "Pass the bar yet, Brennan?"

"Knew I should have stayed in Boston." His hometown's

heavy accent saturates each word, sinking syllables in the lazy drawl. "Things I do for you, Kensington. Especially since I didn't get so much as a cigar from you for graduating from the law school that spews out presidents."

That, I do feel bad about. I was planning to return to Harvard for Jeremy's law school graduation, not just send a gift. Back before my marriage became imminent. "I'll make it up to you."

Jeremy shakes his head. "I'm mostly fucking with you, man. I know the job was you. Everyone in my year wanted the position at Kensington Consolidated. I owe you."

"All I did was mention your name," I tell him. It's true. We both know that's all it takes when your last name is plastered on the building.

"All the gift you need will be watching Crew try to manage his bride at the wedding," Asher tells Jeremy, opening one of the boxes of pizza that's appeared on the granite counter of my kitchen island. "Fucking hilarious," he adds around a big bite of pepperoni and cheese.

I grit my teeth and reconsider opening a beer; mysterious activities be damned. Asher insisted on accompanying me to St. Patrick's Cathedral for the one joint wedding-related event neither Scarlett nor I were able to get out of: meeting with the priest. Neither of us have a wedding party. It was Scarlett's request, and one I was happy to go along with. I would have wanted to ask Asher to be my best man—which I guess he picked up on, given his hat—and would have been obligated to ask Oliver instead.

Since the lack of bridesmaids and groomsmen limits the number of people involved in the nuptials themselves considerably, the meeting also involved going over the logistics of the ceremony. Evidently, Hanson Ellsworth decided he didn't need any guidance on walking Scarlett down the aisle, so it ended up being just the two of us sitting and standing in total silence. I'm surprised the priest didn't suggest couples counseling.

Asher didn't witness any of the awkwardness inside the cathedral. He's referring to the fact that Roman, my driver, pulled up outside the cathedral at the same time as Scarlett's car did. Meaning he had a front-row seat to the tense encounter that marked the first time we'd seen each other since the dinner at my family's estate several weeks ago.

An evening meant to build bridges.

Between me and Scarlett, they burned.

"You remember Scarlett, don't you?" Asher asks Jeremy.

Jeremy grins. "She's hard to forget. I had a class with her freshman year. Managerial Accounting." He grins. "She gave the professor a run for his money. Only reason I understood cash flow analysis."

"You talked to her?" I ask, taken aback. During our college years, I was grateful my path never crossed with Scarlett's. Happy to fuck around with whatever—and whoever—I wanted with no reminder of the responsibilities waiting for me following graduation. I never considered my friends might have talked to her. Done more than talked to her.

Jeremy shrugs as he grabs his own slice of pizza. "A couple of times. I mean, there wasn't a guy in that class who wasn't trying to tap that."

My jaw clenches with something that feels a lot like jealousy.

"I mentioned Crew once, trying to impress her," he continues, then laughs. "Had the opposite effect. It took me until sophomore year to figure out why." He glances at me. "Still don't get the whole arranged marriage thing. Leave that to the royal family."

"Crew isn't all that broken up about it," Asher replies. "Without lifting a finger, he's marrying the hottest woman I've ever seen."

I look Oliver's way. He's remained mostly quiet as he munches on pizza. I'm surprised he agreed to come to this. I'm not surprised he's currently reading on his phone. Something related to work, no doubt.

We finish eating and then head out. Asher holds firm in his refusal to share any details of the evening's plans. When the elevator doors open to the lobby of my building, it's just beginning to grow dark outside. Asher and I follow Jeremy and Oliver —who's still on his phone—toward the doors that open onto the street.

Halfway there, I notice a woman standing at the front desk. Her back is to me, but she's wearing jeans, a white blouse, and a pair of pink heels. I trail my eyes up from the splash of color, tracing her curves up until I reach the elaborate braid her brunette hair is pulled back in. Hair the same color as…

"*Scarlett?*"

The woman's shoulders rise and tense. Lower, like she's letting out a long breath. She didn't come here *to* see me, that much is obvious.

"Never mind," I hear her say before she turns around.

In what I guess is her idea of casual attire, she still stuns me. Nothing about her is what I thought was my type. Not the superiority complex or the snappy retorts. Her red lips are twisted into what could best be described as a sneer as she studies me.

"I was hoping not to see you."

Bluntness is a trait I used to think I *did* appreciate.

Asher does a shitty job of muffling his laugh.

"That explains why you're in my building," I retort.

Scarlett sighs. "Since you're here… I need to talk to you." Her glance at Asher is pointed. "Alone."

"I can take a hint," Asher says. "See you outside, Crew."

My eyes stay on Scarlett as Asher disappears to join Oliver

and Jeremy on the sidewalk. Scarlett holds out the envelope she was attempting to hand off at the front desk. "Here. Store it somewhere safe."

I open it and glance inside. There's a plastic keycard, like at a hotel, and a piece of paper with a series of numbers written on it. "You got me a wedding gift?"

"You'll need the code to call the elevator and the card to get into the penthouse."

"If you want to fuck before we're married—"

Scarlett cuts me off with a laugh, like the idea of us having sex is a ludicrous one. "That's not what this is. I won't be home on Saturday night, and since you were so insistent on living together, I—"

I cut her off. "What do you mean, you won't be there on Saturday night?"

"I'm flying to Paris as soon as the reception ends," Scarlett replies. "For a work thing."

"No, you're not." The dispute is automatic. It's our *wedding night*, and she's planning on flying to France? I probably shouldn't be surprised, but I'm shocked.

"Yes, I *am*. Jacques Deux has a waiting list for years. I called in ten favors to get this meeting with him."

"It's our wedding night. People will talk."

"I don't care. Do *you* normally clear your schedule for the night after a merger closes?"

I exhale instead of saying something I'll regret. "What is your meeting about?"

Based on the way Scarlett sighs—like the question is a major inconvenience—she was hoping I wouldn't ask it. "Why?" she challenges.

I say nothing, just stare.

She sighs again. "I'm starting a clothing line. Jacques Deux has worked with every prominent designer in the last decade. His input, his ideas, they'll make a big difference in the success of the brand."

"This is why you changed the prenup," I realize.

The earning potential for *Haute* is nothing compared to a clothing brand. Especially one created by Scarlett soon-to-be Kensington. Public interest in the both of us has skyrocketed since our engagement was announced. We're a fairytale, minus the ugly stepsisters or the poor beginnings.

"If I hadn't, this could be a conversation. But I *did*, and you *signed*, so it's not. If I need to go to Paris for a meeting, I'll go to Paris."

"It's only the timing I have issue with," I tell her, quietly. I didn't have expectations for our wedding night, but I definitely had hopes. Fantasies that required her to be in New York City, not the capital of France.

Her brow wrinkles for a minute before it smooths. "I can't change the timing, Crew."

"Fine." I don't even know why I'm bothering to argue.

"Fine," she echoes. Glances away from me, looks back, and sighs. "I wrote my cell number down in there too. In case you have questions about the building."

I could lie, but I don't. "I have your number, Scarlett."

She raises one eyebrow. "I didn't give it to you."

"I know. I got it a while ago. I thought about reaching out to you a few times. Thought it might..." I shake my head. "I don't know. It doesn't matter. Go wherever you want, Scarlett."

"I will."

She's getting what she wants, yet she still sounds pissed. Rather than push, I nod toward the door. "That all?"

Her chin jerks up. "Yes. That's *all*." She spins and heads toward the glass doors that lead to the street.

"Great," I mutter sarcastically as I follow. Based on the way her shoulders stiffen, she heard me.

Asher, Jeremy, and Oliver are all waiting out on the sidewalk.

"Leaving so soon, Scarlett?" Asher teases.

"I don't usually loiter around apartment buildings," she replies. "Where are you gentlemen headed to?"

"Crew's bachelor party," Asher replies. He spins his *Best Man* baseball cap around so she can see the front. "I know you lovebirds decided to limit the crowds up front, but I couldn't resist."

"Cute," Scarlett comments.

I *almost* smile.

"You should come," Asher suggests.

Scarlett clears her throat. "What?"

"Crew is way more fun to be around when you're here."

I shoot Asher a sharp glare for that comment. This isn't a wide-eyed socialite he's baiting. In two days, the woman beside me will be my wife. There's a line, and he's crossing it.

"Let's go, Asher."

He shrugs. "Sure. This will be a challenge for us anyway. Let alone a woman."

I close my eyes and mentally call Asher every name I can think of. My best man just ensured my fiancée will be at my bachelor party.

The rock gym is crowded when we arrive. I'm surprised; the number of people here demonstrates a higher interest in the activity than I expected it to have.

This is exactly *not* what I thought my bachelor party might be like: climbing fake cliffs with my fiancée in tow.

Scarlett heads for the small store attached to the gym, probably to swap out the six-inch stilettos she's wearing for shoes with a flat bottom. She says nothing to me before she leaves, keeping the void of silence that's hovered between us intact. It stretched the whole drive here, interrupted by polite small talk, mostly between her and Jeremy. I think she's lying about remembering him from the class they supposedly shared and I hope that means one of my closest friends doesn't know more about my fiancée than I do.

"I can't believe you," I tell Asher, as he pulls out a pair of what are apparently rock-climbing shoes I'm sure he bought just for this occasion. "I told you I didn't want to do anything. Then you plan *this* and invite *her*?"

Asher smirks as he tugs off his sneakers and yanks on the shoes that look like rubber socks. "One, this will be fun. I came with Charles Goldsmith last month and it was a blast. Two, *you're welcome*. Your blushing bride will barely look at you, and it's obviously bothering the shit out of you. You *like* her."

I scoff. "What are you, ten? I don't *like* her; I'm *stuck* with her. My father would permanently disown me if this marriage doesn't happen. Doesn't last. It has nothing to do with Scarlett. Although…" I glance at the display of climbing shoes visible through the glass wall separating the store from the gym itself, where Scarlett is talking to a sales associate. "It doesn't seem like it would *kill* her to act like it's less of an inconvenience."

"What did you expect? You've said for years this is just business."

"It is. And she's making it harder than it needs to be by acting like this is personal, not professional." Although I started it, I suppose. I've never wanted to kiss anyone more than I did in that library.

"Maybe she's worried it is."

I contemplate that for a few seconds. Then dismiss the possibility. "I think *resigned* would be a better adjective. She wants to live separately, for fuck's sake."

"But you aren't. I had to shove twenty boxes aside to get into your place."

"Not by choice. Hers or *mine*." I emphasize the final word, because Asher seems to think I'm excited about this sham of a marriage. The only part I was looking forward to seems to be on a permanent hold. After our encounter in the library, I had my doubts about a traditional wedding night. Following the surprise trip to Paris she just sprung on me, I'm harboring no hope.

"You agreed to move into her place."

"It was that or go another round with the lawyers. If she wants to stay in her penthouse so badly, I don't really care. It's probably just as nice."

"It's *nicer*, actually." Scarlett's voice sounds behind me. "There's a private entrance for the penthouse, and I have my own doorman. I spent five minutes waiting to talk to one of yours before you popped up like some sort of Crew-in-a-box."

I'm glad my back is to her. It makes it easier to hide my smile at her made-up phrase. When I do turn around, it's to discover Scarlett has made her outfit as rock-climbing friendly as possible. Her long hair is pulled up in a ponytail, exposing the elegant column of her neck and the hollow of her throat. The pink heels are gone, replaced with a similar style to what Asher is wearing, and the sleeves of her white blouse have been rolled up.

"A whole five minutes?" I drawl. "What a devoted fiancée you've turned into, honey."

The newfound devotion is expressed with an eye roll.

"Oh, there's Dave!" Asher exclaims, sounding more excited than I've heard him sound about anything that didn't involve women, booze, or cars. Apparently, he was serious when he said he's come here before.

Dave approaches us, matching Asher's enthusiasm. If I passed Dave on the street, I wouldn't be the least bit surprised to learn he works as a rock-climbing instructor. His dreadlocks are pulled back by a purple bandana and he's wearing an easygoing smile that would look wildly out of place in a boardroom. "Hey, dude!" Dave greets. "Back already?"

"Yep. Brought some buddies too. We're celebrating this guy's wedding." Asher claps me on the back, and I force a smile I'm sure comes across as more of a grimace.

"No way." Dave looks like the idea of having a bachelor party here has never occurred to him, and I wish Asher could say the same. "Congrats, man," he says to me.

"Thanks, Dave." Not many people have *congratulated* me about my upcoming wedding. They've acknowledged it. Nodded knowingly. Told me *good work* or *well done*. Every one of them has known why I'm marrying Scarlett. But I don't know how to tell Dave I'm a multi-billionaire marrying for money, so I do my best to act genuinely enthused by the prospect. Made easier and harder by my fiancée's presence a few feet away.

"I'll go grab you guys some gear," Dave says. "There's…four of you?"

"Five," Asher corrects, nodding toward the front desk where Oliver is standing, talking on the phone. He took a call as soon as we arrived and hasn't moved since.

"All right. We usually start in pairs." Dave glances around, then looks at me. "How about you wait for the straggler?" He smiles at Scarlett. "We can work together."

I don't wait to see if it's an arrangement Scarlett will protest. "No. She and I will work together."

Dave raises his hands in an *all good* gesture. "Sorry, man. I get the overprotective brother thing. I'm the same way with my sister."

Asher snorts a laugh. Jeremy starts coughing. If I looked over at Scarlett, I'm guessing she's wearing the same expression of horror I am.

Dave looks between me and Scarlett, his dreadlocks bobbing with each confused movement. "Oh. Are you two not siblings?"

"No," I grit out. "She's my fiancée."

"I just assumed..." he trails. "Never heard of a fiancée attending a bachelor party before."

"We like to do things together." How I manage to say that sentence with a straight face, I have no idea. I'm equally impressed no one laughs.

But Dave nods, looking completely serious. "I get it. My folks are the same way. They each get one activity to indulge the other one on, since they hate doing things separately. My mom hates football and hasn't missed a Giants game in twenty years. My father couldn't draw a stick figure but goes to an oil painting class with her every week." Dave pauses and smiles. "I bet you guys will be just as happy. Whose activity is this?" His eyes bounce between us again.

"Uh..." I'm slow to speak after that. I've never witnessed that sort of relationship in person. I know my father loved my mother. She may have been the only person he's ever loved. When it comes to me and Oliver, he hands out occasional praise, not affection. However he expressed any sentimentality toward my mother, I was too young to remember any of it.

"Crew." Scarlett clears her throat. "This was Crew's idea."

"Excellent choice, man." Dave smiles at me before his attention returns to Scarlett. "And what are you going to pick?"

"Uh…" she stalls. For the first time ever, I see Scarlett look unsure. Rather than revel in it, I scramble to come up with some random hobby I can blurt out. *Golf?*

"It can be anything," Dave urges. "Anything you've always wanted to try?"

"We doing this or not?" Oliver appears, phone in hand. "If not, I'm heading back to the office."

"You can think it over some more," Dave tells Scarlett, then turns to the rest of us. "I'll meet you all by the wall over there." He points vaguely toward the right before heading to the left. We're surrounded by nothing *but* walls. Not just the four typical ones, but lots of additional ones covered with colorful, fake rocks meant as continual handholds.

"Do we think he's qualified to teach people how to scale cliffs?" Jeremy questions.

"Dave's great," Asher replies. "Super chill."

"That's exactly what I'm worried about," Jeremy replies. "*Super chill* isn't the first qualification I'd consider in an instructor."

I ignore their bickering and ask Oliver, "What was the call about?"

My brother grimaces. "Powers wants to come back to the table without the marketing division."

"He's folding?"

Oliver nods. "He held out for longer than I expected him to."

"Me too," I agree.

Dave reappears with ropes and harnesses for a short tutorial on what we're supposed to do in order to leave the ground. Despite Jeremy's misgivings, Dave seems knowledgeable. I'm more concerned with the woman beside me than Dave's laid-back personality. If anything, his ease is a welcome addition to the group. Scarlett seems to be growing tenser by the second.

Once the demonstration ends, we're sent off to a corner of the gym. Asher immediately starts climbing while Jeremy spots him. Oliver is further down, talking with Dave. Probably trying to get out of doing this.

Scarlett clips on her harness and stares up at the rock face that extends fifty feet up in the air. I stare at her. She looks over suddenly, catching me studying her profile.

"Well?" I prompt.

"Well *what*?"

"*Well*, are you going to climb the damn thing or not?" I drawl.

"Give me a minute," she snaps.

"For what? The wall is *right in front of you*. Just grab a handle and get started. It's easy."

"I never said it was hard!"

"Then why aren't you climbing?"

"I'm...preparing."

I scoff. "Preparing for what?"

"Preparing to put my life in your less than capable hands. I'm not exactly overflowing with confidence in your ability to catch me."

"You're wearing a harness attached to a rope above a foam mat. *Of course* I'm not going to catch you. Don't be ridiculous."

"With charm like that, it's shocking anyone tells you no," she retorts. Her words are sharp and her stance is confrontational. But there's something hovering beneath the annoyance, obvious in the way she won't meet my gaze and is fiddling with the strap of the harness.

"Tell me what's really wrong," I demand.

"I told you, I'm—"

"*Scarlett.*"

Her teeth sink into the full, bright red of her lower lip. I've avoided looking at her mouth. The last time I paid it too close attention, I almost kissed her. I'm about to say her name again when she answers. "I'm apprehensive about being too high off the ground."

The meaning sinks in slowly. "You're scared of heights," I realize, then laugh. "Are you kidding me?"

"That is *not* what I said," Scarlett replies hotly. "I just—"

"Six one way, half-dozen the other," I respond. "*Say* it however you want, that's what you meant."

She considers that. "Fine. Heights aren't my favorite."

I laugh again. "Unbelievable. You're really *that* stubborn? You came to a climbing gym and you're scared of heights?"

"One, you're not Mr. Easy Going yourself. Two, I didn't know we were going to a rock-climbing gym. Your misogynistic friend didn't specify when he invited me."

"Asher is far from a misogynist. He loves women."

Scarlett rolls her eyes. "Loving women and respecting women are two different things."

I feel a sudden urge to defend Asher, despite the fact he's the reason I'm standing here arguing with her. "He respects women too."

"Do you?"

I stiffen and glare. "What the fuck kind of question is that? You're marrying me, and you don't think I respect women?"

"I didn't say that you don't, I asked if you do."

"You've got a creative way of saying everything, huh?"

Her chin rises as she glowers right back at me. "You want to know why I came here, Crew? To prove myself. Because I *always* have to prove myself. When you show up at Kensington Consolidated, people don't assume you're there to meet your dad for lunch. They don't think they know more than you do about the company that is your family's legacy. They don't wonder about who you'll marry because they assume that person will have a say in their job one day. We may be similar in some ways, but we are *not* the same."

She unclips the belt and steps out of the harness. I was annoyed she came. Now I'm irritated she appears to be leaving. "What are you doing?"

"Everything okay over here?" Dave appears, his calm face showing only the slightest hint of concern. In his world, things probably go according to plan. He probably doesn't even *have* a plan.

"Fine." Scarlett gives him a small, tight smile that anyone with eyes could see is fake. "Unfortunately, I have to go." She doesn't even make up an excuse. "Thanks for your help, Dave."

"Scarlett..." I start.

She walks away without a word, brunette ponytail swishing. Mocking me with each step. Scarlett only pauses to change back into her heels. Then she's gone, cutting through the crowded street and out of sight.

I'm beginning to wonder if I'll ever watch her leave without a mixture of anger and regret.

For my sanity's sake, I sure hope so.

CHAPTER FIVE

SCARLETT

My mother starts crying when she sees me standing in my wedding dress. I'm not expecting her tears. After almost thirty years of marriage to the emotionless void known as my father, I didn't think there would be much sentimentality on display today. Just appreciation for the hasty planning it took to pull off what every news publication is calling the wedding of the century.

In the past six weeks since my engagement to Crew was announced, every detail of my wedding has been considered. Every possible problem accounted for. Every *minute* accounted for.

This is an unplanned one. Sophie and Nadia snuck into the room off the transept, where I've spent the morning getting ready to say hello. Sophie was the one who begged me to show them my dress. I've only worn it once since I approved the design, for the fitting to confirm my measurements hadn't changed.

I take all three reactions in—Sophie's wide eyes, Nadia's gasp, my mother's tears—before I turn to stare at my reflection. I love this dress. Love it more than I should. Love it more than any other article of clothing I've ever worn.

It's strapless. The line of my collarbone and curve of my shoulder are exposed above the intricately detailed corset. Alluring without being outrageous. The hand-stitched lace leads to layers of cloud-soft tulle and a sweeping train that trails several feet behind me. I've never felt more beautiful than I do wearing this dress. It's a gown meant for a bride who's excited about her wedding. Who has no doubts—about anything, much less her choice of groom.

Somewhat unfortunately, not to mention surprisingly, I fulfill both criteria.

Hovering in the doorway, I watch my mother swipe at her cheeks before she speaks. I figured I had another twenty minutes before she returned from running through every detail with the wedding planner—again. "Scarlett! Why are you wearing your dress already? Your hair still needs to be done."

Nadia and Sophie both startle at the sound of her sharp tone. I know it well, though. It's much easier to mask emotions under harshness than happiness.

"I know. I'll change back." I smile at Sophie and Nadia. "I'll see you guys after, okay?" They take the offered out, slipping back out of the room immediately. I'm left to change and face my mother. I hang my wedding dress back inside its bag and pull on the silk robe I was wearing before, over the white lingerie my husband won't see.

"You're ready?" my mother asks. For more than the hair-dresser, I gather.

I inhale, then make the request I've debated since I woke up this morning. I expected it to feel like an ordinary day. None of it has felt that way. Not showering or eating breakfast or riding to the cathedral where I'll become Scarlett Kensington. "Is Crew here?"

My mother studies me, curiosity burning in the hazel irises I inherited. "Of course." She sounds offended by the mere possibility he might not be. Any hiccup today would be more than a slight against me.

"Can you...get him?"

My mom sighs. "Scarlett, if you're having second thoughts—"

"I'm *not*. I just want to talk to him."

"I don't think that—"

I cut her off again. "*Mom*. Please."

Maybe it's the please that convinces her. I'm not sure the last time that word was spoken between us. From my mouth, at least.

"Okay. I'll ask." She disappears out into the expanse of the cathedral that's filled with people preparing for the wedding or guests showing up extra early for good seats.

I'm all alone in here.

The star of the show and the pariah.

I'm nervous. I didn't think I would be, and it's the final sign that this is not a business deal. A merger like any other. Maybe it is to Arthur Kensington. To my father. To the rest of Manhattan's elite, who have all gossiped about the possibility of this day for years. To Crew. But for me, it's different. Telling myself it isn't won't change that fact.

This is my *wedding*, my *marriage*.

It's personal.

When the door opens again a few minutes later, I know it's not my mother. I can just tell.

He came.

"You're not wearing your dress."

I turn to face him. "You're not supposed to see me in my dress until I'm down the aisle."

"I didn't think you were the superstitious type. Or particularly sentimental." Crew says the words casually, before slipping his hands in his pockets. He looks relaxed. Completely at ease about what is about to happen between us, and it loosens the tight knot in my chest some.

"I don't want our first kiss to be out there." I blurt the statement, which is really more of a request.

Something about today—the dress and the dreaminess and the date itself—has led me to the very real realization today is my wedding. In all likelihood, I'll never have another. I'll be married to this man for the rest of my life. And I've never even *kissed* him.

Should it bother me? Probably not.

But it does.

Something akin to amusement settles in his face. "Is that so?"

It's tempting to back down, but I don't. "Yes." I study him, trying to get a read on what he's thinking. Feeling. I come up blank. He's as effusive as an empty page. "You were basically begging to kiss me a few weeks ago," I remind him of our moment in the library.

A ghost of a smile flickers across his face, as if that memory is a fond one rather than a frustrating one. "I remember."

"So?" I'm growing impatient. Annoyed. *Why can't anything between us be straightforward?*

"Do you?"

"Do I *what*?" I'm rapidly regretting this entire idea. He's right; it's not like me. Maybe this marriage won't last, and it'll never matter anyway.

"*Remember.*"

My spine straightens like it was just injected with lead as the implication hits. "You can't be serious."

Crew tilts his head to the left, showing off the sharp line of his jaw. It tightens as his expression turns daring. "*Beg* me, and I'll kiss you, Scarlett."

"You're…" I search for the right insult and come up short. "I can't believe you."

"I warned you, baby."

"You're just pissed I hurt your pride."

Crew doesn't respond, but a muscle ticks in his jaw.

"Begging is not happening. I'm not that desperate. See you on the altar, *baby*." The nickname holds no sentimentality, only mocking.

He doesn't move. There's a *long*, heavy silence. Weighted down by second guessing and appraisals and regrets. "Ask me."

"Ask you *what*?"

"Ask me to *kiss you*, Scarlett. Isn't that what this conversation has been about?"

Honestly, I've lost track. It's become a push and pull—a battle of wills. Each of us feeling out what we're willing to give up. What we won't agree to concede on. "I don't *ask* for things, either. I take them."

"So do I."

We stare at each other, at a stalemate. I want to kiss him. Badly. I've never wanted to erase the distance between my lips and someone else's more. He wants to kiss me. Just as badly, if his tense posture is any indication.

Pride keeps me in place. He doesn't move either.

"I need to finish getting ready." I say it softly. A fact, not a foot out the door. I'm not backing down. I'm not giving him an excuse.

Crew releases an exasperated sigh, like some major inconvenience is taking place. I'm expecting him to turn and leave. Instead, he approaches me with the conviction of a conquering king, diminishing the few feet separating us with a couple of long strides. He cups my face, his fingers brushing my cheeks, as he tilts my head back and forces my gaze to meet his. "Tell me," he demands.

I question him with my eyes, tempted to sway into his touch. I'm losing ground, and I blame his close proximity for encroaching. It's hard to think—to *breathe*—when he's touching me.

"*Tell me* to *kiss you*, Scarlett." His thumb traces my bottom lip.

Goosebumps rise on my skin. Shivers race down my spine.

He's compromising. Ceding. It prompts a heady rush of power. I didn't capitulate—*he* did. With anyone else, I'd perceive it as weakness. But this doesn't make me think less of Crew—it makes me want him more.

"Kiss me."

The *e* is still hovering in the air between us when he complies. His lips crash against mine, demanding and urgent and commanding. The hands gripping my face are gentle. His mouth is anything but. The wet heat of his tongue invades my mouth, forcing a moan out.

Crew Kensington tastes like whiskey and mint. Sin and seduction. Pleasure and power. And this is exactly why I told him *no* in the library—I knew we would be this combustible. I knew if I let him, he'd burn me. Consume me.

I can respect him.

I can explore my attraction to him.

I just can't care about him.

Success isn't built on good intentions and consideration of others.

His lips leave mine. Too soon. I want to kiss him until I'm out of oxygen. I want to relish the way he makes me forget this is fake.

When I open my eyes, he's staring straight at me. I have no idea what to say, how to reconcile who we were before and who we are after that kiss. A distinction I didn't think I'd have to make before saying *I do*. That's when before and after were *supposed* to start. I'm realizing, as my lips tingle and my pulse pounds, it might have started a long time ago.

I clear my throat. "You should go."

If he's bothered by the immediate dismissal, he doesn't show it. Crew nods once, brisk and business-like. His hands fall away from my face, and I immediately miss their warmth. Their possessive presumptuousness. "See you out there."

I watch him turn and walk away, warring with myself. He gave me an inch. I can do the same. Marriage is about compromise, right?

"Crew." He pauses when I speak but doesn't turn around. My eyes coast over his broad shoulders, stretching the tux jacket tight. Unlike me, he's already wearing his wedding attire. I'm glad he doesn't turn around. It makes it easier to spit out, "Thank you."

He doesn't look back. The door closes behind him a few seconds later, leaving me alone. Surrounded by shoe boxes and cans of hairspray and the products painted on my face, waiting for the hairstylist to appear so I can change into my dress and walk down the aisle.

CHAPTER SIX

CREW

I hear her before I see her. Subtle sounds alert me to Scarlett's approach. There's the glide of satin and silk and whatever else wedding dresses are constructed from across the marble floor. The whispers of the crowd. The swell of the music before it reaches the crescendo that's supposed to signify her arrival at the altar.

According to the one time we practiced this, I'm not meant to turn until Scarlett has reached the final pew. I'm happy to comply. I wouldn't know *how* to look. Stoic is my default setting. That's not how a groom is meant to look, watching his bride come down the aisle. We're supposed to be selling a love story to everyone who is in attendance today. Stock in our families' companies has skyrocketed since our engagement was announced a few weeks ago. Scarlett and I are the faces of the future. The stronger we appear, the better.

Deals fall apart.

Business partners part ways.

Marriages are made of tougher stuff, at least in our world.

Divorce is rare when fidelity isn't expected and each party will end up poorer for it.

My cue to turn appears. I look to the left. Without realizing it, I started holding my breath.

I don't exhale, even when my lungs begin to burn.

I don't move, even though I'm supposed to take a step toward her.

I just stare.

The first time I saw Scarlett Ellsworth, I was fifteen years old. So was she. We were both kids playing adults. I was wearing a custom suit I'd outgrow in a couple of weeks. Scarlett was wearing a floor-length gown, heels, and makeup. I was drunk— off Thomas Archibald's father's scotch. Breaking into studies and sneaking expensive liquor was a common pastime at parties on the Upper East Side.

I thought she was beautiful then.

I've thought she looked stunning every single time I've seen her in the ten years that have elapsed since. Scarlett possesses a classic, timeless poise that provides the same presence as actual royalty.

But today? She's devastatingly, heartbreakingly beautiful. The untouchable sort of regal. An ice queen. A snow angel. A moon goddess. She walks toward me on her father's arm surrounded by a waterfall of white organza, her brunette hair curled in an elaborate updo and her lips painted their signature crimson shade.

Hanson Ellsworth doesn't walk her all the way to me. He stops at the last pew, and Scarlett takes the final steps toward me alone. When she reaches me, I demonstrate more staring. More not moving. It's not customary for the bride and groom to pause before approaching the priest, and the rustling of the audience emphasizes that.

"Hi."

"Hi." I clear my throat. "Ready?"

"Ready." There's no hint of hesitation on her face.

I rely on her confidence like a crutch. "You look..." I flip through adjectives that all fall short. The best I can come up with is "stunning," but it doesn't say everything I'm trying to.

Scarlett looks away after I compliment her, up at the altar where we're about to get married. "Thank you."

We start up the short row of steps that lead to the waiting priest, side by side. The priest launches into a speech about the sanctity of marriage. I don't pay close attention to any of the readings that follow. I'm mostly focused on not looking over at Scarlett. We're on display up here, and I'm no longer worried about appearing too indifferent to her presence. I'm concerned about the exact opposite—giving away too much.

When it comes time for the vows, I have no choice but to look at her. Scarlett hands off her bouquet, and we're stuck staring at each other while the rings are blessed.

I go first. When we met with Father Callahan, he asked if we would be writing out our own vows. Scarlett and I talked over each other in our haste to let him know we'd be sticking with the traditional ones. I wasn't worried about saying them. But suddenly these words—ones that millions of people have said millions of times before during millions of weddings—sound far too intimate as I look at her.

"I, Crew Anthony Kensington, take you, Scarlett Cordelia Ellsworth, to be my wife, to have and to hold from this day forward, for better, for worse, for richer, for poorer, in sickness and in health, to love and to cherish, until death do we part." I slide the diamond wedding band onto her ring finger. "I give this ring as a sign of my love."

The priest looks to Scarlett expectantly. She doesn't need any prompting. Her voice is clear and unwavering, echoing off the glass windows and the marble floor and the dark wood.

"I, Scarlett Cordelia Ellsworth, take you, Crew Anthony Kensington, to be my husband, to have and to hold from this day forward, for better, for worse, for richer, for poorer, in sickness and in health, to love and to cherish, until death do we part." She slides the platinum wedding ring onto my third finger. It's far from heavy but impossible to ignore. A reminder of her I'll always see—whether I want to or not. "I give this ring as a sign of my love."

If I weren't watching her so closely, I would miss the flicker of trepidation as it passes across her perfectly painted face. Scarlett knows what happens next, same as I do. I wonder if she's more or less apprehensive about this kiss following her request earlier.

"You may kiss the bride."

I watch Scarlett smother the urge to roll her eyes. She obviously doesn't appreciate the priest "allowing" me to kiss her. But I'm close enough to see her breath hitch and her eyes widen. She *wants* to kiss me; she just doesn't want to admit it.

I take a step forward slowly. Deliberately.

Actions I don't usually think twice about, I'm second-guessing. The small space between us shrinks to nothing, until the stiff fabric of my tuxedo is pressed against the white material of her dress. This is the closest we've *ever* been, save for that brief moment earlier.

I was annoyed then. At her for asking. At myself for capitulating. Women chase me, not the other way around. And, ironically, the one woman whose attention should be a given is the only person whose lack of it bothers me. I admire her for treating me with a callousness I didn't expect, for not getting swept up in the pomp and circumstance of what is, at the end of the day, nothing more than a business arrangement. However, it's put me in the strange situation of having to pursue what I want from her.

My expectations of this marriage never included a wife who wants nothing to do with me. It would be convenient—if not for the fact I find Scarlett captivating and intriguing. I want her attention.

I have no idea when I'll kiss her again after this, so I intend to savor every second. Most of today—the gold foil invitations and the thousand plus attendees and the flowers covering the end of every pew—seemed unnecessary. This feels *very* necessary.

The thin lace of her veil tickles my palms as I raise my hands. I cradle her face like it's a bubble that might pop. Like it's the most precious possession I own. Her pulse thrums rapidly, just below her jawline. Her eyes turn heated, betraying how her body hasn't moved at all. I hesitate for a few more seconds, letting the anticipation build to a breaking point.

She may want to—try to—forget this day. This moment.

She won't be able to.

Our lips collide. I can taste her surprise, followed by relief the torture has ended. I'm not finished though. I slide my hands down to rest on her waist as I tease my tongue along the seam of her lips. I swallow the slight gasp that allows the entry I'm seeking. Then she starts kissing me back and I forget everything I was trying to accomplish.

Our kiss is fireworks and heat and passion. Combustible. Explosive. Electric. More than a cold fusion of assets. It's a struggle to remember where we are. Why it's not an option to bend her over the nearest available surface.

Ice can be chipped away at. But fire? Only fools trifle with fire. Fire destroys everything in its path.

There's a split-second, right after I pull away and end the kiss, where this feels *real*. When I'm looking at her and she's looking at me and that's the extent of anything that matters. It lingers between us...and then it's gone.

"I present to you, for the first time, Mr. and Mrs. Crew Kensington!"

I incline my head. Scarlett gives me a barely perceptible nod. And we turn, facing the crowd that is clapping and cheering and standing.

We're married. The woman standing next to me is my wife. I've had almost a decade to get used to the idea. It wasn't long enough, clearly, because the words sound strange in my head. Maybe marriage is one of those things that can't be prepared for.

Maybe it's that I *care*—about her, about the significance of the vows we just exchanged—and I didn't think I would.

I take the hand hanging limply at her side, and we start our descent. Past my father and Candace and Oliver. Past Scarlett's parents. Past the politicians and celebrities and the business moguls. People who think they're witnessing a fairy tale and people who know a monopoly was just secured.

The aisle is long. I keep a smile pasted on my face for the full few minutes it takes to traverse from the apse of the cathedral to its narthex. As soon as we pass the final pew, I let the fake expression fall. There's a small army waiting for us outside the doors. Scarlett is ushered away by two women immediately, and I'm left to nod along to the wedding planner as she talks.

It's probably an accurate representation of how the rest of our lives together will look.

The reception is worse than I imagined it might be. Usually, I'm selective about who I socialize with. Tonight, I have no choice. Every person here wants a moment with me. A chance to offer congratulations and earn favor.

Scarlett is surrounded as well. The first time I have a chance to talk to her is several hours after we left the altar, during our first dance. She's looking at me, but she's not *really* looking. I know it's purposeful. I caught a glimpse of vulnerability earlier. Now she's reinforcing her walls. Battening down the emotional hatches.

I shouldn't care.

It shouldn't make me want to push.

"Maybe we should have practiced this too," I suggest, as she moves stiff and unwilling in my arms. For a second, I catch a glimpse of a smile. "I think we should set some ground rules."

"For?" she asks, glancing away. Out at the admiring onlookers surrounding us. A few cameras flash.

"Us."

Scarlett is no longer pretending to pay attention to the crowd. Her eyes fly to mine. "You want to discuss this *now*?"

"You're still leaving tonight, right? I figured it would be best to hammer out some details before then. Plus, you've avoided me since we got engaged."

"I avoided you before then too."

"Well, it ends now, *wife*."

I feel her back tense through the thin fabric of her wedding dress. "And you thought our first dance would be the most appropriate venue?"

"I figured there was a higher chance you wouldn't walk away during the conversation, yes."

"I'm not a coward," Scarlett states.

"I never called you one."

Her chin rises to a defiant tilt. "There's nothing to discuss, Crew. I said I'd marry you, and I just did. That's the extent of *us*."

"The start of us."

"The *extent*," she reiterates.

"I assume you want separate bedrooms?"

She holds my gaze. "I have a chef and a maid. One of them will show you to your room when you get to my place tonight."

"Sex?"

"Be discreet."

"With *you*, Scarlett."

Her throat bobs as she swallows. "I don't know yet. Maybe sometimes."

Maybe sometimes? I shake my head. "You don't want anything from me."

It's not a question. She answers anyway. "I don't want anything from you."

"Okay."

"Okay," she echoes. "We don't need to pretend."

"I'm not pretending."

Those three words linger between us.

The rest of our dance is silent. When it ends, we both move on to our other obligations. Scarlett begins dancing with her father, while I twirl Candace.

It's been years since I wished my mother was alive so viscerally. But this day? This moment? It's one I wish she were here for. From what little I remember and have heard about Elizabeth Kensington, she was sweet and calm. She softened my father's rough edges, which have only sharpened over time. Today would have been romantic, in her eyes. Rather than Candace's endless babbling about the dinner and the cake and the flowers, I imagine she'd ask me if I feel different, as a married man. Lecture me on how to treat Scarlett. Maybe she would have talked my father out of the agreement to begin with. I'll never know.

After the song ends, I ask Josephine Ellsworth. I catch Scarlett's surprised look as we walk onto the dance floor, like the thought of me dancing with her mother never occurred to her.

"You outdid yourself, Mrs. Ellsworth," I compliment as we spin. "Everything was perfect."

Unlike her daughter, Josephine is modest and demure. Pink tinges her cheeks before she glances away at the sea of elaborately decorated tables surrounding us. "Call me Josephine. And it was my pleasure, truly. I'm glad *you* appreciated it."

I half-smile at the emphasis, under no delusions about who Josephine is referring to. I also correct my earlier assumption. She has more fire than she lets on. "I've gathered Scarlett isn't the sort to accept decisions she didn't make."

"Scarlett doesn't do anything she doesn't want to, either."

I feel my brow wrinkle with confusion.

Josephine smiles, and there's an almost daring edge to it. "Don't let my daughter convince you she had no choice in this matter."

"Of course she had *a* choice. Scarlett would have been stupid not to accept this, though. And she's not."

"She's not," Josephine agrees. "But she's smart enough to know her options. She doesn't need you for anything, Crew."

I muffle the smile that wants to appear in response to her earnest expression. This is remarkably similar to the conversation I just had with Scarlett herself. "She may not need anything from me, but she's getting plenty."

"Yes, she is."

I wait, but that's all she says until the song ends a minute later.

"Thank you for the dance, Crew. Scarlett chose well. And she *did* —choose. No matter how she acts. Indifference is a means of survival in this world. I imagine you know that as well as anyone."

With those parting words, she disappears into the crowd. I head for the bar, craving a moment of solitude and a stiff drink. Today has felt endless. Every minute meticulously planned from the moment I woke up.

I order a whiskey from the bartender and lean against the counter serving as a makeshift bar. I stay in place once he hands it to me, sipping the amber liquid and surveying my surroundings.

"Quite the event, Mr. Kensington."

I glance to my left and almost choke. The liquor slides down my esophagus with a stinging stab, rather than the usual pleasant burn. "Mr. Raymond. How nice to see you, sir."

"You can call me Royce," he replies, adopting a similar pose beside me as he orders a drink. I hide my surprise. Royce Raymond is a media mogul, whose production company consistently churns out blockbuster hits. There's not an actor in Hollywood who doesn't want to work with him. He's famous for his hands on approach to everything. Supposedly, not even a PA gets hired on one of his sets without his say so. He's just as well known for his antisocial tendencies, which include snubbing many of the coveted invitations he receives. I'm shocked he's here.

"I'm glad you could make it. Royce."

The older man makes an unintelligible sound.

"Are you in New York for long?" Last I knew, his primary residence was in Los Angeles.

"Long enough."

"Long enough for what?"

"You'll be taking over for your father soon?"

"That's the general assumption. You'd have to ask him for the specifics."

"I've never much cared for Arthur. Too power-hungry for my taste. Although...I suppose you're the one who just married billions."

I hold his gaze as he studies me appraisingly. "Money isn't the only reason I married Scarlett." I expect the words to sound false. To ring with insincerity. They don't.

"A bold statement for a man who just inherited an empire."

"Don't confuse me for my father."

"If that were the case, we wouldn't be having this conversation, Crew."

"What conversation would that be?"

Royce smiles. "You know I have no children of my own."

"I do."

"I'm...entertaining the idea of passing the torch. Would that interest you?"

"A partnership?"

He shakes his head. "Full ownership. It's been fifty years. Nothing lasts forever. When I find the right person, it will be time to move on."

"I assume you know I have no experience in the film industry?"

He chuckles. "I'm looking for someone with good business sense and a moral compass. The latter is difficult to find in this world."

"Thank you?"

Another chuckle. "I'm not looking for a figurehead to collect a hefty percentage. *That*, I could find easily. I've never entertained any of your father's offers because I've seen what happens to companies underneath the Kensington Consolidated umbrella. I know how business works. But it's not how my business works—how it will ever work."

"You would want me to choose," I realize.

"Arthur is…what? Fifty-four? Fifty-six? I wouldn't be expecting him to hand the biggest office over anytime soon, son or not."

"I'm happy in my current position."

"I'm certain you are. But it's different to inherit versus to earn. I built everything I have, same as your great-grandfather."

"Because you had to, in order to succeed. Kensington Consolidated is my legacy. No sane person would turn their back on a thriving birthright to hack it on their own."

"I'm not sure your new wife would appreciate that characterization."

I open my mouth, then close it. "That's different," I finally manage.

"Is it?" Royce challenges. "I find it difficult to believe there wasn't a place at Ellsworth Enterprises for Hanson's only child."

"I believe Scarlett had diverging interests. Ellsworth doesn't own any magazines."

"They offer limited opportunities in other ways as well."

"Perhaps," I acknowledge.

Royce picks up the glass the bartender delivered without me noticing. "Think it over. And congratulations. I expect great things from you and the new Mrs. Kensington."

The end of the reception passes more quickly. The important, older guests begin to leave. I'm left to drink and talk with people I consider friends.

The wedding planner, a petite woman named Sienna, is the one who tells me it's time to make our grand exit.

"Where's Scarlett?"

"Changing. She'll meet you in the lobby."

When I get to the lobby, Scarlett is already waiting. She's wearing another white dress. This one has straps and no train. The silky material clings to her curves, covering her from head to toe in an ivory waterfall.

All I get is a cursory glance. "Good. You're here. Let's go."

I grab her hand before she can take a step. She doesn't ask what I'm doing. Doesn't move as I release my grip and trail my fingers up her arm. Her hair is still pulled back in a fancy knot, baring her shoulders and neck. I trace all the exposed skin, savoring the goosebumps that raise on her skin.

I take another step closer, pressing my body against her side.

She inhales sharply. In the wide, empty space, it's all I can hear. The music and chatter coming from the ballroom sound distant and muffled.

Neither of us say a word. This is a silent truce.

My hand falls away.

Your move.

Scarlett turns, so our bodies are flush. Her eyes scan my face. I have no idea what she's looking for.

I don't know if she finds it or not. But she does kiss me, which is what *I* was looking for.

Her taste hits my system like a drug. Something about Scarlett—her prickliness, her beauty, the fact she's my wife—sharpens sensations. I can't recall the last time I kissed someone else, expecting it to go no further. That's the *only* way I've kissed Scarlett. I pay attention to things I normally wouldn't, not distracted by flying clothes or finding the nearest hard surface.

She smells like lilac and tastes like champagne. Her warm curves crush against me as she deepens the kiss. I slide my hands down her back and settle them on her hips, tugging her closer even though there's nowhere to go. We're already pressed as tight together as two people can be.

If the hem wasn't out of reach, I'd pull up her dress and slide a hand between her thighs. Instead, I journey back north, cupping her left breast and confirming she's not wearing a bra. She moans my name and the sound ricochets around my insides.

This was supposed to be a tease—a preview of what she's missing out on tonight by choosing to fly across the Atlantic. It's turned into torture. She's affected, but so am I. Rock hard and desperate.

Scarlett pulls back first. I let her move away, watching as she straightens her dress and smooths the fabric. I want her—badly. I've never been this affected by a woman before. If she wasn't a former Ellsworth turned Kensington, wasn't my *wife*, I'd tell her exactly how much. Describe exactly what I want to do to her.

Hell, I'm tempted to do it anyway. But then she smirks— triumphantly, *knowingly*. And I'm reminded of just how far out of my depth I am with her.

"You want *nothing* from me, Scarlett?" I pose it like a question, but it's a taunt.

"Nothing," she reiterates. Her voice is as resolute as it was on the dancefloor, but there's no empty edge this time. There's a teasing lilt that calls out my lack of indifference but also tells me there's at least one thing she wants from me.

Before either of us can say anything else, Sienna appears and herds us toward the front of the hotel. She's talking a mile a minute, relaying details I don't care about. I gather the gist is the walk we're about to make to a waiting limo.

A smaller hand slips into mine right before we reach the doors. I have no idea when the last time I held hands with someone was. This shouldn't count. We're the main event in an elaborate show, and this is just one piece of the choreography. But for a few seconds, the warm press of her palm is all I can focus on.

The doors open to a dazzling display of light and sound. A literal carpet—white, not red—has been rolled from the entrance of the hotel to our waiting car. Small potted trees strung with twinkling lights separate the pathway from guests tossing flower petals.

I force a wide smile onto my face. A glance at Scarlett shows she's beaming just as bright and false.

Our families are waiting by the limo. Cameras flash as I shake my dad's hand and hug Candace. I watch as Scarlett hugs her mom and gets a kiss on the cheek from her father. Like a dutiful husband, I help her into the back before climbing into the car myself.

"New dress just for the car ride?" I ask as the limo begins to move.

"You expected me to fly six hours with a five-foot train?"

"I didn't give any thought to the *clothes* you're wearing, actually."

She raises one eyebrow.

I raise one back. "Do you have anything on underneath?"

There's a glimpse of amusement before her expression shutters to blank. "Something you'd see—if we got married for real."

I get what she means, that we're not the traditional love story. We didn't meet at Harvard, bonding over a harsh professor at a study group. We didn't date for years. I didn't propose on a rooftop covered with flowers and pop a bottle of prosecco. But...

"We *are* married for real, Scarlett."

She tilts her head to stare out the window instead of replying.

Fifteen minutes later, we're pulling up to the private terminal of JFK.

"Bye." That's all she says before climbing out.

I watch from behind the tinted glass as she talks to the driver for a minute before an attendant comes over to retrieve her bags. She has three of them, which makes me realize I never asked how long she would be gone for.

The driver gets back into the car. Scarlett heads inside the airport. And the limo pulls back into the busy traffic.

When it stops for a second time, outside a building on Park Avenue, I'm confused. Then, I realize where I am. I step outside into the humid air and walk into Scarlett's lobby. It's expensive and minimalistic. The space is mostly black with gold accents. There's one desk, which a man with gray hair is standing behind. He gives me a respectful nod as I pass.

I use the plastic card Scarlett gave me to call the elevator and then type in the code I memorized.

She was right. Her place *is* nicer than mine.

I step out of the elevator. The far wall is mostly glass, showing off the terrace that spans the full length of the building, overlooking Central Park and the Reservoir.

The floor plan is mostly open, the spectacular view uninterrupted. There's a neat formation of white couches and a gleaming black Steinway sitting in the corner. I walk deeper, discovering the formal dining room, a living room, the library, a study, and then the kitchen.

Finished touring the downstairs, I walk upstairs, peeking into each room as I go. There are eight bedrooms, one of them Scarlett's. My bags and boxes have all been stacked in the corner of the bedroom farthest from hers.

I wonder whose idea that was.

Most of my belongings, the decorations and furniture, were put into storage or left at my old place. The bulk of what I brought along were clothes. Rather than unpacking or sorting through anything, I lie back on the white bedspread and stare out at the shimmering skyline of Manhattan. I could call someone. A woman. Asher or Jeremy. Go out to a club or a bar.

I'm too tired. Too drained.

Looks like I'll be spending my wedding night...alone.

CHAPTER SEVEN

SCARLETT

The warm summer air is tinged with a hint of smoke when we step outside the restaurant. A slight breeze ruffles the hem of my dress and blows my hair back.

Jacques pauses to kiss both of my cheeks. "*Magnifique*, Scarlett," he declares. Loudly enough, the group who exited ahead of us turns to look. "This line will be *magnifique*. A triumph." He pulls me in for a hug. "You need anything—anything at all, you let me know, *oui*?"

"*Oui.*" I return the warm embrace. "*Merci beaucoup.*"

Jacques departs after a few more Frenglish phrases. My French is enough to get by, but I'm far from fluent. Jacques and I learned to communicate through a nonsensical mesh of the two languages while collaborating on my new label.

I loiter outside the bistro where we just ate dinner for a few minutes, debating whether to call a car or walk the few blocks to the hotel where I've been staying for the past two weeks.

"Want a smoke?" The question comes from my left, delivered in a thick French accent. I look over to see a blond-haired man leaning against the brick siding of the building. He's wearing a leather jacket and holding a lit cigarette. I walk over to him, choosing my steps carefully on the cobblestones.

"I'm not a big smoker." I abhor it, actually. It's a gross, grimy habit I associate with the reckless and a disregard for personal hygiene.

Framed by the soft glow of streetlights and distant glimmer of the Eiffel Tower, it suddenly seems more sexy than repulsive. So does the lazy smile being flashed my way, paired with a slightly crooked nose and a jaw covered with a light layer of stubble. "I'm working on quitting," he tells me.

"Seems like it's going well." I look pointedly at the gray smoke curling up from the orange tip and dissipating into the dark night.

He drops the cigarette and snuffs it out with a heavy boot. "I'm Andre."

"Scarlett."

"A beautiful name for a beautiful woman."

"*Merci.*"

His eyes light up. "*Parlez-vous français?*"

"*Je parle un peu français,*" I admit.

Andre chuckles. "Your pronunciation is very good."

"Thank you," I reply. "I've been here for a couple of weeks. It's improved."

"Are you staying much longer?"

"No. I'm leaving tomorrow."

"Headed where?"

"Home. New York."

"The big fruit," he declares.

I laugh. "Apple. Yeah."

"Would you like a memorable final night?" The insinuation is obvious. In the way his body is angled toward mine. The smirk dancing on his lips.

I hesitate. When I approached him, this is exactly where I thought it would lead. We both know it. Now it's on the table, and I'm undecided. The rings decorating my left hand suddenly seem heavier. I didn't expect being married to feel any different. I signed a contract that happened to include a religious ceremony.

My loyalty to Crew can have conditions. I've been gone for two weeks. He's probably had a rotating door of women coming through my penthouse. Growing up, I watched my mother send my father off on business trips with a *travel safe*, knowing full well he wouldn't be traveling alone.

I promised myself I'd be different—wouldn't be the fool who fell for the fairytale. But I angle away from Andre anyway. "All I was looking for was a cigarette."

Andre's hand sneaks into his jacket and emerges with a pack of them. He hands me one. "A smoker, after all?"

I shrug. "We all do things we know are bad for us, right?"

He holds a lighter out and flicks a flame to life. I hold the end of the cigarette out, letting the fire lick the paper until it ignites. "Your husband?"

I follow his gaze to the massive diamond resting on my ring finger. I could have taken it off as soon as my plane left the tarmac in New York. Instead, I've worn the symbols of my marriage every day I've been here. I've adjusted to the weight and the sparkles. If I ever do take them off, it will feel strange. My hand will feel naked. "No."

"Pardon. I assumed…"

"Wrong," I finish, taking a single drag of the cigarette before I drop and snuff it. The street is littered with them. "I should go."

Andre says nothing as I walk away, trench coat swishing around my calves. I'm annoyed with myself. A fling with a Frenchman sounds perfect. It's been weeks since I had sex. I can track it to one night, even. After Crew chased Evan away, I didn't cast my metaphorical net out again. I turned down the two men who approached me later that evening. I knew I'd have the same problem with them that I would have had with Andre.

I'd pretend it was Crew kissing me. Touching me. I *refuse* to do that. It would be a concession of the worst sort. I'd rather be celibate than let one man fuck me while pretending he was someone else.

It would let Crew win in the worst way.

He only has as much influence over me as I allow him to have.

The street is crowded with chatter and laughter. I don't stop at any of the rowdy bars I pass, which are all filled with Andres with arousing accents and smooth suggestions. The only spot I stop at is a wine shop on the same block as my hotel. I pick up a bottle of Bordeaux and carry it like a newborn into the lobby and up the stairs to the third floor.

My room is spacious, and yet I head out onto the tiny balcony that juts off the side of the hotel and overlooks the Seine. It's barely large enough for the one chair out here. I kick off my heels, shed my coat, and use the corkscrew provided in the room to open the bottle. I rest my toes on the wrought-iron railing and stare at the city lights, occasionally taking sips of the tart wine.

I could be in Andre's bed right now, having sweet nothings whispered in my ear in French and warm hands running across my skin. Instead, I'm quickly nursing the bottle equivalent of my third glass of wine. I'll feel like shit in the morning.

My flight leaves early tomorrow, so I'll be back in Manhattan by noon. I'll likely have to face *him* before brunch with Sophie and Nadia the following morning.

It's been complete and total silence from Crew since I left after the wedding. No asking if I landed safely. No wondering when I'm coming home. Nothing at all.

Exactly what I wanted—what I thought I wanted.

Instead, I think of him saying *I'm not pretending.* Recall the feel of his lips against mine. Chastise myself for doing both.

Crew is a cliff. Dangerous. Challenging. One wrong step could be catastrophic.

You're stronger than this, Scarlett.

I'm not, though. Not when I'm alone with no chance of facing consequences. That's confirmed when I slip my phone out of my pocket and log into the security app for my penthouse. It's just past one a.m. here. Crew is reliably home by seven p.m. Earlier than I ever used to return. I wonder if his schedule will change once I'm back in New York. If he'll avoid being in our shared home, the same way I will.

I flip through the cameras until I find him. He's in the kitchen, talking to Phillipe. There's sound but I don't turn it on. I drink wine from the bottle and watch my husband—still bizarre to think, let alone say—talk to Phillipe while eating a plate of pasta. His suit jacket is off, but his tie is still on, hanging slightly crooked as he twirls pasta on his fork and smiles.

He's home and alone.

I fall asleep watching him.

I missed Manhattan.

I didn't realize how much until I step onto the tarmac outside the private wing of JFK. The sight of the skyline is an unexpected relief, like treating a wound you just realized was inflicted. My lungs fill with the scent of exhaust and wet cement. The commotion wakes me more than the espresso I downed on the plane.

A car is waiting. I climb inside and instruct the driver to take me to my office. Leah, my assistant, and Andrea, the head of my editorial section, both know the real reason why I spent the past two weeks in Paris. The rest of *Haute*'s employees know it was a work trip, just not as part of a new endeavor.

I'm going to need to delegate most of my responsibilities at either *Haute* or *rouge*—what I've decided to name my clothing line—but I haven't decided how to handle either yet. Managing both might be possible once I have more of a design team in place for the clothing label. I'm happy to spend as little time at my penthouse as possible. Juggling two demanding roles is a certain way to accomplish that.

My arrival back at the office causes a stir. I stride past the cubicles and down to my corner office, half-listening to Leah as she trots beside me, spouting off everything I'm supposed to handle today.

I feel like shit. I changed out of a wrinkled sundress on the plane, into the tight sheath dress I'm wearing now. The stiff fabric feels constrictive. My head is pounding and my limbs feel heavy. Three hours of sleep and most of a bottle of wine might not have been setting myself up for success today.

Crew's fault.

Two weeks away from him were supposed to settle me. Remind me of how little my life has changed and that my priorities haven't shifted. Scarlett Kensington can be the same person as Scarlett Ellsworth was.

Three thousand six hundred and twenty-five miles sounded like a lot. Sounded like plenty of distance.

They weren't.

I thought about him. While I was attending photoshoots. When I was picking out fabrics. As Jacques was showing me sketches. Last night, when I went home alone.

Leah keeps talking. Rather than admit I haven't been paying much attention, I tell her I have to make a phone call. She scurries out of my office, shutting the door behind her and leaving me in silence. I sink down into my desk chair and lean forward to massage my temples. For the first time since taking over *Haute*, I don't want to be here.

I want to go home. Not out of wifely obligation or because I missed sleeping in my own bed. I want to get seeing him over with. The anticipation is worse than anything he might say or do. A couple of months ago, I'd expect him to act entirely indifferent to my departure and return.

Now I don't know what to expect. It's annoying and nerve-wracking.

I shake a Tylenol out of the container I keep in my top desk drawer and swallow it. Even if I went home right now, Crew wouldn't be there. He's been returning to the penthouse reliably at seven, although that might change, now that I'm back. I know Leah gave his secretary my travel itinerary. If he wanted to, he could have known the second my jet's wheels hit the tarmac. But that would suggest a level of interest in my whereabouts I don't think he has. His behavior before and during our wedding was probably a novelty.

Crew may have experience with women. He doesn't have experience with a wife.

That title comes with weight, even in an arrangement like ours. And I know I'm complicating matters by withholding sex. If I had already slept with him, that would have been that. By waiting, I'm giving it significance. Importance. Maybe even meaning. My intentions for waiting were to achieve the opposite.

If I'd stayed for our wedding night, I would have had the sound of him promising to honor and cherish and love me running through my head while he was inside me. I needed time to establish emotional distance before I allow the physical distance to disappear.

At least, that's what I told myself at the time. I'm no longer certain it will make any difference at all.

I stare out at the New York skyline until my head stops pounding. Then I stand and head into an endless slew of meetings. Everything I have to approve—which *is* everything—has stacked up during my absence. Photo format and models and photographers and products and samples and articles.

When I'm finished with the final batch of approvals, I ask Leah to order me lunch from the cafe down the street and head back to my office. A familiar figure is waiting on the couch in the seating area just outside the door.

I sigh, my headache returning in full force. "Hi, Mom," I greet when I reach her.

"Scarlett." Her green-brown irises skate over my appearance with a discerning eye.

I got dressed on an airplane, but she won't find anything to critique. "What are you doing here?"

She's only visited me at *Haute* once before. My father threw a small fit after I purchased the magazine without his permission— not to mention money—and my mother is skilled at self-preservation. I don't blame her for deferring to my father; Hanson Ellsworth is a formidable opponent. I promised myself a long time ago I would never defer to my future husband the way my mother has always acquiesced when it comes to my father.

"I wanted to see how married life is treating you."

"It's fine." A query that would be easier to answer if I'd actually seen or talked to Crew since our wedding.

"Hmmm." Something in my mother's voice makes me think she might know that already.

I didn't tell her or my father about my trip to Paris, but I wouldn't put it past her to dig it up. As far as my father is concerned, I'm Crew's problem and responsibility now. But my mother is the ringleader of the New York gossip circuit. Nothing happens on this island without her hearing about it.

I break the pointed silence. "Was there anything else, Mom? I've got a lot of work to get done."

"No, nothing else. Let's get lunch next week. I'll have your secretary set something up."

"Fine." I agree, knowing arguing will be pointless.

My mother pauses. "You chose well, Scarlett."

I sigh. "Chose what well?"

"Crew."

The sound of his name hits me unexpectedly. I tell myself it's because I wasn't expecting that to be her response. "We both know he wasn't a choice, Mom."

"We both know you've never gone through with a thing you didn't want to, Scarlett." She raises both of her perfectly manicured brows, as if daring me to disagree with her. I tell myself I don't because it doesn't matter what she thinks.

"I've got a lot of work to get done…"

"All right, all right, I'll get going. Just—he's your chance, Scarlett."

I tell myself not to answer. For the third time, my brain doesn't listen. "My chance for *what*? I already have everything I need."

"Your chance for *happiness*, sweetheart."

I scoff at that, then glance at Leah's desk. She's trying very hard to act like she's not listening to this conversation. "Crew Kensington? He's…he's a means to an end. Nothing more. Treating this like the business relationship it is *will* make me happy."

My mother purses her lips, but she doesn't argue. I'm used to her small bursts of maternal concern buried between critiques and strict instructions. "You'll be in the Hamptons for the Fourth next weekend, right?"

Shit. How is that already next weekend? My parents throw a massive party at their house in the Hamptons for the Fourth of July every year. I've been dreading it more than usual ever since I learned I would already be married to Crew by the beginning of July. We'll be expected to act like the united, loving couple we aren't for a couple of days.

"Yeah. I'll be there."

"And Crew?"

I look away. "I assume so." That sounds better than *I'll have my secretary ask his secretary.*

The small shake of her head makes it clear that's not the answer my mother was looking for, but she doesn't comment further before she turns and leaves.

Rather than head into my office once she disappears, I walk toward the kitchenette around the corner. I pull a sparkling water out of the fridge and carry it into my office, pressing the cold glass bottle against my forehead as soon as I'm out of sight from the rest of the floor. I take a seat at my desk and spin around so I'm staring out at the skyline. My vision blurs as my focus disappears, turning the sharp angles into a jumble.

Home feels different now.

Three hours later, I leave my office. Leah looks up as soon as the door opens, ready for a request or a question. Instead, I tell her, "I'm headed out for the day."

If she's trying to mask her shock, she's doing a poor job of it. Her coffee almost gets upended and sticky notes go flying as she struggles to comprehend my statement. "You're—I mean, you're —it's—" Leah glances at the clock on her computer, as if I'm unaware it's not even five p.m. yet.

"I have some personal business to take care of. I've been gone for a while."

"I—sure, of course."

Despite the fact I'm feeling worse instead of better, I manage a smile. "I have a life outside this office, Leah."

That makes her panic more. "Of course you do. I didn't mean —I... Please don't fire me."

I laugh, then wince as my head gives a particularly painful throb. "I'll be back in first thing tomorrow."

Leah nods. "Before you go..."

I pause. "Yes?"

"Your, uh, your husband's secretary called earlier. While you were in the meeting with Lilyanne Morris."

"And?"

"She called about the Rutherford gala for the children's hospital on Friday. Mr. Kensington is requesting you attend with him."

"Fine."

Leah looks relieved by my answer. "Okay. I'll let Celeste know."

"No need. I'll handle it." I'll have to talk to Crew eventually. It might as well include a conversation about how we'll handle our joint social calendar.

Leah very obviously wants to ask me what I mean by that, but doesn't. I want my employees to feel comfortable approaching me, but I don't invite or indulge speculation about my personal life. That policy has been more difficult to enforce as of late, for obvious reasons. I let the news coverage inform my employees of my hasty engagement and marriage.

Telling someone something invites an opinion on it.

I say goodbye to Leah and head for the elevators, texting my driver to let him know I'm leaving. Twenty minutes later, I climb out of the car and walk into my building to take another elevator up to the top floor.

When the doors open, exhaustion hits me so fast I feel dizzy. This penthouse has always been a safe space for me—somewhere I can be Scarlett. Not poised or prepared or professional or anything anyone expects from me. I resent Crew for taking that sanctuary away from me.

Around him, I feel the compulsion to be perfect, more so than I've ever felt with anyone else. I care what he thinks of me. I can't genuinely say that about anyone else, even my parents. It's a problem—one I don't have the energy to think about right now. Especially since he doesn't appear to be here. There's nothing indicating he ever has been.

I'm not sure why I expected my home to look different—but I did. I thought there would be some obvious evidence a man lives here now. Maybe boxers on the floor or a tie draped on the couch or a strip of condoms on the coffee table. There's nothing. Not even a water stain on the teak coffee table I picked out. The tidiness is really all I absorb before I flop face-first onto the white couch. It's uncomfortable, having my face smushed against the cushions. The construction crew hammering away at my skull isn't all that relaxing either. I'm too uncomfortable to fall asleep and too comfortable to move upstairs.

I must fall asleep, though, because when my eyes blink open, I'm no longer alone. At first, I think the shadowy figure must be Phillipe or Martha. Then, I realize it's too broad and tall to be either my chef or my maid. Recognize the way my traitorous heart starts beating faster for no good reason at all. I'm lying down—no exertion in sight.

"Rough trip?" Crew asks. The low, rough timbre of his voice washes over me, temporarily taking care of the headache. Adrenaline erases exhaustion. I forgot how stupidly symmetrical his face is.

I groan in response. My head still hurts. My throat is dry and my muscles feel stiff. "I feel like shit."

"I gathered." There's a dry note to his voice that makes me think I must look as terrible as I feel. I shouldn't care. I do. Crew Kensington is the last person I want to exhibit any sort of weakness in front of.

He approaches me hesitantly, like I'm a rabid animal likely to attack. If I could move my head, I would. I'd stand up and go far, far away. Somewhere I can't smell him and sense him and see him. I close my eyes, like shutting off that sense will help. "I just need a minute before going upstairs. Go...do whatever. Have a drink in the library like usual."

"How would you know what my usual is?"

Crap. Shit. Fuck. I keep my eyes closed and hope my face doesn't say *I browsed the security footage instead of watching Netflix while I was in Paris.* "You're just predictable, I guess."

Crew hums. It's an infuriating sound that gives no indication of whether or not he believes me. I consider opening my eyes and decide I'd rather not know what he's thinking. A warm palm presses against my forehead. I flinch. The physical contact is unexpected. So is the gentle way his hand brushes my hair off my face. My skin prickles, reacting to his touch even after it disappears.

"How long have you been like this?"

"I don't know. I'm hungover or tired or jetlagged or all three.

The couch was closer than my bed. I haven't left the office before five...ever."

The last sentence isn't necessary. I feel some strange compulsion to justify the fact I'm splayed out on the cushions like a starfish while it's still light out. To prove I don't sit back and collect a paycheck. Once again, I shouldn't care. But I *do*. I care that my mascara must be smudged and my hair matted, and my work ethic appears questionable.

Crew doesn't reply. Then, suddenly, I'm not lying horizontal on the couch. I'm weightless—at least that's how it feels at first. A few seconds later, I'm rocking. I focus on the solid press of his chest and arms. My head isn't appreciative of the movement. The rest of my body embraces the sensation of Crew carrying me. But I protest anyway. "What the hell are you doing?"

"How out of it are you? I thought it was obvious."

I'm not out of it at *all* anymore. I wish I were. Every sensation I'm experiencing right now are ones I'm fully present for. Worse, I'll be able to remember this later. The way he smells good and feels even better. The press of a metal band against the skin of my thigh that symbolizes he belongs to me in a way many people would consider permanent.

I clear my throat. "This is sort of sweet of you, but I'm *fine*." I pack as much conviction into the last word as I can muster.

"I think that couch would disagree."

Crew starts up the stairs. I stop arguing. If he's going to be stubborn about it, I'm best off pretending this is no big deal. Like I let men carry me bridal style all the time.

He turns to the right as soon as we reach the top of the steps and heads straight into my bedroom. "You explored?" The question comes out dry. There are seven guest bedrooms, minus the one he's claimed as his own. This wasn't just a lucky guess.

"What's yours is mine, baby."

"Don't call me that," I mumble. The heat of his body is seeping into mine, and it's making me sleepy. Sleepier. I haven't slept well in weeks. Before I left for Paris, I was riddled with nerves about the wedding. In Paris, I worked late and was woken up early by the market underneath my balcony. I'm the sort of tired that blurs reality. I wouldn't be shocked if I wake up on the couch in an hour to learn this was a dream.

Rather than dump me on the bed, Crew carries me into the attached bathroom and sets me down on the marble that surrounds the tub. "What are you doing?" I question.

He doesn't answer. Either with an explanation or by telling me I'm asking the obvious again. It *is* obvious when he starts the tap running and dumps in an assortment of the salts and soaps from the glass containers set along the windowsill. Steam starts to rise from the water, swirling with the fragrant scents of rose and eucalyptus and steadily building bubbles.

Once the tub is filled, Crew shuts the water off and pulls me standing. I'm worried I might fall asleep mid-bath. I'm far more concerned this sweet gesture might make me say or do something very stupid.

Crew's eyes hold mine hostage as he reaches behind me and tugs at the zipper of my dress. I feel the back gape open and slide down. He pulls the fabric over my shoulders. With a quiet *whoosh*, the silk hits the floor, leaving me standing in my bra and underwear. He doesn't drop his gaze. Blue burns me, roots me in place.

His touch is clinical and detached. Neither hand lingers as he unsnaps my bra and lowers my thong. In seconds, I'm naked before him.

"Do you need me to get you anything?" He holds eye contact, not looking lower.

"I…" I clear my throat and shake my head. "I'm good."

Arousal is a better stimulant than caffeine. I'm no longer worried about falling asleep and accidentally drowning. I'm standing in front of him, totally naked, while he's completely dressed. After he ran me a *bath*. And Crew is acting like all of this is a normal occurrence.

"I'll be having a drink in the library if you need me." There's no missing the teasing in his tone. I hope it's because I called him predictable and not because he suspects I spent nights in Paris spying on him.

"Okay." The word flies out fast.

He needs to get out of here. Before I find out how serious he was about the begging. Before I beg.

Crew disappears, closing the bathroom door behind him. I climb into the tub, letting the hot water envelop my body inch by inch until I'm accustomed to the temperature. It feels like heaven. The steam clears my head and the warmth chases away the long day of travel followed by work.

I sit in the tub until the water starts to cool. Once it's tepid, I climb out and pull on a silk robe, not bothering to dry my hair or brush it. When I walk back into my bedroom, there's a glass of water on the table next to the bed. Along with a bottle of Tylenol. I stall in place for a few seconds, unexpected emotions threatening to overwhelm me.

After taking two pills, I slip between the cool sheets and immediately fall asleep.

CHAPTER EIGHT

CREW

Her eyes widen she sees me. Barely, but I'm watching her closely enough to see the subtle shift in her face. Aside from her eyes, Scarlett's expression remains sanguine. Two women are trailing her. One is typing frantically on her phone, probably taking notes. The other is balancing a tall stack of binders.

Scarlett's steps don't falter as she strides straight toward me. As they near, I can hear what she's saying. "Hopkins should be booked for Thursday. Tell him I want two locations, preferably three. I handled the models already and all the samples from Chanel should be arriving on Monday. Tell Jeanette Richardson I need her piece on the wildlife foundation next week or she'll be bumped until next year. Same with the travel feature. I'll need final versions by Wednesday."

She stops at my side. "Crew."

"Scarlett."

"Ready?"

"You're not going to introduce me?"

Scarlett shoots me an annoyed look before turning back to the two women. "Crew, this is Leah, my main assistant."

A petite woman with a blonde bob and black glasses gives me a small smile.

"And Andrea, my head of editorial content."

"Lovely to meet you both." I smile.

Andrea gives me an unimpressed look, while Leah looks away. Working with Scarlett has clearly rubbed off on them.

"I'll be in the office tomorrow, if you need to reach me," Scarlett says. Her tone is brisk. Both women hang on to every word. "Did you bring the Lorenzo sketches?" she asks Andrea.

Wordlessly, Andrea hands over one of the binders. Scarlett opens it and flips through a few of the pages. "Perfect. Good night."

"Good night," they both chorus, ignoring me. Whatever impression Scarlett has given them of me, it hasn't been complimentary. And they're loyal to her, the sort of loyalty that can't be bought, only earned. It makes me admire her more, and there wasn't a lack of it to begin with. She bought this flailing magazine and turned it into a thriving enterprise. I'm impressed. Proud —despite the fact I have no credit to claim. My sole contribution is that Scarlett seems set on spending as little time in my company as possible. If she's actually spending the bulk of the time she's not at the penthouse working, she's logging ninety-hour weeks.

I move, straightening from the side of the limo I've been leaning against, and open the door. Andrea and Leah disappear back inside the building that houses *Haute*'s offices, leaving us on the bustling street.

"What a gentleman."

"You'd think differently if you trusted yourself to be alone with me."

Scarlett's eyes flash as she slides onto the leather seat,

arranging the blue organza so it covers up the flash of calf I just caught. The gown she's wearing is off-the-shoulder with a sweetheart neckline that dips between the curves of her breasts. Standing while she sits offers one hell of a view.

"It has nothing to do with trust."

I hum before shutting the car door and rounding the rear of the car to climb in the other side. As soon as my door shuts, the limo pulls out into traffic.

"Good day?"

She's already started flipping through pages in one of the binders Andrea left her with. "Yeah. Fine."

Stubbornly—stupidly—I press her. "What did you do?"

"More than fetch daddy's coffee."

Scarlett is trying to piss me off. Ever since the night she got back from Paris—when I carried her upstairs and demonstrated an incredible amount of self-control by not stealing a glimpse of her naked—she's been prickly and combative every chance she's had. I have a feeling if I'd come home to find her in heels and standing, not curled up on the couch, the animosity might be dialed down a notch. She's definitely not indifferent toward me. I'm not sure if this is an improvement though.

I got up for a glass of water at three a.m. two nights ago. Scarlett was standing in the kitchen in her standard attire of a dress and heels, making a cup of tea. I haven't seen her in jeans since my bachelor party, much less sweatpants or pajamas.

She's already turned back to her binders, but I feel obligated to respond. "I'm the Vice President of—"

"I don't care, Crew. Do whatever you want at work. Do whatever you want when you're not at work. Just don't tell me when I can or *can't* work."

"I didn't tell you couldn't work. I asked you about work, Scarlett." I let some ire leak into my voice. Me being nice freaked her out. I can be short instead. "But let's just sit in awkward fucking silence, same as we have every day since you got back."

"Great. Let's." She flips a page so aggressively the corner tears.

I snort and look outside.

Tonight's gala is being held on Carnegie Hall's rooftop terrace. Our arrival attracts more attention than I'm expecting. This is our first official outing as a couple—much less a married one. Neither Scarlett's parents nor mine are attending tonight, which makes us the sole representatives of New York's two wealthiest families. Attention is something I'm used to. But the scrutiny feels different with Scarlett by my side. I battle the contrary urges to shield her and to step away.

Scarlett makes the decision for me. As soon as we're inside, she snags a glass of champagne from a passing waiter and heads for a large group of giggling women. They accept her into the circle with ease, a few glancing back at me.

It shouldn't surprise me. This is how we've acted at every other event we've both attended in the past. I doubt Scarlett considers any of the women she's now chatting with to be friends, but you wouldn't know it based on the way she's laughing and nodding along to something one of them is saying.

I order a bourbon and start to make the rounds, beginning with the Rutherfords, who are hosting tonight. Donald Rutherford is the chair of the board at New York General Hospital. His wife, Jennifer, is an heiress involved with half a dozen charities around the city. I compliment them on the evening and hand Jennifer a check for the fundraiser before moving on and getting sucked into a conversation about upcoming events in the Hamptons.

My summers are spent in Manhattan. If I need an escape, I travel upstate or to Europe. Our Hamptons house is the only one of my family's many properties that contains clear memories of my mother. I spend as little time as possible there. Being there with Candace and the current state of my relationship with my father and brother would be like spilling water on writing. I want to preserve my memories, not ruin them.

When Daniel Waldorf mentions the Ellsworth Fourth of July party next weekend, I realize I might not have much of a choice. Scarlett hasn't brought it up to me, but there's no way her parents won't expect her—won't expect *us*—to attend.

Daniel is describing his new sailboat to me when Hannah Garner sidles over to us. "Nice seeing you, Crew."

Daniel smiles and bails, leaving me alone with Hannah.

She doesn't spare Daniel a glance, assessing me with clear blue eyes. Hannah is probably the closest I came to willingly entering into a committed relationship. Her family is wealthy and well-connected—her father founded a sports agency that represents a whole host of athletes set to become future Hall of Famers. He also owns the Los Angeles Titans. Last fall, Hannah and I attended a game together. She deep-throated me during halftime. That's how our involvement has always been, picking up when it was convenient and nonexistent when it wasn't.

"Hello, Crew." Her long, blonde hair is curled tonight. One piece dips between the valley of her breasts, pulling my attention to her cleavage. She smirks, tracking my gaze.

"Hannah," I reply. "I didn't realize you were in town."

"I convinced Dad to let me handle some business. There's a guy on the Mets he wants to sign." She pauses. "I would have called…but you got *married*."

There's no mistaking the bite in the word, but I don't owe her an explanation. "Were you at the wedding?" I'm guessing the Garners were invited.

Her whole expression tightens. "Couldn't make it."

"That's a shame."

"You never said a word."

I sip some bourbon. "Would it have mattered, Hannah?"

"Scarlett Ellsworth? *Really*, Crew?"

"Kensington," I correct. Hannah's brow furrows. "Her name is Scarlett *Kensington* now."

At that, she scoffs. "Changing her last name doesn't change the fact she's uppity and entitled, with the emotional capacity of an iceberg. You could have done better."

The rush of anger takes me off-guard. Our sexual escapades aside, I consider Hannah a friend. I rode here next to evidence that Scarlett is cold and closed-off. But iceberg or not, she's still my wife. I tighten my grip on the glass, allowing plenty of ire to infiltrate my voice. "Insult my wife again, and this will be our last conversation, Hannah."

"Come on, Crew. No one expects you to be *loyal* to her. You married her for her money."

Guests start filing inside the banquet room where dinner will be served. "Try me," I tell her, then start to walk away.

Her hand grabs mine before I make it more than a couple of steps. "I'm here through Wednesday. Staying in my usual suite at The Carlyle."

I shake her hand off and keep walking.

Scarlett is already seated at our assigned table when I enter the large hall. I say nothing as I take the chair beside her. Polite chatter echoes around us.

Her finger traces the rim of a champagne glass, filling some of the silence with a subtle hum. She sighs, then downs the contents with one final gulp.

"Thirsty?"

"Bored."

"I'm finding the evening highly entertaining," I reply, just to needle her.

"I'm sure you are," she mutters, looking away at the stage.

She must have noticed me talking to Hannah. With any other woman, I'd think she was jealous. Since it's Scarlett, I'm guessing she's miffed I'm enjoying myself.

Jennifer Rutherford—the hostess tonight—appears on stage. Everyone still standing hurries to their seats as the crowd quiets. I zone out as she starts speaking, thanking everyone for coming tonight and sharing plans for the renovations they're fundraising for tonight. It's not until I hear my name mentioned that I zone back in on the conversation.

"...and Crew Kensington, whose generous contributions ensured we've already met tonight's goal."

Contributions? I glance at Scarlett as loud applause sounds around us. "You wrote a check?" I ask, quietly enough no one else at our table can hear.

"It's a *fundraiser*," she whispers back in the *you're an idiot* tone I'm becoming quite familiar with. "Of course I donated."

"You could have told me. It looks strange for us to make two separate donations."

"I didn't feel like elbowing my way past the blonde."

I want to scoff at that, but I keep a smile pasted on my face instead. It remains in place for the rest of Jennifer's speech and through dinner. I'm seated next to Howard Burton, a hedge fund manager a few years younger than my father. He prattles on about market trends while I shove lemon risotto and seared duck into my mouth.

Once dinner ends, seats get rearranged. Howard and his wife gravitate toward the silent auction set up in the next room. Scarlett is talking with Katherine Billings, who is sitting on her other side. I'm about to go get another drink when Asher takes Howard's empty seat.

I raise both eyebrows at him. "I thought you weren't coming tonight."

He slouches in his seat. "Eh, changed my mind."

"Your dad?"

"Yep." Asher rolls his eyes. His father loves the status of getting invited to events like this, but rarely has the follow-through to actually attend. It's the same reason Asher ended up working at Kensington Consolidated—his father ran a thriving company into the ground, thanks to sheer neglect. And he always expects Asher to step up and save his ass.

"Let him handle his own messes, man."

"Yeah. Maybe," Asher replies. We both know he won't. "Hannah is here."

I stiffen at the attempt to change the subject and to gauge my reaction. "Yeah, I know."

"She pissed?"

I shrug. "She's not thrilled." I look over at Scarlett to confirm she's still talking with Katherine. She's not. Katherine is gone, and Scarlett is scrolling on her phone. Her expression is blank, giving me no indication of whether she's listening to or absorbing our conversation.

Asher makes an annoying humming sound in response.

Scarlett stands. "Excuse me."

I watch her walk away, then look back at Asher. "Thanks a fuck ton for that."

He looks confused. "Since when do you care what a woman thinks?"

"Since I married one," I reply. "I'm stuck with her for more than one night."

"You said you barely see her. That you're leading separate lives."

"Both true."

"So? Stop making an effort. I invited her to the climbing gym, and she left after fifteen minutes. Doesn't seem like she'll care about Hannah or not."

"She won't." That's all I say though. I don't explain I inexplicably *want* her to care. That jealousy—an emotion I've always abhorred in women—would thrill me coming from Scarlett.

"Then what's the issue?"

"Just...don't mention other women around her, okay?"

He studies me for a minute before he agrees. "Fine."

I feel his eyes remain on me as I make a point of looking around. A string quartet has set up in the corner and started playing, providing a muted soundtrack to the evening. A few couples gravitate toward the dancefloor and begin to twirl.

"How's the sex?"

I say nothing.

Asher scoffs. "Come on, Kensington. You're not the shy sort."

"It's different, and you know it."

"Different because you don't know?" he teases.

I rub my finger against the rim of my glass.

Asher laughs. "Holy fuck. You don't."

"It hasn't come up," I mutter.

"How the fuck does having sex with your wife not come up?"

I stand. "I'm getting a refill."

But rather than head for the bar, I somehow end up approaching Scarlett. I interrupt the group she's talking to with a polite smile.

"Would you like to dance, *dollface*?"

"Sure, *sugar*."

As soon as we're out of earshot, she mutters, "Dollface? That's your worst one yet."

"Funny. I think sugar might be my new favorite."

Scarlett looks away, but not before I catch the ghost of a

smile. She never attempts to hide any negative emotions, I've noticed. When she's angry or upset, it's all on display. It's the few pleasant moments we've shared that she schools her reactions to.

As soon as we reach the dance floor, I test the theory. There are about a dozen other couples dancing, most of them middle-aged or older. All waltzing with a respectable distance between them.

I spin Scarlett so our chests are touching. Her expression doesn't change as we begin to dance, nor as I tighten my grip on her hand and her waist. My thumb leaves her palm and drifts down to her wrist. The only jewelry she's wearing tonight is a pair of diamond earrings and the rings I gave her, leaving the smooth skin below her palm bare. I settle my thumb on top of her pulse point, feeling it pound at a rapid pace.

I smile, feeling her heart race. She may not *want* to want me, but she does. I know the feeling well.

She doesn't pull away, but she won't meet my gaze either. This is the closest we've been since I carried her upstairs after discovering her on the couch. Scarlett isn't the only one acting unaffected. I want to haul her lips to mine. I want her to be naked and be allowed to look. I want to talk with her without having to extract any syllable that isn't cutting.

Instead, I just twirl her around the dancefloor. Silence is usually neutral. Between us, it shimmers. It has shape and substance. The quiet is weighted by all the things we aren't saying and all the emotions we aren't expressing.

The song ends and transitions into a new one. After a few minutes, she swallows and looks right at me. "I have an early day tomorrow."

After our conversation in the car earlier, I know suggesting she take Saturday off is a bad idea. "So do I." I don't.

"I want to take the car back, Crew."

"Fine." I stop dancing. "Let's go."

Surprise flickers across her face. "You're coming home tonight?"

"Did I tell you otherwise?"

Pink heats her cheeks. "I assumed you made plans."

"You know what they say about people who make assumptions."

"No, I don't," she challenges. "What do they say?"

"You want me to call you an ass?"

"I've been called worse," she replies, then starts walking toward the exit.

I catch up with her at the coat check. "I'm getting sick of this, Scarlett. Does every conversation we have need to turn combative? You want to leave? Let's leave. I'm not fighting you."

"You're making a scene."

I grab her arm to stall her in place. "You're mad I'm coming home? I didn't think you'd care either way."

"I *don't*."

"Then why are you being so difficult?" I hiss.

"Difficult?" she echoes. "I'm not the one who—"

"Are you two in line for the valet?" *Fuck.* I know that voice. I turn to see Hannah aiming a sweet smile my way. There's no authenticity in the expression. "Oh. Crew." She lets out a small, fake laugh. "I didn't realize that was you."

I raise one eyebrow, silently calling her out on that bullshit. "We're not in line for the valet. Our driver is on his way."

"Oh. All right, then."

Still, she doesn't move. I press my lips together, annoyed. "Hannah, this is my wife, Scarlett. Scarlett, this is Hannah Garner." This is the first time I've ever introduced Scarlett as my wife. It's bizarre to say, and equally strange to realize I like the way it sounds.

"We've met before," Hannah says. "Lovely to see you again, Scarlett."

Scarlett stares at her. "Where?"

"Excuse me?"

"You said we've met before. Where?"

Hannah looks flustered, but recovers quickly. "Oh. Um, it must have been at some event here? Crew loves visiting LA, but it doesn't seem like your sort of place."

"New York isn't for everyone, either," Scarlett replies.

"I prefer to visit in the summer. I hate the cold."

"I can see why." Scarlett's eyes flit over the short hem and low neckline of Hannah's dress.

Hannah stiffens. "For such a busy city, it can also feel lonely." She glances at me—deliberately.

I'm torn between doing something and saying nothing. It's obvious what Hannah is doing and why. She's jealous and hurt I married someone else, despite the fact it's been months since we were in the same state and we were never a couple. What I *don't* understand is what Scarlett is doing—why she's engaging rather than ignoring. At every turn, she's made it clear she sees our marriage as nothing more than a business relationship, if that. I'd go so far as to say she treats her business partners with more warmth than she's shown me. And yet—she's sparring with Hannah rather than walking away. Not possessive per se, but not displaying total indifference either.

"If you're so desperate for some company, maybe you should go back inside and find some," Scarlett suggests. "Seeing as *we* are leaving."

I smother a smile, not missing the way she emphasizes *we*.

Hannah doesn't miss it either. She sizes Scarlett up, not bothering to cloak her dislike. "I didn't know you were capable of caring about anything other than business, Scarlett."

"I wasn't aware you knew anything about me," Scarlett shoots back. "Especially since you seem far more interested in my husband."

Hannah smiles. Small, yet flashy and fake. She looks to me. "I hope to see you around, Crew." Her smile turns genuine for the first time before she passes us and heads back inside.

I keep studying Scarlett.

"What?" she snaps. I think her tone was warmer toward Hannah.

I smile. "Nothing."

Scarlett shakes her head before heading toward our car. Roman pulled up at some point during the encounter with Hannah. He climbs out to open the door, but I wave him off and open the door for Scarlett myself. She grumbles a *thank you* before climbing into the backseat. I slide in on the opposite side, then knock on the privacy divider to let Roman know we're ready to depart.

We haven't even reached the end of the block when she speaks. "You have horrible taste in women."

I look over. "What does that say about you?"

She ignores me. "I don't want her in my penthouse."

I bite back the *our* I want to correct her with. Instead, I tell her the truth. "It won't be an issue."

"I have work lunches at The Carlyle."

It takes me a minute to realize what she's saying. Another to wonder how the hell Scarlett knows that's where Hannah stays when she's in the city. "That's not what I meant. She and I are done."

"Does she know that?"

"Yes," I reply. Then, for some stupid reason, that feels a lot like the loyalty she doesn't seem to want, I elaborate. "I told her if she insulted you, I wouldn't talk to her again."

Scarlett scoffs. "Don't do me any favors."

I exhale loudly. "Now you're annoyed I'm *not* fucking her?"

"No! I just—"

"Are *you* sleeping with other people?" I finally voice the question that's been bothering me for weeks.

"Not sure," she responds.

I gnash my teeth together. "Not sure *what?*"

"Not sure you would call it sleeping."

Fuck. She is. "Who is he?"

"You don't know him."

Yeah, right. "I know a lot of people."

"His name is Kyle. He's a surgeon."

That's her type? A science nerd with a superiority complex? It bothers me more than I'm expecting. More than it should. If he's not part of our world, maybe she actually has real feelings for the guy. "He sounds like a tool."

"Jealous?" she taunts.

"That would require me caring what you do."

"Exactly."

I force a chuckle out. It sounds empty to my ears, but I doubt she can tell the difference. "That's not something you need to worry about."

"Great."

"Great," I echo.

It's become predictable: the cycle of our conversations. The joking and the taunting and the silence. The way one of us is a little more open than the other. We're never in sync—never both willing to give without wanting to take.

I pull out my phone and start to sort through emails that could all wait until Monday. At least my father will be happy about my initiative. He and Oliver got stranded in Miami due to a tropical storm. They traveled down south for some golfing and to meet with a commercial developer about offices for a new acquisition. In their extended absence, everything goes through me. I got home at three a.m. last night, or this morning, technically.

"I finalized the branding for my new clothing line today." The sound of Scarlett's voice is so unexpected, it startles me. I figured she was working on her side of the car. "It's called *rouge*. That's what these drawings are for. I'm choosing a design team. I also approved the proofs for the August issue of *Haute* and chose the articles for the September one. That was after I interviewed five secretaries, because Leah already has her hands full running my schedule at *Haute* and I need more help."

Questions form. I know nothing about what she does on a daily basis. That's why I asked earlier. But that was before I knew how much of a sham she sees this marriage as. Before I knew she's fucked another guy with my ring on her finger.

Anger and jealousy pool in my stomach like tar—dark and toxic. "I don't give a single fuck what you do, Scarlett. *Remember?*" I drawl the words like I have something better to do than to bother to say them, then continue scrolling through the hundreds of emails that have piled up.

She flinches. I catch the subtle recoil out of the corner of my eye before she turns away from me to stare out at the city lights. Troublesome emotions harden, sinking down through me like an anchor.

Why do I care?
Why can't she?
The rest of the ride is silent.

CHAPTER NINE

SCARLETT

I t's hard to say which is more oppressive: the July heat or the five women staring at me with the intensity of a firing squad. "Are you and Crew trying for kids?"

I bite back the sarcastic retorts that come to mind in response to Eileen Waldorf's probing question.

I'm still a virgin.

My husband is too busy with his mistresses.

Maybe in a decade or two.

Any of those comments would spread across the patio of my parents' Hamptons house like wildfire. I may have clawed my way to relevance and respect in parts of the business world, but it's come at the detriment of my standing among most of the women in New York society. My attempts to break out of the mold of marriage and kids haven't made me any friends.

Eileen is only a year older than me. Before she married Daniel Waldorf last summer, she worked at a public relations agency. She had their first child a few months ago. It's not uncommon for women to work—until they get married. I'm supposed to be joining the boards of charities and picking out nursery colors now that I'm Mrs. Kensington.

Instead of answering Eileen's question with a sharp retort, I laugh and toss my hair. Just because I hate the game doesn't mean I can't play it. "No, not yet. We're enjoying this time together, just the two of us."

Seeing as we got married a month *ago.* I keep that last part to myself. I know what's expected—and what passes as appropriate conversation—at these sorts of events. It's why I avoid as many of them as I can. But there was no avoiding the Fourth of July party. I've attended every year for as long as I can remember.

Eileen nods and smiles, accepting my bullshit answer without batting an eye. I have a feeling I'll be repeating it a lot. *Enjoying* is a stretch, but it's not a lie I'd like to wait to have kids. It's not that I don't want them—I do. But kids will erase distance between me and Crew. Things between us are uncomfortable and awkward and I don't know how to change that. It should be what I want. It's exactly what I *did* want.

I didn't realize he was making an effort until he stopped.

"Excuse me, ladies." His voice makes me stiffen. It gives me goosebumps, despite the fact temperatures today are hovering in the eighties. "Would you mind terribly if I steal my blushing bride away for a moment?" Crew wraps an arm around my waist, acting the part of the doting husband so convincingly even *I* believe it for a second. I'm sure he can feel how tense I am.

The ladies who were previously interrogating me all coo variations of *how sweet* and *newlywed bliss.* A couple of them are close to my mother's age. And yet they're all eyeing Crew with the same appreciative gaze he seems to coax out of every woman who sees him. I add his annoying attractiveness to the long list of things I'm currently bothered by.

As soon as we're out of sight from the nosy women, his arm

drops. I don't thank him for pulling me away—don't say *anything* to him. It's strange and uncomfortable having him here. Having to act like a happy couple when we're the furthest thing from one.

We've barely exchanged twenty words since the car ride home from the Rutherford gala. I'm pissed—at him, at myself. He's acting like the cold, aloof asshole I expected to find myself married to.

And it bothers me.

I miss the glimpses I got of the guy I don't think many people see. I hate how he's acting like I promised fidelity—like me and other men is more than just a blow to his male pride. I want to tell him it's a ridiculous double standard, that no one here would be surprised to hear he's cheated on me but would be scandalized if I repeated what I told him in the limo.

What I *lied* to him about in the limo.

And that's the main reason I haven't made any attempt to repair the damage that ride home inflicted: the indifferent expression Crew wore. I thought my lies would at least dent his ego. I lied, and I don't want to lie again. I was hurt and mad, so I made up a "Hannah" of my own. I was hoping for distance. Just not this heavy, oppressive sort where it feels like we both might care we're barely speaking.

"Did you need something?" I take a sip from my glass, trying to ignore the spot on my back that still tingles where he touched me just a minute ago.

He studies my movements. "You're drinking?"

I raise both eyebrows, then deliberately look at the glass I'm holding. "You expect me to get through this sober?"

"Not at all. The more wasted you get, the fewer people will ask me if you're pregnant. We both know what the chances of *that* are. With my kid, at least."

I seethe as Andrew Spencer rounds the corner and nears

where we're standing, erasing any opportunity to retort. "Was that all, darling?"

"For now, sweetheart." Crew has spotted Andrew as well. His tone has turned cordial. "I'm sure I'll find another excuse to steal you away later."

"Can't wait," I chirp.

"Crew! I thought that was you!" Andrew stops directly in front of us, blocking my immediate escape route. "How have you been?"

"Fine," Crew replies smoothly. "You? How's Olivia?"

"Good, good." Andrew's voice and expression are jovial as he looks at me. "Scarlett. Wonderful to see you."

I smile, but he's already turned back to Crew. I finish off my champagne while they talk.

"Haven't seen you since the wedding," Andrew says, frowning. "How is everything at the company?"

"The usual."

"Must be more hectic than usual. You haven't been out in a month. Everyone has been asking about you."

Crew's eyes flick to me and away, so fast I almost miss it. I find fresh interest in the conversation.

"Yes. I've been busy."

I didn't realize Crew and Andrew were this friendly. Honestly, I've never paid close attention to anyone he socializes with at the events we've overlapped attending over the years. I talk to everyone out of obligation, even those close to me in age. The girls I attended boarding school with always gossip and the guys will slip in a suggestive comment or two between bragging about their investments.

"*Busy*. Right." Andrew's gaze is back on me. He's smirking, leaving no question as to how he took Crew's response.

"I should have known seeing Crew is why you wanted to

come." Olivia Spencer saunters over to where the three of us are standing.

I had every intention of making a hasty excuse and leaving Crew and Andrew to talk about whatever they want. But something—possibly the way Olivia is looking at Crew—keeps me in place.

At least Olivia is being somewhat subtle in her appraisal, unlike Hannah Garner. But I can still see the interest in the way her eyes widen and her lips turn up coyly. Before we got married, I made a deliberate effort not to pay attention to gossip about Crew when other women were involved. I'm starting to recognize that might have been a mistake. These women think they know everything about me, while I have no idea what history they share with Crew.

"You've been complaining Crew hasn't been coming out," Olivia adds, when none of us say anything. I don't miss the look she gives me as she does. It's obvious she blames me for the fact Crew hasn't been frequenting New York nightclubs, and I'm tempted to tell her I've actually done everything I could to ensure he spends as little time around me as possible.

The petty part of me clinging on to the notion Crew Kensington is a means to an end, not someone who will mean something, is tempted to walk away. Instead, I decide to drop the act. Especially since Crew *will* think it's an act.

I step closer to Crew. He's wearing a white button down with the sleeves rolled up. His bare arm is pressed against mine now, sending small shockwaves across the surface of my skin. The electrifying sensation is almost enough to make me forget the purpose of this.

I take the glass from Crew's hand and take a sip, almost draining the remnants of the smoky alcohol. Bourbon. My painted lips leave some red residue behind, and I place it back in his hand.

Not the most subtle of gestures, and neither is the choice to use my left hand. Diamonds glint in the sunshine.

"I'm surprised you're still hitting the nightclubs, Olivia. Don't you think we should leave that to the teenagers?"

I feel Crew's eyes on me.

"Oh, I do. Aside from the occasional girls' night out. I'm sure you can appreciate that, Scarlett. You're so…independent." Olivia's voice holds just as much sugar as mine as she edges back a half-step from Crew.

"Yes, I am."

"Well, it's lovely to see you. This has become the only event I know I'll see you at."

"Work has been busy."

Olivia's lips purse at the mention of *Haute*. "You've worked miracles with that little magazine. I'd hardly even heard of it, and suddenly I see people mentioning it everywhere."

"I prefer to think of it as wise investing and effective marketing than miraculous," I reply. "And didn't your father place a bid on my 'little' magazine?"

I know he did. I outbid Joseph Adams by ten million and have already made it back tenfold.

"I believe he considered it," Olivia replies. "He decided print is a dying market."

"Pity. Our earning statements tell a different story," I respond, savoring the way her lips tighten.

"Just what you need. More money," Olivia retorts, a bit of her sweetness dissolving.

"My thoughts exactly," I reply.

Awkward silence falls. "I'll let you two catch up," I add. But before I walk away, I turn my head and whisper into Crew's ear. "I'm not getting wasted tonight. We're sharing a bed, after all."

I don't wait for his reaction to the implication. I smile at the Spencers and then head toward the pool.

When we reach the sand, I kick my heels off. The feel of the rough grains between my toes lightens the anxieties I've carried around all night. Rachel and Penelope, two women I went to boarding school with, are laughing and stumbling as we approach the roaring bonfire built on the beach. A bottle of Dom Perignon dangles between Rachel's fingers as she talks a million miles an hour, occasionally almost falling flat on her face.

The bonfire is an annual Fourth of July tradition I've never participated in, which is something Penelope has pointed out three times in the ten minutes it's taken to walk the boardwalk from my parents' place to here in the dark. It's exactly what I pictured it to be. Forced small talk with my social peers is one thing. Drunken debauchery is another. I've seen too many fake smiles followed by back-handed compliments.

As an Ellsworth, I've always been held to a higher standard. I know it. So does everyone else. People on pedestals appear perfect. Until they fall.

I'm no longer an Ellsworth, though. I'm a Kensington. Untouchable. Not only is Crew rich and connected, people *like* him.

We reach the group loosely gathered around the flickering flames. I glance over familiar faces, taking a quick inventory of everyone here—basically everyone who was at my parents' party under the age of thirty. I catch Crew's gaze across the fire. He's standing with a group of guys, looking more relaxed than I've ever seen him. There's no tie or suit in sight. Just a pair of navy swim trunks and a white button down that's mostly unbuttoned. His hair is mussed. By the wind...or by something else. Would he do that? At my parents' party with me present? I don't know. I haven't seen him since our interaction with the Spencers. If he wanted to, he easily could have slipped away for a while.

Rachel pops the champagne with a squeal, drawing my attention back to her and Penelope. Sprays of white foam hit the sand as she directs the stream of golden liquid into the crystal glasses Penelope carried down. I take the offered one with a thanks. Bubbles tickle my throat as I down half of it in one sip.

Down here, in the dark, I feel different. I don't feel on display. The compulsion to appear perfect and know exactly what to say is gone. Familiar warmth trickles through my veins as I drain my glass, lightening and loosening my movements.

I'm comfortable enough to chime in on Rachel and Penelope's commentary. Soon, they're taking bets on who is most likely to go skinny-dipping. I laugh as they recount previous years' anecdotes while deciding who's likely to go for a repeat.

"What about Crew?" I ask, when he's the only guy they haven't mentioned.

Rachel and Penelope exchange a look. "Crew never comes to the Hamptons in the summer," Rachel tells me.

"Oh."

"People had bets on today, you know." She laughs at my surprised expression. "Don't worry, I bet he'd be here. Only idiots didn't. They're the same people who call you a stuck-up bitch— they should know better."

Penelope hisses, "Rachel!"

I don't react. I know that's how people see me. It's different to hear it spoken in such blunt terms though.

Rachel shrugs. "What? It's hard not to hate someone who gets everything she wants."

My walls go up. "I'm going to find a restroom."

The nearest house is the Kingsleys'—technically we're on their stretch of private beach—but I don't actually have any intention of going to the bathroom. I'll stay long enough to make it clear no one chased me off, and then head back to my parents'.

My plan all along was to go to bed early tonight. For the first time, I'll be sharing a bed with my husband. Ideally, I'll be fast asleep by the time he heads to bed.

I pause by the fire. Now that the sun is gone, the heat from the flames counters the cool sea breeze.

"Got chilly, huh?"

I don't turn right away. A second seems necessary. When I glance back, he's closer than I expected. "You sure you never wanted to become a meteorologist? You seem to have a strange fascination with the weather."

"I'm sure."

"No one else finds your fascination strange?"

Crew sort of laughs, but it quickly turns into a sigh. "I don't know what else to say to you, Scarlett."

I look away, like I always do when we gravitate toward anything meaningful. "You don't need to check in on me. Go have fun."

He's so close I can feel his sigh. His chest expands and his breath weaves through my hair as he exhales. I wait for his retreat —for his body to move away. Instead, he puts his hands on my waist and spins me around. So fast I have no time to react or protest.

We're even closer now. Mere inches separate our faces as his hands loosen their grip on my hips. "I don't do things I don't want to do, Scarlett. If I don't want to check on you, I won't. If I don't want to spend time with you, I won't."

"Okay." I say the word softly. Too loud, and it might shatter this moment the way words have done before.

"Okay." His echo is just as quiet.

The first firework startles me. It explodes in a spectacular display of sound and color, illuminating the shore and the sea and all the surrounds previously hidden by the night. The burning wood and the moonlight were weak in comparison. Distant strains of music from the house and the rhythmic battering of waves on the sand seem muffled.

Another explosion lights up the sky, sending pink arcs flying that fizzle and drift back down. Followed by another and another and another. Laughter and shouts are audible nearby, but I pay them no attention. I'm consumed by the sight of the dazzling display that keeps replacing the lingering smoke. I turn so I'm facing the fireworks, but I don't pull away from his hold. I lean into it—literally—resting my back against his front. Crew's arms remain looped loosely around my waist. Warm and secure and strong.

This moment feels magical, and I know it's not the fireworks I'm watching or the champagne flowing through my bloodstream.

I *resigned* myself to marrying Crew. He was the best of decent options.

It wasn't supposed to be like this. Our relationship is supposed to be based on mutual understandings and airtight legal documents. Not on trust and lust and all the other things squeezing my chest right now. Exciting, terrifying feelings. I can't leave him, can never walk away. When he gets sick of being the doting husband and domestic life, I'll be the one stuck waiting at home.

That will only hurt if I let it.

I tell myself I won't, even as I relax my body against his and ignore the envious looks aimed my way. Crew may have married me for my money and my name, but he *did* choose to marry me. He doesn't do things he doesn't want to, like he just said.

"Who do you think came up with this?"

I tilt my head back so I can see his profile. "Came up with what?"

"The fireworks for the Fourth. What about a bloody war says *let's light up the sky?*"

"They're celebratory," I reply. "My mom wanted fireworks for our reception."

"Really?" His hand glides around the curve of my hip. It's an innocent movement, a shift in position. Yet it sets my skin on fire. It's been months since I had sex. I blame that for the awareness pooling in my stomach.

We're sharing a room tonight. A bed. Up until now, I didn't think there was a chance anything might happen. My comment earlier was a tease, a reminder that we haven't before. Now, I'm consumed by the possibility that something *could* happen. That I might want it to.

"Really," I confirm.

"Why didn't we have fireworks at our reception then?"

"I told her no."

"You weren't celebrating." It's not a question, but a statement.

"They're bad for the environment."

He chuckles against my hair, and I feel the vibrations everywhere. "So is flying private."

"Nobody's perfect."

He's still laughing. There's a strange gooey sensation in my chest, like something is melting inside of me.

Rapid bursts of color pepper the heavens, signaling the start of the finale. We're both silent through the end of it, staying still as the final flashes fade.

When the display ends, the magic disappears with it. I feel awkward, standing here with him holding me, not comfortable the way I was moments ago. I clear my throat. "I should head back up."

Crew doesn't move or react for a few seconds. When his hands do drop, I experience disappointment, not relief. "I'll walk you back up."

He's expecting a *you don't have to do that.* I bite it back and turn so I'm facing him. "Okay."

There's no triumph on his face, only excitement. "Let me grab my shoes from the gazebo."

"You changed," I state. Like an idiot who blurts out the obvious.

"Yeah. Some of the guys wanted to swim earlier."

"Just the guys?" The clarification is out before I can stop it.

"Just the guys," he confirms.

I manage a small, jerky nod. *This* time, there's relief.

"Be right back."

I watch him spin and walk away, admiring how his shoulders shift as he strides. The way his swim trunks hug his thighs and butt.

It's one night. People have one-night stands all the time. I've had one-night stands. It doesn't have to mean anything. I have another trip to Paris next week. That will force some distance between us. I can do this. I can *not* care.

Commotion distracts me from the internal pep talk. I squint in the direction of the Kingsleys' gazebo, trying to make out the two figures standing near it. One of them throws a punch and the shape on the receiving end goes down like a parachuting stone.

I react without thinking, running in that direction along with everyone else in the vicinity. The upper class prefers back-stabbing to brawls. If you have a problem with someone, you say it to their face in a sweet tone. You don't rearrange it.

And the last thing I'm expecting when I reach the huddle that's formed around the fight is for Crew to be the one standing, sporting red knuckles and a murderous expression. I rush forward, my path unencumbered as soon as everyone realizes who I am. People are scrambling to get out of my way.

"What the fuck are you doing?" I shout once I reach him, looking between Crew's furious face and Camden Crane, who's sitting in the sand sporting a split lip.

Blood dribbles from Camden's mouth as he begins laughing. "I would have said it to your face, Kensington. She must have a—"

Crew lunges forward and hits him again. Camden will have a black eye tomorrow to match his swollen mouth. I make the stupid decision not to walk away and ignore whatever is happening. Anyone else, I would. Instead, I shove Crew's chest, feeling the adrenaline and animosity radiating off him. He's breathing heavily.

"*Crew*. What is going on? What are you doing?"

He doesn't answer either question. Just keeps glaring at the guy on the ground. I look around at the assembled onlookers, trying to read the situation. Obviously Camden said something that pissed Crew off. Badly enough to convince Crew to disfigure his face.

Penelope and Rachel both have hands over their mouths, looking shocked. But it's the men that I linger on. They all look cowed—nervous. Even Andrew Spencer, who I thought considered Crew a friend. None of them will make eye contact with me.

Camden laughs again. He wipes his bottom lip, smearing blood across his chin. "Didn't think you were the type to get your hands dirty."

"I thought *you* were the type who knew when to shut your mouth," Crew snaps.

"I just had the balls to say what everyone else here was thinking."

"That true?" Crew's gaze lifts, roving across the assembled onlookers. Heads shake everywhere. A cruel smile twists Crew's lips as he looks back down at Camden. "Try me again, Crane. *Please.* I'd love to make you completely irrelevant, not just mostly—the way you are now."

Once that parting shot has made its mark, Crew turns and strides in the direction of the path that leads back to my parents'. After a minute of hesitation, I follow.

My mind is spinning in circles. Based on the whispers and side glances, I had some unintentional involvement in what just took place. I can't recall the last time I spoke to Camden Crane. I have no idea what he could have said to set Crew off. I had no idea Crew *could* get set off by something about me. He was protecting me—defending me. And I have no idea at all how to process that.

The walk back is dim. My eyes adjusted to the brilliant fireworks and the glow of the bonfire. The weak moonlight is barely enough to pick my way along the boardwalk that weaves between stalks of beach grass. Salty air blows strands of hair across my face. I breathe deeply, trying to center myself.

I thought things between me and Crew would settle naturally. That we would find some routine that allowed us to reap the benefits of this arrangement without compromising our individual goals. But more and more, it's feeling like things between us are being permanently decided. The disconnect between us feels like it's hardening and callousing. The decisions we're both making feel like they'll matter—like they'll define what the rest of our relationship looks like for however long it lasts.

When I reach the edge of the patio, I hesitate. I should slip inside and rejoin the party. Play the perfect hostess and give Crew a chance to cool off. I walk inside, but instead of following the sound of talking and laughter, I slip up the back stairwell that leads to the second floor.

The door to my usual bedroom is ajar, even though I'm certain I closed it before heading downstairs earlier. I push it open to reveal the room is empty and dark. But the bathroom light is on. I close the door behind me and drop my heels in a heap, announcing my arrival.

Silently, I pad across the jute rug over to the doorway that leads to the en suite. Crew is standing at the sink, washing his hands. The water runs pink.

I lean against the doorway, debating what to say. I settle on, "Are you okay?"

"Fine." His tone is as short as his response.

I stay in place as he shuts off the tap and dries his hands, avoiding the cut on one knuckle. "You should put some hydrogen peroxide on that."

He doesn't reply. I shove away from the doorframe, walking over to him. Tension is still radiating off him as I brush against his arm so I can lean over and pull the brown bottle out of the cabinet. I grab a few cotton balls as well.

"Sit." I nod toward the edge of the tub as I soak the cotton with liquid. The harsh chemical smell burns my nose.

Crew hesitates before he complies. I watch him out of the corner of my eye as he perches on the marble. The bathroom is big—as large as the one in my penthouse—but it feels tiny with his presence. I study the golden hairs on his tan arms. The way his shirt pulls taut across his shoulders. The blue eyes that see more than I mean to show.

Satisfied the cotton is soaked, I cross the tile and crouch down so I can dab the ball on the split between his knuckles. For a few seconds, the only sound is our breathing.

Crew speaks first. "You know, I've imagined you in this position before. Never doing this, though."

I meet his gaze for a minute. A few retorts are on the tip of my tongue. Some dirtier than he probably thinks I'm capable of. But I don't want our first time to be like this. So I ask a question I'm pretty sure will douse any more innuendo. "Why don't you like the Hamptons?"

"I like them fine." His response is nonchalant. There's emotion underneath it though, underscored in the way his jaw tightens and his eyes darken. This close, I can't *not* register the subtle changes.

"Then why don't you come here in the summer?"

"Who told you that?"

I keep dabbing. "Rachel Archibald. It's a good thing we had a short engagement. If the number of *you're not good enough for him* comments I heard today are the amount *after* the wedding, who knows what it would have been like before."

"Who said you're not good enough for me?" Rather than gloating, his expression is more of a glower.

"I know what people think of me. I get everything I want without working for it, apparently."

"You work hundred-hour weeks, Scarlett. Fuck anyone who says that."

I don't say what I'm thinking: *you probably already did.* I'm sick of the jibes.

He uses his uninjured hand to tilt my chin up. "I mean it. You're Scarlett Ellsworth. You don't care what anyone thinks."

"I'm good at acting like I don't." More honest than I meant to be.

"You don't have to act around me."

I don't answer at first. I lift his right hand so I can inspect the cut on his hand more closely. His knuckles are pink and swollen, but at least he's no longer bleeding. "Kensington."

"Huh?"

I drop his hand and throw the cotton balls into the trash can before I stand up. "You called me Scarlett Ellsworth. It's Scarlett Kensington." His smile makes me wish I'd stayed sitting. "I'm going to head back downstairs."

He nods; I flee. I put my heels back on and step out into the hallway. I need space. Time. Distance.

Crew is confusing. Everything about him is confusing. What he says. What he does. What he doesn't say. What he doesn't do. And the way I feel around him is the most confusing of all.

Going into this marriage, I had one goal: to make Crew see me as an equal. I've retained all the power I had when I agreed to marry him. I didn't consider any of the other ways I might want Crew to see me. I'm worried—terrified—what the repercussions of admitting I want things between us to be real might be. But continuing along the way we have isn't tenable.

Rather than walk downstairs, I head into one of the other guest rooms down the hall. I feel like being alone. There's a loveseat in the corner I curl up on. I lose track of time as I lie there and replay today in my head.

Once the sounds downstairs grow quieter and quieter, I stand and walk back down to my room. The bedroom is dark and the bathroom light is on, just like before. But there's a big lump in the left side of the bed.

I tiptoe into the bathroom to brush my teeth and wash my face.

When I step back into the bedroom, Crew's asleep. Or he's doing a convincing job of pretending he is. He's not wearing a shirt either. Until this evening, I'd rarely seen my husband in anything but a suit. I lean against the doorframe and look at him. His skin is golden. I'm not sure when he has the chance to absorb any Vitamin D. He seems to work almost as much as I do. His tan stands out against the white sheets loosely draped over the abdomen that's impressively defined even while relaxed. He must work out. When, I have no clue. That realization bothers me. I've spent the past couple of weeks living with him, and I learned more when I was spying on security footage from across the Atlantic.

Getting to know Crew terrifies me. The little I already know intrigues me. The reasons for this marriage were supposed to be the real part. The money, the opportunities, the empire our combined resources would form. Me and him were supposed to be fake.

Instead, the empire feels fake.

Leaning against Crew earlier felt very real.

What happened to her? That girl who didn't care? There was a very recent time when I didn't second-guess anything. When I wasn't tempted to leave work early. When I didn't get distracted. When blue eyes didn't haunt my thoughts.

A tiny corner of my heart whispers the answer. *She married Crew Kensington.*

I turn off the bathroom light and tiptoe across the floor until I reach my suitcase. It takes me a few minutes to sort through my belongings in the dark, but I finally find a silky nightgown.

Slipping under warm sheets feels foreign. The bed is usually cold when I climb into it. I huddle as close to the edge of the mattress as I can without falling off it. Even though I can't see or feel him, I can *sense* him. Smell his shampoo. Hear his breathing.

Once I've accepted I won't be falling asleep anytime soon, I slip out of bed and pad toward the door. The hallway is empty and quiet. I head downstairs and cross the cold tile of the entryway that leads into the living room. French doors line the far wall overlooking the pool. I pause by the bookcase to grab the well-worn copy of *Gone With The Wind* and then type the security code into the keypad by the fridge. It flashes green, indicating the alarm has been disabled.

There's no sign of the party that took place earlier. Every surface gleams, spotless. I grab a wineglass, an unopened bottle, and an opener, then head outside. The moon casts a luminous glow that coats everything.

I settle on one of the chairs that line the edge of the pool. The cork pops on the first try. I pour myself a generous glass and then settle back against the cushions, taking the occasional sip as I stare out at the stretch of private beach that buttresses the backyard from the ocean.

Then I pick up the book and start to read.

CHAPTER TEN

CREW

When I wake up, I'm the only one in the bed. I stretch one hand out, feeling the cool fabric where Scarlett should be. My sore knuckles protest the movement. I wince, both from the pain and the memories of how I ended up with a swollen hand. A glance at the clock on the bedside table tells me it's just past three a.m.

I flip onto my back, trying to fall back asleep. Eventually, I give up. I climb out of bed and pull on a pair of athletic shorts. I don't bother with a shirt before heading out into the hallway. Josephine and Hanson's room is in the opposite wing of the house. Unless they make it a habit of wandering around in the middle of the night, which I very much doubt, I don't need to worry about running into my in-laws.

It doesn't take long to find Scarlett. The lights are on in the kitchen and the door leading out to the patio and pool is ajar. As soon as I step outside, I spot her sprawled out on one of the chairs, holding a wineglass in one hand and paging through a paperback with the other.

"Couldn't sleep?" I ask as I take a seat at the end of the lounge chair she's lying on.

She shoves her book aside and takes a sip of wine before she answers. "You snore."

"No, I don't."

Scarlett sighs. "No, you don't. But you were *there*."

I know what she means. We have yet to sleep together, in the literal or the sexual sense. The forced proximity of this trip isn't unwelcome, but it's definitely weird. I never know how to act around her. Every time I think we might have made some progress, we slide right back. She can't even sleep next to me.

I rest my elbows on my knees and stare at the flat surface of the pool. The filters form small ripples that refract the moonlight beaming down. "Is this how it's going to be, Scarlett?"

"Is this how *what* is going to be?"

"*Us*. Is this what you want?"

"We've never been about what *I* want."

I laugh. "Bullshit."

Her eyes flash. "Excuse me?"

"You heard me. If you didn't want this, we wouldn't be married." I stare her down, daring her to deny it.

She looks away. "I expected this to be different."

"Different how?"

"I don't know. Just...different."

I sigh. Nothing is ever simple or straightforward with this woman. "I'd like to know what it's like to fuck my wife, Scarlett."

She doesn't flinch at the crude statement. Doesn't react at all. "You can get that elsewhere."

"Are you? Still?" I add that last word just to be an ass. To see her angry expression. She's more forthcoming when she's mad.

"None of your business."

I laugh. "But it *was* my business after the Rutherford gala?"

She's silent.

"What about kids?"

"You mean heirs?" She scoffs. "I'm not ready. Between *Haute* and the new clothing line, I barely remember to eat. I can't handle a baby right now."

"Okay."

She eyes me, clearly suspicious about my lack of argument.

"Do you want me to move out?" I ask.

"What?" Scarlett looks genuinely shocked by the question. "After you insisted on moving in with your two closets worth of suits and filling the fridge with cow milk?"

She sounds more disgruntled about the second fact than the first, and I almost smile. Phillipe already informed me Scarlett prefers non-dairy milk to the real thing and wasn't happy about my lack of substitution appearing in the fridge.

"I moved in because we're married, Scarlett. If you want to pretend like we're not, that's fine."

She sits up. "I *know* we're married. And I'm holding up my end of the bargain. I don't know what else you want from me."

"Nothing you're willing to give, clearly."

"Sex. Right." She snorts. "You're such a guy."

"Yeah. I want to have sex with you. I also want to know why you asked me to kiss you before our wedding. Why you fight me on everything. I don't know shit about you, Scarlett."

"You know everything that matters."

"Or everything that doesn't," I counter.

She sighs. Looks away. Fiddles with the pages of her book. "Were you named after the sport?"

I blink. *What?* Scarlett stares at me. I raise a brow. "That's what you want to know about me?"

Scarlett takes another sip from her wineglass. "Answer the question."

"No, it's a family name." I shift so I'm facing her, not the pool. "Were you named after the color?"

The amusement is brief, but it appears. "My mother was a Margaret Mitchell fan." She flips over the book beside me, revealing the faded cover of *Gone With The Wind.*

"So you were named after a tease hopelessly in love with a guy who married his cousin?"

She narrows her eyes, but not before I see she's surprised I've read the book. "Scarlett is strong. She's a survivor. She saves herself over and over again, never accepting defeat or relying on a savior."

"It suits you."

Her pink-tipped nails tap the edge of the crystal she's holding. She sucks on her bottom lip, and I imagine doing the same. "I don't want you to move out." Color rises in her cheeks, but she holds my gaze.

"Scarlett..."

"I'll try, okay? I'll try."

"It wasn't an ultimatum," I say softly.

"Good."

She abandons her spot on the chair, crawling into my lap and shocking me into stillness. She settles directly on my crotch. Just like that, I'm uncomfortably hard.

"Thank you."

"For what?" I choke out.

She looks down at my red, swollen knuckles. "For that."

"I've wanted to punch Camden for years. Guy's an ass," I lie. Camden Crane *is* an asshole. But I've never contemplated punching him until I overheard him speculating about what Scarlett is like in bed.

I can tell from her expression she knows the truth, but she doesn't dispute it. "People will talk."

"Let them."

"Won't your father be upset? He does business with Sebastian Crane."

Upset? More like furious. "Contrary to what *some* people think, I don't make my decisions based on my father."

Rather than reply, she kisses me. She tastes like tart wine. Sour and sweet. *Intoxicating.*

The last time our lips touched, we were standing in a lobby with hundreds of people on the other side of the wall. I was wearing a tux, and she was wearing a white dress. Now it's the middle of the night. There's no one else around. She's grinding on my lap, wearing a silk nightgown that barely covers her ass.

Heat surges through my veins. Sparks between us catch, burning with intention. With want and need and other consuming emotions that wash away rational thought.

I don't usually pay much attention to kissing. It's a courtesy, a stop on the way to the final destination. Sprinkled between desperate touches and tearing clothes off. But with Scarlett, I savor it. Maybe because it's been a month since her lips were on mine. Kissing her feels like a gift—a privilege.

Just like with everything else, she challenges me. Her teeth scrape my lower lip and I can't contain the groan that spills out. I feel her smile, even though her face is too close to see it.

I'm close to coming from this alone—her taste, her hands in my hair, the friction between our bodies. When her right hand slips out of my hair and slides down to my waistband, I curse my lack of planning. These shorts don't have pockets. I grab her wrist before she journeys down far enough I won't be able to think straight. Blood is already rushing south. There's no way she's oblivious to how hard I am.

"I don't have anything." I wait to see what she'll say.

Something passes across her face. It looks like regret, mixed with some uncertainty. Then she shrugs and moves away. "Okay."

Okay?

I'm pissed. Annoyed she'd kiss me like that and then turn it off just as fast. Blood is racing through my veins as fast as my heart is pounding, and she's leaning back on the chair, looking the same as she did when I came out here—completely unaffected.

This push and pull has become a predictable pattern between us. But this time, I push harder.

I crawl over her, rubbing my erection against the inside of her thigh. Her breathing quickens, like she's struggling to pull in enough oxygen. Scarlett can control her words. Her body is another story.

I kiss her—hard, deep, and bruising. She kisses me back. I can feel her fighting the urge to arch against me. I stop kissing her, pulling back so I can study her face for a minute. Her cheeks are flushed and her dark hair is spread out in a wild tangle.

Seeing Scarlett in her wedding dress was a shock. This feels like another new experience—like I'm seeing her for the first time. She consumes every thought without even trying.

Her skin is as smooth as the silk she's barely wearing. The transition between the two is subtle. Her soft gasp when I slip my hand up and under the hem of her short nightgown is the only sound I'm aware of. I keep my eyes on her as I trace the wet lace between her thighs, watching as her eyes close and her lips part.

"Look at me, Scarlett," I command. Like hell is she pretending this is some other guy touching her.

She fights me for a minute, keeping her eyes stubbornly shut. I wouldn't expect anything less. But then she's looking at me. Electricity crackles between us, as consuming as anything I've ever felt.

Scarlett bites her bottom lip. She's still fighting—not to react, not to make a sound.

"Show me your tits."

Her eyes widen. Not just with surprise, but with arousal. She likes being bossed around in bed.

Slowly, Scarlett reaches up and tugs at the thin straps holding her nightgown up. The fabric slides down, revealing more and more of her pale skin. My dick jerks as her breasts come into view. The hard points of her nipples pebble under my gaze. Her dress is pooled around her waist, only covering a small strip of her stomach. The rest of her body is bare, laid out before and beneath me.

I've fantasized about seeing Scarlett naked an embarrassing number of times. Unlike most things, the reality exceeds my imagination. Her body is perfect. But it's the fact it's *her* body— that it belongs to the woman who fights me on everything but is letting me see her like this—that has me feeling like I've never seen a naked woman before.

I don't move. I look, soaking in my fill of her feminine curves and creamy skin. Another woman might shirk from the appraisal. Cover herself or look away. Scarlett does neither. She holds my gaze with a hint of challenge sparking in her eyes, looking at me like I'm the vulnerable one.

Maybe she's right. Maybe I am.

She's perfect. And in one permanent way, she's mine. "Spread your legs for me, baby."

There's no hesitation this time. No pet name in an annoyed tone. Eagerness is the predominant emotion on her face as she parts her thighs as wide as they'll go, opening herself up to me.

I slide lower, yanking her panties off so they're out of the way. Her breathing turns fast and ragged. I lower my head and lick her with a long, thorough drag.

Her hips rise and roll, her legs falling further open. Trying to coax me where she wants me. Chasing pleasure and offering temptation. I like her like this. Under me. Focused on me. For all her posturing about property and prizes, I don't think Scarlett realizes how much power she holds. Over everyone. Over me.

She inherited. But she also built. Conquered. Expanded. Like an empress, not a queen. That's rare in our world, where people hide unhappiness under cars they don't drive and houses they don't live in and vacations they don't enjoy.

She's a force, my wife, and right now she's writhing. Silently begging for my fingers and my tongue because she's too proud to say a word.

I tease her slowly and seductively, avoiding the spot I know will set her off. The hard ridge of the chair digs into my knee and my aching cock presses against the cushion, desperate for some attention. The pool lights cast shadows over the patio, the steady *glug* of the water filter the only sound aside from Scarlett's fast breathing. Her skin tastes like salt and sin as I coax her close to the edge and then pull back.

When—and I'm betting it's a when, not an if, based on how wet she is—we're in a position like this again, I'll pay for this slow torture. I'm sure of it. But right now, she has no choice but to lie back and take it. I'm guessing most guys she's been with have been too horny and desperate to pleasure her like this. To drag anticipation out every sweet second.

She tries a new method the next time I look up, tracing her fingers between the valley of her breasts and then cupping her left tit. Her lips tilt up, mischievous and enticing.

We're playing with fire. She's asking to be burned.

I slip one finger inside her, then two. A breathy gasp falls from her lips, which are a natural, rosy pink rather than her signature red. She clenches around my fingers, squeezing them tight. I curl them, and she explodes, convulsing and moaning. Panting and primal.

She holds my gaze as she comes, and it's the hottest thing I've ever seen. Her thighs tremble with aftershocks as I raise my head to meet her gaze. She blinks at me, sleepy and satisfied.

We stare at each other to the soundtrack of waves pounding sand, reconciling what just happened with who we were before. I'm expecting a dismissal. For her to adjust her pajamas and pick up her book and act like nothing just happened. Instead, she sits up and reaches for my shorts.

I snag her wrist and hold it. "I'm *okay*." My dick wants to get acquainted with her mouth. Very, very badly. But if I let her blow me, this will feel transactional. Even scores. I want things between us to feel unfinished. I want her to wonder what *I* look like, fully naked. When *I* come.

Scarlett laughs, pulling out of my grasp to deliberately graze her hand across my crotch. "You're kidding."

"Doesn't sound so great, does it?" I hold her gaze, not leaving any question about what I'm referring to.

Her lips tighten. "Real fucking mature, *Sport*."

I lean forward to press one final, bruising kiss to her mouth. She kisses me back, then bites down on my bottom lip. I chuckle as I pull away, running my tongue across it to check for blood and tasting a sharp, metallic tinge. I reach out and tug her nightgown back into its proper place, covering her naked body from the moon and the stars. "Good night. *Red*."

Then I stand and walk back inside, leaving her to stew.

When I wake up, sun is streaming in through the windows and Scarlett is beside me in bed. Fast asleep and curled on her side with one hand tucked under her cheek. Her dark hair is a tangled mess fanned across the pillow. Her lips are parted and one strap of her nightgown has fallen off her shoulder.

I picture her writhing beneath me last night.

I'm painfully tempted to pull that other strap down and pick things up right where we left off last night.

Scarlett likes a challenge. She may have wanted me last night, but I'm certain any intimacy would have lasted about as long as the sex did. I want her desperate for me. I want her to admit there's more than attraction between us.

We're not there yet. Before last night, I wasn't sure if we ever would be.

I slip out of bed, trying to be as quiet as possible. I didn't hear her come to bed last night, so it must have been late. After our encounter, I lay awake for a while, too worked up to fall asleep. Probably should have jerked off, but I wasn't sure how long I'd have before she'd follow me up here.

Scarlett is still sleeping when I finish using the bathroom and getting dressed. I head downstairs alone. Her father is seated in the formal dining room. The table is spread with an assortment of every breakfast food imaginable.

Hanson Ellsworth closes *The New York Times* with a crinkle when he sees me.

"Morning, Crew."

"Hanson."

"Sleep well?"

I force all thoughts of the time I didn't spend sleeping from my head. "Yes, sir."

"Good." With that, I'm all but dismissed. Hanson turns back to his paper as I fill a plate with fresh fruit, pancakes, and bacon.

Josephine Ellsworth enters the dining room a few minutes later, balancing a teacup and a half of a grapefruit. She visibly brightens when she sees me. "Crew! Good morning."

"Good morning, Josephine."

Scarlett's mother launches into a recap of the party yesterday as I eat breakfast, one that requires little input on my part. I nod and grunt between bites as she goes on about the catering and flowers.

Hanson completely ignores his wife as she talks. I realize this is the romantic relationship Scarlett grew up witnessing. A few more pieces of her prickliness start to make sense.

She appears as I'm stealing seconds, dressed more casually than I've ever seen in a pair of jean shorts and a tank top. Her hair is up in a ponytail that swings as she walks. "Good morning."

"Good morning, dear." Josephine is speaking to her daughter, but her eyes are on me. No doubt she's taking this opportunity to observe how we interact with each other.

Hanson merely grunts a response, not bothering to look up from his paper.

This table could comfortably seat a couple of dozen people, but Scarlett takes the seat right next to me. Her hair brushes my arm as she leans over and pours herself a glass of orange juice.

"I'm glad you slept in, sweetheart. You've been working too hard," Josephine says.

"Mm-hmm," Scarlett mumbles, grabbing a croissant and some strawberries.

"I was thinking we could do some shopping in town today. And Marcy Whitman said her daughter is back in town. She wants to get lunch. What is her daughter's name? I couldn't remember last night."

Scarlett rolls her eyes. "Lucy." She pops a strawberry in her mouth.

"Right. Lucy. We'll leave right after you get changed."

There's a quiet sigh beside me. "Fine."

"I was thinking you and Crew could come down next weekend as well. The country club is having a—"

"I'll be in Paris next weekend, Mom. I need to approve the final designs for *rouge*."

It's news to me—the trip to Paris and that Scarlett told her parents about her new business venture—but I say nothing.

For the first time since Scarlett came downstairs, Hanson speaks. "Are you sure this is a good idea, Scarlett?"

Her hand tightens around her fork. "Yes."

"The magazine might be doing well for the time being, but that's no reason to get ahead of yourself. Especially now that you're married."

"I fail to see what my marriage has to do with it." Scarlett's voice is icy.

"You're too smart to play dumb, sweetie." Hanson's tone is condescending. "You know what the expectations are."

Scarlett stabs another strawberry. "Thanks for the unsolicited advice, Dad."

"If you won't listen to me, I hope you'll listen to your husband. This arrangement took years. Don't destroy it to play dress-up." Hanson glances at me. "Surely you agree this is ridiculous."

"If I thought it was ridiculous, I wouldn't be going to Paris next week to help out however I can." Without thinking it through —*at all*—that's the reply that flies out of my mouth.

Hanson is too practiced of a businessman to show any surprise. But it's obvious he's taken aback in the way he doesn't say anything right away. Whatever he was planning to say clearly no longer applies.

"How exciting!" Josephine jumps into the conversation. "I

hope you two will make time for some sight-seeing. You never went on a honeymoon."

"I love sight-seeing." I don't; I can't recall the last time I actually took in the sights on a trip. My international travel for Kensington Consolidated usually consists of quality time spent at a hotel and in a boardroom. It's worth saying so to see the dubious expression on Scarlett's face, though. I resist the urge to laugh.

Josephine goes on and on about her favorite spots in Paris while Scarlett and I eat. Hanson stays focused on his newspaper. Scarlett eventually excuses herself to go up and change. I give her a few minutes head start and then follow.

When I walk into the room, Scarlett has already dressed in a pink sundress. She glances up in the midst of slipping on a pair of wedges. "Hey."

"Hey," I repeat.

"I'm leaving the car here if you want to go out. Keys are on the dresser."

I slip my hands in my pockets, watching as she straightens and smooths her dress. "Okay. I might go see Andrew for a bit."

"Okay," she echoes. There's some curiosity on her face—I'm sure she wants to ask about what happened with Camden again—but all she does is grab her phone.

"You want to head home when you get back?"

Our original plan was to spend another night, but I'm happy to head back early.

Relief washes over her face. "Yeah."

I nod. "Okay."

She glances around the room, checking to make sure she has everything. Then she walks toward the doorway where I'm standing. Rather than pass, she pauses. Her mouth opens. Closes.

Scarlett shakes her head. "Fuck it."

She kisses me. I'm too shocked to react at first. By the time I start to respond, she's already pulling back.

One small smile, and she's gone.

CHAPTER ELEVEN

SCARLETT

As Audrey said, Paris is always a good idea. And ever since I became editor-in-chief of *Haute*, trips to France's capital city have become common.

This particular visit is one I've been dreading and anticipating. I'm here to approve final designs and fabrics for *rouge*. Once everything is in place, I'll go public with the announcement. It's a daunting prospect. I'm worried I'll fail. Fashion is a hard industry to break into, no matter how much money you have. You can't buy success. And if I fail, I'll fail as Scarlett *Kensington*.

Right now, I'm more focused on my companion for this trip than anything else. I wasn't expecting for Crew to back me up with my dad in the Hamptons. I was expecting for him to stay in New York. Apparently, he meant it when he said he was coming with me.

Things have been tenuous between us since the Fourth. Not awkward, the way they were before we left for the Hamptons. It took me a few days to process everything that happened in the short span of time. Those same days were spent logging long hours finalizing the September issue of *Haute* and preparing for this trip. And then he was waiting at the airport when I arrived for my flight, since Leah shares all my travel details with his secretary. I made the mature decision to pretend to sleep for the duration of the six-hour flight.

Crew hasn't said much since we arrived. So far, we've checked in at the hotel, met with two of my fabric suppliers, and now we're at the French Open. Jacqueline Perout is a friend from Harvard and heiress to Europe's premier department store. Securing her interest in *rouge* will be paramount to its success, so turning down an invitation to watch a morning match from her box wasn't really an option.

"Scarlett Ellsworth! How lovely to see you!" Richard Cavendish has come to stand beside me in the executive suite I'm watching the match from.

Richard is the vice president of a prominent French publication. Our paths inevitably cross at many of the social events I attend here. I believe he's the only person who considers himself charming.

I take a sip of mimosa before answering. Just like with most of the men in my social circle, it's less painful to converse with Richard slightly buzzed. "Nice to see you too, Richard."

"Here on business?"

"Always," I reply cooly, watching his gaze sweep up and down the white eyelet dress I'm wearing. It's modest, with capped sleeves and falling to my calves, but Richard's eyes are heated by the time they arrive at my signature red lips. His bottom lip curls as his gaze moves to the left hand holding the glass. And the large diamond resting on my ring finger.

"So the rumors are true. You got married."

"Rumors? You don't trust the hundreds of papers that reported on it?"

Richard's eyes fill with annoyance. "I have more important things to do with my time than troll the society pages."

The merging of the Ellsworth and Kensington families made it into plenty of respectable European papers, as Richard well knows. Kensington Consolidated and Ellsworth Enterprises both have international holdings.

I could have ignored my father's wishes and married Richard. He wouldn't have contributed as much to my net worth and I find him irksome and boring, but he would have been better for my sanity than Crew Kensington.

Because if Richard Cavendish had spent the last half an hour talking to a pretty blonde tennis player, I would feel relieved not to have to engage in a bothersome exchange of words with him. Crew choosing to do so has left me marinating in a mixture of rage and jealousy.

This is why you shouldn't marry for love.

Not that I love Crew. I just find him mildly entertaining and annoyingly attractive. And after he made me come in seconds, I might have strong feelings toward his tongue.

"Your husband seems to be enjoying the match," Richard comments, following my gaze.

I don't reply. I turn back to watch the green ball get smashed over the net, and I wish I also had something to hit right now.

"Is Kensington here on business too?" Richard needles.

A possessive hand slides to the small of my back. Even before the scent of his expensive cologne reaches me, I know it's Crew. A trail of heat lingers behind the pressure of his palm, and I suppress a shiver by taking yet another sip. At this rate, I'll need a refill soon. Which would probably be a bad idea, since, as was just established, I'm here on business.

Not pleasure.

"Nope. All pleasure, Cavendish." Crew's deep voice rumbles

from behind me. "At some point, you should sit back and enjoy the spoils, don't you agree?"

"I couldn't agree more," Richard replies. I know his agreeable tone means he thinks the opposite. "But I find it disheartening you're ready to sit back so soon. You wouldn't want anyone to think you only got the job because of your father. Are you planning to live off your wife?"

I feel Crew's hand flex against my spine, but his voice is smooth as butter when he replies. "I must have missed you becoming a self-made billionaire, Cavendish. Must be because the papers you own don't really talk about you at all."

Richard's face turns an ugly shade of puce. "Scarlett, lovely to see you, as always. My condolences on your choice of groom."

He stalks off in the direction of the private bar. I turn my gaze back to the tennis match. Crew's hand remains on my back, searing through the thin material.

"Interesting choice in conversationalist."

"I could say the same to you," I reply loftily.

I can hear a smile in Crew's voice. "She approached me."

For some stupid reason, I feel obligated to respond. "So did he."

"I know. I saw."

"You were watching?"

"Always, Red."

He can't see my face, so I don't bother to hide my smile.

After the tennis match ends, I promise Jacqueline I'll meet her for breakfast tomorrow morning. She spent most of the match flirting with Henriq Popov, who is the odds-on favorite to win the French Open, instead of discussing business.

"Where to next?" Crew asks as we leave the private box.

"Um…" Truthfully, I don't have anything definitive planned until dinner with Jacques tonight. Admitting that feels like a weakness, as stupid as that sounds. I rely on looking busy around Crew. Work is always an excuse, something I know he'll respect. "I have nothing planned until dinner," I admit.

"Dinner with who?"

"Jacques. He's—"

"The super in-demand guy you skipped our wedding night for. Yeah, I remember."

He sounds jealous. "You can come, if you want."

"I don't want to get in the way."

I smile. "If anyone will be in the way, it's me."

His brow creases with confusion, interrupting his previously bored expression.

"Jacques is gay, Crew. If you come to dinner, I guarantee he'll hit on you."

Jacques's sexual orientation is a pointless clarification, one I only make because I still feel guilty for lying to him about my pretend lover. His only response is to walk toward the exit. I scurry after him a few seconds later.

Crew weaves through the crowds without so much as a jostle. Even among people who have no clue who he is, he's not the sort of guy you mow over.

He halts when we reach the sidewalk, leaning down to talk to a driver of one of the many cabs lining the street. After a minute, he stands and beckons me over.

"What are you doing?" I ask, pulling out my phone. "I can call—"

"Get in."

"I have a car here."

"I know you do. We rode here in it. Get in, Scarlett."

Part of me wants to argue for the sake of it. I don't like to defer to anyone about anything. But a bigger part of me wants to listen—craves the dominance Crew commands so easily.

Silently, I listen. He doesn't walk around to the other side of the cab. I realize he's waiting for me to slide over. There's something normal about it, so different from the limo rides we've shared in the past. I slide, feeling the fabric of my dress bunch up around my thighs as I glide across the leather. Crew pays more attention to my bare legs than he did to the tennis match.

"Where are we going?" I ask as the car begins to move.

"You'll see," is all he says.

I focus on the scenery passing by. We drive by the Louvre and the Arc de Triomphe. When the car stops, it's by an even more iconic landmark.

I look at Crew. "Seriously?"

"Yep. We can send a photo to your mom to prove we went sight-seeing."

At that, I smile. Reluctantly. Crew pays the driver, and we join the long line of people walking toward the Eiffel Tower.

"Have you climbed it before?" Crew asks as we walk.

"No," I admit.

"Me neither."

Crew navigates us to the one ticket window without a long line. I stare up at the wrought-iron lattice tower as he buys our tickets. Minutes later, we're approaching the start of the steps. Crew is studying the map he took from the ticket window. It's annoyingly adorable.

All of a sudden, he stops walking. "Shit."

I stop too. "What?" I glance around, trying to figure out what's wrong.

When I look back at Crew, he's staring at me with wide, worried eyes. "You're scared of heights."

I stare back at him, shocked that he remembered. Then I smile. "It's okay. As long as we're not parachuting when we get to the top, I'll be fine."

"Are you sure?" He still looks concerned. "We can go do something else."

It's going to be a real challenge to see Crew as cold and callous ever again. "I'm sure. It's more of a control thing. I have more faith in the Eiffel Tower staying upright than I did in that one rope at the rock gym keeping me in the air." I don't share the other difference between that outing and today's: the state of my relationship with Crew.

Crew starts walking again. "Okay. Stairs or elevator?"

I wore flats today. Even if I hadn't, I still would answer, "Stairs."

He grins. "That's my girl."

I know he doesn't mean it literally—at least I don't *think* he does—but the words still send a silly thrill through me. Butterflies flock in my stomach like the most popular guy in school just handed me his letterman jacket to wear.

As we climb, more and more of Paris is spread below us. I spot Parc de Belleville and Champ de Mars. We reach the first observation deck and start up the second set of stairs.

"Do you work out?" I ask, halfway up the third flight.

Crew laughs. "Your pick-up lines need work."

I roll my eyes because I'm too short of breath to scoff. "I'm serious."

"Yeah, I do. You have a private gym, you know."

"I know. I just don't use it."

"Yeah, I realized that when I cleared an inch of dust off the treadmill."

I smile. "Bullshit. Martha would never let that happen."

"Fine. It was more like a quarter inch."

"When do you work out?"

He slants a glance my way. "After you leave. I work out, shower, eat breakfast, and then head into the office."

"Why after I leave?"

His eyes are still on me. Mine stay straight ahead.

"You try to avoid me. I'm not going to make it more difficult for you."

"I left for work at seven before we got married."

I dance around what he's really saying, and he doesn't press the point.

We reach the next landing. Crew pauses. I halt too, watching as he grabs the railing with one hand and grabs his ankle with his other. He balances on one leg and bends the other back.

"What's wrong?"

"I have an old knee injury. Just need to stretch for a minute."

"A knee injury from what?"

"I played football in high school."

I snort. "*Of course* you did. The patron sport of jerky jocks everywhere."

"That's awfully judgmental."

"I *am* awfully judgmental."

"Yeah." He smirks. "I've noticed."

I don't like the familiar way he's looking at me. And I like it too much. "So what happened?"

"Huh?"

"Your knee. What happened to it?"

"Oh. Chris Jenkins hit me with an illegal tackle junior year. I twisted a tendon, and it still flares up sometimes." He shakes his head with a smile. "Asshole."

"Is there film footage of you getting knocked on your ass?"

"No."

"I think you're lying."

"I think you'll never know."

"You should have played a non-contact sport in high school. Like…crew, maybe?"

He *laughs*. And it's not a laugh I've heard from him before. It's a warm, rough, masculine sound that feels like standing in front of a fire drinking hot chocolate. A comforting burn. "Pretty proud of yourself for coming up with that, Red?"

I smile. "A little."

We climb the final few flights in silence. If Crew's knee is still bothering him, he doesn't say anything about it. He keeps up with me easily as we reach the top observation deck and glimpse Paris spread out in front of us.

"Wow." I'm used to closing off my emotions and reactions. I'm always ready with a right answer or a snappy retort, never caught off guard or confused. Never *appreciating* where I am or what I'm doing. It's exhausting, and a guard I usually only let down when I'm alone.

I never expected to be myself around Crew Kensington. I've seen plenty of people navigate arranged marriages with minimal interaction. I expected us to be no different. It's disconcerting, realizing we might be. That I *like* him. Might have chosen to marry him even if his net worth was half of what it is—or nonexistent.

A couple of girls who look like they're in college ask Crew to take a picture of them. I lean against the railing and eyeball their interaction. Everywhere we go, Crew seems to command female attention. The women at Proof, Hannah Garner, Olivia Spencer, the blonde tennis player.

It's not that I don't see Crew's appeal—I do. It's that I'm torn. Staking a claim—admitting my attraction—comes with risks.

Once I lay down my metaphorical cards, that's it. I'll have skin in the game. And it will get rubbed raw when Crew cheats.

For all the attention he gets, I've never seen him flirt with a woman. At most, he seems to allow women to flirt with him.

Even now, with two pretty girls in their early twenties drooling over him, he seems uninterested. He's smiling, but it doesn't reach his eyes. He doesn't look at them the way he was just looking at me. I wish I could blame the happy feeling on the fact I'm standing at the top of the Eiffel Tower on a perfect summer day.

I think it has more to do with him.

Rather than continue spying, I look out at the city. There's a light breeze that counteracts some of the summer heat, blowing my hair out of my face.

"Scarlett!"

I glance over to see Crew beckoning me over. I walk over to where he is standing with the two women. Neither of them appear thrilled by my appearance.

"This is Natasha and Blair," he introduces. "They're from New York too."

"Awesome." You could hear the fakeness in my voice from outer space.

I don't have to see Crew's smile; I can hear it in his voice. "Natasha goes to Parsons." He looks to the lighter of the two blondes. "Scarlett is the editor-in-chief of *Haute*." There's an unmistakable note of pride in his voice that wreaks havoc on my nervous system.

"Oh my God! Really?" Suddenly, Natasha and Blair are looking at me with awe, not annoyance. "I love *Haute*. I read every issue cover to cover. The articles, the photography, the *design*? All my friends are obsessed with it."

Each month, I get the number for *Haute*'s circulation. I judge the success of the magazine on how much money it is making and which models or actresses want to be featured on the cover. But I've never seen the hero worship on someone's face as they realize I approved every page.

"Can you sign this?" Natasha pulls a worn copy of the July issue out of her bag and holds it out to me, along with a pen.

"Um, sure." I take the pen and scribble my signature just below the bold font spelling out *Haute*.

Natasha takes the magazine back like it's a priceless treasure.

"Would one of you mind taking a photo of us?" Crew asks, holding his phone out.

I'm surprised but I try not to show it. Aside from our wedding photos, we don't have any together. I didn't think he would want any.

Blair takes Crew's phone as he pulls me toward the railing. I trip over nothing and slam into his chest.

"If you wanted to stand this close, all you had to do was ask," he whispers as he pulls me to him. I smile as his arms tighten around my waist, pinning me against him.

"Got it," Blair announces. Without looking, I know what moment she captured.

Crew thanks her and we say goodbye before moving farther down the observation deck. I snap a few photos of the view while Crew fiddles with something on his phone.

"Do you not have an Instagram?"

"What?"

"There's a Scarlett Ellsworth, but I seriously doubt you posted this." He shows me the screen of his phone. It's a photo of me walking down the street talking on the phone.

"What the hell?" I grab his phone and squint at it. The photo got forty-three thousand likes.

Crew takes his phone back. "So, no?"

"Technically, I run *Haute*'s account, but I have someone who posts content for me."

He smirks as he types. "Of course you do. I'm not tagging a fashion magazine."

"Tagging in what?"

"I'm posting the photo of us."

I'm not sure what to say to that. *Why?* is the only response I can think of. Then I come up with a worse one. "Does Hannah Garner follow you?"

"I don't know; I've never checked. Why?"

When I muster the courage to meet his gaze, his eyes are dancing with mirth he's not even attempting to hide. "You know why," I mutter.

He grins. "Want me to check? Block her?"

"No." I start walking toward the exit.

It takes us half the time to walk down the stairs that it did to climb up. Once we're back on solid ground, Crew leaves for the restroom. As soon as he's out of sight, I open the Instagram app on my phone and search for his name. Despite the fact he's only posted a handful of photos, he has millions of followers. The photos are mostly of scenery: Copenhagen and London and New York City. A couple feature the two guys from his bachelor party, Asher and Jeremy. One was taken in Boston; I recognize the bar from college.

And then there's the photo of us he just posted. I bite my bottom lip when I see what he wrote as the caption. *Exploring Paris with the most beautiful woman in the world. She outshines all the sights.*

I scroll down through some of the comments. A good number of them are suggestive ones involving Crew. Those don't surprise me. The ones that do are the ones that read *gorgeous couple* and *you guys look so happy* and *marriage goals*. I tap back on the photo, trying to scrutinize the image the way a total stranger would.

We do look happy. We're both smiling. I know mine wasn't forced, and Crew's doesn't look like it was either. His arms are wrapped around my middle and his chin is resting on the top of my head. Thriving greenery and stone monuments are obvious in the background behind us. I search his followers and learn Hannah is one of them. A petty part of me is pleased.

"Ready to go?"

The sound of his voice startles me. "Yep." I slip my phone back into my bag.

"You're free until dinner?" Crew confirms as we cross the lawn and head back toward the street.

"Uh-huh."

"Are you dying to go back to the hotel and do work?"

For once, I'm not. I try not to read into the realization. "Not if you make me a better offer."

Crew shoots me a shocked look that I'm not certain is entirely exaggerated. "Something can trump work for you?"

"Shut up." I shove his shoulder. "I'm not that bad."

"You're worse. But I respect it. Anyone who says you've had everything handed to you...they're *wrong*, Scarlett."

"*You* were handed to me." I point out.

He stops and pulls me to the side of the walkway so quickly I crash into his chest again.

I step back like he scalded me.

Crew grins, but it disappears quickly. "Just to be clear, there are times I disagree with my dad. I argue with him. I don't listen to him. Those moments don't make it into the press. They aren't on display in public. I get why you think I'm Arthur Junior. But I'm *not*, Scarlett. When I step up as CEO, I'll make changes to the company. I could have married Hannah, or some other woman. I could have married anyone. I married *you*, Scarlett. That means something, even if you want to pretend that it doesn't."

"Okay." Honestly, I no longer view Crew as an extension of his father. I only *wish* I did. It would make a lot of things easier.

Crew sighs like my answer is a disappointment. "Okay."

I clear my throat. "Uh, can you send me the photo?"

"What?"

"The photo of us. Can you send it to me?"

Surprise flashes across his face. "Yeah. Sure."

We start walking again. My phone vibrates with a message as we reach the sidewalk. Crew heads for the line of taxis while I wait. I check my phone and see the photo came through from him. It's the first message he's ever sent me.

I text the photo to my mom. It's the first photo in our chain of messages, mostly ones she sent me related to the wedding that I never responded to.

I tuck my phone away and walk over to where Crew is standing.

"He needs to know where we're going," he says, nodding toward the driver.

"Versailles?" I suggest. I've been before, but it's been years.

Crew's smile is blinding. "That sounds a lot like sight-seeing."

"I heard you love sight-seeing."

He smiles. "Is it a better offer?"

I nod. "Let's go."

Jacques is already seated at the table when we enter the restaurant. Our trip to Versailles ate up most of the afternoon. I fully intended to head back to the hotel and change before dinner, but there wasn't time.

Not that it matters. Jacques is far more focused on Crew than what I'm wearing.

I get a cursory greeting before he starts bombarding Crew with questions. I mouth *told you* at Crew when he glances at me. His answering smile makes my insides feel like shaken champagne.

Today has been wonderful and terrible. I've thought about starting my own fashion line since college. This trip is the culmination of years of planning. *Haute* served as an unplanned springboard to making connections in the fashion industry that made *rouge* more attainable.

A clothing line might be a pursuit most people look down upon. It's not as refined as finance or any Wall Street dealings. My father certainly thinks it's shallow and silly.

But that's the beauty of dreams: they're yours. No one else's. You don't need permission or justification to pursue them. You can give them relevance and importance and meaning all by yourself.

Unfortunately for my heart, Crew doesn't seem to share my dad's opinion. Between strolling the gardens and wandering the halls of the palace, he asked me questions about *rouge* and listened to the answers.

Either he's *extremely* dedicated to getting me into bed, or he actually cares how I spend my time, energy, and money.

I spend most of dinner studying him. This is the first time I've seen Crew in what isn't his element. He's not here to pursue a deal for Kensington Consolidated. I doubt he knows much, if anything, about the fashion industry. Jacques isn't someone he'd have common acquaintances with.

And yet, he's thriving. *Charming.* This was meant to be a business dinner. Every meal I shared with Jacques during my last trip here was spent brainstorming or flipping through sketches. Tonight, there's no sign of the manic energy usually buzzing around him like a swarm of bees, tossing out ideas at the speed of light. Jacques is relaxed and laughing. So is Crew. I'm the interloper growing more and more annoyed as they chat like old friends instead of strangers.

This is my trip. My endeavor. My domain. Our lives were supposed to stay separate. Suddenly, they're so entangled I can't look past him.

I excuse myself and head to the restroom after we finish eating, not even sure they'll notice my disappearance. After I've used the bathroom, I linger at the sink, dabbing my face with a paper towel and checking my teeth for food.

When I open the restroom door, Crew is leaning across the opposite wall with his arms crossed.

"I know your French isn't great, but you're not blind. The stick figure wearing a dress means this is the women's restroom. Men's must be down there." I jerk my head to the left, where the hallway extends. On a scale of one to bitchy, I'm at an eleven.

He says nothing at first, which is the worst possible response. Crew has become the one person I can rely on to challenge me. I crave that from him, more than financial security or fidelity. I want him to see me as an equal and as a partner—because that's the way I see him. The muscles of his jaw shift as he visibly clenches it, holding in whatever he was going to reply with. I wait, and it spills out. "What the fuck, Scarlett?"

The question is basically spat at me. I want to smile, but I don't. "What the fuck *what*, Crew?"

"I can't win with you. No matter what I do. I came here to support you. And I watch tennis for hours and try to get to know you and make small talk with your—I don't even know what Jacques does for you—and you act like I'm in your way!"

He's too good. At all of this. I know how to play the game of secrets and lies and deceit. Of betrayal and sweeping mistakes under the rug. I know how to handle the Crew I talked to at Proof, who looked at me with total indifference. The guy who would greet me with a perfunctory, bland *You look nice* and then ignored me for the rest of the night. I'm not equipped to handle the Crew who came here to *support* me. Who makes me feel special—same as he does with everyone else. He's the sun and I'm Icarus, after he learned his lesson.

"I didn't ask you to do any of that!" I snap. "I didn't *ask* you to come. I didn't *want* you to come."

He shakes his head. Laughs. Scoffs. "If this is you *trying*, I can't imagine how you'll act when you're about to file for divorce."

I don't react to them, but I feel the words hit me like a physical slap. I meant it when I told him I'd try. He's staining that moment, that memory, dragging it through this ugly argument. I spent all afternoon *trying*. If I hadn't, I would have been holed up in the hotel working. Ignoring each other except to exchange insults wasn't tenable. Neither is the happy couple we pretended to be today. I'll always have one foot out the door—always be waiting for him to turn into some version of my father—focused on nothing but keeping the keys to the kingdom.

Crew told me he could have married someone else earlier. We both know why he didn't. If my last name wasn't formerly Ellsworth, he would have. He has qualities that can't be bought, like charisma and charm. More to offer than a handsome face and a bank account trailing zeroes.

People genuinely like him. They indulge me because they know I can be a powerful friend and a ruthless enemy. Because I've found fear far more effective than love.

He wouldn't have married me if not for an arrangement.

But I would have married him.

That realization is why I can no longer look at him. I study the stucco floor tiles instead. "I'm not going to file for divorce."

Maybe the most honest sentence I've ever said to him. I won't be the reason this marriage ends. Fails, maybe. But not the one who flags the dotted line to sign.

Not because my father would be furious I destroyed the future he arranged.

Not because I'd lose everything I gained.

Not because my other prospects would be dismal.

Because I'm selfish.

I want him and I don't want anyone else to have him.

Crew pushes away from the wall, looming over me. For one wild, thrilling second, I think he's about to kiss me. Force me to admit I *do* want him here. Instead, he turns to his right, toward the exit.

"You're leaving?"

One eyebrow cocks infuriatingly as he glances back. "Using the restroom. Is that allowed, *honey*?"

The harshest word in the sentence is the sweetest. The *honey* slaps. Our nickname game was entertaining. But after hearing him call me Red with feeling, with genuine affection, *honey* just sounds insulting. I sigh, the fight draining from me as his bitter tone registers. That's one of our many problems: one of us is usually in the mood to spar. "You can leave, if you want."

I'm not only talking about the restaurant, and I know he realizes that when determination flashes across his face. "I'm not a quitter. For better or worse, Red."

"I thought the only vow you meant was *for richer*."

His lips twitch, his bad mood temporarily fading like the sun peeking out behind clouds. "You're still wearing your sticker."

"Huh?"

Crew steps forward and tugs the green admission sticker from Versailles off my dress. I snag it from his fingers before he can crumple it.

He watches me tuck it into my clutch with an unreadable expression. "It's okay to care, you know."

"I know."

"Do you?" Crew counters.

Then he leaves me standing here, gaping after him like a goldfish.

You wouldn't know it's summer based on the iciness in this car. The rest of dinner with Jacques went smoothly. Crew stayed quiet as Jacques and I went over everything that needs to get taken care of this week.

I hoped Jacques was oblivious to the tension simmering between me and Crew throughout dinner. But he whispered *Amore is not easy, ma cherie* in my ear as we said our goodbyes, making me think you might have needed to be blind *and* deaf not to notice we weren't behaving like newlyweds. Jacques laughed at the scowl I answered his advice with.

After dinner, the driver drops us off back at the hotel. I stride across the marble lobby, not bothering to wait for Crew. I need some space. Unfortunately, his long legs carry him into the elevator mere seconds after me. The golden doors slide shut slowly, sealing us inside, and we begin to rise.

I expect him to talk, but he stays silent, leaning against the shiny metal wall and acting as though I'm not standing two feet away.

We arrive at the top floor of suites a couple of minutes later.

"You have my room key?" I ask when the doors open, annoyed I had to break the silence first. He was the one who checked us in. Unless I want to sleep in the hallway or pat him down like a police officer, I have no choice.

Wordlessly, Crew plucks a plastic rectangle from his pocket and hands it to me. I nod a *thanks* before I head toward the number emblazoned on the plastic. I hold the key against the sensor. It flashes green, allowing me inside. I shut the heavy door behind me and lean back against it for a moment. *What a day.* Parts—most—of it were good, which is bittersweet. I'll remember his pissed-off posture in the car just now when I think of climbing the Eiffel Tower side by side. My fault.

I head deeper inside the plush suite, kicking off my stilettos with a heavy sigh that doesn't release any tension. My bags have all been piled in the living room, next to unfamiliar luggage that should not be in here. I turn around at the same time as the door beeps again. Crew enters the room.

"What are you doing in here? I thought you had your own room."

"There were none available," Crew says breezily, pulling off his suit jacket and tossing it across the back of the gilded couch.

"You're lying," I inform him, crossing my arms.

"Am I?" He gives me an infuriating smirk.

"You're *not* sleeping in here."

"Why not? Worried you won't be able to control yourself, Red?"

I bite the inside of my cheek so hard I taste blood. "I've *controlled* myself for the month we've been married. So no, I'm not."

I expect him to bring up how loudly I moaned next to my parents' pool. The only reason we didn't have sex that night was because he didn't have a condom and thought I'm sleeping with a surgeon. Rubbing up against him wasn't exactly the pinnacle of self-control. But instead of a reminder, all he says is, "Great. I don't see what the problem is then."

"You're sleeping on the couch." *Fuck.* I don't negotiate. Ever.

Crew's triumphant smirk is maddening. He untucks his shirt and starts unbuttoning it. Looks at the fancy Victorian-style sofa that appears about as soft as a wooden board. "The bed looks more comfortable."

"I'm sure it is. If you want a bed—" Another suggestion to get his own damn room dies on my tongue as he discards his khaki shorts and strides to the bed in nothing but a pair of black boxer briefs. My mouth goes dry as he climbs in on the side of the bed I usually sleep on.

Golden skin rippling over defined muscles assaults my vision and hijacks my thoughts. He did most of the exploring the last time he was shirtless. I'm ogling and he appears indifferent, climbing into bed and rolling onto his stomach. He tugs a pillow under his head, closes his eyes, and that's *it*.

No touching. No teasing. No taunting. No talking.

We feel like a married couple—fifty years in. Not a loving one who cherishes every moment they share. A resigned one where time together is a chore and at least one person always has somewhere they'd rather be.

I'm completely off-kilter, but if I protest more, it will essentially be admitting I can't handle his proximity. That I'm affected by being near him while he's *unconscious*. I am, but I would rather sleep on the floor than give him that information. Than give Crew the satisfaction of pushing me out of my bed—of winning.

I stomp over to my bags to retrieve my toiletry kit and pajamas. I make sure to slam the bathroom door shut behind me, well aware I'm acting like a petulant child. More than being annoyed with Crew, I'm pissed at myself. If I really wanted to, I could make him leave. I'm choosing to allow this because a part of me wants it. I can feel the cracks appearing in my walls. And I know it.

Worse? So does he.

I just won't admit it—to him or to myself.

I wash my face and slather it with moisturizer. After I go through the rest of my evening routine, I slide out of the dress I've been wearing all day and pull a sleep set on.

Then I pad back out into the living room, tossing my white dress over the same couch where Crew abandoned his jacket. I continue into the bedroom. The lamp is still on, but Crew appears fast asleep, his back rising and falling steadily with each breath. I hover in the doorway, taking the rare opportunity to study him, the same as I did last time we shared a bed. Something I *thought* would be an infrequent occurrence.

I head to the left side of the bed and slip between the silk sheets. It's a king size bed, but it feels tiny. Crew and I are nowhere close to touching, but I can feel the heat radiating from his side of the bed. Hear his rhythmic breaths. Instead of counting sheep, I'm thinking about having sex with him.

It takes me a long time to fall asleep.

CHAPTER TWELVE

CREW

S carlett does *not* like being surprised. I knew that before I set this plan into motion, and my ears are still ringing with her questions when we land in Italy. Her tone grows more and more annoyed with each vague response.

Where are we going? "You'll see."

How long are we staying? "Not sure."

My personal favorite, which I don't bother answering: *Will there be WiFi?*

I know she feels badly about what went down in Paris that first day. Telling me she didn't want me there, pouting while Jacques hit on me. She's too stubborn and prideful to actually *apologize*, but she agreed to extend our trip past the few days it was originally supposed to last. I lied and told her I needed to take a meeting on behalf of Kensington Consolidated, and it made more sense for me to cross the French-Italian border than put someone else on a plane from New York to Florence. After four days of avoidance and silence, I think she was just shocked I asked.

Maybe it's hypocritical of me, expecting honesty from her

while I make up meetings. But the difference is I'm lying to keep her close. Scarlett lies to push me away. And, call me insane, but I keep trying over and over again.

I'm as stubborn as she is. Having my wife ignore me isn't just a point of pride. Scarlett fascinates me. Her beauty is captivating, but *she* is enthralling. I want more than a superficial relationship with her. More than a physical one, although my body wouldn't completely agree.

I want to know why she's a multi-billionaire working hours like she's struggling to pay rent. I want to know whether her relationship with her parents was ever different than it is now, if their unhappiness bled into her—and now into us. I want to know why she agreed to marry me when she seems intent on ignoring her father's wishes and is hostile toward commitment.

After she asks about the WiFi, I stop answering her questions, which only annoys her more. She's still grumbling as she follows me off the jet and toward the waiting car.

The late-afternoon air is warmer and drier than it was when we left France. Dapples of golden light filter down from the blue sky, bathing the tarmac and the distant buildings that make up the airport with a subtle glow.

I exchange pleasantries with the driver before sliding into the air-conditioned car. He finishes loading our luggage into the trunk, and then we're pulling away from the airport and turning onto a busy road.

"You speak Italian?" Scarlett sounds surprised.

"Some." I ask her where the nearest train station is.

She appears impressed, telling me she doesn't speak *any* Italian.

I catch our driver smiling in the rearview mirror as traffic thins and we coast along the road connecting the port city of Salerno and clifftop Sorrento before we enter Amalfi. The car winds past scenic views of terraced vineyards and cliffside lemon groves.

The villa is one of the few international properties my family owns that I ever bother staying at. When we pull up out front, I'm reminded why. It used to be an old rope factory producing fishing nets. The workers undoubtedly enjoyed the same view of aquamarine waves dotted with boats with a shoreline framed by the colorful houses staggered on the cliffs, looking as precarious as Jenga blocks. Years of renovations and wealthy owners have made the house unrecognizable from its humble beginnings. The majolica cladding was custom designed for this property alone.

Scarlett walks across the terracotta floors toward the terrace. She says nothing, which is a first. I've brought other women here before, and they've all spent a minimum of twenty minutes *oohing* and *aahing* over every detail. None of them grew up with the level of luxury Scarlett is accustomed to. All of them knew their time here would be limited and singular.

Technically, Scarlett has a claim to this property. Our ironclad prenup distributes our substantial assets in the event we get divorced. As long as we're married, they all belong to the other— with the exception of the magazine she asked me to sign away. Possessing something often causes it to lose its luster. It's human nature to covet what we can't or don't have. Appreciating what we do own is much rarer.

I watch our driver stack the suitcases in the entryway, then turn back to Scarlett. She's twisting her long brunette locks up into a bun, looking around like she's stepped inside a museum and is observing its artifacts. Appreciative, yet detached.

"I'll be back by six."

She spins, paying attention to me for the first time since we arrived. "Where are you going?"

A question I didn't ask her once in the past four days, most of which I spent in a hotel room in Paris, working remotely so as not to interrupt her business. "Out."

"I came all this way and now you're just leaving?"

"Sound familiar?"

Her eyes flash and her mouth drops. I walk out before she responds. A low blow. An admittance—that her absence and detachment the past few days bothered me. Annoyance—because I want to spend time with her, and rather than man up and admit that to her, I lied. And now I'm having to act like it wasn't one.

I instruct the driver to leave me at a tiny café in town. Happy chatter fills the street in a smorgasbord of languages. I order a cappuccino from the waitress and take a seat at one of the tiny tables—Europe is the opposite of Texas, it seems—and look out at the stucco buildings and the expensive cars and the ocean sparkling in the sunshine.

My phone starts to ring. I debate answering, but it's Asher. I haven't talked to him since I left for Paris.

"Hey."

"Why aren't you answering my texts?"

"Why are you acting like a clingy ex?"

He chuckles. "Fuck, dude. I miss you. You coming over tonight?"

I blink, then realize. *I was supposed to be back in New York hours ago.* "No. I'm at the villa."

"The villa? Does your dad know?"

Most of the time, I like the fact that my best friend's office is right down the hall from mine. This is not one of those times. "He's not my warden. If I want to go to Italy, I'll fucking go to Italy."

"I was just asking, man. He was pissed you left for Paris without warning, and the Lancaster acquisition is supposed to close Friday. We're supposed to run through the final reports tomorrow. The whole team."

"I'll review the reports and send my feedback."

There's a beat of silence. "It was that bad, huh?"

"What?"

"Traveling with Scarlett. I knew it would be a disaster. You couldn't even come back together."

The insinuation chafes. For who knows what reason, I feel the need to defend her. "It wasn't a disaster. She's here with me."

"She *is*?" Asher sounds shocked.

"We never went on a honeymoon. It's just for a couple more days."

"So you're finally getting some? Must be good if you're risking Arthur's wrath."

My molars grind. I'm not sure when, but my marriage to Scarlett became something I don't want to discuss with anyone. More than just her, I'm protective of *us*. I've avoided committed relationships like the plague. Even if I'd developed feelings for Hannah Garner or any of the other women I've been with, I still would have married Scarlett. At the time, I couldn't envision putting someone else through watching me marry someone else. Now, I can't picture putting Scarlett through seeing a woman leave my bedroom. Cheating, because that's what it would feel like.

The moments between us that felt like they mattered have been fleeting. The kiss before our wedding. Carrying her upstairs when I found her on the couch. Dancing at the Rutherford gala. The Fourth of July. Climbing the Eiffel Tower and exploring Versailles.

They're like us. Messy and scorching and confusing and thrilling and consuming.

We've only been married for a little over a month. And yet, I can't imagine my life without her in it. It would be like living with bad vision for years, getting glasses, and then losing them for good. Living with sharp clarity and then returning to dull blurs, knowing what you were missing out on. Scarlett makes me see things differently. Clearly. I can't explain it to anyone, and I don't want to. I'm different around her, and I'd like to think she's different around me too.

Asher clearly doesn't know what to make of my elongated silence. I'm not the passive aggressive type. I say what I mean. I told him my marriage to Scarlett wouldn't change a thing, and I believed it. He believed it.

I was wrong.

"Did you call to discuss anything besides my sex life?" I ask.

"I heard you punched Camden Crane on the Fourth. Sebastian showed up at the office this week. Feel like discussing that?"

"No."

Asher sighs. "You went to the Hamptons, man."

"They're my in-laws. It would have been rude to skip it."

"She's not worth it, Crew."

I clench my cup.

"I know you're a decent guy, and so does she. She's using it. Playing you. Everyone says she's an ice queen. Even if the sex is good, cut your losses. Just—"

"Stop. Talking."

"Crew..."

"She's not an ice queen. You should trust *me* on that, not the guys bitter she never gave them the time of day."

"If you say so." Asher's voice is skeptical.

"If you don't believe me, ask Camden Crane what he was saying right before I punched him," I suggest. "If you want to discuss anything related to *work*, email me. I'll answer once I've thawed out." Then I hang up.

I can't look away from her. Candles dance between us, casting a soft glow over Scarlett. Across her sharp cheekbones and long lashes. Her red lips and blue dress.

She was quiet when I returned from the café. Agreeable when I suggested going out to dinner. We're at my favorite restaurant. The railing to my left is built into the cliff itself. A glance to the side, and all you can see is the churning sea. We're suspended on solid ground.

"So everything is all set? With *rouge*?" I ask.

"Yes. The website will go live tomorrow as soon as it's announced."

"Are you excited?"

I'm expecting a glib retort. Not, "Terrified."

For a second, I think she's messing with me. But the tiny shrug before she takes a bite of bucatini is genuine in its vulnerability.

I lean forward. "Don't take this the wrong way—"

She interrupts. "Terrible way to start a sentence."

I smile. "Why are you doing it? I know *Haute* has been lucrative, but you don't need the money. You were already handling the jobs of three people, and then you went and added more work for yourself. At first, I thought it was me—us. You were avoiding being at home. But at dinner with Jacques…you've been planning this for years. *Why*, Scarlett? I get proving yourself, I do. But pushing yourself like this seems…I don't know. Excessive?"

Scarlett looks out at the water. The sunset is smeared across the sky behind her. Splashes of tangerine and peach mingled with golden light. Her profile is just as stunning as the rest of her.

Sighing, I lean back. "Never mind. I—"

"I feel like I need to earn it." She turns back toward me, her hazel eyes appearing more green than brown tonight. "My whole life, I've had everything handed to me. Yeah, I worked for things, but I would have gotten them, regardless. Harvard wasn't going to reject an *Ellsworth*. Applying was practically a formality. I saw *Haute* was for sale, and I... I don't know. I knew I could turn it around. Even now that it's doing well, I haven't fully let myself trust it. The harder I work, the more I feel like I deserve the success. But I took it over. The pieces were all in place; I just used money and connections to make them shiny again. With *rouge*...it's mine. All me. I want the clothes I design to make women feel powerful. I want them to be made in cities where people need work, in a building where people are excited and proud to be working there. I want to feel like I did something that mattered, and that I did it myself. When I donate to charities, that's all I can do. Sign the check. I'm not healing the kids or flying the plane with emergency supplies. But I know clothes. I can design the outfit that someone wears when they get their dream job. Or on the first date with the person they're going to marry. Or—" She stops talking and looks away, cheeks flushing. "It's silly, I know."

"It's not." That's all I say until she meets my gaze. "It's not silly, Red." I lift my glass and tip it toward her. "To *rouge*."

"To *rouge*," she echoes, tapping hers against mine.

We maintain eye contact as we both drink, and it feels more intimate than I can recall sex ever being.

"Royce Raymond wants me to take over his production company." A subtle rise of her eyebrows is the only indication she heard me. "He made the offer at our wedding. Said I should carve out my own legacy. I don't think I'll take it. But…it's an option."

Scarlett drains her glass and refills it. "An option in LA?"

"I wouldn't consider it if it was in LA."

"Why not? It's warm. Sunny. You could surf."

I smirk. "I don't know how to surf."

"You could learn."

Somehow, Scarlett always manages to say what I least expect. "Do *you* want to move to LA?"

She scoffs. "Of course not. New York is home. I'd never move to California."

"Like I said, I wouldn't consider it if I had to move to LA."

That confession sits between us for a minute. "You don't know anything about the film industry."

"How do you know?" I counter.

"You read or you watch baseball when you have free time."

She's right; I can't even come up with the name for the last movie I watched. I'm surprised she noticed. "I said the same thing," I admit. "He said he has people who do. He wants me for my business sense." I leave off the bit about my moral compass.

Scarlett nods, as if that answer makes sense. "No crack about how I don't have any?" I tease.

"I've seen the department reports. I know you do."

"Why were you looking at the reports?" *How?* Those aren't public record.

"I was curious. And I'm a Kensington."

"What does that mean?"

"You're wondering how I got access." She takes a bite of her pasta. Chews. Swallows. "That's how."

"Oh," is my brilliant response.

She hasn't shown any interest in Kensington Consolidated, but she's right. As of our marriage, she gained a substantial share of the company. More than enough to gain access to company reports, or anything else she might request.

"I don't think you should take it," she continues.

"Take what?"

She rolls her eyes. "The Royce offer."

"Really? I thought you'd want me to."

Her eyes narrow. "Why?"

"Because of everything you just said to me. About earning your own accomplishments. Not being my dad's bitch."

"I never meant any of that shit, Crew."

"Yes, you did."

"No, I *didn't*. I wanted to hurt you and I didn't know how else to do it. Kensington Consolidated is your birthright. Your family's legacy. You deserve it. Anyone else would destroy it."

I process that. "What about Ellsworth Enterprises? I could say the same to you. You're the sole heir."

She shrugs. "We'll figure it out when that time comes, I guess."

"*We*, huh?"

Pink stains her cheeks. "If there's a we, then."

"I didn't have a meeting today." I blurt the confession with no prelude, no further explanation.

She studies me. "Where did you go earlier?"

"I read at a café for three hours."

"Why?"

I know she's not asking why I read. "I wanted to bring you here. I didn't think you'd come otherwise."

"I'm a Kensington now."

I blink at another rapid turn in conversation. "Yeah, I know. I was at the wedding, remember?"

She doesn't smile at the lame joke. "If *rouge* fails—if *I* fail—

your last name will be associated with it. That's why I got so upset in Paris. I don't want you to be disappointed in me."

I'm so stunned I can't speak. It feels like I'm hearing these words through a wind tunnel—*I don't want you to be disappointed in me*. From a distance and a shout. "Scar—" I clear my throat. Once. Twice. "Scarlett, how could you—I could never be disappointed in you, okay? I swear. You could murder someone, and I'd bury the body, no questions asked. If *rouge* doesn't do well, I'll be fucking proud of you for trying."

A few seconds pass where she says nothing, and I become convinced I should have said nothing. They add up to fifty, and I spend most of them rewinding our conversation, spotting all the ways I could have avoided this.

"I spied on you."

"What?"

She half-smiles and gulps more wine. "If we're sharing secrets... When I was in Paris, I spied on you every night. Through the security cameras. With the time difference, I was back at my hotel when you got home from work. I spied. Every single night."

"Why did you?"

"I was curious, I guess. What you would do. How you'd act. What you were really like."

"And what did you learn?"

"Not much. You're pretty boring."

I smirk. "Not boring enough not to spy on, apparently."

Making Scarlett blush might be my new favorite hobby. Every time, it feels like a gift. An accomplishment.

"Whatever."

My grin widens. She laughs and looks away.

"You ready to go?"

"Yeah."

I flag a waiter and pay the check, stealing glances at Scarlett the whole time.

By the time we leave the restaurant, it's pitch black out. I didn't realize how much time had passed. When I'm with her, I don't focus on anything else. A disconcerting realization for someone used to being in control.

The later hour hasn't dampened any activity. The streets are just as busy as they were earlier. We walk side by side, closer than is called for. I glare at every guy who does a double take at her.

Scarlett stumbles over absolutely nothing, and I reach out to grab her arm. She laughs. "I thought we didn't touch."

"You're drunk," I realize.

She thrusts one hand in my face, holding her thumb and pointer finger tightly pressed together right in front of my face. "Only this much."

I tug them a few inches apart. "I think you mean this much."

I've never seen Scarlett tipsy before. Usually, she's the picture of poise and snark no matter how many glasses of champagne she's downed. It's oddly endearing, how her eyes twinkle and her nose crinkles. She looks younger. "Nope." She pops the P and closes the gap. Between her fingers and between us. "I meant this much."

Before I can reply, she kisses me. She's unsteady on her heels, leaning on me and off-center as she loops her arms around my neck and sucks on my tongue on a busy street.

Most of our kisses have been hurried. This is no exception. She kisses me like there's a timer. Like the world is ending and we're the only two people who still exist.

She pulls back after a couple of minutes of public indecency. Before I have the willpower to, despite the fact I only had one drink at dinner, not however many glasses of wine it took to put this sloppy grin on her face.

Halfway to the pier where we left the speedboat we drove from the villa, Scarlett stops and slips off her shoes. And then she starts *skipping* toward the sand. Her brunette hair waves in the wind and her blue dress flies around her thighs.

For the first time since I met Scarlett, I think she looks care-free. Happy. The wine probably deserves more credit than I do, but I still claim some. Especially when we reach the sandy beach and she reaches out and tangles her fingers with mine. "I wish there were fireworks."

"Maybe next time."

"You'd come back here?"

"If you want to."

She stands and stares at me as the breeze blows her hair into a wild disarray. "It scares me."

I feel my brow furrow. "What scares you?"

"How much I want to come back. How much I want...you."

She immediately regrets the confession. I read it in how her shoulders tense. The way she looks away from me and out at the ocean instead.

"Scarlett." I step closer.

"What?"

She still won't look at me, so I grip her chin and turn her face toward me. "I want you. I'll *always* want you."

Her face twists with disbelief. "You don't know that. This will—"

I don't loosen my hold. "I *do* know that. You're my *wife*. I meant those vows. You're the only woman I've ever approached in a bar. I wouldn't have given anyone else my mother's ring. Risked a massive business contract because some drunk dick described how he would fuck her. You're different, Scarlett. You matter to me, Red. I'd choose you over anyone. Anytime. Anywhere. Don't doubt that. *Ever*."

"I don't want you to matter." The statement rings with a sincerity her words usually lack.

"I know." My response is instantaneous. But the words are filled with so much heat and longing, I expect them to leave scorch marks on my lips. I'm not sure when we became this. When *she* started to matter so damn much.

"But you already do."

"I know that too."

She shoves me. "Have a conversation with yourself, then." Her tone has returned to the bossy one she usually uses with me.

I chuckle and pull her back to me. "You get your fill of the beach?"

She sighs and droops against me. "Yeah. I'm tired."

I scoop her up and carry her down the dock bridal-style.

"What are you doing?" she murmurs.

"Carrying you."

"Don't stop," she instructs, her voice sleepy.

"I won't."

"Don't give up on me."

"I won't," I repeat.

Scarlett is silent for the rest of the walk to the pier. She curls up on the boat's seat as soon as I lay her down. The drive back to the villa takes ten minutes. I tie the boat up and lift her again. Her arms loop around my neck as she snuggles her head beneath mine. The neediness should feel constricting. Instead, I savor it. I slow my steps as I climb the stone stairs and cross the backyard, delaying the inevitable destination.

Most of the villa's lights are on, shining through the dark-ness like a beacon. Scarlett blinks as we draw closer. Once we're through the front door, I set her down. And she starts undressing. Her shoes go flying first. Then she's twisting and yanking at the zipper of her dress. It falls, faced with her stubbornness. All of a sudden, there's a whole lot of skin on display.

I scrub a hand across my face as she strolls across the living room in nothing but a pair of matching pink lace.

Fuck. Me. Of course, *this* is the night she decides to give me a goddamn lingerie show.

And then that's gone too.

Words get stuck in my throat as she walks toward me, totally naked. "Why are you still wearing clothes?"

"Because I'm not drunk."

"I'm *not* drunk."

"Okay," I agree. Arguing with a drunk person is usually a fruitless exercise. Arguing with a drunk Scarlett would be like hitting my head against a brick wall: pointless and painful.

"I want you to fuck me."

Jesus Christ. I was in no way prepared for a proposition. Yeah, I definitely thought about this happening tonight, but not like this. Not when I have no idea what she's really thinking. Feeling. "Not like this."

Annoyance flashes across her face, followed by hurt. It feels like a rusty knife. No matter what, we're never on the same page at the same time. "Is it because I have to *beg* for it?"

If she does, I'll really lose it. "Fuck. *No.*"

Once again, I've said the exact wrong thing. "Guess you won't be finding out what it's like to *fuck your wife.*"

She throws my own words at me and then stalks into the master bedroom, slamming the door behind her for good measure.

I rake my fingers through my hair, trying to erase the memory of what just happened. Two steps forward, three steps back.

The guest room next to the master is a foreign sight. I haven't set foot in here for years. When my father sets up a "family" vacation, it's always to the Alps for Christmas or on some tropical island. Whenever I've spent time here, I've stayed in the master. There's no way I'm setting foot in there tonight.

I strip down to my boxers and face plant into bed.

I wake with a dry throat while it's still dark out. I roll around in the sheets for a few minutes, trying to find a comfortable spot that will lull me back to sleep. Eventually, I give up. I stand and leave the bedroom, heading for the dark, silent kitchen.

It takes me three tries to find the cabinet with the glasses in it. I fill one with cold water from the tap, drain most of it, refill it, and then turn to leave.

Scarlett is leaning against the doorway, staring at me. My heart rate accelerates, slows, and then picks up again.

"Do you want any water?"

She scoffs and turns away.

I cross the kitchen in a few strides and grab her arm. "Scarlett. Look, I—"

She whirls on me. "*What?* What do you *want* from me, Crew? Because I thought it was sex. But I offered that to you on a platinum fucking platter and you decided to sleep down the hall."

"You weren't thinking clearly."

"No shit. I *can't* think clearly around you."

"That's the sweetest thing you've ever said to me, baby."

"Don't get used to it."

"I'd like to."

That seems to pierce whatever armor she's wearing underneath her flimsy nightgown. These scraps of short fabric will be the death of me, I swear. "Will this end once we have sex?"

"What?"

"Forget it."

"Just say what you mean, Red. I'm not a fucking mind reader."

She chews on her bottom lip. "I want to sleep with you. I don't want it to change things."

"Change them from what? Not talking in New York?"

"From..." She shakes her head. "Never mind."

I make the first move. I erase the space between us and press my palm against her waist, guiding her against me.

She makes the second. Her hands run up my arms and shoulders before sliding in my hair. "Just warn me, okay?" she whispers. "Warn me it's going to end. I'll be fine, as long as I have a warning."

"What the hell are you talking about?"

Scarlett doesn't answer. She kisses me. Heady and deep and arousing. The sort of kiss that can be the main event. I could kiss her for hours. Memorize exactly how it feels, how she tastes, the little sounds she makes, and it still wouldn't be enough.

But I realize this won't be the main event when her hand slides south. Before I can *think*, much less react, she's fisting my cock. And I'm done. I won't be the one stopping this. The brakes aren't working. I want her. I've wanted her for so long it's hard to remember a time when I didn't.

She makes quick work of my boxers, and I tug off the silk that barely covers her. I'm not thinking clearly, but I'm aware enough to realize this doesn't have to happen in the kitchen. I haul her up against my body, and her legs wrap around my waist. Maneuvering through the dark house while carrying her isn't easy, but I manage.

I toss her down on the bed, in the midst of tangled sheets that suggest tossing and turning. "Couldn't sleep?"

"Stop talking." Her hand grips my hair as she steers me back to her lips.

I want to savor this: her feel, her taste, the sight of her spread beneath me. But it's dark in here, meaning I can't see much more than her shape. I haven't had sex in months, which isn't helping matters.

Scarlett isn't exactly slowing things down. She writhes beneath me until the tip of my cock slides through her wet heat. Her hips rise, teasing me. Pressing us closer together. Fingernails dig into my back. My name breaks the silence in a ragged moan.

I start to sink inside her and realize what feels different.

I pull away, trying to remember where I left my luggage.

"Don't stop." Her voice is unlike I've ever heard it. Desperate. The vocal equivalent of stepping in someone's way.

"I need a condom."

"No, you don't."

It's not the response I'm expecting. We haven't discussed birth control or kids—aside from her saying she isn't ready to have them. Not to mention, there's the surgeon she's supposedly screwing. I'm clean, but she doesn't know that. All things we'll need to discuss eventually, but not right now.

Her answer is reckless and irresponsible, neither of which are adjectives I'd normally use to describe Scarlett.

My shock must show on my face. Abruptly, she drops her hands from my back, lying on the white sheet like she's about to make a snow angel. Open, but not vulnerable. "Forget it. Get one."

She's silent as I stand and locate my suitcase. I can feel the annoyance radiating clear across the room. I feel like I missed something and I'm not sure what. There's a good chance I won't need the foil packet I return to the bed with.

"We don't have to do this tonight."

In answer, she takes the condom from me, rips it open, and rolls it down my dick. Then she straddles my lap and sinks down. Her heavy exhale is half-whimper, half-moan as I fill her. I mentally recite every finding from the latest quarterly report to keep from immediately coming like a horny teenager. She's wet and hot and *Scarlett*.

I let her control the pace. Let her take me deep and fast and frantic. Let her use me like a toy to get herself off. Part of me is pleased she wants me as much as I've been wanting her. Part of me is just caught off guard. I don't give up control—during sex, when it comes to anything.

Except when it comes to her, apparently.

When Scarlett doesn't care, she shuts down. Her desperate movements aren't indifference. She wants this, and she's showing me just how much. I trace the length of her throat with my tongue, tasting the hint of salt on her skin from our trip across the waves. She smells like lemon and something floral, almost sweet.

When I trail my tongue down between her breasts, she gasps and circles her hips. I grunt. "You're close, Red. I can feel you clenching around me." Wet, greedy sounds fill the room as she impales herself on me over and over again, chasing her release.

"*Crew*." She says my name like a curse.

"Are you going to come on my cock, Red?"

Our lips meet in a dirty, messy kiss. And then she's convulsing around me, making sounds that almost push me over the edge after her.

I flip her over so she's beneath me and lift one of her legs as I sink back inside her. My lips find the shell of her ear. I don't look at her face, I just use her body the same way she just used mine. "You came fast, Scarlett. Do your boy toys not get the job done?" She yanks my mouth back to hers and bites my bottom lip so hard I taste blood.

Scarlett can't be owned or tamed or controlled. It's part of her appeal. Wild, raw beauty is the most devastating sort. She's a storm, the cataclysmic kind you can't help but respect even as you mourn its upheaval.

"What's it like to fuck your wife, Crew?"

Adrenaline floods my system. I'm high—on sensation, on thrill, on *her*. I rub her swollen clit as I keep fucking her with quick, brutal thrusts. "Do you always get this wet, or is it for me?"

Scarlett fights it, but I hear the moan slip between her lips. Goose bumps pebble her bare skin, despite the fact the air conditioning isn't on in here. I take and take and take, speeding up the pace of my thrusts with each stroke. And she spreads her legs as far as they'll go, letting me in deeper. Begging without words.

I pound into her like I'm winning our battle of wills, like I'm claiming her as a prize. Scarlett claws at my back and meets my thrusts, spurring me on. She can lie to me all she wants, but her body can't engage in the same deception. Setting aside the mess of other emotions between us, the things we haven't said, our chemistry is the combustible sort. It crackles in the air like a summer storm.

She's wearing my ring, but she's never felt like mine. This is the only way I can claim her, fucking her as hard and as thoroughly as possible. The headboard taps a cadence against the wall. Sweat builds between our bodies.

I slow my movements, not ready for this to end yet. Scarlett swears. I'll have marks on my back tomorrow.

"Please, Crew. *Please*."

She *begs* me before she starts to convulse again, and I don't have a prayer of making this last any longer. The throaty pleas set me off. A tsunami of pleasure hits, rolling through my body in a powerful wave. Heat erupts in a white-hot fire that shoots through me and erases everything else. Thoughts, fears, worries? All gone.

There's just me and the woman making me come harder than I ever have before.

The aftermath of sex is usually predictable. I'm used to clinginess and questions. With Scarlett, I've learned to expect the unexpected.

So when I pull out and toss the condom and the first thing she says is, "You're good in bed," I laugh.

"You don't sound surprised."

"I'm not."

Close to a compliment. "I can go…"

She shifts so her head is on a pillow. A slight breeze shifts the air as she drags the sheets over her naked body. "If you want."

It's not what *I* want, and I know the word choice was deliberate. So I lie down beside her.

I stare up at the ceiling, trying to reconcile how it's possible for something to surpass every expectation and to also fall short.

In the darkness, there's no metric for time passing. Seconds, minutes, maybe hours later, Scarlett's breathing hasn't evened.

"Do you want to talk about it?"

Her leg jerks, hitting mine. "I thought you were asleep."

"Nope." I pop the P, just to extend the one word I have to offer.

"It was…different than I was expecting."

I tense. Debate responding. Grind my molars. "Your surgeon makes you come three times?" I sound jealous—sound like I care —and I hate that I do. I should be relieved she's not clingy. That I'll never need to feel guilty for taking other women up on their offers. Instead, I'm marinating in a disgusting mixture of rage and annoyance.

"That's not what I mean."

"What do you mean?"

She's silent. For so long, I wonder if she's managed to fall asleep.

"Don't hate me," Scarlett whispers.

"I don't."

She sighs, and it's the saddest sound I've ever heard. "You will."

Then she rolls over, so all I can see is her back.

CHAPTER THIRTEEN

SCARLETT

I'm not this girl.

I don't get giddy or nervous or change my dress three times. I look down on women who are willing to change anything and everything about themselves for a man. If it's not something you're willing to do for yourself, why would you do it for someone else?

Rather than pathetic, I feel lighter and looser than I ever have. Fizzy, like a bottle of champagne that's been shaken but not yet popped. Feelings—excited feelings—bubble to the surface. I've always had opportunity at my fingertips, and yet this is what spins my insides into a frenzy: spending time with the guy I married for a lot of logical reasons and even more illogical ones.

I smooth the ruffled hem of the pink dress I'm wearing. It's an outfit I would never wear in New York—it screams girly and innocent and naïve. Today, I've forgone my red lips, left my hair down in waves, and I'm wearing sandals. For once, I look my age. Maybe younger. I've dropped my guard, and my appearance reflects that.

When I step out into the bedroom, I panic for a split-second.

Maybe Crew wants the woman with high heels and higher walls. Maybe any allure is how I've been hard to get. I told him *no*, and it was a novelty. Last night, I acted like his cock was the only one in the world. And I *definitely* made it obvious I'm not indifferent toward him. I basically admitted to stalking him.

A breeze wafts through the open terrace doors, rubbing the soft cotton against my skin. Every time I see a room in this house, I fall in love with the villa a little bit more. If it were possible to run *Haute* from here, I'd never leave. As long as Crew stayed too.

He's standing by the front door, typing something on his phone. Things feel different between us. Not better or worse, just different. What we share—what we don't—used to be clearly defined. It's now a blur.

When Crew smiles at me, the bottle gets shaken a little more. "Ready?"

"Yeah."

I follow him outside. We're not pretending last night never happened—the confessions, the sex, the waking up in bed together—but we haven't discussed it either. I wasn't all that drunk last night. I remember every second. My behavior was mostly because I let down my guard and acted the way I wanted to act without worrying about consequences. They don't seem as glaring in the light of day.

We could have flown back today. Instead, Crew asked if I wanted to go to a football—soccer—game over breakfast. Despite my low interest level in sitting in the hot sun watching a bunch of guys run around and listening to spectators pretend they could play better, I agreed. Because *he* suggested it.

Driving past dramatic cliffs and dazzling ocean views, it doesn't feel like much of a hardship. Crew drove a gray Maserati convertible out of the garage, which is what we're riding in now.

I try and fail to recall another time we've been alone in a car together. Everything that would feel commonplace with anyone else feels meaningful with him. I don't speculate on why that might be. We may be in a decent place right now, but I have no delusions it will last.

Happy for now is more than I expected.

Happy ever afters aren't realistic.

I spy on Crew under the pretense of studying the scenery, beneath the shade of my sun hat and the cover of Gucci sunglasses. My recent trips to Italy have all been for work, mostly to Milan. I forgot how the craggy coastline can take your breath away, with blue water that's startlingly clear and vibrant. The color of Crew's eyes—so pretty you think it is fake.

Crew appears relaxed and alert as we drive. He's dressed casually, in a white cotton t-shirt and a pair of navy shorts. Wayfarers shield his eyes. This guy is unrecognizable from the Crew Kensington who sidled up to me in Proof. Tan, relaxed, maybe even happy.

Flashes of last night play across my memory as I trace his profile, lingering on the shift of tendons in his arms as he turns the wheel to take a right. I can list the number of guys whose forearms I've previously ogled on zero fingers. For some reason, the sight of Crew's is one I can't look away from.

He seems content to sit in silence, not making any attempt at conversation. Warm wind zooms past, occasionally carrying strains of conversation or notes of music as other cars pass by. My hair flies around my face. I keep twirling and tucking it behind my back, and after a few minutes, the breeze tugs it free again.

I huff an exasperated sigh, and the corner of Crew's mouth twitches. My purse is a mess, the same as it always is when I travel. I dig through lip gloss, Euros, hotel chocolate, and my passport—probably should store that somewhere else—before locating a hair tie.

My hair gets wound up in a messy knot, finally staying in place. This feels so different from the climate-controlled interior of a town car. Vacations are usually museum tours and wine tastings. Set itineraries and work calls. Riding in a convertible on a summer day is something I easily could have experienced before. But something in me whispers it wouldn't feel like this with just anyone.

I can't ignore Crew. Can't pretend he's just the guy chauffeuring me around. Rather than fight it, I embrace the giddiness his presence incites. I recline my seat and prop my bare feet on the dash and fling my hand out the window so it can surf the wind. The hem of my dress creeps up my thighs as I lean back. I watch Crew glance before he white knuckles the steering wheel. I turn my head to the side, not making any attempt to pretend I'm not looking at him.

"See something you like?"

He looks at me before he takes another turn. The sun backlights him, spreading beams of golden hues. "Lots."

His grin is boyish. Not calculating or predatory, and I realize I'm not the only one who might be sick of perfection and pretenses.

I smile back, and something shifts. There's a tangible moment where he's not a Kensington and I'm not an Ellsworth. Where we're just Crew and Scarlett.

And then his phone rings. It's connected with the car's Bluetooth, so the sound blares through the speakers. *Isabel* flashes across the screen.

Crew answers. "Hello." His tone is flat, slightly annoyed, and I take some solace in that.

"Crew! Hi!" Hers is peppy and cheery. I roll my eyes before rolling my head so I'm looking out the window instead of at him.

"What is it?"

"I don't mean to bother you, it's just—are you in a wind tunnel?"

"Driving," Crew replies.

"Oh. Uh, well, Asher mentioned you're extending your trip?"

"Yes."

"We have the meeting on the Lancaster acquisition this afternoon."

"I sent you my feedback on the reports this morning. Anything inadequate, flag and I'll handle when I get back into the office."

"I saw your email. I just…"

"Just *what*, Isabel?" Crew sounds impatient.

"You've overseen this from start to finish. I'm just surprised you're not here and instead you're…well, no one is actually sure what you're doing. Is everything okay?"

"Yes."

"Okay…" She drags the word out for as long as it will last. "We have a board meeting on Tuesday. Will you be back by then?"

"Yes," Crew repeats.

"Your father isn't happy."

"So…business as usual?"

Isabel laughs. "Pretty much. I'll send you the minutes from the meeting by the end of the day."

"I'll be offline until tomorrow. No rush."

There's a beat of silence, heavy with disbelief. "Okay."

"Bye, Isabel." Crew ends the call.

"Slacker," I mutter.

He laughs, but neither of us say anything else for the rest of the ride to the stadium.

I knew soccer—or football, as the Europeans call it, which makes logical sense, just like the metric system—was a popular sport in Italy. The huge crowds that surface before the towering structure is even in sight are still unexpected. Long lines of fans sporting jerseys and wide smiles fill both sides of the sidewalk.

Crew appears unconcerned by the busyness. He pulls into a lot surrounded by a chain-link fence after a quick exchange of Italian with the man guarding the gate. From there, we're led through a private entrance and into the heart of the stadium. I ask, "How much of the team do you own?"

He smirks at me. "Twenty percent."

"It wasn't in the disclosures."

Crew blinks, brimming with false innocence. "It wasn't?" I roll my eyes. "I used my trust fund. Technically, that wasn't covered in the mutual considerations."

"Looked into every loophole, huh?"

"I wasn't the one who had the prenup rewritten."

"Would you have signed, if I'd told you about *rouge*?" It was in the preliminary stages when I brought the paperwork to Crew. Nothing I *needed* to disclose—legally speaking—but something I should have.

"If you'd told me, you'd know."

"I didn't know what you'd do then."

"And you know now?"

His question sounds like a lot more than just the one decision. Like he's asking if I know *him*.

"I don't know." It's not a lie, but I can't help but feel the honest answer is *yes*.

Crew's gaze lingers on my expression for a few seconds, but he says nothing.

Our seats are right at the edge of the field. I stare out at the expanse of green grass as Crew talks to the man who brought us to them in Italian. My French might be iffy, but my knowledge of the native language doesn't extend beyond *Ciao*.

Even though the game hasn't started yet, the field is filled with activity. Players at both ends are running drills and stretching. Others are jogging in place or talking to coaches.

Crew takes the seat next to me. "You know much about soccer?"

"What is there to know? You try to kick the ball into the net."

He chuckles softly as he leans back. His bare arm brushes mine, and it *sears*. The sun has nothing on the surface of Crew's skin. "I think you missed your calling as a coach."

I scoff. "Do you come here a lot?"

"Come where?"

"The villa. This stadium."

His legs spread out, crowding the plastic barrier that separates us from grass. "A few times a year. In college…the guys would always want to party. London, Copenhagen, you know. And my dad only wants to go to the Alps or to a good golf course."

"This is better."

"And here I thought we'd disagree about everything."

It's not exactly a smooth segway, but I blurt the question anyway. "Are you expecting last night to happen again?"

"Which part? When you admitted to stalking me, the skipping, or when I carried you up three flights of stone steps?"

I'm not exactly cool, sitting in the sun. But my cheeks still manage to overheat more. "Forget it."

"I hope so."

Against my better judgement, I meet his gaze. And since he's no longer driving, he holds it without worrying about crashing.

"I really hope so. All of it, plus the sex."

I pretend that doesn't merit a response, choosing to focus on the figures on the field instead of the one next to me. It works for a while, until the actual game starts.

Crew either thinks his commentary is invaluable or is trying to prompt a response out of me, because he spews an endless stream of facts about different players I couldn't care less about.

I alternate between smirking and sighing. Professional soccer games last for longer than I thought.

The most excitement is when the black and white ball bounces off a post with ten minutes left. But I'm not entirely bored.

It's hot and loud. We spent the French Open in the shade sipping champagne. Yet I'd rather be here than back there.

Nearly three hours pass before the game ends. Scoreless, neither team makes a single goal. Crew continues his analysis—until the same man reappears and asks him something in Italian.

He turns to me. "The team owner wants to talk. Do you mind waiting?"

Days—maybe even hours ago—I would have given an honest *yes* because sitting around here for even longer is one of the last things I feel like doing. Warming toward Crew isn't the equivalent of a personality transplant, though, so I don't say *no* either. "I'll come with you."

Something in Crew's expression suggests my middle ground isn't what he considers a compromise, but he doesn't argue, just nods.

We leave our seats, following the mysterious Italian who must work for the team. Halfway up the stairs, Crew grabs my hand, tugging me closer so that his body is the one cutting through the crowd. Once again, I tamp down the urge to fight him. I feel like I've proven to Crew I can handle myself. He knows I'm fully capable of shoving my way through rowdy fans. If he wants to do it for me, fine. A more concerning realization is how much I like the way it feels—having him take care of me in some small way. I've fought hard to establish independence. Relying on others is often setting yourself up for disappointment. I tell myself this isn't a slippery slope, that letting Crew lead me through the stadium isn't an indication I'm knocking down boundaries I carefully built.

I lie to myself.

The crowds thin the deeper we get into the stadium. Most people are leaving, not entering. We pass into a private section that requires our silent guide to flash his badge. The hallway is empty and quiet, the only sounds muffled by concrete walls.

Crew keeps hold of my hand, and I don't let go either. We step into an elevator and then out into another hallway, this one carpeted and plush. Full-size photos of players line the walls.

"Antonio, can you give us a minute?"

The man accompanying us—Antonio—nods and keeps walking down the hallway for a few dozen feet before stopping.

I glance between him and Crew. "What is it?"

"I need you to wait in here." He opens the door to our left, revealing an empty suite overlooking the field.

My eyes narrow. "Why?"

He sighs. "The team owner...well, he's a dick. His father ran things when I got involved, and it's been a rocky transition. I was hoping to avoid him. Someone must have told him I was here."

"I can handle dicks."

Crew's smile is brief. "*I* can't. He'll hit on you, or worse, and I'll hit him." His voice is grim honesty. "I'd just gotten access to my trust fund when I invested in this team. It was a stupid whim, and I'm lucky it paid off. My involvement is minimal. If it becomes a mess, it will be a real pain in the ass."

"You could just, you know, *not* punch the guy," I suggest.

"I'm not going to stand by and let someone insult you."

"It sounds more like he'd be *complimenting* me."

He exhales. "Please?"

That's what gets me. The *please*. I'm curious to meet this guy.

But my inclination when Crew asks me to do something has become to listen, not to argue. So I agree. "Okay."

It happens fast. There's less than a foot of space between us, so Crew only has to take one step forward before his lips are crashing into mine. It's nothing like an obligatory farewell kiss. His tongue teases mine. His teeth tug on my lower lip. His hands pull my hips flush against his.

The sigh when he steps back is heavy with regret and annoyance, neither of which appear to be aimed at me. "It'll be quick, okay?"

He's striding away toward a waiting Antonio before I can reply. I wander into the suite, feeling a little dazed. It doesn't appear anyone watched the game from here today—everything is spotless.

I walk to the far end of the suite, looking out over the field. This is a very different view than the one from the edge of the grass. The entire field is spread out in a symmetrical rectangle, green grass separated by stark white lines.

I snoop around the suite. Drink some water. Answer some work emails. Sophie texted me this morning, asking about getting together. Aside from one short brunch weeks ago, I haven't seen her or Nadia since my wedding. I reply, suggesting they come over to my place for a girls' night next week. My mother responded to the photo I sent of me and Crew in Paris with an invitation we come over for dinner soon. I don't know whether to be resentful or appreciative of the effort. Anything regarding my parents usually comes with strings attached. Before Crew and I got married, requests to see me were usually predicated on events where they thought my absence would be offensive.

Finally, Crew returns. Alone, Antonio has disappeared.

"Sorry. It took longer than I thought it would."

I stand and walk over to him. "It's fine. Means *your* investment is doing well, right?"

His smirk has nuclear side effects. "Right."

My plans for a quick exit rapidly rearrange. I have no idea why I notice the details I do. Crew has a single freckle beneath his left eye. A dark brown circle that is slightly thinner at the top than the bottom. Not perfectly round.

"Are you ready to go?"

My response surprises us both. "No." This outing was all him. To plan, to control, to end. Suddenly, I don't want it to.

To Crew's credit, he reacts fast. "You discovered a deep love of European football?"

"Not exactly." I press up against him, forcing him back. He doesn't have to acquiesce, but he does. I guide him back to one of the couches and down.

Crew's eyes are molten pools of blue as he realizes where this is heading. It's good—fantastic—for my ego.

I straddle him and discover he's already growing hard. I feel heady with power as I rub against him. He hisses and grabs my hips. "Favorite position?"

"Have we been here before?" I tease.

"*Scarlett.*"

I've always liked my first name, the way the syllables sound. Every time Crew says it like this—as if saying it is a precious gift—I fall in love with it more. And maybe not just with the eight letters.

"I didn't lock the door," he murmurs.

"I don't think this will take long." I stand. Kick off my sandals and pull down my thong.

Crew leans back on the leather couch, his Adam's apple bobbing and his eyes half-lidded with lust as I return to my spot on his lap and unzip his shorts. He makes a low grunt as I grip him, his throat working as he fights the urge to thrust in my hand.

His hands creep up my thighs.

"No touching," I whisper. "Unless you *beg.*"

One of his famous mouth curls makes an appearance as his hands fall away. There was a time when I didn't think Crew Kensington was capable of backing down about anything. His reputation is a ruthless one. People like him, but they also respect him. He's a worthy opponent and a powerful ally. But for *me*, he bends.

He clenches his jaw as he grows harder. I keep stroking him, teasing him with slight drops of my hips that almost allow him to slide inside. His breathing grows faster and quicker. We're both fully clothed, the skirt of my pink dress spread across his lap, covering everything we're doing. Somehow, that makes it that much hotter. Crew looks pained as he studies my boobs, just inches from his face.

"No touching," I repeat, before I let him slip inside me. Only the tip, and then I raise my hips out of reach.

He groans and I grin.

"You told me to fuck you bare last night. Why?"

Crew asking about sex right before we have sex feels strangely intimate. I've never discussed the act with other guys I've slept with. It just happened. "It was our first time."

He doesn't reply with a *duh*. But his "I know" isn't much better.

Crew isn't touching me. I'm still setting the pace. But all of a sudden, I no longer feel like I'm in control. "I figured you didn't…usually. And I'm clean and on birth control." He's young, hot, and heir to a multi-billion-dollar empire. If he's not wrapping it up, he's an idiot. And I don't think he is.

Talking in circles isn't my usual mode of communication, but I think Crew knows what I'm saying. I wanted our first time to be something special, something different. Just the fact it was him wasn't supposed to be enough, even though it felt like it was.

I won't so much as allude to this, but I also want him to trust me. Stupid, considering I've given him several reasons not to. Considering I've lied. I'm worried fessing up now might destroy any shaky trust we have built.

Crew holds my gaze as he reaches into his pocket and pulls out his leather wallet. Silly disappointment fills me, but I keep a neutral expression plastered in place.

"We should be careful." He says the words as he rolls the condom on. I focus on what he's doing, so I don't have to look him in the eye.

"We should," I agree. Instead of telling him I haven't slept with anyone else in months. Instead of asking him whether *he* is sleeping with anyone else.

I tease him with a few more rolls of my hips, and then I drop my pelvis again. I'm dripping, and he slides in with no resistance. Even deeper than last time.

Crew is swearing, his hands clenched into fists as he visibly restrains himself. "Please, Scarlett. Fuck, I—*fuck*. Move, Red. Please."

I comply, and my release starts to build instantly. I'm close, so close, and I feel the dredges of my willpower snap. I no longer care about being in control. About his insistence on wearing a condom. About the fact this trip is a respite from the reality we'll have to face soon.

"Touch me, Crew, please."

I beg, and he doesn't tease me about it. He's suddenly every-where. His lips suckle their way along my neck. One hand massages my breast, and the other sneaks between my thighs to touch the soaking spot where he's sliding inside me.

I detonate in seconds. Hot, blinding pleasure washes over

every inch of me, lighting up every cell and spreading heat. Crew takes over, impaling me on himself again and again. Prolonging my release and jerking inside me as he finds his own.

I collapse against him, breathing heavily. My limbs feel loose and languid, wrung out.

His hands run up and down my calves.

"And they say reality doesn't live up to fantasy," Crew whispers to me.

I smile against his hot skin.

CHAPTER FOURTEEN

CREW

When I walk into the conference room for the weekly eight a.m. chat on Monday morning, my father and brother are uncharacteristically silent. I'm uncharacteristically cheerful. Scarlett and I returned from Italy on Saturday. Things between us are good—shockingly good. She wandered into the home gym when I was working out this morning and we ended up having sex on a yoga mat. But our relationship hasn't become just physical. We agreed we'd both be home by eight p.m. and eat dinner together. It feels like the start of a new normal, one I want a surprising amount.

I take a seat at the table meant for thirty. "Morning."

Oliver looks uncomfortable while my father appears grim. Something is wrong. For once, I wish someone else was in charge to handle whatever problem has surfaced. The final vestiges of the peace I felt with Scarlett last week slip away.

"What's wrong?"

Apprehension grows when neither of them answer.

"Is this an actual problem or did one of you lose to a potential client on the course?"

My father speaks first. "I've been talking to Nathaniel Stewart about some investments."

I look from my father to Oliver, searching for some clue of why that's an issue. "Okay."

Nathaniel Stewart was a couple of years ahead of me at Harvard. He's built up a solid reputation on Wall Street for smart investments in up-and-coming companies. Not the sort of business my father usually bothers with, but I could not care less. It's not something that should rise to the level of these meetings. There must be more to the story.

"How are things with Scarlett?" my father asks abruptly.

I tense, realizing the lack of transition means this must have something to do with her. "Fine."

"Really?"

"Yes. *Really*," I reply. "I don't think my marriage is any of your business."

"Of course it is. She serves a purpose." My father tosses a manilla envelope onto the shiny wood separating us. "She's cheating on you, Crew."

Shock freezes me for a few seconds.

"What?"

"My best PI took these two weeks ago. They met outside The Chatwell and were inside for over an hour. He had a room booked. It wasn't the first time. All the records are in there. They've been meeting regularly for the past year."

I don't say a word as I open the envelope and let the glossy photographs spill out. They're bad. Nathaniel's hand resting on Scarlett's lower back. His lips on her cheek. One shows them standing in the lobby while he whispers into her ear. I can't see her expression in any of them, but Nathaniel looks smug.

Two weeks ago. These were taken before Italy, before we slept together. It doesn't feel like much of a consolation. We were already married. The surgeon was bad enough, but at least I didn't have to see evidence of it. Nathaniel Stewart rarely pops up at parties, but he attends some events. I'll have to see his smug face in person at some point—and not plant my fist in it.

"Do you spy on all of your business partners?"

My father leans back in his chair, studying me closely. "Yes. I'm not about to climb into a crowded bed. A man about to be bled dry by a vengeful wife isn't of much use to me. Not every woman is as understanding as Candace." The cavalier way he talks about his second wife looking away from his affairs would bother me if I could look away from the photographs.

I gather them up and stuff them back into the envelope so I don't have to keep staring at them.

"Scarlett can do whatever the hell she wants. I do." The words taste bitter on my tongue.

"No, she *can't*, Crew. She's a Kensington, part of the future of this family. Spreading her legs for potential business partners is not an option. Keep her in line."

I work my jaw. "I'll handle it, okay?"

"Handle it how?"

"I don't know yet. Give me more than five minutes to think about it." I may disagree with plenty of the things my dad says and does, but he's my father, my boss, and arguably the most powerful man in the country. The sharp tone I snap those two sentences in isn't one I've ever used with him before.

He doesn't call me out on it, even when Oliver's eyes widen. "I spoke with Sebastian Crane last week. Talked him out of taking his business elsewhere, after you assaulted his son."

"Camden had it coming."

My father shakes his head. "This spell of stupidity ends now, Crew. She may be beautiful, but she's just a piece of pussy. Pull it together, before you embarrass this family."

I've never wanted to hit my father more. "I said *I'll handle it*."

Brown eyes pin me in place. I've never been more grateful I inherited my mother's blue ones instead. I look more like her than Oliver does, and I've always wondered if that's why my father heaps me with *more*. More responsibility, more praise, more disappointment. It all depends on the day. Whatever he finds seems sufficient.

"Good."

Oliver was too cowardly to interject in our conversation before, but he does me a solid and brings up some production issue with an overseas company. I pretend to listen, scratching out notes on a legal pad and stealing glares at the manilla envelope that puts Scarlett and me right back where we started: strangers.

My mood hasn't improved by the time I stalk into my office. I nod at everyone who greets me, not even bothering with a *hello*.

Asher is in his usual spot: feet propped up on the corner of my desk. He grins when he sees me, waiting for me to comment. I'm too pissed to care where he sets his shoes. My skin hums with restless energy that simmers in my blood.

The last time I felt this unhinged, I punched Camden Crane. Before the Fourth of July, I'd been in one fight. It was in a Boston bar. A guy bumped into me and was drunk enough to think I shoved him. He threw the first punch, and I dropped him in one blow I'd consider self-defense. I'm not an irrational guy. I have a temper but I keep it closely leashed. Or at least I *used* to, before I married Scarlett.

"Good morning to you too, sunshine," Asher says. When I

don't reply, he adds, "I thought people were supposed to come back from vacation all relaxed. You look like you just attended your own funeral. I mean..." He lifts his feet and raises his eyebrows. "You didn't even say anything."

Sunshine. I snort. He should have seen me before eight a.m. I was fucking *whistling* when I walked into the building. Now, I yank my chair away from the desk so hard it almost topples. "I'm fine."

Asher's eyebrows are close to his hairline. "Holy fuck. What the hell happened? I've never seen you so pissed."

"Just some bullshit with my dad," I half-answer. "Forget it."

"Bullshit about what?"

I shake my head.

"So...how was your trip?"

"Great."

"*Really?*" He drawls the question in a disbelieving tone.

"Yep." I log into my computer and start sorting through the stack of papers Celeste left on my desk.

"What about things with Scarlett?"

I force myself to keep sorting through the papers. "Good."

The second "*Really?*" sounds even more dubious than the first.

There's a knock on the door of my office. "Come in," I call out.

It opens to reveal Isabel. I'm not surprised to see her; I half-expected she would be waiting in my office next to Asher.

"Hi, Crew."

"Morning, Isabel."

"Welcome back. You have a nice trip?"

"It was fine."

"I thought it was *great*?" Asher interjects. I shoot him a glare, and he wisely shuts up.

"If you have some time this morning, I thought I'd catch you up on where the projects stand."

"I'm free until ten. Take a seat." I nod toward the open chair next to Asher.

"Guess that's my cue." Asher stands and buttons his suit jacket. "*Great* to have you back, buddy."

I grunt a response as I grab a fresh sheet of paper to take notes on.

The four changes to a five. Quarter to eight, instead of 7:44. I've spent all day debating whether to honor the promise I made to Scarlett this morning—that I'd be home by eight. It was an easy one to, especially since she usually works later than I do. I was happy to; wanted to. But a big, petty part of me now wants to show her that I can be indifferent too.

I can put other things first.

Except I can't, apparently, because I'm standing and grabbing my briefcase and heading for the elevators. All day, I've battled the urge to confront her. To show up at *Haute*'s offices and demand answers. But I didn't. And now that the chance to get answers about the photos in my briefcase is approaching, I don't know if I really want them.

The drive to the penthouse takes thirteen minutes. I step out of the elevator at 7:58. There's commotion in the kitchen, so I head there first. Phillipe is standing in front of the stove, manning three pans at once. "Good evening, Mr. Kensington."

"Evening, Phillipe. Is Scarlett home?"

"I don't believe so."

I glance at the clock. 7:59. "Okay. I'll wait until she gets home to eat."

"I'll make sure everything is ready."

"Thank you."

I head upstairs. I've slept in Scarlett's room for the two nights we've been back, so I go there first. My only detour is to the library to pour myself a drink.

There's a loveseat in the corner of her bedroom. I drop my briefcase next to the closet, strip off my suit jacket, loosen my tie, and take a seat. Most of the far wall is glass. The skyline of Manhattan twinkles in the distance, the outlines of buildings lit up like Christmas trees.

I sit and swirl whiskey and stew as minutes tick by.

Scarlett appears in the doorway at 8:47. When she sees me, she smiles. I savor the sight for a second.

"You're late."

She kicks her heels off and drops her phone on the dresser. Sighs. "I know."

I watch the whiskey paint the inside of the glass before it drips down. "We agreed on *eight*, Scarlett."

"I know," she repeats. "I'm sorry, okay? I've been gone for a week and a lot has piled up. It had to get done tonight."

I learn it's possible to admire and despise someone all at once.

"Get on the bed."

She studies me, starting to absorb something has shifted. "I don't take orders."

My control is dangerously close to snapping. I want to watch this glass shatter against the wall. I want to yell at her, to ask how she manages to keep doing this. Keep reeling me over and over again. I thought Italy was a turning point.

I down the glass, savoring the smoky burn as it sears a path down my throat. I stand. "*Get on the bed*, Scarlett."

Holding my gaze, she reaches behind her dress. I can hear the slide of the zipper as the teeth separate. The fabric pools at her feet, leaving her in a matching set of black lingerie. My dick twitches.

My control snaps. I advance on her like a predator hunting prey. I attack her lips, kissing her with punishing pressure and plenty of nips. She moans as her nails press into the back of my neck, biting down on my lip and sucking it between her teeth. I haul her up against me, moving toward the bed and dropping her unceremoniously on the mattress.

I yank my tie over my head and undo my pants. "Hands and knees."

Scarlett hesitates. She knows something is wrong. But she doesn't ask, just moves into the position I requested. I yank her lacy underwear down and pull out my cock. I'm painfully hard, like I always seem to be around her.

I hate how much I want her. My jaw clenches as I roll a condom on. Protection was already a tense subject between us before I saw those photos this morning.

I slam into her without warning, bottoming out on the first thrust. I grip her hips as I pound into her over and over again, trying to pretend she's someone else. Just a warm body I'm using to get off.

I don't touch her anywhere else besides her waist. My thrusts are selfish and primal and desperate. Right now, I'm chasing the chance to forget. The irony of the fact I'm using Scarlett to try to forget Scarlett doesn't escape me. I could have gone out to a bar or a club and found a random woman—or two—to distract me from my train wreck of a marriage for the night. Instead, I came home and waited for her.

Scarlett moans as her inner muscles tighten around me. She's close to coming. And I can't forget it's her I'm fucking.

Her scent is familiar. So are the greedy little whimpers she's making.

Annoyance quickens my movements. I thought this would make me feel better, treating her like the property she's set against becoming. But this—screwing like she's a woman I met for the first time tonight—isn't impersonal. The sound of my name falling out of her mouth as she clenches around me is what sends me over the edge right after her. She's still spasming when I pull out of her and stalk into the bathroom to get rid of the condom.

Scarlett is sprawled out on the bed when I walk back into the bedroom. I ignore her as I buckle my pants and pick my tie up off the floor.

She sits up, naked aside from her bra. "What the fuck, Crew?"

"What the fuck *what*, Scarlett?" My response is caustic, and I watch her flinch at my tone. I didn't think it was possible to feel worse right now, but that subtle movement managed to do so. I need to get out of here.

"If this was some role play shit, you can drop the act now."

I chuckle darkly.

"You want me to pretend that was normal?"

"Do whatever you want," I retort. "You always do anyway."

She stands and walks over to me. Despite the fact I came minutes ago, my body reacts. My dick hasn't gotten the memo she's a liar and a cheater.

"Tell me what's wrong."

"Nothing." I turn away.

"Where are you going?"

"Out."

"Where?" she presses.

"None of your business."

"Sure. I'm only your *wife*." That's probably the worst thing she could say right now.

I laugh, and the dead sound of it scares me a little. "It's awfully fucking convenient, when you're my wife and when you're not. When we're an arrangement and when this is a marriage."

"I told you I would try, Crew. I'm *trying*."

I shake my head and stalk toward the door.

"You said you'll always want me," she tells me. I still, hating how she's bringing that up now. Marring that perfect memory with the anger and hurt swirling between us. "In Italy, everything you said—"

"I *do* want you, Scarlett. That's the fucking problem."

"Guess I was right about you hating me. I did think it would take a little longer." The words are harsh, but I don't miss the sadness not far beneath. It cuts deep.

"We both know you're an overachiever."

I walk out of her bedroom without another word.

"You look terrible," Asher tells me when I walk into the conference room for the monthly board meeting the following morning. "More trouble in paradise?"

"I don't want to talk about it," I clip. I only left my office for meetings yesterday, going so far as to skip our usual lunch.

Wisely, Asher doesn't push. My dark mood from yesterday is still hovering, fueled by the copious amount of whiskey I drank last night and the little sleep I got in my penthouse. I'm used to sleeping beside Scarlett. My old mattress felt cold and empty.

Oliver studies me closely as he enters the room and takes a seat across from me. I keep my face impassive. He and my father will want an update. Results from a confrontation I'm not ready to make. At least the surgeon was before we started to feel like a real couple. Knowing she was with someone else right before we left for Europe? That will be far worse than simply simmering with the possibility.

"Did you see the email about the company party?" Asher asks me.

"Yes." The reminder doesn't improve my mood. An annual event I was looking forward to—our first outing as a *real* couple. Up until yesterday morning, when time spent with Scarlett became slow and painful torture. As the future CEO and son of the current one, there's no way I'll be able to get out of going.

"Did you watch the Giants game last night?"

"Not really, I…" My voice fades when a familiar face strides into the conference room. "What are you doing here?" I ask Scarlett, far louder than I mean to.

Her face is an indifferent mask. Exactly how she used to look at me. "I'm here for the board meeting. Same as you are, I'd imagine."

"*Why* are you here for the board meeting?" I grit out as she pulls at the chair beside me and takes a seat.

"Because I'm a member of the board." The light floral scent of her perfume surrounds me.

"No you're not." The dispute is automatic.

"Yes, I am. The company bylaws state the number of shares I need to hold, and I do. Thanks to our *marriage*."

I pinch the bridge of my nose and let out a long exhale, ignoring the confused looks from everyone but Asher.

This is payback for last night. I ran that show, so now she's taking counter measures to prove I'm not in control. Our relationship is an endless chess match.

Scarlett opens a folder, signs some paper with a flourish, and sets it aside before looking at me, challenge dancing in her eyes. I can feel a headache forming. I'm pissed. "Last night, you seemed to think I should act more like a wife," she tells me. "Here to support you, Sport."

"This is not what I meant, and you know it."

"Maybe you should have clarified, then. Not walked out."

"Do you want me to show up at one of your magazine meetings?" I demand.

Scarlett smirks. "*You* can't. Because I own all the shares of *my* company, remember?"

Always two moves ahead. I lean forward, trying not to get distracted by how she smells. How I can't help but react to her proximity. "Scarlett—"

Her phone rings. She answers it, like I'm not trying to talk to her. Like we're not in a boardroom waiting for an important meeting she shouldn't be attending.

"Hello?" A pause. "No that won't work. I don't care. It's unacceptable." Whoever she's talking to replies. "Put him through. I'll handle it."

She stands and strides out of the room with the phone pressed to her ear. Everyone watches her leave.

If I were alone, I'd bang my head against the table right now.

Asher leans closer. "*Dude.*"

"Not now." I grit my teeth as I open one of the folders that's been distributed around the table, pretending to look through the graphs and expense reports.

The coffee cart comes around, delivering drinks. Asher orders an espresso, and then it's my turn.

"Plain coffee, please. Black." The middle-aged woman who works the small cafe on this floor complies, placing a steaming cup of dark brown liquid in front of me.

"Anything here?" She nods to Scarlett's bag beside me.

I'm so tempted to say no. But I got into this mess by pissing her off. I sigh. "Do you have non-dairy milk? Soy or something?"

Asher chortles, and I give him a look that promises a slow and painful death if he utters another sound.

"Yes. I have soy."

"She'll have a soy cappuccino."

Isabel walks into the conference room as the barista is making Scarlett's drink. The look on her face suggests she already knows who owns the stuff strewn beside me. Scarlett must not have gone far to wrap up her phone conversation. There's only one hallway that leads down here.

Scarlett reappears a couple of minutes later, capturing the attention of the room once more.

"Did he cry?" I mutter sarcastically as she sits down beside me.

"Nope. But he did discount his fabric to half cost when I was willing to pay double."

"How exciting," I drone.

"What's this?" She's looking at the cappuccino.

"What you think it is."

"You got me a coffee?"

"There's a cart," I reply, excruciatingly aware of how everyone in a ten-seat radius is listening to this conversation.

"I can't drink this."

I sigh. "It's soy, okay?"

Her eyes burn into me as I continue to pretend to look at papers. In reality, the numbers are blurring together.

"You think dairy substitutes are ludicrous."

"They are. I just didn't feel like listening to you complain about how you can't drink dairy, despite the fact you're not lactose intolerant."

"The way I had to listen to you complain about the missing carton of two percent?"

I close the folder. "It's not *missing* if you threw it out."

"I relocated it."

"Into the trash."

"You don't even take coffee to work in the mornings. *I* do."

"There's more oat milk in our fridge than ten people could drink in a month. But my *one* carton—"

"There were three," Scarlett interjects.

Asher laughs. He tries to hide it in a cough, but it's too late.

Scarlett glances past me. "Hi, Asher."

"Scarlett. Pleasure, as always. I haven't enjoyed a board meeting this much...*ever.*"

"It won't be a regular occurrence. I've got plenty of work already. But I'm an *overachiever*, so..."

I grit my teeth as she delivers that little dig.

"I saw the announcement about *rouge*. Congrats."

"Thanks, Asher." Scarlett sounds genuine.

"And it already sold out? No pressure, huh?"

I look over at her, ignoring Asher entirely. "It sold out?"

"Yes."

She doesn't meet my gaze, sliding a folder back into her bag.

"You didn't tell me."

The words are out before I've thought them through, nothing more than a reflex. I know they're a mistake, even before she scoffs. "I was going to tell you last night. Part of why I was late. You had other plans for the evening, apparently."

Before I can decide how to respond or deal with the guilt, my father appears. The room falls silent as he takes his seat at the head of the table. There are no round tables at Kensington Consolidated. The pecking order might as well be spraypainted on the walls in here. Even among the board, the hierarchy is clear.

His eyes linger on Scarlett, but he doesn't react to her presence. I knew he wouldn't. I'll hear about this at our next "chat" though.

Arthur Kensington doesn't bother with pleasantries. He delves right into today's agenda, taking updates from different departments on current projects and different acquisitions. The projectors display a series of graphs and charts disclosing profits and margins.

Scarlett seems engrossed in the material. I wonder if this is how she acted at Harvard.

I'm sipping my coffee when she speaks.

"Where are the November earning projections?"

Total silence follows Scarlett's question. It's carpeted in here, but if someone dropped a pen, you could hear it fall. You don't interrupt Arthur Kensington. Not while he's leading a meeting. Not when he's complaining about the weather. Some of the executives sitting at the table have never said a single word during a board meeting, they're so petrified of my father.

Scarlett isn't stupid; she's making a statement.

My father holds her gaze while the rest of us hold our breath. I have the bizarre urge to make a sound and break the quiet. To protect Scarlett from the heavy weight of Arthur Kensington's disapproval.

Ridiculous on many levels, not the least of which is that Scarlett doesn't need my protection—doesn't need me for anything. She's made that clear.

The rush of pride is also unexpected. Not many people have the confidence to question my father about anything, let alone business.

Silence continues to stretch. If I had to guess, I'd say that my father is wondering if dealing with Scarlett's boldness is worth the billions we gained. He should try being married to her. I don't regret agreeing to it—don't hate her, the way she implied last night—but I most definitely underestimated what a challenge it would be.

"Isabel?"

I wonder if Scarlett knew Isabel is responsible for calculating the projections for our new projects. She definitely knew my father approves the packet before the meeting. I flip to the section containing the projections. *September, October, December. No November.*

My father missed a mistake, and Scarlett caught it.

"Yes, Mr. Kensington?" To Isabel's credit, her voice doesn't waver as she gets called out.

"Did your department exclude November from the projections?"

"It appears so. My apologies. I'll correct the section and recirculate a copy to the board."

My father nods. "Do that." He looks to Scarlett. "I'm glad to see your talents extend beyond designing clothes and networking, Mrs. Kensington."

The muscles in my jaw protest from how tightly I'm clenching it. I know exactly what he meant by networking, and the mention of fashion wasn't a compliment.

"Even a CEO can make mistakes, Arthur."

People don't interrupt my father and they don't call him by his first name either. Scarlett managed to break both rules in a span of two minutes.

My father tilts his head. He underestimated her. I knew it before; he knows it now.

The rest of the meeting passes without incident. I get pulled into a conversation with the head of our finance department as soon as it ends. I watch as Scarlett talks to Asher for a minute, then turns and leaves the conference room without sparing me a glance. A stupid part of me wants to chase after her. But I let her go.

When I walk out of the conference room, Oliver is waiting for me.

"What the fuck was she doing here, Crew?" He whispers the question angrily. "Dad is pissed. What if she's leaking information to Nathaniel Stewart?"

I grind my teeth at the insinuation and the name. "She's my wife. She's entitled to a spot on the board; she owns the necessary shares."

"She's making a fool of you."

"Butt out of my marriage, Oliver. I'm *handling it*."

He *tsks*, and it's grating as fuck. "Interesting you call it a marriage now, not a business arrangement."

"Business arrangements are what I handle at the office. I don't go home and sleep next to it."

"You sleep in the same bed?"

"None of your fucking business." I spin and walk away, headed toward my office. I need a minute to fume in silence. Except, when I enter my office, it's not empty. Scarlett is leaning against the front of my desk.

"What are you doing in here?" I slam the door shut.

"Lock it."

I don't move at first. My emotions are all over the place. I care way too much.

Scarlett is the strongest woman—person—I know, and she weakens my resolve whenever she's involved. Against my better judgment, I flick the lock shut. "You shouldn't be here."

"My last name is on the side of the building."

"*My* last name." I can't resist the jab.

She clucks her tongue. "Are we an arrangement or a marriage, Crew?" She throws my words back at me, making me tense. Even more so as she walks over to me. "Which is more *convenient* right now?"

I hold her gaze, and we wage war with our eyes. I know I'll break first when she sinks to her knees and unzips my pants. All the blood in my body rushes south.

She's not actually going to... She *is.* She *does.*

We're in my office. Scarlett is kneeling in front of me. I should feel in complete control. Instead, I've never felt more powerless, more awed. She walked into this building like she owns it, and now she's sucking my cock like she owns it too.

She does.

I haven't so much as kissed another woman since we got married. Not out of loyalty or obligation or love, but because I know they would fall short. That I would picture fisting brunette hair and the red lips currently wrapped around my dick.

I've never fooled around in my office before. I keep work and pleasure separate—for good reason. I want people to think I earned the CEO position, not that I had it handed to me. But I'm in no position to think clearly right now. To consider consequences.

Scarlett pulls back to lick and swirl the sensitive tip of my shaft, her hand rubbing my length before she guides me back into the wet heat of her mouth until I hit the back of her throat. I give up on acting indifferent to the warm suction—acting like I'm not already embarrassingly close to exploding.

I'm glad her hair is up. It allows me an unobstructed view as I focus on the mesmerizing motion of her mouth. One of her hands stays wrapped around the base of my dick, while the other moves lower to cup and caress my balls. I groan as I feel the familiar tingle form at the base of my spine. I'm going to come soon. Embarrassingly soon.

My hips start to rock, instinctually driving my cock deeper and deeper into her mouth as I get closer and closer.

Her name falls out of my mouth with a raspy growl. "I'm going to come." She keeps sucking and pumping, swirling her tongue around the slit in the tip. My breathing grows ragged and my heart pounds as heat spreads up my spine. "*Scarlett.*"

I gave her two warnings, which is two more than I'd give anyone else. I come with a groan, filling her mouth. Her throat bobs as she swallows everything I give her. I lean back against the door, letting it support most of my weight as the pleasure slowly dissipates.

My muscles feel loose.

My mind: blown.

Scarlett sits back on her heels and wipes her lips with the back of one hand. Then she rises, strolling over to the purse she left on my desk. She pulls out a tube of lipstick, and—*fuck me*—slicks a fresh coat of red on her plump, full pair.

I clear my throat. "Scarlett—"

"I have to go." She glances at her watch. "I have a meeting in ten minutes. This took longer than I expected."

"The meeting or the blowjob?"

She smirks. Then she brushes past, leaving me to zip up my pants and wonder—once again—what the hell just happened?

I'm sitting at my desk debating whether I should go home yet when Oliver opens my door.

"Ever heard of knocking?" I snap.

"She's meeting with him."

"Who is meeting with who?"

"Scarlett. The PI Dad hired just reported she's at a hotel with Nathaniel Stewart."

I bite the inside of my cheek. Is that what earlier was about? Guilt? "Right now?"

"That's what I just said. Come on, let's go."

"Go where?"

"To the *hotel*, Crew."

"I told you I would handle it."

"Yeah, well, you handling it seems a lot like you doing nothing. I'm going. You can stay if you want."

That gets me moving. Oliver showing up alone won't end well.

The drive starts out in silence, but it doesn't last long. "Is she like that with you? That shit in the meeting earlier? Dad actually *read* the two company emails 'he' sent out earlier, you know." Oliver laughs.

"It's complicated."

"Sounds like a lot of work."

"Guess I don't see the appeal of being with a doormat, the way you and Dad do."

"What's that supposed to mean?"

"Aren't you sleeping with Candace?"

Oliver's Porsche swerves to the right and then back straight as he corrects the steering. "Who told you that?"

"You just did." I laugh. "Wow. Seriously?"

His hands look white thanks to the pressure he's exerting on the wheel. "Does Dad know?"

"Considering he hasn't punched you, I doubt it."

Oliver scoffs. "He doesn't care about her."

"He doesn't," I agree. "But he'll definitely care his son is having sex with his wife. If that got out…it would be a PR nightmare for the company."

"It's not going to get out."

I'm not so certain, but I don't say so. "How did it start?"

He sighs. "I went over there a few months ago, when Dad was in Chicago. I thought Candace had gone with him. She hadn't. She was there, asked me to stay for a drink. Things evolved from there."

I shake my head. "Jesus. Is it still going on?"

"It happened a few more times. It was kinda hot, you know? She's—"

I interrupt. "I don't want any details. I can't picture you two together, and I don't want to."

Oliver is silent for a few minutes. "I can picture you together. You and Scarlett. Not like *that*, just in general. And you can deny it all you want, but it's obvious you care about her."

"I don't." My response sounds empty, even to my own ears.

He hums. "I heard she was in your office after the board meeting."

I squint over at him as another pair of headlights illuminate the car. "Where did you hear that?" His office is on the opposite end of the floor.

"From at least ten people. Overheard some of the secretaries talking about it too."

I scoff.

Oliver pulls over opposite the hotel and shifts the car into park. We sit and stare at the building.

"Well?" I ask.

"Well what?"

"This was your idea. What's next, Sherlock Holmes?"

"Maybe we should go inside. Or you should."

"*Why?*"

He shrugs. "I don't know. Maybe if you catch her, she'll feel guilty and tell you what is really going on."

"That's the stupidest idea you've ever had."

"*My* wife isn't the one cheating on me."

"No, you're the Nathaniel in your scenario and I'm Dad." I lean my head against the glass and close my eyes. "Fuck."

"There she is."

I raise my head and open my eyes, fully prepared to see Scarlett kissing another man. Instead, she walks out of the hotel alone, wearing the same dress she had on this morning. Her hair is up in the same fancy twist I was careful not to disturb while she was blowing me. She doesn't look like she was just rolling around in hotel sheets or engaging in a passionate affair, but looks can be deceiving.

Rather than head straight for the car waiting along the curb, she hesitates. I watch her give the driver a *wait a minute* gesture and then retreat toward the hotel. She doesn't walk back inside. Instead, she leans against the brick exterior of the building with her head tipped upward.

After a couple of minutes, she pulls her phone out of her pocket. She stares at it for a few more minutes, then starts tapping on the screen. Eventually, she raises it to her ear.

Oliver swears. "Dammit. I told Dad he should have the PI tap her phone. She's probably calling Jonathan. Now we won't—" He stops talking when my phone lights up in the cupholder. Scarlett's name and the photo of us at the top of the Eiffel Tower light up the screen. "She's calling *you*?"

I'm just as shocked as he is.

"Answer it!"

Silently, I grab the phone and tap the green button. I pull in a deep breath as the call connects.

"Crew?"

I shove the anger and jealously and turmoil far, far down and attempt to sound normal. "Hi."

She clears her throat. "Hi."

I watch her closely. Her head is still tipped back. She's chewing on her bottom lip furiously. "Did you need something?" I ask.

A beat of silence. "I, uh, I'm about to leave the office," she says. *Lies*, rather.

"I won't be home for a while." I look at the car dash. It's almost eight.

She doesn't call me out on breaking our promise. "Oh. Okay. I'm going to pick up Chinese on my way home. Do you want me to get you anything?"

Her expression twists as soon as she's spoken the question. It's strange, seeing her reactions to what she's saying. She sounds normal. She looks pained and unsure. Not guilty. *What does* that *mean?* "Sure. Thanks."

"Want anything specific?"

"You know what I like." I don't mean for the words to sound suggestive, but there's definitely some innuendo.

"Do I?" Rather than confident, she sounds unsure.

"I'll try to get out of here soon, okay? We can...talk."

"Okay. Bye." She hangs up but doesn't move. Her posture doesn't change until she swipes at one cheek. She's crying. The realization hits me like a bolt of lightning and flattens me like a two-ton weight.

"Let's go," I tell Oliver.

"What did she say?"

"Nothing relevant."

"Are you going to—"

"Oliver. I swear to God. For the last fucking time. This is none. Of. Your. Business. Coming here was a mistake."

The rest of the ride back to the office is silent. I don't bother going back upstairs. I say good night to Oliver and then head straight into the garage and my waiting car.

Scarlett beats me back. When I walk into the penthouse, she's sitting cross-legged on one of the couches that overlooks the terrace, poking at a takeout box. Her expression is blank when she looks up, and I hate it. I want the smile she gifted me with last night.

"You're home."

I strip my suit jacket and toss it on the couch. "Yes."

"Are you hungry? Your food is—"

"Do you know Nathaniel Stewart?"

I watch her reaction closely. She coughs. Swallows. Takes a sip of water from the glass on the coffee table. *Incriminating.* "Yes."

"When was the last time you saw him?"

"Earlier tonight." She holds my gaze. At least she's being honest. Although she's smart enough to know I wouldn't be broaching this topic unless I knew something.

"Are you sleeping with him?"

"No." Her answer is swift.

"Don't lie to me, Scarlett," I warn. "If you're screwing him, just tell me the fucking truth."

"That *is* the truth." She shoves the chopsticks in her food and stands, crossing her arms. "I swear."

"If you're not sleeping with him, then why would you meet him at a hotel? *Multiple* times."

Her eyes narrow. "You're having me followed?"

"My father is. And not you. Stewart. He's interested in a business opportunity and wanted to make sure the guy was clean."

"When did you find out about this?"

"Yesterday morning," I admit. "He has photos."

237

"Of me *fucking* Nathaniel?"

I wince. "Of course not."

"That's why you…last night. You believed him. You thought I was cheating." The anger I can handle. The hurt in her voice is worse.

"It looked bad, Scarlett. And it's not like you *haven't*."

She breaks eye contact for the first time. "That was before, Crew."

"I know."

"And I'm sick of having that flung in my face. Like you haven't been with anyone since we got married."

"Actually, I haven't."

She looks shocked. "You haven't?"

"Nope." I roll up my sleeves and head for the couch, pulling the takeout containers I assume are for me out of the bag and grabbing a pair of chopsticks. My chest feels lighter for the first time in thirty-six hours. And I'm starving as a result.

"I—why?"

I shrug and start eating. "Wasn't interested."

That admission is met with a long beat of silence as she sinks back down on the couch and picks up her food. "He gave me money," Scarlett finally says. When I look over, she's fiddling with her chopsticks again. "For *Haute*."

"Why the hell would you need money?" I ask. Even before she married me, Scarlett was set to become the richest woman in the country.

"I'm going to inherit a lot. My parents paid for everything: cars, penthouses, tuition, credit cards. But I don't have direct access to anything. Or I *didn't*, until I got married."

"What?"

"I'm an only child. If I didn't get married and have kids, there wouldn't be an Ellsworth heir." She purses her lips. "My father didn't want to take any chances, apparently. He put some strict conditions on my trust fund. I'm sure *Haute* turning profitable gave him quite the scare."

"You wouldn't need to get married then," I realize.

She nods. "I wasn't...opposed to *this*." She gestures between us. "I just wanted to do it on my own terms, I guess. And if I'd waited until we got married, then *Haute* would have already sold. I didn't have many options."

"I would have given you the money."

"Like I said, I didn't have many options."

I half-smile at that. "Is he still involved?"

"No. I paid him back as soon as we got married. In full."

"Did you sleep with him? Back then."

"No. I don't mix business and sex."

"So he tried to."

"Yes," she admits.

"And tonight?"

"He wants to pursue another investment together." She leans back and tucks her legs underneath her. "I took the meeting as a courtesy, but I told him no. That I have my hands full with *Haute* and now *rouge*. And." She clears her throat. "I mentioned that I'm happily married."

Like hell is this guy getting involved in Kensington Consolidated.

"He made another pass at you?"

"Yes." She catches sight of my expression, and hers turns amused. "I handled it, Crew."

I sigh. "I'm sorry. Last night...I was pissed."

"Yep. Figured that out."

"I thought we were finally in a good place. And then I saw those photos and I just...if it was true, I wasn't sure if I wanted to know. That's why I didn't say anything to you until now."

"I should have told you about it. Possibly when you insinuated I didn't earn *Haute*."

I wince. "I'm an ass sometimes."

"Sometimes?"

I set my food down on the coffee table and move closer to her. I tilt her head up and trace my thumb across her bottom lip. "Scarlett." Her name is my favorite word in the English language. I love saying it. Caressing the syllables.

I'm about to kiss her when she asks, "Where were you last night?"

"My old place. Alone."

She holds my gaze. "Okay."

"Would it bother you? If I hadn't been?"

"Yes."

I smile. "Good."

For the first time, all our steps feel forward.

CHAPTER FIFTEEN

SCARLETT

"Morning." I smile at Leah and Andrea as I step off the elevator.

"Mor—morning," Leah stutters, then looks to Andrea. "Did you, um, did you not get my message?"

"About the delay with the delivery?" I glance down at my phone to respond to a text from my mother. She's still been badgering me about dinner. "I saw it. I requested they send everything straight to the park. We should still be on schedule."

"Okay. Great." When I look up, Andrea and Leah are exchanging surprised looks.

I hide a smile. They're both probably wondering why I'm in such a good mood. "I just have to grab a few things from my office and then I'll head over there. Everything else is on schedule, right?"

Andrea nods. "I'll see you both at one."

I head into my office. The samples I was supposed to look through last night are hanging from a portable rack. Leaving by eight every night has cut into my productivity. I'm more happy about that than I ever imagined being.

I didn't realize how unbalanced my life was until Crew straightened the scales. My drive to make *Haute*—and now *rouge*—successful bled into everything else. Dedicating every thought and decision to that goal is the reason the photoshoot today in Central Park will feature the hottest designers, most talented photographers, and most coveted models. It's a point of pride—the pinnacle of my identity outside of being Crew Kensington's wife. But it's not a title I feel the urge to separate myself from as much as I used to. Crew is someone I'm proud to be attached to.

As I flip through each sample, I type up my comments and send them to the design team. I read through the article submissions for the next issue. Photos for the cover get flagged based on preference. And then I leave for the shoot.

Central Park is more crowded than I'm expecting. I rarely am out and about in the city during daylight hours—at least on a weekday. Joggers and families fill the winding paths that I weave through on my quest toward the carousel, where the shoot is set to take place.

Set-up has only just begun when I arrive. The area is being cordoned off as props and cameras are strategically placed. I confirm there are no issues and then take a seat on a nearby bench.

A few emails have already piled up. I answer them all, and then let my finger hover over Crew's name. He's probably busy.

Things are good between us right now—really good—and I'm scared to trust it. Just because things feel stable doesn't mean they'll stay this way. I saw how quickly his favor can shift during the debacle with Nathaniel.

Sexual attraction isn't an enigma to me. It's everything else: the way we're both home by eight, the fact we sleep in the same bed, the two percent milk in the fridge. They symbolize things I thought we'd never be.

I've accepted it, embraced it even. But that's different from relying on it. Perpetuating it. If it disappears, it will be that much harder to revert back to what our relationship used to look like.

I shut my phone off and focus on my surroundings. The lighting team is still getting set up by the carousel, so I people watch instead. Few people bother to glance over at the scene taking place off the path. Most are joggers or walkers. Frazzled moms or babysitters promising ice cream to screaming kids. One woman passes me with six dogs pulling her along. She stops at the bench next to mine and proceeds to tie them up to the metal armrest one by one. She manages to secure five. The sixth is a puppy with floppy ears, large paws, and fluffy golden fur. It can't stop getting tangled up in its leash.

The woman lets out an exasperated huff. "Goldie! Hold still!"

"I can hold him for you." The words are out without any conscious decision on my part. I'm a typical New Yorker. With the exception of my stints at boarding school, I've lived on the Upper East Side my whole life. I don't stop and talk to strangers; I stride past them like I'm chasing the gold in a speed-walking competition.

A grateful smile erases any chance of taking the words back. "Really? That would be great. Thank you!" The woman, who looks to be in her late twenties, takes a couple of steps closer and hands the green leash to me. The puppy immediately turns its attention to me, alternating between licking my leg and sniffing my shoes.

The woman redoes her sloppy ponytail and bends down to tie her sneaker. "I was worried they'd pull me over." She knots the wayward laces and then checks the other shoe. "I'm only supposed to walk three at a time, but the other volunteer called in sick this morning...so here I am."

"You're not a dog walker?"

"No. Well." She stands and smiles. "I guess I sort of am. I volunteer at the Loving Paws Rescue. Dog walking is like less than five percent of the job. It's mostly feeding and brushing and poop scooping and, well, you get the picture."

I look down at the dog that's stopped licking and settled by my feet. His little tail wags as he rests his head on a tiny paw. "These are all rescues?"

"Yep. Our landlord has a strict no-pet policy, and my roommates would kill me if we got kicked out of our shoebox." She rolls her eyes. "So I volunteer and get to spend time with animals that could use some TLC. Most of it's great. Some of it sucks." She studies the dog attached to the leash I'm holding. "This guy is headed to a kill shelter in the morning."

"What? Why?"

"Space. Only so much money and lots more hungry mouths to feed, you know?"

"They'll *kill* him?" I look down at the face that looks like it's smiling. Lolling tongue. Wagging tail.

"Goldie will have a few weeks there. But if no one adopts him…then yeah."

"That's so sad. He looks so happy."

The woman's face falls. "I know. At least he won't know it's coming. Not much to worry about when you're a dog."

"Yeah. I guess so."

I've never had a pet in my life. When I was younger, I asked for a kitten. An animal that claws furniture and uses the bathroom indoors was my mother's worst nightmare—or so she claimed. I can only imagine asking for a dog would have gone over far worse.

"Thanks for holding him." The woman smiles and takes Goldie's leash back from me. "Have a good day."

"You too."

I watch her walk away, tugged forward by the dogs as they strain and bark. Then shake my head and look back at my phone.

But the furry face stays with me throughout the shoot. As I'm looking through photos and selecting accessories. Consulting photographers and deciding on angles. By the time the shoot ends, it's close to five p.m.

For some reason, I Google *Loving Paws Animal Rescue* as I walk toward my waiting car. It's close, only a few blocks away. I figured it must be, since the woman was walking. Taking six dogs on a miles long trip doesn't sound realistic.

I climb into the back of the town car. "Back home?" my driver today, Eric, asks.

For a few seconds, I deliberate. Leaving work at a reasonable hour is one thing. A living, breathing animal is another. But something possesses me to reply with the animal shelter's address. Traffic is heavy. It takes fifteen minutes to make the short trip. The exterior of the building is nondescript. If not for the small, white sign, I wouldn't have known I'm in the right place.

A bell rings above the door as I walk inside, past the five folding chairs and a display of pamphlets on rabies and neutering. The woman behind the counter isn't the one I met this morning.

She looks up, her brow creasing. "Can I help you?"

I stride up to the desk and clear my throat. "I'm here to adopt a dog. Goldie?"

"We close in ten minutes."

"He's getting sent to a kill shelter tomorrow. I'll pay extra. Whatever it takes."

The woman studies me as she scoops her brown hair up in a ponytail and ties it. She's wearing a t-shirt that reads *I Brake For Squirrels*. I take that as a promising sign she's not in favor of the whole kill shelter concept. A brown clipboard gets unearthed from the papers littering the desk. "Fill this out."

I exhale, relieved. "Okay."

The form is basic. I fill out all the sections, leaving the one on former pets blank. I hand the clipboard back, watching as the woman scans it over. "There's a two hundred dollar adoption fee," she informs me.

"You take donations?"

"Yes."

I pull my checkbook out of my handbag and write a check before handing it to her. The woman's eyebrows fly upward as she reads the amount. "Lucky dog." Her cheeks flush, making me think she didn't mean to say that out loud.

"Can I take him tonight?"

"Yeah. Let me grab him."

She disappears into the back, leaving me alone in the small lobby. I panic a little, looking at all the pamphlets. I know absolutely nothing about dogs. Barking sounds from behind the door. The woman reappears, holding Goldie. She sets him down, and he bounds over to me, tail wagging.

I scoop him up, letting him lick my face. That seems to pass muster, because the woman's expression is softer when she hands me a folder. "Here are all the papers. His medical history. Vaccination schedule. Training tips. Veterinarian suggestions. Any questions, just call here. He's already had dinner. Feeding amounts and times are in there as well."

I take the folder from her. "Okay. Thank you."

"Congratulations. He's a sweetheart. I was dreading the pickup tomorrow."

I look down at the puppy snuggled in my arms. "Thanks."

"I read *Haute*."

When I look up, she's smiling sheepishly.

"Before and after you bought it. It's really impressive what you've done with it."

I smile. "Thank you. That means a lot."

Then I turn and head back outside. Eric steps out to open the door. His eyes widen as he takes in the dog, but he doesn't comment. Just asks where the next stop is.

Goldie thoroughly explores the backseat as we drive back to the penthouse. I look through the folder, feeling overwhelmed by the amount of information. I don't even know if Crew likes dogs. He could be allergic, for all I know.

When the elevator doors open to the penthouse, I can hear his voice coming from the kitchen. I set Goldie on the fluffy living room rug and walk down the hall.

Crew is standing at the kitchen counter, studying some papers and talking on the phone. His eyes light up when he sees me. I smile at him before I walk over to the fridge and pour myself a glass of water. On second thought, I fill a glass bowl with water too.

"Yes," Crew says. "Send the expense reports when you can, and I'll take a look later." There's a pause. "All right. Bye."

He sighs, and then I hear him move. He drops his chin on my shoulder and kisses my neck. "Hi."

"Hi." Embarrassingly, my voice comes out breathy and high.

"How was the shoot?"

"Good." His question distracts me from the feeling of his lips against my skin. I pull away. "I have something to show you."

"Oh, really?" He raises one brow.

"Yeah. Follow me." I start toward the living room, then remember the water. I spin back around to grab the bowl. Crew eyes it but doesn't say anything as we walk down the hallway.

We enter the living room. The *empty* living room.

"*Shit.* Where did he go?"

"Where did *who* go?"

"I, uh." I set down the bowl of water and look at him. "I sort of got a dog today?"

Crew looks shocked. "You *what?*"

"I was at the shoot—in the park—and there was this woman with all these dogs. And there was this one. He's super sweet and really mellow, and they were going to *kill* him, Crew. So, I—I went there after the shoot and I adopted him." I pause, assessing his expression. "Are you mad?"

"I, ah, where *is* it?"

Nothing is out of place, and no dog is in sight from my position in the living room. "I don't know. I left him on the rug."

"And you thought he would just stay in one spot? It's not a stuffed animal, Scarlett. It's a real one."

"I know that," I snap. "You're getting awfully judgmental about a dog you've never even met."

He smiles. "Okay. I'll look upstairs. You take downstairs."

I sigh. "Fine. He's tiny. Like a golden fluff ball."

"I know what a dog looks like."

Rolling my eyes is very tempting, but I refrain. "And his name is Goldie."

"*Goldie?*"

"What's wrong with Goldie?"

"We're changing his name," Crew says.

"Let's *find him* first, okay?"

Crew doesn't reply before he heads for the stairs. I smile when I hear him call "Goldie" upstairs.

I look under the couch and behind the armchair in the corner of the living room. The kitchen doesn't have any hiding spots. I head into the study next, crawling on my hands and knees to look under all the furniture in there. I'm walking toward the dining room when I hear "I found him!"

When I reach the top of the stairs, Crew is sitting on the runner that traverses the length of the hallway. Goldie is between his legs. His little paws peddle through the air as Crew scratches his belly.

Once I'm a couple of feet away, I sink down to my knees.

"He's cute," Crew comments.

"I know."

"You wanted a dog?"

"A cat, when I was younger. My mom said no. I don't know anyone with a dog. Anything about dogs." I wrinkle my nose. "It was stupid. Impulsive. I wasn't really thinking."

And it's Crew's fault. Lately, I've changed. I leave work at a reasonable hour. Worry less. Smile more. Make the spontaneous decision to adopt a puppy. They're healthy changes. Changes I wouldn't have made on my own. Reconciling who you are with who you were is uncomfortable. Especially when you're not certain it's a permanent change.

"I've always wanted a dog," he tells me.

"You have?" Surprise saturates the question.

Crew scratches Goldie's chin. The puppy stretches. "Yeah."

"They gave me a whole packet of stuff. He needs food and training and vaccinations."

"Okay. Let's go."

"Go where?"

"To a pet store, Red. To get all the shit he needs."

"Like what?"

"Like a bed and a crate and toys and a collar and a leash and food?"

Yeah. Definitely didn't think any of this through. "Oh."

"We don't have any of that, right?"

I appreciate the *we*. "No."

Crew stands and holds out a hand to pull me upright. "Let's go shopping then."

"You were trying to work earlier. I can just…"

He leans down and scoops up the dog. "You coming?"

Without waiting for an answer, he heads for the stairs, carrying Goldie.

An hour later, we stand side by side, staring at the wall covered with dog toys.

"Wow."

"Should we get him one of each?" Crew jokes. There are dolphins and condiments and emojis. Dinosaurs and beer bottles.

Our dog will be spoiled. There's no other logical conclusion, looking at the overflowing cart. It took us fifteen minutes to decide on the right brand of puppy kibble. We spent another ten minutes in the treat aisle. Choosing a crate was quick because we got the biggest one. Ditto with the bed, because there was only one that fit the largest crate. And now we're stuck in the toy aisle with way too many options.

"Who would buy their dog an eggplant emoji?"

Crew smirks. Grabs the purple plush toy and tosses it in the cart.

I laugh. "We're *not* getting that."

"I'll give it to him when you get home from work."

I fight it, but I'm smiling when Crew's phone rings. He tugs it out of his pocket. "Asher." He doesn't answer it.

"Work?"

"Nah. He probably wants to go to a bar."

"You can…if you want to. Not that you need my permission."

With one sentence, I spread the insecurities I've tried to bury. In the two months since we got married, Crew hasn't gone to a club.

He works, and he spends time with me. I'm waiting for it not to be enough.

"I don't want to." He grabs a bear and an orange rope. "Good?"

"Sure."

We move to the next aisle. Crew looks through the harnesses as I pick out a blue collar and matching leash. In line for the checkout, his phone rings again. This time, he answers. "Hey."

I pet Goldie and pretend I'm not listening.

"No, I can't." A pause. "Asher...we're too old for this shit." He glances at me. "Okay. Fine. I'll be there in twenty minutes." Crew hangs up the phone and sighs. "Asher needs a ride. He went to dinner with his folks. His dad, well, he makes mine look like a teddy bear sometimes."

I look down at the dog resting his chin on my shoulder. "Teddy."

"Huh?"

I nod toward the dog. "You said you wanted to rename him. What about Teddy?"

"I like it."

"Good."

"I can drop you guys off before I get Asher."

"I don't mind."

"You're sure?"

"Yeah."

We check out and load everything into the car. It takes me most of the drive to figure out how to put Teddy's new car harness on. I snap the carabiner to my seatbelt right as Crew pulls up outside Pastiche.

"This place is nice," I comment.

"You've been here before?"

"Once. With some friends."

Asher appears.

"Ignore anything he says about us," Crew advises.

I raise both eyebrows, but I don't think he can see in the dark car. Asher walks my way, veering toward the backseat at the last minute, when he sees me sitting up front.

"Can't go anywhere without the missus these days, Kensington?"

"Yeah, *you're welcome.*"

Asher laughs as he spreads out in the backseat. A bag crinkles. "What the hell?" A light shines. "Why is your backseat filled with...stuffed animals and bones?"

"We got a dog," Crew replies, smoothly turning into traffic.

"A *dog*?"

"Yep."

"*Why*?" Asher asks.

"Scarlett is a sucker for a cute face."

I roll my eyes. "Whatever, Mr. I've Always Wanted A Dog Let's Buy Out the Whole Pet Store."

Crew chuckles.

We drive a few more blocks before Teddy wakes up and starts whining. "What do I do?" I ask Crew, as his cries grow louder.

"What did the shelter tell you?"

"Basically nothing. I haven't read through the whole packet yet, and I left it at home. He already ate."

"He probably needs a patch of grass," Asher suggests in a bored tone.

I look at Crew. "Pull over."

"Here?"

"You want him to go on *me*?"

Asher laughs as Crew mutters under his breath.

He pulls over in front of a tree surrounded by mulch. "This is the best I can do."

I work at unclipping all the straps of the car harness I just slid into place.

"Can't he pee in that?"

"It's attached to the seatbelt, Sport."

Asher laughs again. "I get why the press is obsessed with you two. You're a real riot."

Both Crew and I ignore him as we struggle with the harness. "This one had the best reviews," Crew mutters.

"You looked up the reviews?"

Based on the illumination from the streetlights, he looks affronted.

"Of course I did." Crew keeps fiddling with the harness, petting Teddy as he does. I give up on helping and watch him struggling to free our dog.

I think I love him. It's a terrifying realization.

"There!"

"You realize we're going to have to put it back on him, right? Don't celebrate yet."

Crew rolls his eyes before climbing out of the car with Teddy. He sets the dog down in the mulch, and he immediately squats.

"Didn't see this coming when we went to that climbing gym."

The sound of Asher's voice startles me. "What do you mean?"

"I figured you two would end up divorced or not speaking. Crew likes things done a certain way—his way. I got the sense you were the same way. Basically, a recipe for disaster."

"It's only been a couple of months. Who knows how we'll end up."

"Anyone with eyes could make a good guess," Asher replies.

Crew climbs back into the car before I have a chance to reply. He hands me Teddy, who wriggles and licks my face.

"He went."

"I saw." I give his soft head a rub. "Who's the best boy?"

"You never say that to me, Red."

"You're housebroken."

Asher makes a gagging sound.

Crew leans over to help me reattach the harness. "And you like it when I'm bad," he whispers in my ear.

"If you're done with the displays of affection, can we go?"

Crew sighs. "Your place?"

"Nah, drop me off at Proof. I need a drink."

"You could have called a fucking Uber, man. I'm not a car service."

"Right. You were so busy being a *dog dad*. I figured if I called you, we could go get a drink. You didn't tell me you were bringing the wife, and I didn't even know you had a puppy."

Crew sighs, but I think he hears the same thing I do. Asher wanted to talk to him, not just a ride. I thought their relationship was more work colleagues than anything, but it seems like they're genuinely friends. "Fine, I'll drop you at Proof. You had better not be late for the Danbury meeting in the morning."

"Don't worry, boss. I'll be in your office bright and early, feet on the desk."

"Feet on the desk?" I ask.

"Crew hates it when people touch his desk," Asher tells me.

"Oh." I glance at Crew. He appears amused, not annoyed. I've touched his desk. Leaned against it. Sat at it.

A few minutes later, Crew stops in front of Proof. I look at the line of people standing outside, decked out in short dresses and expensive attire. Not too long ago, that might have been me. With the exception of waiting in line. I was always on the list.

"Thanks, man," Asher says. "One of these days, I'll actually tell him to fuck off." He clears his throat. "Seriously, I owe you. Bye, Scarlett."

"Bye, Asher."

Asher climbs out of the car and disappears inside.

"You should go with him," I tell Crew.

He looks surprised. "Why?"

"He obviously wanted to talk to you, and that's why he called. About whoever he's trying to tell to fuck off. You guys are friends, right?"

"Depends on the day." Crew smiles, telling me he's kidding. "Yeah, we're friends. We've known each other for a while. His family is *almost* as messy as mine."

"So, go. Seriously. I can handle all this." I wave a hand at all the dog supplies we just bought.

"You lost the dog last time."

"He has a leash now. Plus, he seems tired." I glance down at Teddy, who's methodically licking at his paw.

"Asher is a big boy. He has other friends he can call."

"He called *you*," I point out.

Crew considers that. Smiles a little. "I can't believe you're encouraging me to go to a club with Asher, of all people. Half the stupid shit I've done was his idea."

"I trust you," I whisper. It feels like the right thing to say and also happens to be true.

It captures Crew's attention. "Yeah?"

"Yeah."

He looks at me and I look back. And something very tangible and very real passes between us before Crew unbuckles his seatbelt. "Text me when you're home."

I nod. He leans forward and kisses me before he opens the door and steps out of the car. I watch his confident strides eat up the distance between the curb and the entrance of Proof, only stopping to say something to the bouncer before he disappears inside.

I climb into the driver's seat and drive home.

CHAPTER SIXTEEN

CREW

When the elevator doors open, it's to the sound of loud female laughter. It's not Scarlett's, a sound I unwittingly memorized, despite the fact I've only heard it a few times. This is higher-pitched.

I pass the entryway tables and walk into the living room, following the sound. Scarlett is sitting on the sectional couch, poking at a container of Chinese food with a fork. At the sound of my footsteps, she looks up. Her eyes widen with surprise—she wasn't expecting me home this early.

"Crew!"

"Red." I look at the other two women on the sofa. One has blonde hair, the other, light brown. I recognize them, surprisingly. They were with Scarlett that night at Proof, when she scared that woman off and I responded in kind. Had anyone else done that, I would have been pissed. With Scarlett, I found it amusing. The first of many exceptions where she is concerned.

I stroll forward and give the two women my most charming smile. "I didn't know you were inviting company over."

"I thought you had a meeting tonight."

"Plans changed." More like I pushed the meeting to tomorrow morning so I could come home earlier and screw Scarlett senseless. I take a seat beside her on the couch and focus my attention on the two other women. "Nice to meet you both. I'm Crew." I'm assuming they were at our wedding, but I don't recall seeing either of them.

The blonde gives me a saucy smile that immediately tells me why she and Scarlett are friends. "It's *very* nice to meet you. I'm Sophie, and this is Nadia." She nods to the woman to her right. "Scarlett has been stingy with details about her hot husband."

I glance at Scarlett in time to see her roll her eyes and then take a healthy sip of wine.

"Hot husband, huh? Are you ladies married?"

"Nadia is practically engaged. She and Finn have been together forever. And I'm seeing where things go."

"Seeing where things go? You said you were going to break up with Kyle weeks ago!" Nadia says.

The name Kyle and the way Scarlett tenses beside me tickles something in the back of my brain. "How long have you and Kyle been dating?"

"About four months now," Sophie replies. "But it feels like less. He's a surgeon, so I barely see him."

"A surgeon, huh?" I glance at Scarlett, who's intently studying her dinner. When your wife tells you she's sleeping with someone else, details tend to imprint. Our conversation in the car after the Rutherford gala is burned into my brain. She told me his name is Kyle, and he's a surgeon. That's too much of a coincidence, right? Unless she fucked her friend's boyfriend behind her back, she lied to me. Deliberately. Convincingly. "Sounds like a real catch. Have you met this Kyle, Scarlett?"

"Nope." She shoves a forkful of sweet and sour chicken into her mouth.

"We should go on a triple date!" Sophie exclaims, making it seem like the most revolutionary idea to ever exist. "We've never all been in relationships at the same time before."

"Sure, sounds fun," I agree. I doubt it will be fun, but getting on Scarlett's friends' good side can't hurt.

Sophie beams. "Perfect. I'll ask Kyle about dates."

"Can't wait to meet him."

If possible, Sophie's smile brightens. I am definitely on her good side. Nadia is harder to read, but seems agreeable enough. Scarlett's fingers are basically strangling the fork.

"Let's start a movie," Scarlett suggests.

"I'm going to the bathroom first," Nadia says before climbing off the couch.

Sophie stands as well. "I'll come with you. Last time we were over here, I got totally lost."

Nadia and Sophie disappear. Neither Scarlett nor I move. I don't speak first. I wait to see what she says. Finally, she sighs. "I lied, okay? I haven't been with anyone else since we got married either."

I thought I'd made peace with the knowledge she had. The rush of euphoria—of *relief*—at the confession she hasn't is unexpected. "Why did you lie to me?"

"You know why. I was mad at you that night. This wasn't supposed to be...*this*. I assumed you were sleeping around, and so I told you I was. I didn't think you'd believe me if I didn't give you a name, so I stole Sophie's hook up." Another long exhale. "Just forget it."

There's no chance I'll be doing that. "Were you ever going to tell me?"

"I almost did. In Italy, after we..." She glances at the doorway her friends disappeared through, like she's worried they'll overhear us. "I wasn't sure how you would react. If you'd still—" I watch her play with a stray thread on the hem of her tank top.

"If I'd still what?" I nudge in a soft tone.

"If you'd still be interested."

I blink a few times as those words sink in. "Interested?" I echo. *What the* fuck *is she talking about?*

"Don't play dumb, Crew. We're married. I'm basically a sure thing. Guys want what they can't have, not what they *have*."

I laugh. "You're serious?" Based on the way her eyes flash, she is. "You think *I* think you're a *sure thing*?" Saying the words makes me laugh again. I've never worked harder for a scrap of a woman's attention than I do with Scarlett. Every time she touches me, I feel like the luckiest guy in the world. I grasp her chin in my hand and tilt her face up, so she has no choice but to look right at me. "I've never wanted *anyone* the way I want you, Scarlett. Thinking you were with other guys didn't make you more desirable or keep my attention. It made me want to punch every single one of them in the face."

"We made it through the maze!" Sophie announces, bouncing into the room.

Scarlett jerks her face out of my grasp and faces her friend, pasting a wide, fake smile on her face. "Great. Where's Nadia?"

"Here." Nadia walks into the room and settles back in her original spot on the couch. "What are we watching?"

I study Scarlett as Sophie and Nadia debate options on Netflix.

"We can talk more later," I tell her quietly. "Did Teddy get fed?"

She nods without looking at me. "Yeah. And walked. Your dinner is in the kitchen, if you're hungry."

"Thank you." I lean over and kiss her shoulder. "I'll be upstairs."

"You don't have to." This time, she's looking at me when I glance over. "You can stay down here. Eat with us, if you want."

I don't ask if she's sure. Scarlett doesn't make offers she doesn't mean. "Okay."

Both Nadia and Sophie glance over when I stand. "Just going to grab some dinner and change," I tell them. "Do you ladies need anything?"

They both shake their heads, giggling.

When I walk into the kitchen, there are three paper containers on the counter. I open one, finding Mongolian beef inside. The next has kung pao chicken. I've eaten Chinese with Scarlett once, and she remembered everything I liked. It does something twisty to my insides. Something that's more than attraction, more than loyalty. My role models, when it comes to romantic relationships, have all been shitty ones. Men who know they can get away with anything and women who let them.

Scarlett and I are different. I *want* us to be different. For the first time, I feel some real confidence that it's something she might want too.

Nothing has changed when I reenter the living room in sweatpants, dinner in hand. Teddy trails on my heels. I love the little dog, who's steadily growing every day. The papers from the rescue only guessed at his heritage. There's definitely a lot of golden retriever in him. Beyond that, he's a mystery.

Scarlett smiles when she sees him. Teddy sniffs around her and then heads over to Sophie and Nadia on the other couch.

They both gush over him. Sophie even climbs down onto the floor to pet him.

I take a seat beside Scarlett and dig into my dinner.

"You softie," she accuses, looking at Teddy, who is basking in her friends' attention. "He's supposed to have a routine with his crate."

"Says you," I reply. "The doggie daycare said you picked him up three hours early."

She shrugs, but I see right through it. "It was on my way home."

"Admit it, you missed him."

"You came home early too."

"Not to see Teddy."

"What are we watching?" Nadia asks, interrupting our side conversation.

Scarlett leans forward to grab the remote off the coffee table. Her tank top rides up, exposing a strip of skin. Just like that, I'm envisioning peeling the thin material off her body. Changing might have been a mistake.

The girls settle on a comedy. A few minutes in, I know I won't be paying much attention to it. I finish my dinner and spread out on the couch. After hesitating, Scarlett lies down beside me. Her ass rubs directly over my crotch, and I groan into her ear. "Unless you're willing to finish it, don't start it, Scarlett."

"Who said I'm not willing to finish it?" she whispers back.

I slip a few fingers under the hem of her tank top, tracing circles on her smooth skin. Nadia, or maybe Sophie, laugh at something happening on the screen. I don't look over to check. "I don't want to share you. I'm the only one who fucks you, Red."

Her breath hitches. I hear it, and I feel it. The quick rise of her rib cage.

"Say it."

She turns her head, so it's tucked under my chin. "You're the only one who fucks me," she whispers.

I tease the underside of her breast, and then slip my hand back down to rest on her stomach. "Watch the movie."

She huffs, annoyed. I smile, sliding my hand to curl around her hip and staring at the screen without registering a single pixel.

The next thing I know, Scarlett is shaking me awake. I blink, scrub my hands across my face, and yawn. "Shit. I fell asleep?"

She nods. "Somewhere between the shoot out and a sex scene, so you must have been exhausted."

"I thought the movie was about a bachelorette trip?"

"Thing escalated, I guess. I wasn't paying very close attention."

"No?" I ask, the picture of innocence.

Scarlett rolls her eyes. "I put Teddy in his crate. Sophie and Nadia left. I'm heading up to bed." But she doesn't move.

I do.

I tug her closer, flipping our positions so she's caged beneath me. Electricity crackles between us. She doesn't fight me. She spreads and sprawls, raising her arms and tugging her hair out of its bun. Her knees part, so my hardening cock is pressed directly against her soft center. I roll my hips and she moans.

"You want my cock, Red?"

In response, she moans again. Louder. I sit up, pulling my shirt off and tugging down my sweatpants so my dick juts out. Scarlett bites her bottom lip, laser-focused on my growing erection. She's not wearing a bra. I can see the hard points of her nipples as her body responds.

The leggings she's wearing are skin-tight. It takes me three jerks to get them down and off. Her soaked underwear comes off next. I move closer, about to push inside, when I realize, "Condoms are upstairs."

This has always been a tense subject between us. Now that we're not only having sex, but having it as often as possible, it's become an increasingly pertinent issue. It's an ongoing test of trust in each other. Saying you trust someone is one thing. Backing it up with action is another. Especially when transmitting a disease or pregnancy are potential consequences.

"I trust you." She repeats the same thing she told me four nights ago, outside Proof. And it prompts the same swell of a sensation that feels a lot like love.

I kiss her as she works her way down and around my cock. I've *never* had sex without wearing a condom before. Nothing is dulled. I groan at the sensation of her tight, wet heat contracting around me without any barrier. "Holy shit."

"It feels different?"

"Yeah," I breathe, picking up the pace once we've both adjusted. "Feels good. You feel so fucking good."

"It feels different with you," Scarlett murmurs. I know she's not talking about the lack of latex between us.

She winds her long legs around my waist, opening up to me even more. We both moan as I slide deeper, hitting a new spot. My breathing quickens as I start to feel the familiar tingle in my balls. And then I'm coming, harder and longer than I ever have. White spots dot my vision, bringing new meaning to blinding pleasure.

Slowly, reality trickles back into the living room. But I don't move away from her. Scarlett's hand threads through my hair, running through the short strands over and over again. I press my lips against the curve of her neck, right where it meets her shoulder. Inhaling her scent and breathing against her skin.

This is new to me too. Intimacy after the physical act of sex. I wasn't a jerk about it, but I definitely never stuck around to snuggle with anyone else afterward.

"Sophie and Nadia like you," she tells me.

"They didn't judge me for falling asleep like an old man?"

I feel her laugh reverberate against my cheek. "No. They both work a lot too. Plus, you don't *look* like an old man, so that helps."

"Is that a compliment, Red?" I tease, tilting my head back so I can see her face.

"Like you don't know I think you're hot."

"I like it when you say it."

"Fine. You're hot, okay?"

I smile. "Okay."

"Sophie wants to get set up with Oliver. She's planning to break up with Kyle."

"She'd be better off sticking with the surgeon."

Scarlett raises a brow. "Why?"

"Remember when you asked about me and Candace?"

"Yeah."

"Remember what I said?"

"Holy shit. Seriously?"

"Yep." I pop the P. "My dad is going to find out—if he doesn't know already—and I'll get stuck in the middle."

"Wow." She hesitates. "Can I ask you something? Totally unrelated to the whole Oliver sleeping with your stepmother drama. I've just been meaning to."

"Yeah, sure."

"The other night, Asher mentioned your desk. How you don't like other people touching it. Why?"

"Maybe I just don't like people touching my stuff," I tease.

"Is that why?"

I exhale. "No. It was my mom's desk. She came from money too. Her family had a shipping business. She inherited it and handled a lot of the work—had her own office in the house and everything. My dad sold the company after she died. At the time, I thought he was being callous. Now..." I look over at her. "Now, I think the reminders might have hurt too much."

There's a long stretch of silence between us. "Would you sell *Haute*?"

Talk about a loaded question. And it's so *Scarlett*. Testing my feelings for her by discussing business. "No," I reply. "I wouldn't."

She holds my gaze, but I can *feel* how much she wants to look away. I can tell what she thinks I'm saying.

"I would make sure it thrived because I think that's what you would want. My father is a coward when it comes to his feelings. I wouldn't try to forget. I would fight like hell to remember."

I've never seen Scarlett cry. She doesn't now, but there's a sheen covering her hazel eyes that suggests she might be close to it. Her hand is still in my hair, and she uses it to tug me closer, until our lips are just a few breaths apart.

"I wouldn't sell either," she whispers, before she kisses me.

CHAPTER SEVENTEEN

SCARLETT

"Scarlett? Scarlett?"

I blink and glance at Leah, who's giving me a strange look.

"Yes?"

"I was just asking if you had any comments on the October issue before we end the meeting."

I glance down at the pages of notes in front of me. Rub my forehead in an attempt to alleviate the headache building. "No. This all looks great. Good work, everyone."

Silence follows. Silence with a shocked undertone. I *always* have notes. Suggestions. Input. I'm too distracted to come up with any right now.

I stand, needing out of this room. I'm exhausted. I want to snuggle up on the couch in sweatpants with a bottle of wine and Crew.

Except the wine might not be an option. I realized my period was late—two weeks late—four days ago. I've been so busy I didn't realize how quickly time is passing.

I'm pregnant.

I think.

I've thrown up every morning for the past few days. I've been emotional. Tired. And I'm late, which has never happened before. But I don't know if I'm pregnant for certain because I'm afraid to find out. I never thought I'd call myself a coward, but that's exactly who I am right now. I'm terrified to know for sure. Terrified to tell Crew. If I'm this far along, he knocked me up in Italy, possibly the first time we slept together.

He'll probably be proud. Our families will be thrilled.

And I'm…freaking out.

Also, I feel like I'm going to be sick. Again. Lately, my "morning sickness" has felt a lot like all-day nausea. Talk about false advertising. I don't know anything about babies or pregnancy. I thought I would have time. I wanted time. Crew's swimmers clearly had other ideas. Statistically speaking, we've had plenty of sex to make pregnancy a possibility. *Protected* sex. If I'm really six weeks along, we conceived back when he was still wearing condoms. Ninety-nine percent effective? I guess we're part of the one percent in more ways than one.

I'm not against having kids. I knew we would, eventually. Crew wants kids, although I know part of that urge is fueled by his father. It just feels fast. Soon. We weren't a couple before we got married. It took us a month to have sex. We've finally found an equilibrium that this will shake. Sharing responsibility for a dog was an adjustment. Having a child is a huge change for any couple. For us, it will come with a whole host of complications I was happy to put off for a while.

I hobble down the hall in my heels, wishing I could take them off and chuck them at the wall. I'm sleep-deprived. *And possibly hormonal.* As soon as we have sex, Crew is out like a light. I've laid awake the past few nights, worrying about all the ways this will change our lives.

My office is a sanctuary. When I bought this magazine, I spent hours deciding how every inch would be decorated. I hold all my meetings here. It makes a statement, the colors bold but not garish. Abstract paintings line the wall above the white leather sofa. Framed issues of *Haute* are displayed on the opposite wall, above a table that always boasts a fresh arrangement of flowers. They're peonies today. The floral scent usually makes me happy. Right now, it makes me want to hurl.

I take a seat at my desk, firing off a few rapid replies to the emails that came in during the meeting I just left. I have a thousand things to do: photo shoot approvals, communications with advertisers, and arrangements with different vendors. A few months ago, I'd be ordering takeout and settling in for a few more hours here.

All I want to do right now is go home.

My eyes fall to the framed photograph to the right of my computer. I placed it there as a prop, a testament to the *women can have it all* mentality: a happy home life and a successful career. I already had the successful career, and I've always known I have the capability to accomplish whatever project I want to. For the past nine years, I've also known I would probably marry Crew Kensington. I just didn't know what it would be like being married to him. Confusing and thrilling and fun. He's become someone I rely upon and trust and look forward to seeing.

How the hell did that happen?

I thought he'd have no interest in making this marriage work as anything more than a two-hundred-page document spelling out the consequences if it didn't. I banked upon that. *Relied* upon it. The way we've become something so different is both reassuring and worrisome.

The black-and-white photograph of us on our wedding day sitting on my desk doesn't look like a prop anymore. It looks real.

I can even pinpoint the moment it was snapped, when Crew told me we should have practiced dancing before we got married the same way we kissed before speaking our vows. I'm smiling, and so is he.

I try to picture a little kid with Crew's blue eyes and my dark hair. I can't. I've never held a baby before; I can't even remember the last time I saw one in person.

Rather than stop at a pharmacy and put all the second-guessing to rest, I go straight home. *Coward.* I seek out the solace only Crew can provide. It usually includes snuggling on the couch and then sex.

My body has become accustomed to the schedule—to crave it. Crave *him.*

The elevator doors open, revealing Crew leaning against the wall beside the Monet. "Finally! I was about to call you."

I take him in: the combed hair, the tux, and the anxious, *let's get going* expression.

He does the same to me. "You forgot." The two words are flat. Annoyed. Any hopes of talking him into staying home, spooning on the couch, and admitting I might be pregnant flee like leaves on a windy fall day.

"No," I lie. "My meeting just ran long. I came home as soon as I could." The last part, at least, is true. I rushed home because I wanted to see him. "I'll go change."

I can't believe I forgot. Tonight is Kensington Consolidated's company party. I know it's a big deal for Crew, filled with important networking for cementing his status as future CEO.

Crew grabs my hand as I try to pass him. His annoyed expression falters, something softer appearing. "Are you okay?"

I paste a smile on my face. "Of course. Just give me a few minutes, okay?" I can't tell him. Not now, right before we have to go make small talk with important people all night. A part of me is relieved, even. There's no choice but to *not* utter the words.

It's not until I'm inside my closet that I let the smile fall. I read somewhere, once, that smiling tricks your brain. The mere motion triggers happy chemicals into releasing, whether your smile is fake or real. Since I can't drink—possibly for nine months, but at least until I take a pregnancy test—I could *really* use any drugs my body can produce naturally. And I'll be forcing lots of smiles tonight.

I swap the pencil skirt and blouse I've been wearing all day for a floor-length silk gown. The emerald fabric whispers against my skin as I head into the bathroom to freshen my hair and makeup. Once I'm satisfied with both, I grab a matching clutch and a strappy pair of stilettos. My feet cringe at the thought, but the fabric will drag on the floor if I don't wear heels.

Crew is in the same spot I left him in, scrolling through emails on his phone.

"Ready," I chirp.

"You look beautiful," he tells me, before we walk into the elevator.

I bite down on my tongue until the pain turns sharp, battling the urge to tell him what I've been preoccupied by all day. "Thanks."

"Did work go okay?"

"Yep." I hesitate. "I might need to go to Paris next week for some meetings."

Crew doesn't look up from his phone. "Yeah. Sure."

"Okay." I rest my head back against the hard panels of the elevator, following Crew out into the underground garage when we reach the bottom floor. Roman is waiting beside the car. He gives me a respectful nod. "Mrs. Kensington."

I smile at him before climbing into the SUV.

The ride to the Met is silent. I know Crew is nervous about tonight. He's been handling a big acquisition lately, and I'm sure he's bracing for questions from investors. I'm preoccupied by the possibility a tiny person might be growing inside me.

Walking from the car and up the steps is all it takes for my feet to start screaming at me. The climate controlled and smooth lobby floors of the museum are a slight relief. We're immediately escorted into the Great Hall. Polite chatter echoes off the soaring ceiling and stone walls. I barely have the time to take in any of the candles or flower arrangements decorating the space before people start approaching us. Swarming us.

Crew is the golden boy of Kensington Consolidated—of all of Manhattan. The heir to the throne. Emperor-in-waiting.

I've never gotten the impression Arthur Kensington is well-liked. Business savvy, but not approachable. He's the guy you invite because you have to, not because you want to.

Oliver is more of an enigma. I spot him standing in the corner, talking to two other men in tuxedos. He seems like his father's lackey, willing to do whatever it takes to impress and hold his position. But I didn't think he was the type to screw his father's wife behind his back. No matter his intentions, he doesn't have the effortless charisma Crew possesses. The ability to make you feel special just for holding his attention. I noticed it when I was sixteen and told my father the only Kensington I would marry was Crew, and I see it now as he talks to the Spencers.

It feels like every single one of the thousand plus attendees have spoken to Crew by the time we reach our table—in the very center of the hall. Arthur and Candace are already seated, but there's no sign of Oliver.

Arthur rises to kiss my cheek, playing the perfect father-in-law. "Scarlett. Stunning, as always."

"Thank you." I smile at Candace, who looks completely at

ease by her husband's side. Maybe I underestimated her and Oliver both. She certainly doesn't seem like the type to step out on her marriage. Cheating may be socially acceptable for men, but she'd become a pariah if it came out she had.

"You spoke to Justin Marks?" Arthur shifts his attention to Crew, who's pulling my chair out.

I shoot him a small smile as I sink down, immediately kicking my heels off under the cover of the tablecloth.

"Yes." Crew beckons a waiter over and orders a scotch. He looks to me. "You want champagne?"

For some reason, the possibility of this happening didn't occur to me. "No thanks. I have a headache."

His forehead wrinkles. "You do? You didn't say anything."

"I'm fine. I just had a long day. Alcohol will probably put me to sleep."

The line between his eyes doesn't smooth. He knows me well enough to hear the false note in my voice. But before he can ask any more questions, Arthur interrupts, obviously not sharing the same concern for my welfare his son does. I imagine he'd feel differently if he knew my "headache" was the future of his carefully constructed empire.

I tune out as Crew and Arthur discuss business. Oliver appears as dinner is being served, taking one of the two empty seats. He ignores Candace and joins the discussion on some investor. I people watch and pick at my food. I'm hungry, but not for anything on my plate. The steak is so rare it looks raw, and the potatoes taste too rich.

"You're not hungry?" Crew asks me when his father is distracted by a member of the museum staff who's asking him about some logistics.

"Not really."

"Do you want to leave? I can see if—"

For some reason, the offer makes tears pool in my eyes. Some reason probably involving hormones. I know Crew sees when his eyes widen. "No. We should stay. I'm just...going to use the restroom. I'll be back in a bit."

"Okay." Crew's voice is hesitant, but his father is asking him something again. He's distracted.

I slip my heels back on and head toward the exit, following the signs that point to the womens' room. The sinks are all empty. I walk straight into one of the stalls and lean back against the tile wall, relishing the feel of the cold stone against my skin. Deep breaths help with the nausea some.

All night, I've played the role of Crew's arm candy. No one here is interested in my opinions on Kensington Consolidated. I don't owe any of them anything. But I want to support Crew, the way he did when he backed me up with my dad or when he asks about my meetings and listens to my answers. For him, I can suffer through a night of stuffy conversation and overpriced food.

I pee, and then leave the sanctuary of the stall to wash my hands. I'm soaping them when the restroom door opens, and Hannah Garner strolls inside. She's wearing a midnight blue gown that offsets her tan and blonde cascade of curls. I never pressed Crew for details about their past. Honestly, I don't want them. But it puts me at a disadvantage—one Hannah intends to use, if the leer on her face is any indication.

"Scarlett. What a surprise."

"What's surprising?" I rinse and shut off the tap. "The fact that I wash my hands, or that I'm here supporting my husband?"

She giggles, and it's malicious. Grating. "Your husband? He doesn't belong to you. He was *forced* to marry you. It's obvious he doesn't even *like* you."

"You don't know anything about my marriage."

"I know more than you think. I know Crew hasn't been

heading straight home from work." She takes a step closer. Her heel taps the floor like a warning shot. "Want to know how I know that?"

"He's done with you." I repeat what he told me.

Hannah *tsks* and shakes her head. "Is that what you tell yourself? He's *Crew Kensington*. You're a bore so obsessed with working your daddy had to sell you off to the highest bidder. All you're good for is your money. He pretends you're *me* to get off during sex."

My palm twitches, tempted to slap her. But I won't give her the satisfaction. A reaction is exactly what she wants.

"Always so stoic, Scarlett. Acting like you don't care about anything or anyone. But I saw you with Crew earlier. You care about *him*. You think he's being *faithful*? I never thought the Princess of Park Avenue would be so naïve."

"You sound awfully jealous, Hannah. Did I marry the guy you want?"

Her eyes narrow. "Two weeks ago, he fucked me in the bathroom of Proof. Said he'd never come harder. I don't want him. I *have* him."

For the first time, I feel a small flicker of uncertainty, and I hate myself for it. Crew was at Proof two weeks ago, when I told him to hang out with Asher. *Would he have screwed Hannah instead?* It was before he knew I'd been fully faithful. There's nothing but triumph on Hannah's face, confidence with no trace of deceit. But I don't trust her. She has every reason to lie. To sow doubt into my head.

There's nothing I hate more than being played a fool. My whole life, people have seen me as a spoiled princess. They've never considered how much harder excessive wealth can make your life. Everything becomes fake. The pleasantries, the platitudes. Pointed reminders and presumptions. How lonely it can be to always second-guess others' intentions.

I'm lucky in lots of ways, but my life is a long way from perfect.

I trust Crew. I believe he's being faithful.

And if he's not—if I'm wrong—it will shatter me.

I look Hannah straight in the eye. "I don't believe you."

I walk out of the restroom without another word. The muffled music and voices coming from the hall sound loud after the quiet confrontation in the bathroom.

When I reenter the party, my gaze is drawn straight to Crew. He's standing near our empty table, looking sinfully sexy in his tuxedo as he clutches a glass of amber liquid and talks with a large crowd of men. Holding court.

I sigh and head for the open bar. Joseph Huntington, a good friend of my father's, is standing alongside it, watching the bartender mix a martini. He smiles when he sees me. "Scarlett! How are you, dear?"

"I'm well, Mr. Huntington. How are you?"

"Good, good."

"Quite the family you married into, eh?" He waves a hand around at the opulence surrounding us. "Hanson has never thrown this sort of affair."

I shrug. "My father isn't one for pomp."

"Wouldn't have known that, seeing the wedding he paid for."

I smile. "Blame my mother for that."

"Maybe you'll shake things up when Hanson steps down." Joseph peers at me closely. I've mostly ignored the speculation about the future of Ellsworth Enterprises, even as it's grown louder. My father is nearing retirement age. I didn't take a job at the company, the way everyone expected me to. I married Crew, who has an empire of his own to run.

"Maybe."

Joseph smiles at my vague response and picks up his drink. "Have a lovely evening."

"You too."

I turn to the bartender once he disappears. "Hi. Can you make me something without alcohol, please?"

The bartender grins. He's cute, close to my age. With a lanky build and shaggy hair. "First request I've gotten of those tonight."

"I'll bet. Businessmen love their fancy liquor."

"No kidding. If I pawned *one* of these bottles, I'd be able to pay rent for months." He backtracks quickly. "I'm not going to, obviously. Just a bad joke."

I laugh. "Don't worry about it. And I doubt anyone would even notice."

"Do you like ginger?"

"Yes."

He nods and starts pouring.

"Have you bartended long?"

"A couple of years. I'm getting my master's at NYU. It's good money and works with my class schedule."

"What are you getting your master's in?"

He looks sheepish. "Anthropology. You can laugh. I'll be eating Ramen my whole life."

"Good for you," I say, and mean it. "Money is overrated."

"Easy to say when you have it."

"You're right," I agree. "But I bet most of these people aren't very happy with their lives."

"Are you?"

I sigh. "That's a complicated question."

"It is." He studies me for a minute, then holds out a hand. "I'm Charlie."

I shake his offered hand. "Scarlett."

"Do you work for Kensington Consolidated?"

"Not exactly. I'm married to a Kensington."

"I thought I recognized you," Charlie replies. "You had that big, fancy wedding this summer, didn't you?"

"Yep."

"My little sister loves your magazine."

I smile. "Really?"

"Uh-huh. Last time I went home, my bed was covered with old *Haute* issues."

"Seriously?"

"I swear."

"Wow. That's flattering."

Charlie slides a glass with a pink tinge in front of me. "Sort of a Shirley Temple, but I added a few special ingredients. No alcohol."

"Thank you." I take a sip. It tastes like ginger, grapefruit, and rosemary. "It's really good."

"Good."

I keep chatting with Charlie. Occasionally someone comes up for a refill, and he has to work. I often end up in conversation with whoever it is, hearing over and over again about what a fantastic job Crew is doing and how they're so excited for the future.

By the time Crew himself appears, I'm on my third mocktail, chasing ice around in circles with a straw as Charlie makes someone a gin and tonic.

"Hey." He stops beside me, close enough I can feel the heat radiating from his body.

"Hey." Ice clinks against my glass as I keep chasing it round and round. Hannah's annoying lilt bounces around my head.

I don't want him. I have *him.*

Crew looks me over. I know, because I can feel each spot his gaze grazes. "Are you drunk?"

I laugh. "Nope." I pop the P for emphasis. "I wish."

His brow furrows as he tries to decode my words. "Are you ready to go?"

"Are you?"

"I wouldn't be asking if I weren't."

I snort. "Right. We only do what you want. Since I'm just *Crew Kensington's wife*. Nothing more. Nothing meaningful."

Hurt, then anger flash across his face. "I thought we were past this shit."

"Yeah, me too. Then I spent all night getting treated like a *prop*, while you were nowhere to be found."

Charlie finishes making the drink. Now he's pretending like he can't hear our conversation, although I'm sure every word is audible.

"You knew what tonight was," Crew replies. "What this world is like."

"I want us to be different."

"We *are* different."

"It doesn't feel like it right now." I drain the rest of my drink and wave goodbye to Charlie. "Thanks for keeping me company."

He smiles and nods. I stuff a couple of hundreds into his tip jar.

Crew follows my attention, and a muscle jumps in his jaw. I wobble as I step, yanking my elbow away when he tries to steady me. "I'm *fine*."

"You're drunk."

I laugh. "No, I'm *not*. Stone cold fucking sober, thanks to you."

Confusion mars his handsome features. "What? I didn't tell you not to drink."

I begin to walk toward the exit, leaving him to trail after me. The staccato of my heels pounds the marble like an angry march. I'm mad. At Crew, at myself. Mad I might ruin everything. Mad I care if I ruin everything.

He's following me. I can sense it, and I'm mad about that too.

I barely register the feel of his hand gripping my elbow before he pulls me into one of the empty galleries that line the hallway leading to the lobby. In one smooth motion, I'm up against the wall.

"Scarlett. What's wrong?"

It's dark in here. Only the barest hint of light from the hallway creeps in. "Nothing."

"Don't lie to me."

I kiss him. He groans as I tug his bottom lip between my teeth. Suddenly, I'm desperate. Clawing at the jacket of his tux and then fumbling with his pants.

"Scarlett. *Scarlett.*" He says my name again, but I'm focused on one thing. I need a distraction. Intimacy. *Him.*

"I need you."

Another groan as I tug his cock out. I can't see anything. But I can feel the soft skin harden in my hand as I grip him in my palm.

He kisses me the way I want him to fuck me. Skilled and hungry and rough. I started this, but Crew's mouth makes it clear I won't control it. His lips are fierce and dominant as one palm slides underneath my dress and up my thigh. I arch against him as his fingers discover how wet I am, barely aware of the hard press of the wall against my spine.

The silky material of my dress is bunched up around my waist and my thong is pulled to the side and then he's inside of me. I hiss at the intrusion that sates one need and feeds another.

"I'm not wearing anything," he whispers as he starts moving. "I'll make a mess."

"I know." I wrap a leg around his waist, opening myself up further. "It's okay. I want you to."

His lips are back on mine, hard and demanding. All I'm aware of is Crew and how he's making me feel. No matter how many times we do this—and it's a high number at this point—it always feels this way. Like the first time, and the best time.

He's setting a brutal pace. Nothing about this is languid. It's raw and primal and hard and deep.

I close my eyes because I can barely see anything, anyway. It heightens the sensations. The sound of his harsh breathing. The smell of his cologne. The feel of him sliding in and out of me.

His greedy lips swallow my moans.

Distantly, I'm aware of the voices and commotion that remind me where we are. How scandalous this would be. How few of the people milling about down the hall have probably had sex in a semi-public space because they were utterly consumed by the other half of their marriage.

I'm so close. Each thrust pushes me closer to the edge. I can feel the pressure building, the heat forming and my muscles tensing.

Crew's mouth moves to my neck, nibbling and sucking at the sensitive skin. "You're always so wet for me, Red," he murmurs. "So responsive. So eager. Are you ready to come for me, baby?"

Everywhere burns. I use his tie to tug him closer, forcing more friction between our bodies as I grind against him, chasing my release. Pleasure builds and expands, chasing everything else away. I'm so close to the precipice; I'll do anything to reach that point. "Yes."

One more thrust, and I *shatter*. Break apart into a million pieces that act as the sweetest oblivion. I'm still experiencing the orgasmic high when I feel Crew's release fill me.

He pulls out a few seconds later, leaving sticky warmth

behind that leaks down my inner thigh. We're both breathing heavily. He tucks his half-hard dick back into his Armani tux. I straighten. The silk skirt of my dress falls to the floor, covering my legs and the wetness between them.

The only sound in the large gallery is our breathing.

"We should go," Crew says finally. "People came for dinner, not a show."

I don't smile at the lame joke. He can't really see my face, anyway. I just walk out of the gallery and back into the hallway, heading in the direction of the lobby. By some small miracle, we don't encounter anyone. Crew's hair is mussed and his shirt is wrinkled. I'm sure it would be obvious to anyone what just took place between us.

The hot air waiting outside smacks me in the face like a sauna, seeping away the cold, dry air conditioning and saturating my dress and hair with humidity instead.

Roman isn't waiting outside. The car that gets pulled up outside in front of the fountains is Crew's black Lamborghini.

"Where's Roman?" I ask as we climb into the car. I was kind of counting on his presence on the drive home.

"I gave him the rest of the night off," Crew responds.

"Oh." That's all I can come up with. I stare out at the city lights instead, right until we pull up to a gas station.

A quick glance at the gauge tells me there's more than half a tank. We didn't need to stop. But I say nothing as Crew climbs out. Neither does he. There's no knowing smile. No joking words. He climbs out and shuts his door with an ominous thud.

Tears burn my eyes as regret simmers in my stomach. I'm braver than this. *Stronger* than this. My mood—my emotions— used to be my own. It's concerning how reliant I've become on how Crew acts to inform my own feelings.

I step out of the car, not caring the silk hem of my dress is dragging on the dirty ground. "I'm getting a water."

A nod is Crew's only response. The sharp scent of gasoline swirls in the damp air as I cross the parking lot and head into the convenience store. Some pop song streams through the speakers.

"Evening." The woman behind the counter gives me a tired, perfunctory smile.

I nod in response as I pass the register and head for the coolers in the back. I grab a bottle of Fiji and spin to see…pregnancy tests. A whole shelf of them. Different brands and colors promising quick results. I hesitate. Come up with excuses. I scan the shelves, surprised by the number of different options promising accuracy and quick results.

What's the difference? It's just a stick you pee on, right?

With a heavy sigh, I grab three boxes at random and walk to the register, setting the water and the tests down on the scratched plastic counter. The cashier looks at my left hand between ringing the first and second box up. I roll my eyes when she's not looking.

Marriage doesn't make you worthy of becoming a mother.

I pay for everything and take the plastic bag, heading back into the humid night air. Crew has finished fueling, but he's still standing outside the car. His hands are in his tux pockets and his eyes are on the sky. I slow my steps as I approach, drinking the sight of him in.

Watching him, I accept that some part of me wants to hope I *am* pregnant. Wishes that the test will be positive and that Crew and I have the type of marriage where I'd give him a onesie that said something nauseatingly adorable, like *I love my dad*. Where I'd know he wanted a kid because it was a piece of me and him, not an heir to pass an empire of fortune and responsibilities along to.

"Did you get food?" Crew lowers his gaze from the sky and looks at me. Or more specifically, at the bag I'm carrying.

"No." I reach the passenger door and climb inside.

"Dammit." Crew settles beside me and closes the door. "I'm starving. The food is always shit at those things."

Try possibly being pregnant, I think. I say nothing.

"What did you get?"

"Water." I reach down and grab the plastic bottle out of the bag. The boxes of pregnancy tests audibly shift in a scrape of stiff paper. Crew raises his eyebrows but doesn't comment.

I take a long sip as we speed along the street. The cold water hits my empty stomach, causing a loud gurgle. I suffer through an uncomfortable few seconds as the water warms in my belly before taking a few more, smaller sips. We drive in silence for another ten minutes until Crew unexpectedly pulls over.

"What are you doing?"

"I told you, I'm hungry. So are you, it sounds like." He flicks on the hazards. "This place has the best fried chicken in the city."

"There's food at home."

"Nothing prepared. I'm not dragging Phillipe out of bed at this hour to make me something."

"It's his job."

"What's the real issue? You can't spend ten extra minutes in a car with me?"

I don't answer, just look out the window.

He sighs, heavy and exhausted. "Do you want some chicken?"

"Yes. And a chocolate milkshake." This sounds like the sort of place that would have milkshakes.

He looks at me. "I don't think they'll have a dairy-free version."

I almost smile. "I know."

He drops the keys in the cupholder. "Okay. I'll be right back."

I stare out at the passing cars as his door opens and shuts. Plastic crinkles as my foot brushes the bag in the footwell, taunting me. I'm ninety-eight percent certain I'm pregnant. Now that I have the tests, it seems silly to say anything until I know for sure. On the two percent chance I'm not, it will complicate things between us unnecessarily. Complicate things more than the mess my confusing behavior has already caused.

Crew's return comes with the mouth-watering aroma of fried chicken. He hands me a container and sets a to-go cup in the cupholder. "I got it with maple butter. I hope that's…" He trails off when he realizes I'm already devouring it. "…okay."

I don't know if it's because I'm starving or because I'm probably pregnant or because I'm craving comfort food, but the fried chicken tastes like the best thing I've ever eaten. The coating is salty and crisp, and the maple butter is sweet and smoky. I inhale three pieces without breathing and then wash it down with a sip of chocolatey heaven.

"Good?"

I groan and he smiles.

The drive back to the penthouse is silent. Crew parks in the garage and we walk toward the elevator side by side. It feels like days since we left, not hours.

Once we're inside the elevator, I step forward to swipe the card for the penthouse. When I glance at Crew, he's looking down. I follow his gaze. The thin white plastic I'm holding does nothing to hide the purple letters spelling out *Pregnancy Test.*

"You're pregnant?" Crew's voice is quiet. Calm. Unreadable. I didn't expect excitement, but I expected *some* emotion. Instead, the question sounds like it was spoken by a robot. Smooth and unfeeling.

"I don't know," I reply. I overcompensate for his lack of emotion with some snark. "That's what the test is for."

"You think you're pregnant?"

"Well, I'm not taking them for *fun*," I snap. His fingers tighten around the car keys he's holding. I soften my tone, trying to act like apathy and rational questions were the response I was hoping for. "My period is late and I keep throwing up my breakfast. So yeah, I think I'm pregnant."

He releases a long exhale. "Wow."

That word lingers in the air between us for the rest of the ride up. The doors slide open, revealing the familiar entryway. I don't make it more than a few steps inside before he says my name. It's followed by a warm palm that wraps around my forearm and pulls me around to face him. All I can see is blue, his gaze is that intense.

"Scarlett."

"*What?*"

He closes his eyes, then opens them, probably praying for patience. I know I'm being short and unreasonable, but *he* doesn't get to be the one freaking out about this. I'm the one whose body will change. "You can't tell me you might be pregnant and walk off. That's not the way this marriage works."

"How *does* it work then, Crew? If I *am* pregnant, what do you want me to do? Do you want me to wrap up a stick I peed on like a Christmas present? Wait and see if you notice in a few months? I made nice with all of your fans tonight and you're getting laid and I'll probably be popping out an heir for you soon. What else do you want from me?"

The line of his jaw turns taut. "I want you to take the test, Scarlett. And then show me what it says, so I don't spend all night wondering."

I'm in the mood for a fight, but he's being annoyingly easy-going all of a sudden. "Fine." I spin and stalk in the direction of our bedroom, the sharp corners of the boxes swinging against my legs with each step.

The plastic handle digs into my palm. I thought it would be a relief, Crew knowing. Thought it would save me the dilemma of telling him a definitive answer if he knew and asked. I didn't consider it would mean he'd be here when I found out. That there would be no chance to absorb the news myself before seeing his reaction.

The thud of his footsteps stays a steady trail behind me as I reach the stairs and climb to the second floor. The bedroom door is slightly ajar. I push it all the way open, dropping the plastic bag on the floor before kicking my heels off by the chaise lounge and stretching my toes.

Best feeling ever.

My feet sink into the soft rug as I find the zipper of my dress and pull it down. Silk pools around my ankles.

Crew's footfalls have stopped. I can feel his eyes on me, sweeping my bare skin with silent awareness.

I walk over, barefoot, in my bra and thong. I grab one test from the floor before heading for the bathroom. When I turn to close the door, he's standing in the doorway.

"No."

He looks amused. "I've seen you naked before, you know."

"I'm *not* naked."

Blue eyes flick down to the sheer lace bra and back up. "Sure."

I act like he said nothing. "I'm peeing alone."

"How long does it take?"

"Do you have somewhere to be?"

He heaves a sigh. "I'm just *wondering,* Scarlett."

I rip the box open, grab the stick, and hand him the empty box. "Read the directions, then." I shut the door on him and then walk over to the sink. I pull in long, deep breaths as I stare at my reflection in the mirror for a minute.

Despite the full face of makeup, including my red lips, I look young. Nervous. This feels like a big moment. If I were closer with my mom, I'd call her. But she'll tell my dad, who will call his lawyer and start redrafting all the documents that were just finalized following the wedding. Nadia and Sophie would freak out, and any of my other "friends" would probably call the press.

I wash my face and brush my teeth. I'm stalling. I don't know what I want the result to be. In the past few days, I've started to accept that I must be pregnant. If I'm not, I won't be disappointed, exactly, but some other emotion adjacent.

This is soon.

Way too soon.

We've been married for less than three months. Things between Crew and me are new and volatile. I'm supposed to debut my clothing line in the spring. If I'm pregnant now, I'll be *very* pregnant then.

"This one says two minutes," Crew calls through the door. "But the other two say five. Does that mean they're more accurate? Why did you get three? Are you supposed to take three? Did you take that one?"

I don't answer any of his questions, but I do pee on the first stick. Once I have, I don't know what to do with it. Just hold it, I guess? Wave it around like a Magic Eight ball? I peed on it, so I'm not setting it down on the counter surrounding the sink.

"Scarlett?"

It's bothering me less and less that Crew is here. It actually feels nice, not that I'll tell him that. I open the door and hold out the test. "Here. Hold this one while I take the other two."

"What?" He fumbles with the boxes. "Why?"

"Because I didn't want to get pee on the counter." I give him a *duh* look.

"What does it say?" He squints at the stick.

"Nothing yet."

I take the other two tests from him. I pee on them both at once, which might affect the results. At this point, I'm past caring. I just want a somewhat definitive answer before I go to bed.

When I open the door again, Crew is staring at the test in his hand like it will disappear if he looks away. "It's, um, positive." He clears his throat. "Pregnant." It's the first time I've heard him sound unsure about anything, and it's while looking at a black-and-white answer.

After a quick glance down to determine if the two I'm holding show results—they don't—I look back up. He's looking at me now, and I have no idea what to say or do. I think he was hoping for some direction from my reaction, because he stays just as blank and immobile.

"Do you think this is normal? Do other couples stand here holding these?"

He smiles, and I smile back. "Who cares what other people do?"

I exhale. "Yeah. You're right. You…want this, right?"

"A kid?" he clarifies.

I nod.

"Yeah. Do you?"

The tests I'm holding both turn positive. I turn them so he can see. "Three for three. I think we're past the wanting kids conversation."

"We don't have to be."

"We're married and you want a kid and you're telling me you'd be okay with not keeping this baby?"

"I'm saying it's your body and if that's a conversation you want to have, let's have it."

I'm surprised, and I know it shows on my face. We're not a couple of high schoolers who fooled around once. Kids—heirs—are one of the primary goals of this marriage. "Wow. That's shockingly progressive of you. Suzanne Lamonte asked me if I was considering taking time off work to try and *get* pregnant earlier."

"She might feel foolish about that."

I catch the caveat. "I'm keeping it, Crew. There was never a question. Yeah, I wish it had happened later—like maybe when we were actually trying—but it didn't. I don't feel ready, but I probably never will. So…" I lift one shoulder and let it drop.

"So we're having a baby."

A comment about his lack of role in the whole growing and birthing a human process going forward is at the tip of my tongue. His contribution was quick and enjoyable. *I'm* having a baby, not him. But I bite it back, considering he's handling this whole thing far better than I expected.

"Yep. I mean, I'll go to the doctor and confirm, but these all had *super accurate* plastered on the front, so it going the other way seems unlikely, I think? I don't really know."

"You'll tell me? When the appointment is?"

"Oh," I reply, thrown. "Uh, you don't have to—"

"I want to go."

"Okay." My voice is barely a whisper.

"Okay," he echoes.

Then, unexpectedly, he kisses me. It's urgent and eager. There's no finesse and lots of emotion. The stiff material of his tux rubs against my bare skin, sending moans tumbling out of my mouth. Then something shifts. Slows. Softens. Touches linger and drag. Sink into my skin and sear.

"I should go let Teddy out," Crew murmurs, pulling back.

"Are you coming back?"

"Yeah. I'm coming back."

"Okay." I step away and walk back into the bathroom without looking at him. His footsteps fade as he walks down the hall to the guest room that's become Teddy's domain.

I shed the lace I'm wearing and step into the shower. Hot water pounds over me as I wash my skin and shampoo my hair. I rest a hand on my flat stomach as suds slide down it.

I'm pregnant.

Suspecting felt different than knowing. I'm scared and excited and a million other emotions I can't name.

I'm relieved Crew knows. I didn't realize how heavily telling him was weighing on me until it lifted. There wasn't any doubt in my mind he would want this baby. Heirs—for his family's company, for my family's company—were always a pressing goal of this marriage. All the uncertainty stems from how this will affect *us*.

Crew and Scarlett.

I step out of the shower and towel off. My hair gets a quick brush and my skin a sweep of moisturizer. I'm too tired to do anything else. I hang up my towel, pull on one of the silk night-gowns I usually sleep in, and slide into bed.

When the door opens, I'm still awake. I stay curled on my side as I watch Crew's silhouette remove the tux. I close my eyes when he approaches the bed. But I know the exact second he slips between the sheets. His heat radiates. The mattress dips.

I don't move and he doesn't reach for me.

We usually have sex before bed. Technically we already have.

Right now, I'm craving his closeness more than his cock.

Before I can think it through, I roll over. His eyes hold mine as our bodies brush. One warm palm finds the small of my back and pulls me closer. I snuggle against him, tucking my head beneath his chin and tangling our legs together.

"Are you okay?"

"I was nervous to tell you," I admit. "It feels big."

"It *is* big."

I hesitate before I keep talking. "My parents didn't choose not to have more kids. When I was born... I don't know the details, but my mom couldn't have any more. What if that happens to us?"

"Then we'll have one kid."

He makes it sound simple. "My father still resents her for it. Not giving him a son."

"You think I'd care about that?"

"My parents chose to get married. It wasn't an arrangement. The way they went from that to who they are now...that's not what I want, Crew. I know it took more than just not being able to have more kids. But that was part of it, and I—I'm scared. I like who we are now. I don't want it to change."

"If it does, it will change for the better. I promise."

"You can't promise that."

"I just did."

I close my eyes, but I can't fall asleep.

"What else is bothering you?"

Again, I hesitate. "I talked to Hannah Garner tonight."

"Oh?" A lot simmers beneath the single syllable. I'm not sure if it's in regard to her, or that I'm bringing it up. Or because he knows we must have talked about him. But there's no panic or guilt.

"She told me some things. Some lies, I think."

"Like what?"

"Like that you had sex with her two weeks ago, in the bathroom of Proof."

"She was there the night I got a drink with Asher."

"Okay."

"I didn't talk to her. And I *definitely* didn't have sex with her."

"Okay," I repeat.

"You believe me?"

"Yes. I told her I didn't believe her and walked away. I trust you. I'm trusting you. Just...don't make me a fool, okay?"

Crew tightens his grip, so there's no space between our bodies at all. "I hope our kid is just like you," he whispers.

"I hope it has your eyes," I murmur back.

"We'll figure all of it out," he promises.

We. I've never been part of a we. It just became my new favorite word in the English language. I'm in love with the sound.

And the man saying it.

CHAPTER EIGHTEEN

CREW

The conference door opens mid-meeting. To my surprise, my secretary's head is the one that peeks through. "Mr. Kensington—"

I hold up a hand. "Not now, Celeste. I told you no disturbances."

"But—"

"Take a message."

"I real—"

I look up from the presentation for the first time, thoroughly annoyed. "There better be a financial crash or a family death."

"Well, no. But your wife—"

I stand up, almost knocking the chair over. "What about Scarlett?"

"She's here. She fainted in the hallway—"

I'm out the door before she's finished the sentence. "Where is she?" I bark, striding down the hallway so quickly Celeste almost trips trying to keep up.

"In your office."

The cold fist of fear around my heart loosens a bit when I

enter my office to find Scarlett is sitting on my leather couch, looking completely alert and aware.

I shut the door behind me.

She glances up at me and sighs. "I told Celeste not to bother you."

"What happened?" I ask as I kneel beside her.

"I'm fine," Scarlett says. She's holding a bottle of water and playing with the paper label. She tugs at the edge until it rips.

"That didn't answer my question."

Another sigh. "I got a little dizzy in the hallway. I felt nauseous this morning. Didn't have any breakfast."

"*Scarlett.*"

"I know, I know. I'm fine, though." She takes a drink of water. "I just needed a minute."

I stand and walk over to my desk to dial Celeste's number. She answers on the first ring. "Crew Kensington's office."

"I need you to let Isabel know I'll miss the rest of the presentation. Have them extend my apologies to Patrick. And push my meetings for the rest of the day."

"Yes, sir."

"And, Celeste?"

"Yes?"

"Thank you. I'm sorry I was short before."

"No problem. You're welcome, Mr. Kensington."

I hang up.

"I'm *fine*, Sport." Scarlett rises from the couch. "You're over-reacting. Go back to work." She grabs her bag. "I'll get something to eat, okay?"

"Damn right you will." After shutting off my computer, I walk over to her. "I'm taking you home."

"I'm going back to my office. I've got work to do." She starts toward the door.

I ignore her and follow.

"Crew. I mean it."

"So do I."

"I am *not* going home!"

"Yes, you *are*. There's stubborn, and then there's reckless. You're pregnant, Red. You can't keep acting like you're not. You need food and rest."

Her eyes flash. "There's annoying, and then there's over-bearing asshole. Want to know which one you are?"

She strides out of my office without telling me the answer, but I'm betting I could guess right.

I follow her down the hallway. More like chase, really. Scarlett's a lot faster on heels than I'm expecting.

She reaches the elevator and jabs at the button, then looks over at me with a sigh. "It's just a couple of meetings. And I don't know about you, but I don't find sitting in meetings all that strenuous."

"It's also *not* resting."

She looks around and lowers her voice. "The doctor said I was fine to keep working."

"I'm betting you didn't mention fourteen-hour days and forgetting to eat were part of what you consider working during your last check-up." I went to Scarlett's first appointment with her —when the doctor officially confirmed she's pregnant—but I was in London last week and missed her second one.

"I didn't see any reason to."

I rake a hand through my hair in frustration. "How about because your husband and father of your child told you to?"

"Would *you* go home in the middle of the day?" she asks me.

"That's a ridiculous hypothetical."

"Because we both know you wouldn't?"

"No, because *you* are the one who is pregnant!"

"Once we're two separate entities, feel free to co-parent to your heart's content."

I step closer, tilting her head up so she has to meet my gaze. "I can't change the way biology works, baby."

She sighs. "I'll eat lunch, I promise. And if I start to not feel well, I'll try to leave the magazine early, okay? I've got to approve the proofs for the next issue."

"Scarlett…"

"I know you're worried. I feel completely fine now, though. There's a lot I need to get done while I still can."

"You need to hire more people," I tell her.

Scarlett seems to handle the amount of responsibility that would usually be divided among four people. She's a perfectionist and a control freak.

"I know."

Something suddenly occurs to me. "What are you doing here?" I was so distracted by making sure she's okay I didn't think to ask before. There's no board meeting today, and that's the only time she's showed up at Kensington Consolidated, aside from handing me the edited prenup.

She gnaws on her lower lip. "I was going to see if you were free for lunch. I should have called—"

The elevator dings as the door opens. "Okay. Let's go to lunch." I nod for her to walk inside and then follow her.

"You were in the middle of a meeting. Go—"

I hit the button for the lobby. "What are you in the mood for?"

Scarlett gives me an exasperated look. "Crew."

"Scarlett." I say her voice in the exact same tone.

She sighs, and I know that I've won this round.

CHAPTER NINETEEN

SCARLETT

C rew watches me devour the cheeseburger with a wide smile on his face. "Hungry?"

I dip a fry in ketchup. "Your kid is a raging carnivore. All I want is fried food, preferably with meat." I take another big bite. Swallow and chew.

"You took your vitamins this morning, right?"

I stick my tongue out at him. "Sounds like you'll be a helicopter parent."

"Teddy's doggy daycare tells me how often you call to check on him, Red."

"Whatever, Sport," is the best retort I can come up with.

I drop a hand to my stomach, which has become an unconscious action as of late. I have to force myself to keep from doing it at work, since Crew is the only person who knows I'm pregnant. But I'm starting to show, so we'll have to announce it soon.

"A baby feels like a lot of responsibility," I tell him. "Before Teddy, I'd never even kept a cactus alive."

He chuckles, and it's become the laugh I compare all other

laughs to. Just the right mixture of husk and rumble. "Is that why you got him? Some sort of parenting dry run?"

"No. I thought this was a ways off." I play with a fry. "I just... I wanted something that felt like *ours*."

"Isn't that the whole point of marriage? The whole *what's mine is yours* shtick?"

"The money? Cars? Planes? Property?" I shake my head. "I meant something I didn't already have."

Crew's expression is serious. He's studying me like I'm a riddle to decode. A puzzle to put together. A question without an answer. "What else is on that list?" he asks. "Aside from a dog?"

I shift uncomfortably under the weight of that question. "I don't know. This baby." He takes a sip of water, studying me the whole time. I try to bite the question back, but it spills out anyway. "Why?"

His answer comes instantly. "I want to give you everything you want."

That blue gaze should come with a warning label. It sears into every inch of me, leaving a brand behind. I expected these feelings for him to reach limits. Instead, they seem to be spreading like a wildfire that can't be contained.

The waitress chooses this moment to reappear, fussing over our empty plates and rambling on about dessert while checking out Crew. He doesn't look at her. I'm the one who breaks eye contact to study the street.

What I want is...him. This life we're building together with a dog and a baby and inside jokes. I want it so badly it scares me.

I'd rather get nothing than get everything...and then lose it.

It's not until Crew climbs out of the car after me that I realize he's not planning to head back to the office. He badgered me into admitting I could get everything I needed to get done today from the penthouse rather than my office, so we came straight here after finishing lunch.

"You can go back to work," I tell him as I step inside the elevator.

"I'm good here," he replies, following me.

His attentiveness makes me uneasy. A day will come when I can't even reach him and I'll remember this—him dropping everything for me—and it will be that much more painful as a result. "I thought you're the bigshot at Kensington Consolidated? At the company party, everyone told me you're the future of the company. Won't they miss you?"

"Scarlett," he says, with more patience than I'm expecting, "I imagine *me* telling *you* how to do your job would go down about as well as a nuclear attack. Do you still hate double standards?"

I have nothing to say to that, which pisses me off. He's right —him telling me how to do *anything*, much less manage *Haute*, would not go over well.

When did he get so good at arguing with me?

The elevator doors open. "I'm going to take a bath."

Without another word, I head up the stairs and into the bathroom that bears clear signs of his presence. We never discussed it, but we share all the same space now. Sleep in the same bed. His suits hang in my closet. There's a second toothbrush by the sink.

I plug the drain and start the hot water running, perching on the rim of the tub and staring out the window as it slowly fills.

I own more bubble bath than one woman really needs, but I don't bother looking through labels. I squeeze a little of each bottle into the water swirling with steam. A decision I regret when there is suddenly a thick layer of bubbles. I shed my clothes and sink through the fragrant suds into the scorching water, using my big toe to turn the tap off.

Despite my resistance earlier, this definitely beats walking around my office in high heels.

I relax in the tub until the bubbles disappear and the water turns cold. The tub drains as I wrap a fluffy robe around myself and shuffle into the bedroom. And stop.

Crew is sprawled out on the bed typing on his laptop. He's changed out of the suit he was wearing earlier into gray sweatpants and a white undershirt.

Corporate Crew is sexy as hell. Casual Crew gives me butterflies.

"Hey," he greets, glancing up as I walk toward him. His gaze lingers on the fact I didn't knot the robe. It hangs open, flashing him just about everything.

I climb atop the comforter on my side of the bed. "I'm starting to show."

"I noticed." Pretty sure he's staring at my boobs, not my baby bump.

"We should decide, you know, how we'll tell people." I rest a hand on the small bulge between my hips. We won't have a choice for much longer, now that I'm almost five months along.

"Like who?"

"Our parents, for starters."

"We always go to the Alps for Christmas. We can tell my

family then, if you want. And we can spend New Year's with your folks."

"Will the Alps be like Thanksgiving was?" A huge, formal affair, in other words. If not for the food served, I would have had no idea it was a dinner party unlike any other.

"No. My dad doesn't invite other people over when we're there."

"Why?"

Crew shrugs. "No idea. He just doesn't."

"So it'll be me, you, your dad, *Candace*, and *Oliver*?"

"Well, I assume we'd bring Teddy."

I roll my eyes. "That's not what I meant."

"I know. And to answer your question, yes, it will probably be awkward."

"Okay."

"You're okay with going?"

I nod. "Yeah."

"Okay. I'll let my dad know." Crew is acting nonchalant, but I can tell this means something to him. He cares about his father and brother, despite their dysfunctionality. He looks at his laptop. "I've got a meeting to call in for. I'll move downstairs."

"You don't have to. You can stay."

His brow wrinkles. "I'll have to talk for parts of it. I don't want to disturb you."

"I'm not a sleeping toddler. And I figured you'd have to talk, since you're Mr. Future CEO." It's not a direct invitation, but it's awfully close to one. I want him to stay. And so I just say that. "I want you to stay."

"Okay," Crew replies, his voice soft. "I'll stay."

I nod and close my eyes. I have proofs to approve, but they should only take me a few hours. My eyelids feel heavy, and I'm warm and comfortable. Full.

Crew's phone beeps as he types in a conference code and waits for approval. "Crew Kensington, is anyone else on the line?" he asks, once the call connects.

"We're all here, sir," a male voice replies.

"Great. Go ahead and get started."

The same male voice begins droning on about deliverables and staffing decisions. Inch by inch, I shift on the comforter until I'm close enough I can feel Crew's body heat. He asks a question I'm too drowsy to comprehend, simultaneously pulling me against him so I'm nestled against his side.

I fall asleep to the sound of his voice talking through contracts as he plays with my hair.

CHAPTER TWENTY

CREW

My small, dysfunctional family is already seated when we board the plane bound for the Alps. My father raises both eyebrows when he takes in the pile of luggage and the dog we have in tow but doesn't comment.

Candace squeals. "What a cute puppy! Did you just get him?"

"No, we've had him for a couple of months," I reply. I don't have the relationship with Candace—with any of my immediate family—where I'd announce the arrival of a canine companion.

My stepmother is too busy petting Teddy to reply. The staff is moving efficiently about the jet, stowing our suitcases and preparing for takeoff.

I take a seat across from my father. "Hi, Dad."

"That animal better not have an accident on here," he comments, sipping at some amber liquid, although it's not even noon.

Teddy tends to get overexcited easily, but I don't mention that.

Scarlett is still standing by the door, talking to one of the stewardesses. She nods and then heads for me, taking the seat next to mine. "Merry Christmas, Arthur."

My father grunts.

Despite the fact it's warm on the plane, Scarlett leaves her down coat on. She's visibly pregnant now, with a slight bump that I find to be the sexiest sight in the world. There's something primal and painfully arousing about the fact she's pregnant with my child.

"No Oliver?"

"He's running late," Candace says, sitting down across the aisle. "Should be here soon."

I nod, not trusting myself to speak. Now that I know about her and Oliver…I can't unknow it.

My brother shows up a few minutes into the awkward silence. His bags are stowed with the rest of ours as he greets us all and makes small talk with my father.

A couple of minutes later, we're in the air. Teddy seems unbothered by the altitude, napping at Scarlett's feet. She's scrolling through something on her phone. I assume it's work-related, but when I sneak a peek at the screen, I discover she's looking at cribs.

I smile before starting to swipe through the documents on my tablet I downloaded to review.

We're a few hours into the flight when the stewardess appears to serve lunch. She distributes each meal and then comes around with drinks. My father's cognac gets refilled. Then it's Candace's turn. She rejects the offered alcohol with, "I can't drink that. I'm pregnant."

Total silence fills the cabin. Even my father looks up from the paper he was reading. "What did you say?"

"I'm pregnant, Arthur. Isn't that exciting?"

Candace sounds bubbly and happy. My father looks shocked. Scarlett looks to me, wide-eyed. It's the same announcement we were planning to make on this trip. Thunder stolen. But I realize why she looks so shocked when she glances at Oliver. His complexion has turned gray.

And all of a sudden, I realize…I'm not certain the baby is my father's.

As soon as I have a chance to, I corner Oliver. We end up in the living room of the chalet, right between the elaborately decorated Christmas tree and a stunning view of the snow-capped mountains.

"Tell me there's no chance it's yours."

He looks away. "I'll talk to her."

I swear. "Oliver, I swear to God, if you—"

"I know I fucked up, Crew. I don't need the perfect son rubbing it in."

"If perfect is *not* fucking our *stepmother*, then it's a damn low bar," I snap. "You need to handle this. Immediately. If Dad suspects… If Candace talks… This could be a total disaster. And it's the last thing I need right now. I've got enough going on, with—"

"With what?"

I glance around to make sure we're still alone. "*Scarlett* is pregnant."

"Whoa." Oliver blinks. "Are you sure…" My glare cuts him off. He clears his throat. "Right. Congrats."

"Thank you. But between that and the Sullivan acquisition that's supposed to go through right before then, this mess is the last thing I need to be worrying about."

"The Sullivan acquisition is set to go through in April."

"I know."

Oliver counts backward, coming to the same conclusion I did when Scarlett's doctor shared the conception date during our first visit—I knocked her up one of our first times. "Damn. Impressive work, little bro."

I roll my eyes. "Keep it to yourself. I haven't told Dad yet."

"He'll be fucking thrilled. More future CEOs."

"I know." And that's why I haven't told him, because some part of me wants him to be excited about becoming a grandfather, nothing else. I know that's why Scarlett hasn't told her parents either. "Deal with Candace, okay?"

Oliver nods. "Yeah, yeah. I will."

Everyone else is already at the table in the formal dining room when Oliver and I walk into the room. I take a seat next to Scarlett, grabbing her thigh and giving it a quick squeeze. Her eyes are filled with questions she can't ask and I can't answer. Not here.

The servers bring out the first course.

My father appears to be in good spirits, which I'm surprised by. I've never gotten the impression he wanted more kids. He and Candace have only been married for a year, and I was surprised he chose to get married again at all. I didn't think the news Candace is expecting would be welcome. And it complicates the possibility it's not even his kid a whole lot.

Dinner is filled with forced pleasantries and discussions of the itinerary for the coming week.

"Can you ski?" I ask Scarlett, while my father presses Oliver about something involving golf. I've never made much of an attempt to understand the sport.

"Like a penguin," she replies.

"So, you waddle?"

She rolls her eyes as she takes a bite of salad. "They navigate snow successfully, okay? Yes, I can ski."

"Well?" I challenge.

"Let's go on a black diamond tomorrow, and you'll find out."

"Deal," I reply, although there's no chance I'll be allowing my pregnant wife to ski down anything other than a bunny hill. I know that's a battle we'll have later—and elsewhere—considering Oliver is the only one who knows and she doesn't know that he knows.

Dinner is followed by Torta di Pane, a lemony bread pudding that's almost as good as the chocolate-covered biscuits I get here, and then everyone disperses. Candace claims jet lag and goes to lie down. Oliver disappears, hopefully to talk with Candace. Scarlett goes to let Teddy out. My dad takes a phone call.

I wander around the first floor until I end up in the study. I haven't been to the chalet since last winter. This is my father's favorite property, so I tend to avoid it. The holidays are usually the only time of year I visit.

The bookshelves and leather furniture look the same. I pour myself a drink from the bar cart in the corner and take a seat in one of the armchairs, looking out the glass doors that lead to the back patio. It's snowing out. The exterior lights illuminate each individual flake as they drift down from the sky.

Scarlett comes into view, decked out in down and trudging through the foot of snow already piled on the ground from a storm before we arrived. Teddy bounces behind her, barking happily. I smile as Scarlett throws an orange tennis ball and Teddy bounds through the drifts after it.

The door to the study opens and my father walks in. He halts when he sees me, obviously expecting to find the space empty.

"I can go," I offer. Knowing him, he has work to get done.

He surprises me by saying "It's fine," and taking a seat in the other armchair. "You've already made yourself at home," he adds, nodding toward the drink in my hand and sounding more like his usual self.

I watch Scarlett throw the tennis ball for Teddy again.

He follows my gaze, taking in the view of the snowy yard for the first time. "Seems like things are going well between you two."

"They are." I pause. "She's pregnant."

My father's smile is wide and full and more genuine than I've seen in a long time. "Well, how about that? Nice work, son. Congratulations."

I shift uncomfortably. Never did I ever think I would have to say this next part to my father as an adult. "Congratulations to you too. Candace seems excited."

My father is silent for a few minutes, adding layers of awkwardness to what already existed. Finally, he speaks. "I had a vasectomy shortly after your mother died."

"Oh." Rather than address the implications of what he's really saying—because *fuck*—I ask, "You didn't want more kids?"

"Only with her."

In the twenty-five years I've known him, it's the most sentimental statement I've ever heard my father utter. "Mom would probably find that romantic."

Everything about this moment is bizarre: the small yet genuine smile on my father's face, talking about my mother like she's more than a ghost we stopped acknowledging as soon as her funeral ended, how it's come about by way of his current's wife revelation.

"No." He swirls the whiskey in the tumbler, a move I recognize. A move I copy. "She'd be disappointed. So, *so* disappointed in me. Losing her was the worst thing I've experienced. I shunned everything that reminded me of her."

I nod. *Everyone*, he means. "She'd forgive you, Dad."

He hums a sound with a subtle undertone of thanks.

I glance outside to see Scarlett and Teddy have disappeared. "I should head upstairs. Scarlett is a light sleeper. I don't want to wake her up."

My father nods as I down the end of my drink and stand. I'm halfway to the door when he speaks. "Crew."

I turn. "Yeah?"

He's looking outside at the snow, not me. "Don't mention any of this to Oliver. Candace isn't one to turn down attention. There's still a chance he's not the father." I'm sure I look like a goldfish. My mouth is gaping, but no sound comes out. He chuckles. Dark and ominous. "I wasn't sure if you knew. Now I do."

I don't say what I'm thinking. That I didn't think *he* knew. I want to ask if he's planning to say anything to Oliver—or Candace—but I sort of don't want to know. Mostly, I want to pretend this conversation never happened. "I suspected."

He's still staring at the yard. "You should probably request a paternity test yourself. Can't be too careful."

Any sympathy or understanding drains away like liquid down an open drain. If he wanted either, he shouldn't have brought her into it. "You're right, Dad. Mom *would* be disappointed in you."

He doesn't so much as flinch. "We need to talk more tomorrow, Crew."

"Fine." I walk out of the study and slam the door behind me.

When I enter the room I'm sharing with Scarlett, she's a lump under the covers. Teddy is curled up in his crate in the corner. He sits up when I close the door behind me. I kneel beside his crate to scratch his ears through the bars. Scarlett is still in the same position when I stand. I walk into the bathroom to get ready for bed before sliding under the covers next to her.

I lie there and stare up at the ceiling I can't see in the dark, trying to pinpoint exactly when my family became so screwed up.

Whoever said money can't buy happiness was clearly onto something. Most of the rich people I know are perpetually unhappy. Wealth provides security. Too much money makes you feel untouchable. And that can easily become dangerous. Higher highs and lower lows.

"What time is it?" Scarlett's groggy voice comes from my left.

"Little past eleven."

She groans. "I went to bed a half hour ago."

"I'm sorry. I tried to be quiet."

"It's not you. I never sleep well the first night in a new place."

We lie in silence, side by side. This is my favorite part of every day: falling asleep beside her.

"Crazy about Candace, huh?"

I can't muffle the snort that escaped. *You have no idea.*

"What?" she demands.

"My dad isn't the father. But…Oliver might be."

Silence. I wonder if she managed to fall back asleep in the thirty seconds it took me to answer her question. Then, I hear it. Muffled at first, until it becomes unmistakable.

Laughter. She's laughing. Harder and less reserved than I've heard her. And maybe people are right about it being contagious —because I start laughing too.

A few minutes ago, when I climbed into bed, I was tense and uncertain and sad. Cynical about how little of privilege feels *real.* It's zeroes in a bank account—nothing tangible. Complimenting people you can't stand. Pretending you're happy when you're not.

Nothing about laughing with Scarlett feels fake. Not the sound of our amusement or the way I suddenly feel loose and light.

My father married Candace. Oliver slept with Candace. Candace made morally gray decisions. The only one I pity is the innocent child who will be affected by those choices.

"Remember when you told me your family wasn't messy?"

I smile in the dark. "I didn't see this coming."

"How do you know your dad isn't the father?"

"According to him, he got a vasectomy. Years ago, after my mom died."

"You believe him?"

"I don't see why he would lie."

"And he never told Candace?"

"Doesn't sound like it. I didn't ask. I think he assumed it would only become an issue…"

"If she cheated," Scarlett finishes.

"Right."

"And how do you know Oliver might be the father?"

I sigh at the reminder. "He told me there's a chance. I talked to him before dinner. He's freaked out by Candace's announcement…to say the least."

Scarlett scoffs. "Yeah, I guess he would be."

"I told my dad you're pregnant," I blurt. "Before we talked about everything else." That seems like an important distinction to make, given what *everything else* entails.

"Did he tell you to get a paternity test?" It's not what I'm expecting her response to be, and the surprise shocks me silent, giving her the correct answer. "*Wow.*"

I stumble through my thoughts, trying to figure out how to respond. I've been careful when it comes to Scarlett and feelings. Not to accumulate them, because I've stacked up plenty. But to express them. I think about her constantly: when I eat, when I'm at work, when I jerk off. I don't pay attention to other women. My mood revolves around hers. I know what all that adds up to. But *I love you* and *paternity test* aren't two phrases that belong in the same conversation.

"I don't need a paternity test."

"Do you *want* one?" she counters.

"*No.* No," I repeat. I reach over and tug her toward me, so her back is to my front. I rest my palm on her stomach, cradling the slight swell.

"I trust you, Red." Short of the l-word, it's the strongest declaration I can make. The list of people I trust—unequivocally—is a short one. It starts and ends with her. "With everything. About everything."

For an agonizing moment, she's silent and still. Then she shifts away. I roll onto my back, accepting the distance she clearly wants. But the sheets keep moving. I feel them yank and loosen as I squint over at her side of the bed, trying to figure out what she's doing.

I get my answer when her body presses against mine. Heat radiates from her skin as she twists so she's lying more on me than the mattress. My arm curls around her involuntarily, and I realize she's now naked.

She reaches into my boxers and pulls out my cock. I groan. "Scarlett…"

"I can't fall asleep without this now," she informs me. "Without you. It's fucking annoying."

My lips turn up into a grin I doubt she can see. "It's fucking something."

Then I'm swallowing her moans with my mouth and spreading her legs with my hips and pushing inside her with a groan. We both come in minutes, using each other in an unfamiliar yet familiar way. There aren't any dirty words or daring positions. It's sweet without nothings. Tender without lingering touches. Quick without rushing.

Scarlett stays tangled on my side of the bed after we've both come. I run my fingers through the long, silky strands of her hair, matching my breathing to hers. It's deep and even. I think she's fallen back asleep—until she speaks. "I trust you too."

I keep combing through her hair, feeling those four words expand in my chest. I know that she does. She's told me so before. More importantly, she's shown it—when she trusted me about Hannah. But I'll never get sick of hearing it.

My limbs grow heavy as I relax into the mattress. I'm close to sleep, maybe already asleep, when the sharp screech of an alarm jerks me alert.

Scarlett tenses. "What is that?"

"I think it's the fire alarm." I climb out of bed, trying to stay calm when I'm anything but. There are fireplaces in every room of the chalet. One stray spark can ignite fast. Visions of scorched walls and raging flames fill my head. I shove worst-case scenarios away as I climb out of bed and get dressed in a pair of joggers and a sweatshirt.

Scarlett is sitting up in bed, still naked. I toss a pair of sweatpants onto the bed. "Put those on." It takes a minute, but she does. I pick her silk nightgown up off the ground and pull it over her head. Her down coat is draped over a chair. I help her into it rather than rely on her doing it herself.

"It's probably a false alarm," she tells me.

"You think that's a risk I would take with you?"

She doesn't reply, just steps into the snow boots I set out for her. I grab Teddy's leash and collar and open his crate. He bounds out, thrilled by this development. Must be nice to be a dog—woefully oblivious to what might go wrong. Eternally optimistic.

I usher Scarlett toward the door. When I open it, I half-expect for there to be smoke and flames. The hallway appears empty and untouched. But the scent of smoke *does* hang in the air. My grip on Scarlett's hand and Teddy's leash remain tight as we walk down the hall and the stairs. The smoke is thicker downstairs. I can actually see it swirling in the air, rather than just smell it.

The front door is wide open. I herd my little family outside. Oliver, my father, and Candace are all huddled out on the front porch.

"What's going on?" I basically bark, looking at the exterior of the chalet. It appears untouched, the stone façade and soaring windows showing no signs of fire or charred damage.

"Candace was trying to make cookies." My father's voice is dry. Unimpressed.

"Oh."

"I'm so sorry," Candace says. "I don't know what happened." She eyes our mismatched outfits. "You all were already in bed?"

I nod.

Scarlett is falling asleep against me by the time the alarm is shut off and the house has been aired out. She stumbles her way up the stairs, resisting my attempts to carry her. Stubborn, as always.

We reach our room and she pulls off her clothes, leaving them as a trail across the carpet. I put Teddy in his crate and get undressed again, sliding back into bed beside her.

"Not exactly an uneventful trip, huh?" Scarlett teases, as she rolls over and rests her head on my chest.

I chuckle. "Not exactly."

I'm nearly asleep when I hear a buzzing sound. Scarlett stirs. I quickly grab my phone, intent on silencing it. But the screen is black.

More buzzing. Scarlett scoots back to her side of the bed and grabs her phone. Twin lines appear between her eyes as she squints at the screen.

"It's my mom." She answers. "Mom?"

Even before she speaks again, I know something is wrong. Her shoulders tense and her lips press together.

"Okay. I'll be there as soon as I can." She ends the call. Drops her phone on the bed. Stares blankly ahead. "My dad had a heart attack. He's in surgery."

I throw the covers back. "Let's go."

CHAPTER TWENTY-ONE

SCARLETT

Less than twenty-four hours after leaving and days before I was supposed to return, I end up back in New York. I'm sleep-deprived and stressed, to the point the watercolor print I'm staring at has turned into a meaningless blur of pastel. I wonder who decorates hospital waiting rooms. Who gets to choose the framed artwork you'll stare at and the color of the chairs you'll sit in during the worst hours of your life?

The trip back to New York was a blur. I watched it unfold like a movie, not as a participant. And I was able to because Crew handled everything. Our luggage, his family, chartering the flight back, the car waiting at the airport to bring us to New York General in record time. I found out my father was in surgery while I was thousands of miles away. Now I'm in the same building, and he's still cut open on an operating table.

I'm exhausted, but this plastic chair is too uncomfortable to fall asleep in. My mother is sitting next to me, pale and silent. The only reaction I've gotten out of her since I arrived was when she saw Crew came back with me. She was surprised. My parents' marriage doesn't show up during the best of times. Seeing mine do so in the worst of them was clearly a shock.

It didn't even occur to me to fight Crew on coming back with me, but her stunned expression made me think I should have. Made me realize how much I rely upon him now. If he hadn't been next to me when my mother called, he would have been the first person I told about my father's heart attack.

My relationship with my father is complicated. It always has been. He wanted a son, not a daughter. A dutiful child, not the rebel I turned into. I love him, but it's mostly an obligatory sort of affection. I resent him for how he treats my mother—how he treats me. For being embarrassed by my ambition instead of encouraging it. If I'd refused to marry a Kensington, I'm not sure we'd still have any sort of relationship.

He might die. I'm no doctor, but the fact the surgery is taking so long doesn't seem like a good sign. And if he dies, he'll never meet my child. My motivations for not telling my parents about the pregnancy are mostly petty. I wanted my father to see this baby as a grandchild, not an heir. He would have been thrilled to hear his bloodline is continuing. Now he may never know.

My mother keeps checking her watch. It's annoying, the small motion that catches my attention every time she does it. But I don't ask her to stop; I don't have a better way to distract her. The only way I can think of is blurting news that shouldn't be delivered in a somber, impersonal waiting room while she's waiting to learn if she's a widow.

I wish Crew was still here. He went to take Teddy and our luggage back to the penthouse.

A man wearing a set of scrubs appears in the open doorway and heads our way. We both stand in tandem as he approaches. "Mrs. Ellsworth?"

"Yes," my mother replies. Her voice is tight and tense, pulled taut.

The surgeon looks to me. "Are you a relative?"

"I'm his daughter."

He nods. "Well, I'm pleased to report Hanson pulled through the surgery. He's got a long road of recovery ahead, but there's no reason to think he won't make a complete one. He's lucky the ambulance arrived so quickly and we were able to get him in the OR immediately. He's being transferred to recovery right now. I'll have a nurse let you know when you can see him. All right?"

My mother's sigh of relief is audible. "Thank you so much, doctor."

The man smiles before he leaves. My mother sinks back down into her seat. She was cagey on the phone—and when I arrived—on details about what exactly happened. The surgeon's comments—about details my mother didn't already know—clarifies things some. She wasn't there when he had the heart attack.

"He was with another woman, wasn't he? She's the one who made sure the ambulance *arrived so quickly*?"

My mother holds my gaze. Doesn't look away or fiddle with anything or make excuses. "Yes."

I sigh. Shake my head. "Why do you stay with him, Mom? Why do you put up with it?"

"It's how things are, Scarlett. You know that."

"But it's not how they have to be. Dad isn't worth it. Let him go."

"And do what?"

Get a life sounds too harsh. "I don't know... Be happy?" I hear a younger Scarlett in the suggestion. One less jaded. One who believed in happy endings.

She laughs. "Oh, sweetheart. This life *is* what makes me happy. Being

Josephine Ellsworth is who I want to be. Your father is far from perfect, but he's a good man. I knew exactly what we'd be when I met him for the first time. Everything that we would never be. I made my peace with it before we got married."

"What do you mean?"

"We wanted the same things. He needed a wife. I wanted a husband. Our fathers agreed, and that was that."

"I'm aware how an arranged marriage works," I say, tone dry. She used to tell me their marriage hadn't been arranged, that they were in love, and it was just another lie. Part of the perfect family façade to try on when it suited. I pretend I don't care. "I'm in one, remember?"

My mother smiles. It's the same one she always gives me when she thinks I'm being ridiculous. "No, you're not."

I give her a look thick with disbelief. "You planned the wedding."

"Yes, I did. I saw it then and I see it now. That boy is in love with you, Scarlett."

I'm so shocked by her words, I can barely blink. I know Crew cares. Things between us have evolved into a friendship and a comfort I never imagined our marriage might contain. But love? My mother is in shock. Her husband had a heart attack and was found with his mistress. But still… "You're delusional."

"No, honey. That's *you*." My mother has perfected the art of spewing condescension in a sweet tone. It layers every syllable. "Why do you think he came all this way?"

I swallow, and admit, "I'm pregnant."

My mother's face lights up. "Really?"

I nod. "It's…confused things between us. I'm hormonal, and it's just… He's a good guy."

It's not the full truth. Lines blurred between me and Crew long before two of them appeared on the pregnancy test. But it's the story I'm sticking with when it comes to my mother. I wish we had the sort of relationship where I could confess everything that's happened between us. The way Crew makes me feel.

But we don't, and it's never bothered me more than it does right now. I've always prided my independence. I'm not the spoiled rich girl who has her every whim catered to. My default appearance is poised and prepared. But right now, I want to fall apart.

Crew walks into the waiting room, and my heart does a silly little skip.

"Any news?" he asks, taking the seat beside me.

"He's out of surgery. Should make a full recovery." I share the update like it's a weather report. But I don't feel obligated to play the loving daughter in front of Crew. I know he won't judge me.

"Good."

My mother leans forward. "Congratulations, Crew. Scarlett shared the happy news about the baby."

He doesn't look surprised I told my mother. "Thank you. We're excited." His hand squeezes my thigh.

My mother gives me a pointed look. I ignore it; she's in no position to be doling out relationship advice.

"You should go get some sleep, sweetie," she tells me. "You look exhausted."

"I haven't slept in…" I try to count the hours. "A while."

"Go. Your father will be out of it for a while. I'll send you any updates."

"Okay." It doesn't take much for me to agree. Sitting on hard plastic while my mother justifies her money-motivated decision to stay with my father hasn't been a blast.

Silently, Crew stands and offers me his hand.

I take it. "Bye, Mom."

It feels wrong, leaving her sitting there all alone. I can't picture my father holding a vigil if the roles were reversed. Never before have I tried to analyze my parents' relationship this closely. I just took it at face value. I know why I'm peering closer now—I have something to compare it to. I want everything they're not.

Crew says nothing as we leave the hospital and climb into the waiting car. It's dark out. I don't know what time it is. What day it is, even.

I stare out the window, seeing nothing. Even once we pull into the garage, my eyes don't focus. My limbs don't move.

The door on my side of the car opens. Crew leans in, unbuckling my seat belt and lifting me into his arms.

I press my face against his warm neck, inhaling the familiar scent of his cologne. "You smell good."

"I showered."

His steps are sure and solid as he walks over to the elevators. I don't open my eyes.

"He was with his mistress when it happened. Not my mom. She doesn't care. She says she never cared. I hope that's true, or else I'm screwed." I squeeze my eyes tighter. "I can't even remember the last time I was this tired," I mumble. "And I'm always tired." Crew somehow manages to hold me and also flash the card to get the elevator moving. "You're so strong." I sigh. "I feel like everything is falling apart. Like *I* am."

His grip on me tightens. "Nothing is falling apart, Red. Everything is fine. Your dad will be fine."

"I know. I'm relieved. You know why? Because my first thought when I heard he had a heart attack was that if he died, I would have had to take over Ellsworth Enterprises. Or sell it. Or…I don't even know what I would have done. How sad is that?"

"It's understandable. Your relationship with him is complicated."

"*All* of my relationships are complicated."

The doors open with a *ding*. I open my eyes to the familiar sight of the entryway to the penthouse I've started thinking of as *ours*, not *mine*. Crew doesn't set me down and I don't ask him to. He just strides for the stairs.

"Have you talked to your dad?" I ask.

Crew shakes his head. "I'm sure he'll call about something work-related soon. Until then, I'm not getting involved in the Candace drama."

I blink. "Wow. I completely forgot about that."

"You've had a lot going on."

"You should talk to them, Crew."

I used to think that Arthur and Oliver were closer than Arthur and Crew. That Oliver resented Crew for usurping and outshining him. But I realized Crew is the glue holding his family together on the flight to the Alps. Arthur and Oliver both rely on him to handle whatever needs handling. I don't like that I've become another burden Crew has to carry—literally, at the moment. I lean on him, need him, rely on him, and he's never needed my support the same way.

"You should sleep." He lays me down on the soft fabric of my comforter. "Staying up all night can't be good for the baby." I can't distinguish his concern for me from his concern for the baby. He carried me to bed once before I was pregnant. Would he have carried me tonight if I wasn't?

"I tried to sleep on the plane," I mutter.

"I know, baby." The soft tone of his voice temporarily soothes my worries.

"My dad is fine. You can go back to the chalet. Spend Christmas with your dad and brother. Your family."

He says nothing for a long minute. I don't want him to go, and I'm worried he took it the wrong way—that I do. I wish it were brighter in here. The hall light doesn't illuminate his whole face; most of it is shadowed. I can't see his expression, but I can feel something pulsing in the air between us. Before I can decide what it is, he speaks. "My family is right here."

Five words, and they decide more between us than the two-hundred-page document that was supposed to govern this arrangement. If our story had a different start, I'd respond to that sentence with three. I'd admit he's become my whole world. The first thing I think about when I wake up and the last before I fall asleep. The first person I'd call with good news or bad. *My* family.

Pretty promises can be deceptive. All I hear in Crew's words are truth. Not ugly, but real.

Before my tired brain can come up with a response, he stands and moves away. "Get some sleep, Red."

The bedroom door closes, and I'm alone in the dark. I realize maybe you don't have to have already experienced something to know you're experiencing it for the first time. My emotional experience with men is laughably limited, as in nonexistent. I was so busy teaching myself not to get hurt, I never let anyone close.

Crew Kensington doesn't just have the ability to hurt me.

He holds the power to destroy me, if he ever decides to use it.

CHAPTER TWENTY-TWO

CREW

I'm running on the treadmill when Asher calls. I debate answering. I slept poorly in the guest room I used to inhabit. Scarlett is still sleeping. I didn't want to disturb her last night.

When he calls for a second time, I answer. Before I can say a word, he asks. "What the fuck is going on? Is it true?"

I falter. "Is what true?"

"Is Kensington Consolidated getting investigated for insider trading?"

Shock freezes up my limbs. I almost fall on my face. "What? Where did you hear that?"

Asher swears. "Where didn't I? It's all over the place, Crew. Papers, television, online. Lead story. Front page. I had to go into the back entrance of the office to avoid the fifty reporters outside."

We need to talk more tomorrow, Crew.

Realization hits me like a sack of bricks when I recall my father's parting words the last time we spoke. He wasn't talking about Scarlett or Candace. Dread trickles down my spine.

I turn the treadmill off and collapse on the floor, breathing heavily. Talk about a shitstorm of a week. My brother potentially knocking up our stepmother, Hanson Ellsworth's heart attack, and now this.

"I don't know," I admit.

"Aren't you with your dad?"

"No. Scarlett's father had a heart attack yesterday. We're back in New York."

Asher inhales. "Shit. Is Hanson going to pull through?"

"He should be fine."

There's a beat of silence. "This is a five-alarm fire, Crew. People are panicking. Phones are ringing off the hook. Stock is off the cliff."

I scrub at my face. "Who broke the story first?"

"I don't know. Why?"

"I need you to find out."

"Crew, we're way past the point of containment. This shit is everywhere. Discrediting one source isn't going to—"

"True or not, someone leaked this," I interrupt. "I want to know who."

Asher sighs. "Okay. I'll do some digging."

I hang up and call my father. Voicemail. Call Oliver. Same.

My feeling of foreboding grows. They knew about this. Both of them.

My next call is to Brent Parsons, the head of Kensington Consolidated's legal team. Luckily for him—assuming he wants to keep his job—he answers on the first ring. "Parsons."

"It's Crew. You've seen the news?"

"Reading it now."

"What's your gut?"

"There was definitely an investigation. Too many details to be totally fabricated. But if the feds had anything solid, we would have found about this very differently. Whoever leaked this probably did us a favor."

"A *favor*? Stock has dropped ten points in an hour, Brent."

"This came out sooner than they wanted. We can hit back while they still have nothing. Defamation. Document requests. I'm already coordinating with public relations on putting out a statement. Assuming there's no smoking gun, we'll be fine." He hesitates. "Unless there's anything you need to tell me?"

"If there is, I don't know it."

Brent sighs. "That's probably for the best. I'll keep you in the loop on everything. Do you want me to copy Arthur as well?"

"No. Everything goes through me."

"You got it."

I hang up and stalk down the hallway to take a shower. The door to our bedroom is still shut, so I head to the guest room's bathroom. The hot water washes away the sweat, but none of the worries.

I should have taken Royce Raymond's offer. If I had, I wouldn't be in the middle of this shitstorm, all alone. With a pregnant wife. A kid on the way who's supposed to inherit this burning legacy.

When I enter the kitchen, Phillipe is standing at the stove, cooking. "Merry Christmas, Mr. Kensington," he greets.

And...*of course* it's fucking Christmas. 'Tis the season for corporate espionage.

"Merry Christmas, Phillipe," I reply. I rub my forehead, feeling the few hours of sleep I'm running on. "You didn't need to come in today. I didn't even realize..."

He smiles. "It's no trouble. The usual this morning?"

"Yes, please."

I take a seat at the table and scroll through the news as Phillipe cooks my omelet. Asher wasn't exaggerating. It *is* everywhere. I scroll a few articles and get the gist of the story. There aren't any concrete details, and that gives me some reassurance.

After eating breakfast, I end up on the living room couch, working on my laptop. I need to go into the office, but I don't want Scarlett to wake up all alone.

It's past eleven when she comes downstairs with wet hair, wearing a silk pajama set.

"Hey." She stops a few feet away, running a hand through her hair self-consciously.

"Hi." I close my laptop and lean forward. "It's, uh, Christmas."

Her eyes widen. "Shit, really?"

"Really."

"Wow. I'll…I can get dressed. I feel like I should stop by the hospital, but we can go do something after, if you want?"

I *do* want. Badly. I want nothing more than to drink hot chocolate and go skating and look at elaborate decorations and whatever other touristy shit people do here during the holidays that I'd normally look down upon. As long as I do it with her. But I can't. And I have to tell her why. "I can't. I have to go into the office."

"On Christmas? You were supposed to have this whole week off."

"That was before."

"Before what?"

I nod toward the muted television. The banner at the bottom says the words I can't seem to. *Kensington Consolidated Investigated for Insider Trading*, it reads.

"Fuck," Scarlett breathes.

"Yep."

"Is it…true?"

"I have no idea. But I've got to handle it, either way."

"Can this take down the company?"

"I don't know." I rest my elbows on my knees and scrub my hands over my face. "The legal team is working on it. My dad and Oliver aren't taking my calls."

"What does that mean?"

"It means they knew about this and kept me out of the loop."

"Maybe they were trying to protect you," Scarlett suggests softly.

"Fuck that. This is my family's company. My legacy. I'm supposed to be the next CEO."

"You didn't know anything about this. You didn't do anything wrong. If you have to, you can start over. Start your own company."

"If this goes that far, the Kensington name won't be worth much."

"Money talks."

"Most of mine is tied up in this sinking ship."

"*I* have money, Sport."

"And you married me for mine." I stand and grab my laptop. "So I'd better go bail out this ship, huh?"

"Crew…"

"I'm sorry I can't go to the hospital with you. I'm going to drive myself to the office. If you want Roman to take you, just give him a call."

"Okay," she says.

"Okay," I repeat.

I walk over and kiss her. It's brief and sweet.

She grabs the inside of my elbow, holding me in place for a minute.

"Merry Christmas, Red."

"Merry Christmas, Sport."

The meetings last for hours. I'm drained and irritated by the time I head back toward my office.

Asher is waiting. His feet aren't up on my desk. If I'd ever told him why this hunk of wood holds sentimental value, I know he never would have put them up in the first place. Probably why I never did. Not many people challenge me.

"Nathaniel Stewart."

"What about him?" I ask.

"You wanted the name. He was the leak."

I sink down into my chair. "How reliable is your source?"

"Kiera Ellis. Her father is—"

"I know who her father is." The biggest media mogul in the country.

"There's more to come, apparently. Nathaniel claims he has some of our internal documents. Damning ones." Asher raises a brow. "Do those exist?"

"No idea."

Asher shakes his head. "I'll admit the guy made a few good investments. But he's a bottom feeder at best. Coming after Kensington Consolidated makes no sense."

I know exactly why he's doing it, but I keep that to myself. Good leadership is knowing when to share—and when to shut up.

"I'll take care of him."

Asher shakes his head. "Plotting revenge on Christmas? That's the Crew Kensington I know. For a while, I thought you'd gone soft."

"Scarlett is pregnant."

Asher whistles and leans back in his chair. "Already?"

"All it takes is one time."

"*Right.* I'm sure you've had sex with your hot wife just the once." He pauses. "Are you freaking out?"

"No." I don't correct his assumption that this is a recent development.

"Are you experiencing *any* emotions?" His tone is exasperated.

"Some."

"Like…"

"I can't picture my life without her."

"I meant about the spawn you sired, Crew."

"I know what you meant. But the baby isn't here. It's the size of a peach or something. She is."

"Then go home and be with her."

I want to. But I know what I'll have to ask when I do. And it's not a conversation I'm looking forward to.

Scarlett is curled up on the couch with Teddy when I get home, eating popcorn. I shrug off my suit jacket and loosen my tie as I walk into the living room, wishing I was in sweatpants like she is.

"Hey." Her voice is soft. Hesitant. Unsure.

"Hi." I take a seat near her feet. Teddy crawls over to lick my hand.

"How did it go?"

"Too soon to tell. I've got to wait a few things out."

She nods.

"How is your dad?"

"He was sleeping. The doctors said that's normal. There don't seem to be any complications so far."

"That's good."

"Yeah."

I inhale. Exhale. Chew the inside of my cheek. "I found out who leaked the investigation to the press."

"Really?"

"It was Nathaniel Stewart."

I watch her reaction closely. See her eyes widen. Her lips part. "Seriously?"

"I trust my source."

"Why would he do that?"

I hold her gaze. "I think you know why."

Her hazel eyes narrow. "I told you. *Nothing* happened between us."

"I know. I believe you. He and my father were working on a deal. I put an end to it."

"Because of me?"

"Because of you," I confirm.

"Why?"

"Because you're mine."

She scoffs. "Real mature, Crew."

"It was also a risky deal. But I wouldn't have bothered if it were with anyone else."

"Is there a point to this conversation?" Her tone has turned sharp. Icy.

I seethe, silently. "Nathaniel claims he has documents. *Internal* documents. Documents like...the ones you requested."

She sucks in a sharp breath. "Are you fucking kidding me?"

"I'm not accusing you of anything. I *trust you*, Scarlett. I just need to know...did you tell him anything about the company? Is there anything he could use or twist or bluff—"

She stands, toppling half the pillows off the couch. "I can't believe you. Are you seriously asking me this?"

I stand too. "I'm in the dark here, Scarlett. This...*tornado* just landed right on top of the company I'm first in line to inherit. People are relying on me. To lead, to keep their jobs, to save this company. If there's anything you know, I just..."

My voice trails when I realize a horrifying fact.

She's crying. Clear liquid streaks down her cheeks in shimmering trails. "I'm the reason you're first in line."

I step forward. "Red..."

She steps back, swiping angrily at her cheeks. "Fuck. You. Why don't you just make me wear a wire if you think I'm going around spilling company secrets to any guy that so much as smiles at me?"

I rub my jaw, trying to figure out where this conversation veered so far off course. I didn't want to bring Nathaniel up. I knew it would be a sore spot. But I had no idea it would become *this*. "That's *not* what I'm saying. I trust you. I just—"

"There's no *just*, Crew. You're doubting me, and I've *never* doubted you. I can't believe I—" She shakes her head. "Anything Nathaniel knows about Kensington Consolidated, he didn't learn it from me. Happy?"

I'm about the furthest from happy a person can get right now. "No."

"Yeah. Me neither. Merry fucking Christmas."

I watch her stomp up the stairs.

Merry fucking Christmas, indeed.

I end up back at the office. *When in doubt, work*, as the Kensington family motto goes. I'm used to spending late nights and long hours inside these four walls.

I envy the employees who feel like they earned their position here. I still don't. Maybe I never will. Some second-guessing is healthy. I don't think never feeling like you're working hard enough is.

Except, today, maybe for the first time, I saw it.

Respect.

Today was the most tumultuous day Kensington Consolidated has experienced since my great-grandfather took a small loan and turned it into an empire. Yet no one asked where my father was. Where Oliver was. They did exactly what I asked without question. Listened to me without questioning or whispering behind my back. And the one person I'm endlessly trying to impress—my father—wasn't even here to see it.

And this same shitstorm made a mess between me and the one person whose feelings I care about.

I spend a couple of hours going through emails and reports. Today was spent doing damage control. Everything else was shoved to the back burner, but still needs to be dealt with.

When I finish, I pour myself a generous splash of bourbon and sprawl out on the leather couch in the corner of my office, debating whether I should go home or just sleep here. I sip and stare at the ceiling.

The knock on the door startles me. I was certain I was the only one here at this hour. I'm not entirely shocked to see Isabel is the one opening the door. She was here all day, by my side, doing anything she could to help. "Hey."

"Hey," I reply. "I didn't realize anyone was still here."

"Same. I saw the light on under the door on my way back from the restroom."

I sit up and run a hand through my hair. "What are you still doing here?"

She walks over and takes a seat on the couch next to me. "Working."

"At…" I glance at the clock. "Ten thirty? On Christmas?"

Isabel shrugs. "I'm not a big holiday person."

That doesn't surprise me at all. Although it occurs to me, I know hardly anything about Isabel outside of her professional aspirations. "Me neither."

"Is that why you're here?"

I sigh. Down more bourbon. "No. I fucked things up with Scarlett."

"Oh?"

"We had a fight. It was my fault. I just—I didn't expect it to be like this, you know? She—we—weren't supposed to feel so real." I drain the rest of my glass before standing and walking over to the bar cart, refilling my glass before I sink down beside her, slouching back against the couch. "Quite the damn day, huh?"

Isabel leans back, mirroring my posture. "Yeah." She pauses. "The board's vote will be unanimous, you know."

"Vote about what?"

"Making you CEO."

"I've got the right last name."

"You've got a lot more than that, Crew." Her left hand migrates to my knee. Before I've had time to process the touch, she's sliding up my thigh with a clear destination in mind.

I'm frozen. Shocked. For some reason, this wasn't an outcome I imagined when she entered this office. And it would be easy to let this unfold. Emotionless and empty, exactly what I used to expect from sex. Scarlett would never need to know. Maybe she wouldn't even care after our argument earlier.

But *I* would know. *I* would care. My brain is processing what my body already knows: I only want Scarlett. My dick isn't even reacting. And I haven't had *that* much to drink.

I stand abruptly, leaving Isabel on the couch with a wounded expression. "Go."

"Crew…"

"I said *go*, Isabel. I'm your boss. If you want to keep your job, you'll never touch me inappropriately again."

She stands, some defiance mixing with the hurt. "I won't tell anyone about us. You can trust me."

"There is no us, and I don't trust you, Isabel. I'm *married*."

Isabel scoffs. "Not happily."

"I. Don't. Want. You. Don't test me, Isabel. You won't like the consequences."

Reality and stubbornness fight for space in her expression. "I've had a crush on you since I started here, you know. I should have made a move sooner. Apparently, I was the only person in this city unaware you were engaged to Scarlett Ellsworth. What I get for avoiding gossip, huh? But then everyone said she was cold and detached and only in it for the money. So I thought I still had a shot."

I sigh, suddenly exhausted. "I *am* happily married, Isabel."

She gives me a small, sad smile. "Yeah, I figured that out when you jumped away like I'd set the couch on fire."

"I didn't know you felt that way. If you want to transfer to another team, I can—"

"*No*. No, it won't be an issue. I promise."

I study her for a minute, weighing her sincerity. "I don't give second chances."

She swallows and bobs a nod. "I know."

"Good."

I watch her leave, then sink down behind my desk. If Asher

ever caught wind of what just happened, I wouldn't hear the end of it for a while. He's the one who insisted Isabel had feelings for me. After her questions about Scarlett, I thought we'd moved past it. Thought she knew it would never happen. Even if Isabel had expressed interest sooner. I kept sex uncomplicated—and sleeping with a member of the board wasn't that. And now... I've never explicitly promised Scarlett fidelity. But up until the opportunity to cheat was dropped in my lap—literally—doing so didn't occur to me.

My phone vibrates with a text from my brother.

Oliver: *I know you've seen the news. We're back in NY. Meet you at the office at 8.*

I stumble as I stand, either from the whiskey or the exhaustion catching up to me. But my steps are steady as I leave my exit and head toward the elevators. There's no sign of Isabel, nor anyone else.

I know driving is a bad idea, so I flag a cab once I reach the street and give the driver the address for my family's estate just outside of the city. The trip takes twenty minutes. I start to feel the buzz of alcohol about ten minutes in. But it doesn't deter me.

After paying the driver and punching in the code, I walk through the front door. Automatically, my feet veer to the right, toward my father's study. There's already a light on, but I'm more focused on collapsing onto the couch than squinting at my surroundings.

"I hope you didn't drive here," my father comments, rising from behind his mahogany desk and walking over to the fireplace. He pours himself a glass of scotch and takes a seat in one of the chairs that flank the stone façade.

"Is it true?" I ask the ceiling.

My father sighs. Ice clinks as he swirls his glass. "It's not quite as bad as the press is saying. But yes, there were some questions being asked. It was being handled."

"Dammit, Dad. Why didn't you tell me?"

"So you could say exactly what you've been telling everyone all day: you had no idea."

"You should have told me. I'm supposed to be the future CEO!"

"Nothing future about it. I'm stepping down. It will be official by the end of the week."

"I—are you fucking kidding me? You're handing me the keys to the castle...while it's under attack?"

"Don't be so dramatic. The company will be fine."

"And if it's not?" I snap. "What the fuck then?

"They can't touch our personal fortune, Crew."

I exhale and sit up, relieved the walls stay where they should. "Did you do it?"

"No." My father's answer is swift and sure. "But...it happened."

"What do you mean, *it happened*?"

"Beckett Stanley was leaking information. I found out what he was doing, and I took care of it."

"Not by telling the authorities, I gather."

"You know the issues that would have caused. I got rid of him and appointed Isabel to the board in his place."

I scoff. "*Issues*. Sort of like the issues we're dealing with now?"

"There's no evidence. They won't be able to do anything."

I press my palms to my eyes and groan. "Jesus, Dad."

My father studies me like I'm a science experiment. "What's the real issue?"

"There needs to be another issue other than being investigated and having stock in free fall and—"

"*Crew*."

"She married me for my money," I bite out. "She married the future CEO of a billion-dollar company. Not…this. She'll get questions. It might even affect *Haute* and *rouge*."

My father blinks, appearing genuinely off-guard. "This is about Scarlett?"

"Do I have another wife?" I snap. I look at my hands, clenching them into fists. "I love her, Dad. I love her so fucking much. I'm pissed at you and I'm worried about the company, but I'm fucking terrified this will change everything between us."

A slight raise of his eyebrow is my father's only response to the whiskey-fueled declaration. Normally, I'd rather chew on razor blades than discuss this with my father. "You have more to offer her than money, Crew."

One of the nicer things my father has ever said to me. But… "She married me *for* my money," I repeat.

"She's the sole heir to billions and is making tens of millions off that magazine and clothing line. You really think she married you for money? She didn't need to get married, and she didn't need the money. Scarlett picked you. She chose to marry you."

"Her father told her to," I mumble.

"Because they're so close? Because she's easily manipulated?"

I scoff.

My father knows how to employ sarcasm. Who knew? "You must have wondered why the engagement was between you and her, not Oliver and her?"

"Oliver needed to travel and manage the international holdings, while I would make New York my home base and strengthen the family business brand." I parrot the line he told the two of us for years.

"I decided that later. When Hanson and I first spoke about a potential arrangement, the agreement was that *Oliver* and Scarlett would get married. He's oldest and stands to inherit just as much as you do. It was the logical choice, on the face of things."

I look up. "What?"

My father strokes his chin, looking at the fire, not me. "Hanson came back to me a year later, when you were sixteen and Oliver was almost an adult. Said he would honor the agreement, but only if it changed to *you* and Scarlett. He was adamant about it. Something—someone—changed his mind. The only reason I ever figured he changed the terms was…he told her."

I'm the reason you're first in line.

I thought she meant our marriage when she said that.

"Don't assume she didn't choose you, Crew."

With those parting words, my father leaves me in his dark study with a head spinning from a lot more than just alcohol.

CHAPTER TWENTY-THREE

SCARLETT

I wake up alone. Crew's side of the bed is empty and cold. If he came home last night, he didn't sleep next to me. I tossed and turned most of the night, so I'm confident I would have heard him come in. The realization he didn't creeps in slowly, with plenty of other doubts I try to push aside.

I shower, then dry my hair and apply a light layer of makeup. Enough to cover the dark circles below my eyes and, of course, some red lipstick.

Armor feels especially important today. I pull on a pair of black tights and a gray sweater dress. It's off-the-shoulder and loose without being baggy, camouflaging my small bump. At this point, my pregnancy is somewhat of an open secret. I doubt anyone I work with has missed the fact that I stopped drinking coffee, walk around carrying a granola bar, and occasionally run to the bathroom at inopportune times. Despite how strained our relationship is, it feels strange to tell my employees I'm pregnant before my own father. He was sleeping when I visited him yesterday, which was honestly a relief. My father and I don't have much to say to each other under the best of circumstances.

Before I head downstairs, I peek into the guest bedroom Crew slept in when he first moved in. It's empty, the bed neatly made and unwrinkled.

I'm stunned by how harsh and hard the panic hits. I thought I'd be okay if things between me and Crew ever went south. There's a saying: how you'll never know how much you want something until it's gone. That's not how I feel. I already knew how much I want him. I didn't know the pain of possibly losing him would feel this visceral, how I wouldn't be prepared for falling apart.

So, I do what I always do. I shove the pesky emotions far down and go to work.

The office isn't as busy as it would be on a normal Thursday, but it's far from empty. Prep work for the February issue is in full swing, which has become my professional focus now that *rouge* has officially launched. Approving the groundwork—from the branding to the hiring—has given me some flexibility in how much time I spend juggling my two endeavors. So has the reality I'll have to take a stretch of time off in a few months.

Leah approaches as soon as she sees me step out of the elevator. "Good morning!"

"Good morning." My greeting is decidedly less cheery than Leah's.

"I'm so sorry about your father."

I sigh. "Thank you. He'll be fine, we think."

"Oh, good. How was your Christmas?"

"Could have been better," I admit. "Yours?"

"It was nice. My parents are visiting."

"You should go, then. I told you to take today off."

"But you're here."

"I can manage. Just let me know…" I glance up to see Leah is no longer paying attention to me. She's focused behind me, on something.

Someone.

I glance over one shoulder. Sure enough, Crew is stepping out of the elevator I left minutes ago, headed straight toward me.

Most of the time, *Haute*'s open layout is convenient. I can quickly assess who is at their desk. Different departments can collaborate.

Right now, it's fucking *inconvenient*. More people than I realized were even in the office today are poking their heads out of cubicles and from behind partitions, straining to get a better look. When I've been the subject of office gossip before, it wasn't firsthand.

Up until *now*.

This is primetime entertainment.

"What are you doing here?" I snap.

He looks good. He *always* looks good. Freshly showered and clean shaven, and wearing a pressed, crisp suit tailored to fit him perfectly.

"I need to talk to you."

"Now?" The condescending challenge in my voice would be enough to make most people shrink. Crew is not one of those people.

"Now." His tone is one I haven't heard directed at me in a while. Stern. *Cold.*

"I'm busy."

"I'm not going anywhere."

"You've got a lot of nerve showing up here."

Crew makes a show of looking around the office. "Maybe there's a meeting I could crash while I'm here? *Interrupt* during?"

I glare. He glares back. I spin on my heeled boots and stalk in the direction of my office, not waiting to see if he's following. But he is. I feel his presence as soon as he steps inside my office, filling the confined space.

While he shuts the door, I shrug out of my wool peacoat and toss it on a chair. "Talk."

I don't miss how his eyes skim over my body. We haven't had sex since we left Switzerland, the longest it's been in a while. If he drowned his annoyances balls deep in another woman last night, it doesn't look like it was very satisfying.

His gaze lingers on the framed photograph of us on my desk before he speaks.

"You're mad."

I snort. "I'm pissed, and I don't have time for this. I have a lot of work to get done today."

"Cut the shit, Scarlett. You were supposed to have this whole week off."

"That was before I became the sole breadwinner in the family." It's a low blow, one I almost feel bad for.

Crew doesn't even flinch. "*Please*, Scarlett. I just need to—"

"Nice suit," I interrupt. "Did you sneak in after I left?"

"No. I kept some stuff at my old place. It's closer to my office."

"Contingency plan?"

He studies me. "Is this your way of asking where I slept last night?"

Yes. "No."

He knows me too well.

"I was at my dad's. On the couch in his study, if you want details."

"I didn't ask."

Crew grips the back of one of the chairs that face my desk. "This mess with the feds…there's some stuff there, Scarlett. He said it won't stick, but I can't make any promises."

"Promises about what?" I question.

"You might not want your last name to be Kensington. It could affect *Haute* and *rouge*. Financially, or at the very least, you'll get questions. I might not be the CEO of a successful company. Or a respected one. Right now, we're bleeding money. That's not what you signed up for." I watch his lips tighten. His jaw muscles flex and shift. "So, I guess I'm asking… Do you want a divorce?"

I inhale sharply. "I can't have this conversation right now, Crew. I'm at work! You can't just—"

He steps forward, faster and closer than I'm expecting. "I know. But please, Scarlett. Just answer the question. I can't… I've got to go meet with my dad. The lawyers. The board. And I can handle it. I *will* handle it."

"Okay. What does that have to do with me?"

"I'll fight harder if I have something to fight *for*." He pauses. "Otherwise, I'd consider walking away. I'd take Royce Raymond up on his offer, if it wasn't in LA."

I tilt my head to see his face better. "You told me the job was here."

"I lied. I wanted your honest opinion, and I knew California would tip the scales. It's not an option now though, obviously, with the baby."

"The baby," I repeat. "So, what? I'm worth fighting for until I'm no longer a human incubator? Is that what you're saying?"

"I—God, no! Don't twist what I'm saying. This is exactly what you did last night."

"Last night. Right. When you accused me of downloading

company documents for the sole purpose of blabbing about them to—"

"I didn't *accuse* you of anything!" Crew shouts. "I *asked*, Scarlett. I found out who the leak was. You know him; I don't. We're a team. I was trying to—"

"If we're a team, then maybe you should have trusted me. Maybe you should have believed me!"

"When did I not trust you? When did I not believe you?" Crew retorts.

My phone rings, shrill and loud. I hesitate, but I pick up the receiver. Only a few people have the direct number rather than going through Leah, suggesting it's important. "Scarlett Kensington."

"Hi, Scarlett. It's Jeff. I'm looking through the proofs for the next issue, and I think that…" I tune him out. Crew leans forward and scribbles something on a pink sticky note.

He tilts the photo of us so it's directly facing me, and then walks out of my office. Jeff, *Haute*'s head graphic designer, keeps talking. About image placement and positioning and presets.

I pick up the note and read what he wrote. *If you decide to file, just have your attorney tell mine. I'll be working late.*

My gaze ping-pongs between the photo and the closed door. *Fuck. I fucked up.*

"Jeff, I'm going to have to call you back." Without waiting for a response, I hang up and run over to the door of my office. I scan the floor, but there's no sign of Crew. Not in the kitchenette, not loitering by the elevators.

"Leah!" I rush over to my assistant, who's standing by the main conference room, talking to Andrea. "Did you see Crew leave my office?"

"Um, yeah. A few minutes ago."

"Where did he go?"

She shifts uncomfortably. "Um, he left."

I swear. Loudly. Then keep walking until I reach the elevators. I bang on the down button a couple of times, hoping the doors will magically open. No such luck. That leaves the stairwell. I shove through the door, glad it doesn't set off some alarm. Evacuating the whole building is not on today's to-do list.

The long descent is spent deliberating on how far I should take this chase. If he's not in the lobby—which I doubt, based on how many steps I still have to go—do I go to Kensington Consolidated? Barge in and do exactly what I just chastised him for? He'll be home tonight, I assume. But then I think of the wording in his note. *I'll be working late.* Not *I'll be home late.* Not *I'll see you later.*

Was that a deliberate phrasing?

Finally, I reach the ground floor and burst through the metal door. It takes me a minute to scan the lobby. To my surprise, he's still here. Handing a badge back to a guard at the front desk.

And I'm hit with a whole new dilemma: what do I say? This was the furthest thing from a thought-out plan. Before I can second-guess, he spots me. Even from here, I can see his brow furrow.

I walk over, trying to get my breathing under control.

"How did you get down here so fast?"

"I ran down the stairs." Ran sounds more impressive than panting and slipping.

"You *ran*? Why the fuck would you do that? You're pregnant."

I pin him with a flat stare. "Really? I had no idea," I say sarcastically. "Women have run *marathons* while pregnant, Crew."

He shakes his head. "Well? What are you doing down here? I thought you were so busy."

"You left."

"What you wanted, right?"

"No. I mean, yes, I wanted you to go. I'm annoyed and anxious and I try to keep my personal life totally separate from work, which is basically the opposite of yelling at each other in my office. But the answer to your question...it's no. I don't want a divorce." I hold his gaze. "Better or worse, right?"

Relief floods his expression, smoothing the creases in his forehead. "Richer or poorer seems more fitting for the current situation. Stock dropped more this morning."

I lift and lower a shoulder. "I promised both."

"I won't hold you to it. I won't fight you on it."

"I don't want a divorce," I repeat.

His eyes close for a minute before he shrinks the small gap between us. He cups my jaw and I'm treated to a heady dose of déjà vu. This feels like our first kiss.

The anticipation. The uncertainty. The possibility.

I grip the stiff fabric of his shirt, pulling him closer.

Crew brushes my hair back. Runs his thumb along my jaw. "This mess—it's not about the money or the company or the scandal or my dad. It's about *you*. It's about being the guy that's good enough to stand next to you. You were worried I wouldn't see you as an equal—as a partner? I'm worried about the exact. Same. Thing."

It's so vulnerable, saying *I love you* to someone you choose to love. Love toward my parents was obligatory, stemming from the biological fact that without them, I wouldn't exist and the opportunities their work allowed for. Love toward the baby I'm carrying is instinctual. He or she is my child, a tiny piece of me, my responsibility to protect and adore.

None of that applies to Crew.

I love him because I *want* to. Because he challenges me and confides in me. Supports and softens me. I know the moment he enters the room and the second he leaves.

He sighs when I say nothing. "I know I'm the one who barged in here and demanded to talk to you, but now I really do have to go. If it was just my dad, I'd make him wait, but it's the whole board and most of the legal department. I'll get home as early as I can tonight. Okay?"

I keep holding his shirt. Stay silent.

His forehead wrinkles. "Red—"

"I love you." The words fall out of my mouth and hang between us.

And... Welp, there it is. I said it.

Awkward and unsure, I stare at Crew, waiting for him to react. Say something. Move. He's stunned; that much is obvious. Eyes wide. Lips parted, like he was about to say something that no longer applies.

He clears his throat.

"You don't have to say it back. It wasn't, I didn't, I—"

His fingers tilt my chin up, forcing me to look at him. He kisses me again, firm and warm and unyielding. It lingers on my lips with an invisible brand. *Property of Crew Kensington.* "I love you, Scarlett. So fucking much."

"You do?" To my embarrassment, my voice wavers. I genuinely wasn't sure if he did—does. It's part of why I hadn't said it until now. Not because I didn't want to show my cards, but because I didn't want him to feel like he had to.

His thumb swipes my cheek, caressing my face like it's something precious. "Yeah," he replies softly. "I do."

Crew is looking at me like I'm all he'll ever want. I let myself trust it. Cherish it. Believe it.

"Okay." It comes out as a whisper.

"I'll see you tonight." He tucks a strand of hair behind my ear, as unwilling to leave as I am to let him go.

Reluctantly, I nod.

He smiles. Shakes his head a little. Exhales. "Okay." Then he drops his hand and walks away toward the glass doors separating the lobby from the street. I can see Roman standing outside, waiting next to the car. Crew pauses to say something to his driver before he climbs in the backseat and out of sight.

I turn back toward the elevator with a smile on my face. This time, it arrives quickly. I'm back in *Haute*'s offices in a couple of minutes, with plenty of curious looks being aimed my way. Me running into the stairwell isn't a normal occurrence.

When I walk into my office, it takes a few moments of staring stupidly at my monitor before I remember I have work to do. I start shuffling through papers on my desk, trying to decide what to prioritize. I have to call Jeff back. A pink sticky note goes fluttering to the ground. I reach down to pick it up and freeze.

It's the note Crew wrote. But the side I'm staring at is the sticky back. The side I didn't think anyone wrote on.

Crew did.

And by the way, I love you. That's what he wrote.

I stare at it for a minute, heart pounding. Then I pick up my phone and text him.

Scarlett: *Who writes on the BACK of a sticky note???*

Crew responds instantly. He must still be in the car.

Crew: *I feel like that's a rhetorical question.*

Crew: *Don't feel bad I said it first.*

Scarlett: *You wrote it. Not the same thing.*

Scarlett: *I just saw it.*

Crew: *I figured that out halfway through our conversation, Red.*

Scarlett: *You were just going to drop the l-bomb and leave?!*

Crew: *Drop the l-bomb? How romantic.*

Scarlett: *Let me remind you the sentence started with "and by the way." Hardly Hallmark material.*

Crew: *I'll work on it.*

Crew: *I'm at the office.*

Crew: *I love you.*

I smile like he can see me.

Scarlett: *I love you too.*

I take the pink sticky note and tape it to my monitor, back side facing toward me. And then I pick up the phone and call Jeff back.

CHAPTER TWENTY-FOUR

CREW

"We should focus on a stock options report," Isabel suggests.

"Fine," I agree. "If you talk through that, I can overview the projections analysis." I glance at Asher, who's sitting next to me. "You good?"

"I think I know the song and dance by now."

"And Isabel and I don't?"

Asher sighs. "I'm good."

"Good."

My phone buzzes with a text from Oliver, double-checking on dinner with our dad this weekend. I don't blame him for making certain I'll be there. My father told Candace the baby couldn't be his after Scarlett and I left the chalet to see her dad. Candace admitted to lying about being pregnant, claiming my father wasn't giving her enough attention. They're in the midst of divorce proceedings now. I haven't told Oliver our father knows about him and Candace, and my father hasn't either, it appears. Hardly surprising. Unless it's a dirty secret he can use, my father is happy to sweep anything unpleasant under the rug. Especially ones which can't be bought off.

I reply to Oliver, promising I will be there, then switch over to my thread with Scarlett. The last thing she sent me was the link to the crib she wants.

We've barely started setting up the nursery. She's been busy preparing for maternity leave, while I've been pandering to investors and associates of Kensington Consolidated, trying to do damage control. Like Asher said, it's been an exhausting, frustrating process. As CEO, I have no choice. And now that Scarlett is over eight months along, I also need to find the time to assemble a crib.

Asher glances at the phone screen. Chuckles, when he sees what I'm looking at. "Damn. Never thought I'd see the day, Kensington."

A secretary shows up to show us to the conference room before I have a chance to respond. The meeting lasts an hour. It goes well, which is a relief. Reputations aren't restored overnight, only destroyed. If Nathaniel Stewart had any Kensington Consolidated documents, he never released them. Slowly but surely, the whispers are dying out.

We're all in high spirits as we pass the reception area and head toward the elevators. Isabel is chatting away, discussing improvements and takeaways. Ever since our late-night encounter on Christmas, she's made an effort to be overly professional. And excessively efficient.

The elevator arrives. A middle-aged man steps out, and the three of us walk inside.

"Uh, Crew?" Asher interrupts Isabel's analysis of the stock solutions.

"What?" I glance at Asher, who's making no attempt to brainstorm and analyze. He's squinting at his phone screen.

"Have you checked your phone?"

"No, why?"

"I have a bunch of missed calls from Celeste? Why would she be calling me…"

I'm no longer listening; I'm scrolling through the *hundreds* of missed notifications *I* have. "*Fuck.*"

I jab the *Lobby* button with my elbow as I tap Scarlett's name, as if that will speed up our descent. It rings and rings, finally going to voicemail. I swear again, then think. A quick Google search pulls up *Haute*'s number. It rings three times before a woman answers. "*Haute* magazine, Alexandra speaking. How may I help you?"

"I need to talk to Scarlett Kensington."

"Is she expecting your call?"

"Just transfer me," I grit out.

"I'll see if her assistant is available." Cheery piano music echoes through the line as I watch the numbers tick down. Our meeting was on the ninety-seventh floor. We're only just hitting eighty.

"Scarlett Kensington's office. How may I help you?"

"I need to talk to her."

"Can I take a message?"

"I'm her husband," I snap. "So no, I need to talk to her *now*."

The pleasant tone disappears. I can't remember Scarlett's secretary's name, but it turns out she's pissed at me. "Why the hell weren't you answering earlier?" She shouts the question, and it temporarily shocks me. People don't speak to me like that. "I— oh my God. I'm so sorry, sir. I, seriously. I don't think you can fire me, but she will if you—"

"Where. Is. Scarlett?"

"New York General. Her water broke forty-five minutes ago. I tried to go in the ambulance with her, but she wouldn't let me. She just wanted me to call you."

I pinch the bridge of my nose. *Sixty-three.* "I'm headed straight there."

I hang up the phone, silently cursing the elevator to move faster.

"She's having the baby?"

I give Asher a *duh* look. "No, her secretary just *really* wanted to ask you out."

"We're past the joking point. Got it."

I bang my head back against the wall. "We were supposed to have another month. I have to go straight there. I don't have time to take you two back to the office."

"Dude. You're about to become a dad. I'm coming with you."

I nod, not bothering to respond. One, because I don't really care what Asher does, so long as it doesn't slow me down. Two, because I'm already freaking out enough without letting his answer fully sink in.

The elevator doors open. I basically sprint toward the black SUV parked along the curb. Roman is leaning against the side of the car, reading a newspaper. His eyes widen as I race toward him. I assume Asher and Isabel are behind me, but I don't bother checking to confirm they're keeping up.

"Mr. Kensington, is everything—"

"Keys," I demand. Roman is an excellent driver as it relates to dressing and discretion. But I've never seen him so much as run a yellow. Wisely, he listens, handing them over and climbing into the passenger seat. I round the front of the car and climb into the driver's side. Doors open and slam in the back, and I peel away from the curb like we're fleeing the scene of a crime.

"What hospital is she at?" Asher asks.

"New York General." I swerve, narrowly missing a delivery guy on a bike.

"If we're going to the West Side, you should take 7th. There's an accident on 8th."

"How many blocks?"

"Five, no seven. Wait, no, actually four."

We reach a red light, and I slam on the brakes. Cars are already beginning to cross from the other direction, so I can't run it.

I glance in the rear-view mirror. "Do you or do you not know how to get there?"

"Traffic is always a shitshow, man. You know that. It keeps..." He trails off. "Oh, wait. They cleared 8th. You should go that way now."

I huff and tap at the black screen on the dash. "Does this thing work?"

"Yes, sir. I can connect it." Roman leans over and starts fiddling with the controls on the dashboard. A few seconds later, a map appears on the screen.

The light turns green and I zoom forward, following the directions coming from the speakers. We hit another yellow, so I press down the accelerator and change lanes.

"Damn," Asher comments as I cut off a Mercedes, setting off a series of honks. "We should've gone to Monaco to race like we talked about in college. You can seriously drive, man."

My phone starts ringing, *Incoming Call* flashing across the screen. I'm about to reject it when I see it's Scarlett calling.

"Hello?" My greeting is tentative. I know she must be pissed.

"It doesn't sound like you're dying in a ditch."

In the backseat, Asher snorts. If I could flip him off while driving, I would.

"Scarlett, I swear I'm—"

"An HOUR, Crew. I've been here almost an hour! Where the *fuck* are you?"

"I'll be there in five minutes." I cut off a cab. "Ten, tops."

"Where have you been? Why weren't you answering?"

I sigh. "I had a meeting. My phone was on silent and I wasn't checking it."

"You promised me." All the anger in her voice has drained away. The uncertainty that's left behind makes me press harder on the accelerator. "You promised me I wouldn't have to do this alone."

We hit another red, and I barely restrain another profanity as I tap an urgent beat on the steering wheel, urging it to change back to green. "You won't, baby. I'm almost there."

"I'm scared, Crew." She says the words softly, but they have the effect of a shout for how they hit me. "It hurts so fucking much and they couldn't find a heartbeat at first and I—I'm freaking out."

A tight fist of fear squeezes my chest. I fight through the panic before it can choke me. She needs assurance, not more anxiety. "Red, I'll be there. I swear. But even if I were in a ditch some-where, you can do this. Just breathe. This is what all those classes were about, right?"

"You weren't paying attention during Lamaze."

Scarlett sounds like her usual self again, and I almost pass out from relief. I definitely shouldn't be driving. But I can see the hospital up ahead, only one block away. "Yes, I was," I counter. "You just focus on one thing and then do the really fast breaths."

"Uh-huh. And then what?"

I glance at Roman for help. He shrugs. "I thought you had kids," I hiss. Another shrug. "Exhale?" I suggest.

Scarlett laughs. It's more strained and reedy than her usual laugh, but it loosens the tightness in my chest some. "You're so full of shit. I knew you weren't paying attention."

I stop the SUV with a screech of tires under the ambulance bay. I leave the car running and the keys in the ignition, just grab my phone and run toward the automatic doors into the busy hospital. There are white coats and gurneys everywhere. A child is crying somewhere close. The PA system is crackling, telling some surgeon to report to OR 1. I press the phone against my ear. "What floor are you on?"

"Five."

I rush for the elevator bank, then alter course when I spot a sign for a stairwell. There's a lot of nervous energy I need to burn off. I take the flights two steps at a time and yank open the door with a massive five painted on it. The hallway looks the same as the lobby downstairs, all white tile and fluorescent lights.

There's a desk to the right.

"Scarlett Kensington," I pant. "What room is Scarlett Kensington in?"

The nurse studies me, stern and assessing. "Are you a relative?"

"I'm her husband. The father. Where is she?"

She taps some keys on the computer. The seconds feel like minutes. "Room 526."

I start to the right, only to discover the numbers are going down, not up. I sprint to the left until I reach 526 and burst inside.

Scarlett is sitting up in bed, listening to a white coat-clad man who must be a doctor. When she sees me, her expression collapses. I rush to her side, grabbing her hand and kissing her head.

"You must be Crew. I'm Dr. Summers."

"Is something wrong?"

Dr. Summers looks somber. "I was just telling your wife we

can't wait any longer. I'm afraid the baby isn't positioned properly for a natural birth. We'll need to do an emergency C-section before the baby goes into distress."

"Distress?" I echo. Scarlett's hand tightens around mine.

"We'll do everything we can to prevent that from happening. That's why we need to move quickly."

For the first time since I've known her, Scarlett looks young and scared. Frail. "Can my husband stay with me?" she asks in a tinny voice.

Dr. Summers smiles kindly, but his tone is firm. "I'm so sorry, but no. We don't allow family members in the operating room during emergency surgery." *Emergency surgery.* Those two words permeate the fog in mind. Sharp panic cuts through as dread coils in my stomach. "A nurse will be in shortly to take you downstairs."

I'm frozen. Scarlett's breathing is quick and choppy. "You knew? When we were on the phone?"

"They told me there might be complications when I came in. I knew you'd get here as soon as you could." She gives me a wry smile that falls short. "Sorry for freaking out on the phone."

"I should have had my ringer on. What complications?"

"What Dr. Summers said. The baby isn't flipped the right way. But since my water already broke, they can't wait any longer to see if it will reposition."

I inhale, torn between pelting her with more questions and avoiding freaking her out.

A woman in pink scrubs enters the room. The nurse smiles at Scarlett. "Ready to become a mom?" Her cheer doesn't sound feigned, but it doesn't register as real. This isn't how this was supposed to happen. It doesn't feel like a happy, joyful moment.

Scarlett smiles back but doesn't reply.

The nurse gives an understanding nod. "Ready?"

"Ready," Scarlett replies. Her hand squeezes mine.

I lean down and kiss her forehead, letting my lips linger. "I love you."

Scarlett's grip tightens. "I love you too."

Then she lets go. The nurse wheels her bed away.

"As soon as there's an update, someone will let you know," she tells me on her way out.

All of a sudden, I'm standing in an empty hospital room, alone. My body feels heavy, my limbs disconnected. Breathing becomes difficult. I need out of this tiny room. I'd go outside if I weren't terrified of missing an update.

I walk back into the waiting room in a daze. Asher stands when I appear. Honestly, I forgot he was here.

"Isabel went back to the office. What's going on?" Asher asks. "That seemed sort of fast."

Under any other circumstances, him pretending he knows anything about childbirth, specifically the length of time it takes, would be amusing. I'm too anxious to do anything but pace right now. Back and forth. This waiting room looks the same as the one in the cardiac wing. While waiting to hear if Hanson had made it, I didn't experience any trepidation. His death wouldn't make me lose any sleep.

Scarlett's would shatter me. Just the hypothetical thought has my throat tightening and my eyes stinging. I feel like ants are crawling across my skin. Like my clothes are too hot and too tight. I try to take deep breaths, to pull in the air tinged with antiseptic.

"Crew, you're freaking me the fuck out. What is going on?"

In. Out. In. I keep pacing. "She's in surgery."

"*Surgery?*" Asher's eyes widen. "Is that…normal?"

"No, it's not normal," I bite out.

"Do you want me to…call anyone?"

"I don't care." The honest answer is *I don't know*. Scarlett and I never discussed who we'd invite to the hospital or when we would. I figured I'd be with her, that we'd get to make these decisions together, after we had a healthy baby.

I keep pacing. I don't know what time she went into surgery. How long a C-section takes. I'm totally unprepared, and the only thing that's keeping me from totally losing it is the hope that any minute someone will come tell me they're both fine.

I walk in circles until I start to feel dizzy. Then I sit. Bounce my knee. Spin my wedding ring in circles. Press my palms to my eyes and try to pretend I'm anywhere else.

Vaguely, I'm aware of activity around me. By calling *anyone*, Asher apparently meant *everyone*. My father. Oliver. Josephine and Hanson—who is fully recovered from his health scare. Scarlett's family huddles with mine, whispering. Probably about me. Wisely, none of them approach me.

An eternity passes before Dr. Summers appears. I stand as soon as I see him.

"Your wife is asking for you, Crew."

Relief hits me so hard I feel like my knees are about to buckle. "She's okay?" My voice cracks between the *o* and the *kay*.

Dr. Summers smiles and nods. "She's okay. And you've got a healthy baby girl."

A girl. I have a daughter. The thought feels foreign, even after months of knowing this was coming. "Can I see them?" My voice sounds like my throat is filled with rocks.

He nods. "Of course. Follow me."

Dr. Summers leads me to a different room than before. Scarlett is lying down, with a blanketed bundle resting on her chest.

"I'll give you a minute," he says, then disappears.

Scarlett looks up as soon as I step inside the room. Her smile is wide and brilliant. "She has your eyes."

I reach the bed and catch the first glimpse of my daughter's face. She's perfect. And Scarlett's right. Her eyes are the same shade of blue as mine. The color I inherited from *my* mother.

"The first time I saw you, I thought you had the most beautiful eyes I'd ever seen," she tells me.

I turn my head so I can press my face against her hair, feeling my eyes burn for the first time in my adult life. "I was so scared. So fucking terrified, Red."

"I'm okay," she assures me. "*We're* okay."

I look back at the tiny human we created together. "Wow."

"I know." Scarlett echoes my awed tone. "Do you want to hold her?"

I swallow. "Yeah. I do."

The fake baby from the birthing class felt nothing like the real thing. Scarlett passes me our daughter, and she's tiny and perfect and *real.*

"We should have decided on names sooner."

I smile wryly. "And ordered the crib, probably."

Scarlett's eyes widen. "Fuck."

"I'll take care of it," I assure Scarlett. "She'll have a bed." I look at my daughter. "You'll have a bed."

"Wow," Scarlett comments, staring at us. "You're a total DILF. I mean, I figured you would be. But it's different that it's my kid too, you know?"

I snort a laugh, and it feels good. Expels the last swirls of anxiety.

"What about Elizabeth?" Scarlett asks.

I study the small, innocent face. That same tug from my wedding appears, wondering what my mom might have to say on a day like today. She would have known what to tell me when Scarlett was in surgery. I clear my throat. "Don't feel like we have to—"

"I don't."

"Won't your mom be offended?"

Scarlett scoffs, but then sobers. "I mean…it could be her middle name, I guess."

"Elizabeth Josephine Kensington," I say softly.

"Yeah."

"I like it."

"Me too," Scarlett states.

"She's here," I tell her. "Your mom. Your dad too."

"*Really?*"

"Asher called them along with my dad and Oliver. I was… well, I wasn't in the mood to talk to anyone. And we hadn't talked about who we'd call and when."

Scarlett nods. "You can see if they want to come meet Elizabeth."

"Are you sure?"

"I'm sure."

"Okay." I'm reluctant to relinquish Elizabeth. Loathe to leave this room. But I hand her back to Scarlett and retrace my steps to the waiting room. They're all still there. I wasn't sure if they would be.

I clear my throat. "Uh, Dad? Hanson? Josephine? Do you—do you want to meet your granddaughter?"

All three of them look stunned. Maybe it's just hitting them they're grandparents. Maybe they didn't expect this offer.

To my surprise, Hanson stands first. Josephine follows. My dad is the last to rise, but he does. I glance at Oliver. *Go ahead*, he mouths. Me and my dad trail after Scarlett's parents down the hallway.

"We named her Elizabeth," I tell him quietly, as we walk down the hallway. My father is often unpredictable. I don't want his response to the revelation—positive or negative—to color the first meeting. "231," I tell Josephine and Hanson when we near Scarlett's room. They enter. I hear Josephine exclaiming. My father and I linger outside.

He squeezes my shoulder. "I'm proud of you, Crew. Your mother would be too."

Then he heads inside. I'm left standing in the hallway, crying for the second time today.

CHAPTER TWENTY-FIVE

SCARLETT

C rew is acting strange. He came home distracted, but on time, missing Sophie and Nadia's visit by only a few minutes. Pet Teddy and kissed Elizabeth before they went to bed, but it was autopilot. The same actions he does every night when he returns from work.

I watch him check his phone in the mirror's reflection. Glance out the window. I set down the tube of lipstick.

"You know...we don't have to do this tonight."

That jerks him out of his reverie. Crew glances over, looking surprised. And confused. "What? Why?"

"It's been a long day. And you seem...I don't know, out of it. We can reschedule."

His eyebrows rise and a touch of amusement reaches his lips. "Reschedule? It's our anniversary."

"I know, but it's just a date. Our track record with annual holidays or celebrations or whatever isn't great. And shouldn't we celebrate our marriage every day, not just the day we got married?"

A full-blown smirk is his response to that comment. "Who knew you were such a romantic, Red?"

I roll my eyes. "Shut up. I'm serious."

"I am too. So finish getting ready so we can go to dinner."

"Hungry?"

"Yeah." He slips his phone away, studying me with the expression of a sinner, not a saint. "For *dessert*. I'll be downstairs."

We've fooled around like horny teenagers since Elizabeth was born, but sex hasn't happened. And if someone had told me at my wedding a year ago I'd be leaving my newborn daughter at home to go to an anniversary dinner with Crew Kensington with full confidence we were in a monogamous relationship, I would have laughed in their face.

Yet here we are.

I spray on a perfume, grab a pair of Louboutins from the closet, and head downstairs. My mom has made herself comfortable on the couch. Her enthusiasm toward being a grandmother is nearly as surprising as the state of my relationship with Crew. I was mainly raised by nannies. But my mother dotes on Elizabeth every chance she gets. Even my father has surprised me on occasion, asking to hold her or offering up a genuine smile when he sees her. He's not here tonight, and I don't ask why. My parents' relationship isn't for me to control or judge. Most importantly, it has no bearing on my marriage.

Crew is leaning against the wall next to the elevator, staring off into space. He straightens when he sees me coming, his blue gaze darkening with lust.

I smirk at him before greeting my mother. "Hi, Mom."

She smiles as she looks me over. "You look beautiful, Scarlett."

"Thank you. Do you need anything before we go?"

"No, no." She waves a hand toward the entryway. "You two have a lovely evening. If Elizabeth wakes up, I'll be here."

"Okay." I hesitate for a few seconds, even though she's already turned back to the book open on her lap. Then, I walk over to Crew.

"Ready?" he asks.

"Ready," I confirm as we step into the elevator.

"How was work?" he asks.

"Good. July issue is all set, and the summer line is sold out."

He smiles at me proudly. "Congrats, Red."

"Thanks. How was your day?" Kensington Consolidated has officially weathered the storm. The investigation ended without charges. Stock has risen. Being the CEO of a Dow company isn't your typical nine to five though.

We sound like we've been married for decades. Crew is talking about some deal Oliver wants to take as we walk from the elevator to the bay of the garage for the penthouse where our cars are kept. We climb into Crew's Lamborghini.

Impulsively, I lean over and unzip his pants. He stops talking immediately, zeroing on my hand palming his cock. The growl of the metal teeth parting is the only sound in the car.

"Did he show you their deliverables?" I ask, tracing the outline of his erection with my fingers.

Crew's breathing is fast and ragged. "I can't even remember what we were just talking about, to be honest."

I laugh a little before I tug his cock out and lower my head, running my tongue around the crown.

"*Scarlett*." My name comes out in a garbled groan, full of grit and gravel and want.

The garage lights are motion-activated. They flick off, plunging the car into near darkness, not shadows. The lack of light feels taboo and erotic. Heat pools in my stomach and dampens between my legs, making me feel needy and desperate. I clench my thighs together.

I suck him deeper, hollowing my cheeks and grazing the underside with my teeth, the way I know he likes it. I'm rewarded with a husky growl. One hand glides into my hair and tugs. "God, you're the sexiest thing I've ever seen, Red," he rasps. "You suck me so good, baby."

I moan around him, knowing the vibrations will travel down his shaft. His hips jerk, telling me he's close. Heavy breathing fills the car before he groans and fills my mouth. I swallow and lean back, letting his half-hard dick go after a final, wet suck.

Crew's head is tilted back. He rolls it to look at me, his eyes lidded and hazy with pleasure. A lazy, satisfied grin on his lips. His cock still out. Still hard. Every woman's fantasy.

"Come here," he grits out.

I glance around the dark, empty garage, and then I crawl across the gearshift and settle in his lap. His dick settles against the soaked lace of my underwear as my dress fans out around our laps. I moan at the contact.

Crew's hand slides up my thigh and between my legs. He growls when he feels how wet I am, the rumble deep and possessive and followed by my name.

He just came, but I'm so worked up I think he could breathe on me and I'd explode. His hand moves to his cock, fisting the long length and rubbing against my center. "You want this, Scarlett?"

"Yes." I pack as much need into the three letters as I can manage, drawing the word out into a whimper as he starts to nudge inside me.

"This is okay, right? You're okay?"

Forget breathing. The slight pressure and the concern in his voice causes me to ball my fists to fight off my orgasm. "I'm fine," I gasp. "Fully recovered. Just fuck me. *Please*."

He does, moving my thong to the side and filling me with the delicious glide I've missed. His mouth finds the spot between my neck and my shoulder, pressing warm, wet kisses and whispering dirty words against my skin. I rock and grind against him, meeting every thrust until I fall off the peak of pleasure. Waves of warmth spiral and spread, leaving me sated and spent. I feel Crew shudder as he comes inside of me.

I don't move from his lap, wanting to stay in this moment for a little while longer. Connected, feeling the rhythmic rise and fall of his chest as he breathes.

"Not bad for an old married couple, huh?"

My lips tug up into a smile as I lean back and pat his abs. "Glad you haven't let yourself go."

His smile is wide and genuine as I slide off him and back to my side of the car. We both fix our outfits before Crew starts the car and rolls out of the garage. He drives with one hand, keeping the other tangled with mine.

I recognize the restaurant he stops outside, even though I've never eaten here before. It's known for being trendy and upscale.

Crew hands the keys over to the valet and we head inside. There's another couple waiting at the hostess stand we stop behind.

"Have you been here before?" I ask.

He shakes his head. "They have the best view."

"Best view of what?"

"You'll see," is his cryptic answer.

I look around, taking in the brick walls and the black accents and the metal chairs. And the blonde woman walking toward us.

"What a surprise!" Hannah's voice is peppy, filled with false confidence.

Crew says nothing.

"Is it?" I question, keeping my voice short and dry.

"How are you? I heard you had a baby?" Hannah glances at my stomach, like she's looking for evidence.

Before I have to respond, another woman approaches us. "Han, the table is ready."

"Oh, okay," Hannah replies. "I'll be right there, Savannah."

Savannah has focused on Crew. Her eyes widen appreciatively, then slide to me. "Oh my God. I *love* your dress."

"Thank you." I look her over and hide a smile. "I like yours too."

"Thanks." Savannah glances down at the beaded bust. "It's from *rouge*'s summer line. I just love their stuff."

Hannah's mouth twists like she's sucking on a slice of lemon. Savannah is clearly oblivious, but it's obvious Hannah knows who owns *rouge*.

"That's one of yours?" Crew asks, sounding surprised. Nothing he works on has a tangible output you can run into on the street. I've seen strangers reading my magazine and wearing my clothes before, but it still feels strange.

"Holy shit!" Savannah suddenly exclaims. "You're Scarlett Kensington, aren't you?"

"Yep," I reply. "And this is my husband, Crew. We're celebrating our wedding anniversary."

"Aww. That is *so* romantic," Savannah gushes.

"Crew is *super* romantic," I praise. "And so supportive. On the drive here, he said the sweetest things to me." I don't look over, but I'm sure he's stifling some amusement.

"You made it *hard* not to." Humor dances in those blue depths, obviously proud of the innuendo.

Hannah looks annoyed and uncomfortable. Savannah is beaming at us like we're couple goals come to life.

A waiter approaches. "Mr. and Mrs. Kensington? Your private table is ready, if you'd like to follow me up to the terrace."

I give Hannah and Savannah a little wave. "Enjoy your evening, ladies."

"So I'm *super romantic*?" Crew teases as we follow the maître de through the restaurant.

"You have your moments," I reply. "And it was brag about that or trade insults with your jealous ex."

"Hannah isn't my ex-anything."

"Whatever."

"It's cute when you're jealous, Red." Crew leans in, his lips brushing the shell of my ear. "Especially when you're full of my cum."

I suppress a shiver that has nothing to do with the fact the air conditioning is on full blast in here. The tuxedo-clad maître de keeps walking toward the elevator, completely unaware of the fact my husband's mouth is the exact opposite of everything else in here: filthy.

The elevator's silver doors part to reveal the rooftop. Gray stone covers the ground. Artfully placed trees and flowers interrupt the spaced tables. Twinkling lights illuminate the space. We're the only people up here. Crew must have rented out the whole terrace.

"Wow," I breathe.

"A server will be up shortly to take your orders. Enjoy your evening." The man steps back into the elevator, leaving Crew and me standing alone up here. He walks over to the edge of the roof, overlooking the whole city. I follow.

"You like it?"

"I love it." I glance over at him. "Since you accused *me* of being jealous, I've always wondered: what did you say to that guy

370

in Proof? The night you came over to the booth, right before we were engaged?"

"Technically, we got engaged when we were sixteen."

I roll my eyes. "You know what I mean."

"I told him you were mine," Crew replies.

"That's all you said to him?"

"*Him*? You don't even remember the guy's name, do you?"

"Stop changing the subject."

"Do you?"

I think back to that night. Try to remember the guy who came over to my booth and talked to Sophie and Nadia. But all I remember about that night is Crew. How he looked. What he said. "No," I admit. "I don't."

He grins, pleased. "I might have threatened *Evan* with a little bodily harm if he got handsy with you that night."

The possessiveness in his voice elicits a contrary mixture of contentedness and annoyance. "I wasn't *yours*. We weren't even married then."

Crew shrugs. "It felt like you were."

I remember how pleased I was when he dismissed that redhead. I shouldn't have cared who he screwed back then. But I did. "See? I knew you were romantic."

"You said *wasn't*."

I raise a brow. "What?"

"You said, 'I wasn't yours.' Does that mean you are now?"

"Yeah," I tell him. "I am."

In the past year, I've learned a lot. One of the things I've discovered about Crew is that his assurance means he is rarely without something to say. This is one of those rare moments. Where he gifts me with a sentimental smile that tells me he's as much mine as I am his.

"Did you think we would be here the day we got married?

371

Like *this*, I mean." I gesture between us, as if love is a tangible connection you can see between two people. "Ever wonder what it would be like if you'd married someone else?"

"Do you?"

"I asked you first."

He ignores me. "You know one thing about us that was always confusing? Why *me*? Up until my father told me I'd be CEO, it made some sense. But once he did, I always wondered…"

His musing is too pointed, too precise. "Your dad told you."

"He mentioned you…*requested* me."

I smile wryly. "Hanson Ellsworth doesn't grant requests."

"So…"

"So, it was more of a threat. I told him I'd marry you…or no one."

"Why?"

I shrug. "Part of it was rebellion. Back then, everyone assumed Oliver would end up at the top. Asking Arthur to change the terms after they'd been set would be embarrassing for my father."

"And the other part?"

"I wanted you." I chew my bottom lip. "I wanted you," I repeat.

The aftermath of that confession leaves me embarrassed.

"Come on." I try to tug Crew toward the table. "We should look at the menu."

He doesn't budge. "Not yet. Wait."

I look around the rooftop. "Wait for wha—"

Loud flashes of color light up the sky, cutting me off. I stare at the spectacular sight.

"We're celebrating," Crew tells me.

I realize, if anything, I was *underselling* his soft side earlier.

Money can buy a lot. Importance. Accolades. Relevance.

Lavish vacations and expensive dinners and a dazzling display meant for two people in a city of millions.

Love is immune to currency. Money isn't why there's a soft half-smile on Crew's face. Why there are butterflies in my stomach and a total certainty in my head that we'll last.

Side by side, we watch fireworks explode over the Manhattan skyline, illuminating the city we call home. And there's nothing fake about any of it.

THE END

You can read Oliver Kesington's story in *Real Regrets.*

AUTHOR'S NOTE

Thank you so much for taking the time to read *Fake Empire*. I hope you enjoyed Scarlett and Crew's story!

Please take a moment to rate or review this book. It's the best way to help me reach new readers, and I'd love to hear your thoughts!

All the best,
C.W. Farnsworth

ALSO BY C.W. FARNSWORTH

Four Months, Three Words

Kiss Now, Lie Later

The Hard Way Home

First Flight, Final Fall

Come Break My Heart Again

The Easy Way Out (The Hard Way Home Book 2)

Famous Last Words

Winning Mr. Wrong

Back Where We Began

Like I Never Said

Fly Bye

Serve

Heartbreak for Two

For Now, Not Forever

Friday Night Lies

Tuesday Night Truths

Pretty Ugly Promises

Six Summers to Fall

Real Regrets

ABOUT THE AUTHOR

C.W. Farnsworth is the author of numerous adult and young adult romance novels featuring sports, strong female leads, and happy endings.

Charlotte lives in Rhode Island and when she isn't writing spends her free time reading, at the beach, or snuggling with her Australian Shepard.

Find her on Facebook (@cwfarnsworth), Twitter (@cw_farnsworth), Instagram (@authorcwfarnsworth) and check out her website www.authorcwfarnsworth.com for news about upcoming releases!

ACKNOWLEDGMENTS

I loved writing this book. It's the first one I've written that *flowed* from start to finish. I was excited to open my laptop and type, to get lost in the glitz and glamour and decadence of Crew and Scarlett's world. I hope you had as much fun reading this book as I did writing it.

Huge thanks to the team of incredible women, all of whom I've been fortunate enough to work with before, for helping me polish this book into its best possible version.

Mel, your notes put the biggest smile on my face. This book is different from everything else I've published so far, and hearing positive feedback from someone familiar with my writing was so nice to hear. Thank you for all your meticulous, detailed comments!

Tiffany, you've been included in the *Acknowledgements* for nearly all of my books, and I still don't feel I've managed to fully express how grateful I am to you. You never fail to impress me with your attention to detail. Passing off a manuscript for edits is a mixture of relief and second-guessing. Sending this book to you, I was confident it was in the best of hands. Thank you for another amazing job.

Writing this book became a personal challenge for me. It pushed me out of my comfort zone in several different ways, and I'm so proud to see the finished product and so grateful to everyone in my life who allows me the time and the space to write these stories I can't stop thinking about.

Ingram Content Group UK Ltd.
Milton Keynes UK
UKHW010750130623
423359UK00004B/68